WORK WITH ME

AN ENEMIES-TO-LOVERS STANDALONE OFFICE ROMANCE

SYNERGY WORKPLACE ROMANCE
BOOK 1

MICHELLE MCCRAW

lazy dog
BOOKS

BOOKS BY MICHELLE MCCRAW

40 and Fabulous

Fashion and Passion

Frenemies and Lovers

Books and Hookups

Conspiracies and Chemistry

Synergy Series

Work with Me

Friend Me

Trip Me Up

Boss Me

Forget Me

Tempt Me

To my grandmothers, Ruby and Nancy, and all the other working women who blazed the trail, who held the door, who fought the fight so that I—and my daughter—can keep fighting to make our own ways in the world.

1

ALICIA

THE SKY WAS the color of pea soup. Angry pea soup.

Having lived in Texas all my life, I knew the sky turned that color and the clouds boiled only when they were brewing something especially violent.

I gauged the distance from the overhang of the parking garage to the building entrance across the cracked pavement of the four-lane street. There'd be no sprinting across in my four-inch heels.

"Trying too hard," I muttered. "Flats would've been fine. Or even boots." But I'd wanted to make a good impression at my first gig for my brand-new company. Serious. Capable. Flawless. Ready to use my pointy-toed shoes to kick ass and create a name for myself by turning around this troubled project.

This was my stick-it-to-em moment. To my old boss, Lowell, who'd said I was too "sensitive" to be management material. To Dr. Fletcher, who'd told our entire class—while I, the only woman in the room, sat there, too flummoxed to object—that women didn't have the drive to succeed in technology. To every coworker who'd ever talked over me, taken credit for my work, or tried to mansplain programming to me. I was walking into Synergy Analytics, a Fortune 1000 company founded by two Stanford grads and now worth over six *billion* dollars, to use my smarts to help them succeed.

Not bad for a local girl who went to a state university. I brushed invisible dust off my shoulder.

My phone pinged. Thirty minutes until the meeting. Plenty of time to get through security, shake some hands, and take my seat at the head of the table. I drew myself up. For the first time in my life, I was my own boss. I was more than qualified to do this gig, and I could beat the rain, too.

As my shoe hit the sidewalk, I heard the first plink. *Ha! Missed me!* A good thing, since I was wearing a white blouse, my suit jacket folded over my messenger bag to keep cool in Austin's early-September heat. A see-through shirt at my first meeting would not be a good look. Another quick step, and I checked the street for cars. Clear, if I went fast.

I stepped off the curb, and a raindrop bounced in front of me. *Bounced?* Another one to my right. A blur of white zoomed in front of my nose. That wasn't rain; it was hail. Pea-sized. No sweat. Hail wouldn't even get my blouse wet.

Crossing the second lane of traffic, I kicked a hailstone. That one was bigger, about the size of a marble. An anomaly. *Still, better watch out.* If I stepped on one that size, I'd probably go down in the middle of Sixth Street. And then I'd get run over by a car. I couldn't let Noah lose another parent. Besides, I hadn't yet bought life insurance to replace the policy my old employer had provided. "If I get into this building safely," I murmured, "I promise I'll call the insurance company as soon as I get home."

Gritting my teeth against the pelting stones, I took two big steps to cross the last lane before hopping up onto the curb over the pile of white hailstones that had drifted against it. Two more steps took me under the building's sheltering overhang. I glanced up at the green clouds. "Thank—"

A flash of white, and pain seared my forehead right at my hairline. "Ouch!" Cradling my face, I scuttled further under the awning. That'd teach me to practice gratitude.

"Are you all right?" A tall figure loomed up in my peripheral vision.

"Fine, I'm fine." But when I pulled my hand away, my fingertips were smeared with blood. I dug in my bag for a tissue.

"Scalp wounds bleed a lot. Hurt like a motherfucker, too. Hang on, I've got something." The man set down his duffel bag and rooted around inside. His faded black T-shirt with AC/DC's distinctive logo rode up on his back, revealing a vee of lean muscle that disappeared into his jeans. Between working a desk job and hanging out at soccer fields, I hadn't seen a lot of physiques like that. Not since Rick. I shook off the memory. I couldn't let Rick ruin my you-go-girl attitude.

The man turned, a heather-gray T-shirt in his hand. "It's clean, I promise. Mind if I—?"

Not sure whether my lost power of speech was due to his Greek-god bod or blood loss, I shook my head. Gently, he brushed away my hand holding the blood-soaked tissue and pressed the shirt to my face. The shirt smelled like fresh soap and something else. Leather. Like a boot shop. Or the inside of a luxury car. I inhaled, wishing I could wrap myself in that scent.

When he stepped closer, he kicked a hailstone. "What is this? It's not snow."

"It's hail." The shirt covered one eye, but I checked him out with the other. He was tall, a good three or four inches taller than me, even in my heels. Ah. It wasn't all his laundry soap. He was wearing some fancy cowboy boots; thus, the leather scent. Ostrich. Expensive. Faded, broken-in jeans that showcased narrow hips, and the shirt I'd already noted that stretched tight in all the right places. Dark hair, somewhere between brown and black. Dark eyes, too. Sharp. Assessing. But also kind. My cheeks heated under that stare.

"Hell? You mean, as in frozen over?" He spoke crisply, like the people on TV, not like anyone I'd ever met in real life.

"No. Hail. H-A-I-L. You're not from around here, are you?"

He smiled, the right side higher than the left. "Nope. Still trying to get used to some of these Texas accents."

"Just visiting, or do you live here now?"

That lush mouth tensed a little. "A little of both. I've been in Austin for three months, but I hope I can go home soon."

"You hope?" I flashed him an easy smile. "Clearly, you haven't had the full Austin experience. Most people never want to leave." Except me. After living my whole life here, my hometown had started to feel a little like a favorite shirt I'd outgrown. Soft and cozy, but a little too tight.

The tension disappeared, and his right cheek kicked up again. That smile should've been illegal. "Maybe I haven't had the right tour guide." His gaze started to trail down, and his eyes widened when they reached my chest. He blinked back up to my face. "You've, ah, you've got some blood on your blouse."

"Oh, shit." I put my hand over his on the T-shirt. His hand was warm and dry. Smooth skin, like he also worked at a desk. He slid it out from under mine so I could survey the damage. Dammit, two red drops right over my left boob. Holding one hand to the cut, I tried to unfold my jacket with the other.

"Let me help?"

I nodded, and he shook out my jacket. While he held it out behind me, I slid in one arm, swapped hands over my cut, and then slid into the other sleeve. When he pulled the sides together, we stood close, like we were dancing. That heavenly scent of his surrounded me, and the hail, my meeting, everything faded around me.

He looked familiar. I'd seen those full lips before, quirked to one side. The short, dark beard, thick on his chin and a little scraggly on his cheeks. The genuine smile seemed different, but I'd seen those eyes crinkled at the corners. How did I know him?

"Have we—"

He spoke at the same time. "You work around here? I don't think I've seen you before."

"It's my first day. I have a big meeting this morning." Clearly, I wasn't all that memorable if he didn't think he'd seen me before. Where had I met him?

"In there?" He tilted his chin toward the Synergy building behind me.

"Yes, I'm a consultant. I own my own business." Even bleeding there on the sidewalk, I felt my chest expand.

"Consultant." He stepped back, taking the glorious scent with him. The hailstones plinked outside the awning. "Let me get you a bandage. I've got one in my bag."

"No. Thank you, though." I couldn't walk into a meeting with Cooper Fallon with a bandage on my face.

"Would you rather have blood dripping down your forehead during your big meeting? That chunk of ice really got you." He rummaged in his bag and pulled out a small plastic first-aid kit.

"Are you a Boy Scout?" I carried a first-aid kit in my car for Noah, but I didn't know too many men who did.

He chuckled. "They kicked me out when I was nine. Marlee. My assistant. She takes care of me."

An assistant? My first-aider in jeans and a T-shirt didn't look like someone with that kind of power. But now that I thought about it, his voice did carry a slight imperious edge like he was used to giving orders. And having them followed.

He clicked open the kit and pulled out a bandage. When he peeled apart the wrapper, I caught a flash of red.

"What's that?"

"Oh. Lightning McQueen. You know, from *Cars?* She has a twisted sense of humor."

Of course I knew *Cars*. It had been Noah's favorite movie since he was three. "You're not putting Lightning McQueen on my face."

"Show me that smile. The one you gave me when you talked about your business. The one you'll show them in that meeting."

I couldn't help it. I smiled, big and broad, every time I thought about Weber Technology Consulting.

"That's it. No one will be looking at old Lightning McQueen here when you flash that gorgeous smile." He lifted the shirt away from my face, brushing my fingers. It wasn't blood loss that made them tingle.

"Thanks..." I raised my eyebrows.

"My friends call me Jay."

"I'm Alicia."

"Alicia." He rolled my name in his mouth. Then, with a light press of his warm fingers, he adhered the bandage to my head. "We match now, see?" He held up his arm, and, sure enough, across his elbow was a Lightning McQueen bandage.

"The hail didn't get you, too?" I'd been too focused on my own injury, my own problems, and I hadn't been paying attention. Jay's arm bulged with lean muscle, and a vein wrapped around his forearm. I'd only seen that on TV, too.

"Nah." He rubbed it. "Got too close to a tree on my run." He stepped closer again. "May I?"

I nodded, my throat too dry to speak. He tugged my jacket so the sides met in front. Then he slid a finger into my hair near the cut and smoothed it down. He scanned me from my head to my toes, and every spot his gaze hit tingled.

"Good as new." He stepped back. "Feel okay? Not too dizzy?"

Dizzy? Yeah. I blinked. Had I said that out loud? "I'm good."

"Good." He opened his mouth and then closed it again. Was he about to ask me out? He had to be feeling what I was. That thing he'd said about my smile was definitely flirty. An invisible tether kept either of us from moving toward the door or out onto the sidewalk.

My sister's words echoed back to me from years ago. *Life is short. Don't wait for what you want. Ask for it, and then take it.* She hadn't lived long enough to follow her own advice. But I'd taken her words to heart, and I knew what I wanted: more time with this guy's gentle fingers and bottomless eyes. "Hey, Jay, I've got that meeting now, but maybe you'd like to get a coffee sometime?"

He glanced again at the door behind me. "I'm sorry, I...can't."

My belly went tight and heavy, and my cheeks heated. "Oh, okay." Did he have a girlfriend? Was Marlee more than his assistant? Or maybe I was in shock and had hallucinated the signs of his attraction. Served me right for putting myself out there. For following Melissa's advice.

I needed to get out of there. Regroup and focus on my meeting. I hitched my bag higher on my shoulder. "I have to go. Thank you for your help."

When I held out the shirt to him, the gray fabric was smeared with blood. Gross. I snatched it back before he could touch it. "I'll wash this out tonight and bring it back tomorrow. I'll leave it here in the lobby in the morning?"

"Sure." He bent again, showing that tantalizing sliver of his back, and picked up a golf ball–sized hailstone. He pulled a sock from his duffel and wrapped it around the hunk of ice before dropping it back into his bag. I had to smile despite my embarrassment. If he was anything like Noah, Jay would stash it in the nearest freezer and pull it out to examine later. Scientific curiosity always melted my nerdy heart.

Though this scientist-slash-first-aider's heart didn't feel the same about me. My cheeks blazed again.

He opened the door and held it for me.

I walked through, careful not to brush against him. The heat had spread down my neck to my chest. I spotted a sign for the restrooms to the right and turned toward it without looking at him. "Thanks again."

"Anytime, Alicia."

A few minutes later, I clipped a visitor badge to my lapel, mentally donning my armor again. *Back on track. Kicking ass. No more distractions, no matter how sexy.*

Another tall man strode through the security sensors, extending his hand to me. "You must be Ms. Weber. I'm Cooper Fallon."

I sucked in a breath. Chiseled jaw, sandy-blond hair, eyes the color of bluebonnets. I'd seen photos of him—the CEO of Synergy Analytics had been on the cover of *Forbes* at least twice, plus I'd Googled him, of course—but photos hadn't prepared me for six-feet-something of tanned skin and trim physique accentuated by a crisp blue shirt, tailored slacks, and a creaseless sports coat. I passed my hand over my slim black skirt, wrinkled from the drive over.

Mentally giving myself a shake, I grasped his hand. "Pleasure to meet you, Mr. Fallon."

He didn't ask me to call him Cooper.

"Stairs okay?" he asked. "We're meeting on the second floor."

"Sure." A little cardio might settle out my nerves. Taking a deep breath, I followed him through the security sensors to a wide, open staircase. Climbing, I looked around me. Wide wooden planked floors, exposed ductwork in the ceiling, bright reds, oranges, and blues in colorful splashes on the walls that reminded me of the Hill Country in spring. "How long have you owned the building?"

"Not long. We bought it from a company that decided to move to a remote workforce. We're living in the space for a while before we decide to make any changes."

"But Synergy didn't go remote?" I almost smacked my forehead. *Obviously, Alicia. They're here.*

He waited for me at the top of the stairs. "No, we take a collabora-tive approach to software development. Jamila says that's what you prefer, too?"

I smiled at the mention of my mentor. I could almost feel her standing next to me, saying, *You got this.* "Absolutely," I said. "Teams can get so much more done when they're located together, when they don't have to rely on email or even instant messaging for communi-cations."

"I'm glad you think so. I'm sure you'll fit right in with the team."

He pulled open a frosted-glass door to a conference room. Inside, most of the chairs were taken. A quick glance told me the meeting attendees were all men; no surprise there. And at the head of the table—

"Jay?" I lifted a hand to my forehead. Was he one of the devel-opers I'd be working with?

"Alicia!" Jay stood, his smile quickly turning to a frown as he glanced from me to Cooper. "What's going on, Coop?"

Maybe that hailstone had done more damage than I'd thought. Or maybe I'd been too infatuated by a pair of sharp, dark eyes. But seeing the two men together, the puzzle pieces snapped into place. Cooper Fallon and my-friends-call-me-Jay *Jackson* Jones, cofounders of Synergy Analytics. The business brains and the programming muscle that'd started the company in their dorm room at Stanford and had grown it into a Fortune 1000 company in less than a dozen years.

Why the hell did Jackson Jones need *me* on a programming project?

Beside me, Fallon straightened. "Ms. Weber is here to help set direction and move the project forward."

Over the phone, he'd told me I was there to rescue a struggling project. Huh.

Jackson's stare went flinty. "As the project lead, it's my role to set direction."

Next to Jackson, a young programmer slumped into his seat like he was trying to melt into the polyester mesh. I wanted to do the same. These two were supposed to be best friends, and now they were arguing. Because of me. Actually, because Cooper Fallon hadn't told his business partner he was hiring a consultant. Me. And who the hell was in charge here? I eyed the seat at the head of the table, the one I'd planned to occupy. The one where Jackson Jones now presided.

Something that wasn't my fault had suddenly become my problem. Nothing for it but to woman up and solve it. I stiffened my spine. *Showtime.*

"Mr. Fallon, would you like to brief Mr. Jones while I get to know the team?" I said, with what I hoped was the smile Jay—Jackson— had admired and not a teeth-baring snarl.

"Great idea, Ms. Weber." Fallon tilted his head toward the hallway. Jackson circled the table and followed his cofounder out the door.

A second before the door swung shut, Jackson's low tone floated through. "This is bullshit, Coop—"

I spoke loud enough to drown him out. "While Mr. Jones and Mr. Fallon talk strategy, we'll get to know each other. I'm Alicia Weber of Weber Technology Consulting, and I'm here to help get this development project back on track so we can deliver on schedule. I'm looking forward to getting to know all of you.

"Would you like to start the introductions?" Waving at the young guy who'd been sitting next to Jackson, I circled around to the head of the table. I moved a Synergy mug of coffee out of the way and sat in the power seat, surreptitiously lowering it so my feet touched the floor.

As the guys took turns introducing themselves, the arguing on the other side of the door eventually quieted, and before we'd finished, Jackson and Fallon slipped back inside. Fallon took the empty chair across the table, his expression serene as he listened to the team provide status updates on their assignments. Jackson leaned against the wall, arms crossed, the color still bright on his high cheekbones. He said not another word, but heat seemed to radiate from him, and the programmers closest to him squirmed in their seats. But to me, at least, there was no mistaking the hurt in his eyes. What the hell was going on between those two? They needed a couples therapist more than a consultant.

"Now that everyone has met," Cooper said as he stood, "I'd like to review the project constraints. With Alicia joining the team, I'm confident you'll be able to complete development by November 15 as originally planned."

Two months. I had two months to turn the project around and deliver shippable code. I could do it. I knew I could. Unless...

"Alicia?" Cooper asked.

What had he asked me? Something about the date, I thought. "Absolutely, Mr. Fallon. We'll get it done."

Jackson snorted.

I narrowed my eyes at him. He wouldn't sabotage me, would he? It wouldn't be the first time someone had tried. I'd seen it all before: deliberate slowdowns, bugs introduced "accidentally," even calling in sick at a critical point on a project. All because a woman threatened their fragile egos. They'd closed ranks and manspread around the table until there was no room for me.

I couldn't let that happen here. If we succeeded, Cooper Fallon's recommendation would open doors for me in Austin, in Silicon Valley, wherever I wanted to work. I'd write my own ticket. If I failed, though, that'd be the end of Weber Technology Consulting. I'd head back into someone else's cubicle to churn out code, something I'd been trying to escape for the past five years.

So when Cooper Fallon shook my hand and said, "See you at eight tomorrow morning?" I said, "Absolutely. Can't wait to get started."

It's always good to start a new job lying your face off, right?

As if he could see the guilty thought race across my forehead like a marquee, Cooper narrowed his eyes at me. "Until tomorrow, then." He turned to talk to Jackson, who stared at me with an unreadable expression. Gone was the tenderness he'd shown when he'd pressed that ridiculous bandage to my forehead.

I stared right back. It didn't matter how nice he'd been. Or how famous a programmer he was. No way was I going to let Jackson Jones ruin this make-or-break opportunity for me.

2

ALICIA

THE SECOND I pulled up at the U11 soccer field, I knew something was wrong.

It wasn't a tingling mom-sense like my best friend, Tiannah, had. I figured that was something that washed into the bloodstream in the delivery room, like oxytocin. I was proof you couldn't get it simply by holding your sister's hand as she gave birth.

No, I could tell because the kids weren't running around. They were sitting in the grass while Tiannah cradled Noah in her lap, wiping his tears and kissing his forehead. Behind her, her husband, the coach, paced, his phone to his ear. I ignored my buzzing phone to leap out of the car and wobble across the gravel parking area in my heels. I swore I'd burn them. They'd slowed me down twice today.

"Noah!" I dropped to my knees next to him in the grass. "What happened?"

Tiannah reached out and took my hand, her motherly reassurance flowing into me. "He tripped. Went down hard. He says his arm hurts."

The skin had already reddened along his forearm. I might not have a mom-sense, but Noah had broken enough bones that I knew my next step.

"Hey, buddy," I said in a soft voice. "Think you can stand up?"

He wiped his face on his sleeve. "Yeah."

"We'll go see Dr. Ruiz. She'll fix you up." I supported him under the uninjured arm, and Tiannah gripped him from behind as he stood on wobbly legs.

While the other kids clapped, Tamika ran up, her braids flying. "Noah, you okay?"

"Yeah."

She hugged him, ignoring his arm sticking awkwardly out at his side. "Feel better, 'kay? I'll see you at school tomorrow."

He nodded and untangled himself from her hug. Poor guy had to be really hurting. Normally, he'd have talked to his best friend until we dragged them away from each other.

"Alicia!" The familiar voice made my stomach clench. Running feet approached, and Rick stood there, barely breathing hard from his jog across two soccer fields. "What happened?"

I looked up into his rugged face. I used to think he was handsome; now the sharp angles of his cheekbones looked harsh. Nothing at all like the soft crinkles around Jackson Jones's chocolate brown eyes. I blinked away the memory. "Noah fell, and I'm taking him to the doctor."

Gently, he lifted the arm Noah cradled and examined it. "Hurts a lot, huh?"

"Yeah, Coach—I mean, Rick." Noah's mouth pinched tight.

Rick ruffled his hair. "I might not be your coach this season, but you can still call me that."

I grimaced. I'd pulled strings to ensure Noah wouldn't be on Rick's team this season. I'd hoped never to see him again after we'd broken up earlier in the summer, but I should've known better, considering how much time we all spent at the soccer complex.

"Looks like it could be broken. I'd take him to the doctor."

I blinked hard to avoid rolling my eyes. Hadn't I just told him that's where we were going?

"I can go with you. Talk to the doctor. Palmer's staying with his mother tonight."

"No." I'd said it louder than I'd meant to. "I mean, we're fine. I've got this." When Rick didn't release Noah's arm, I said, "I'd like to get him there before they close."

"Sure." He ruffled Noah's hair again. "Good luck, Noah. Hope to see you back on the field soon."

"Thanks, Coach." Noah's eyes were narrow with pain, but they still shone at Rick. Shit. I'd known it was a bad idea to date a man who was both his coach and the father of one of his friends. Noah probably hoped we'd get back together. But I wouldn't be doing that. Not even for him.

"You sure you don't need me?" Rick's voice was low, only for me. His green eyes glinted.

"Thanks, Rick. We're good."

"But—"

Tiannah's voice cut over him. "She said she's good. Besides, I'm going with her."

I blinked at her. "But what about—"

"Orlando's got the kids." In a lower voice, she said, "You could use some help. But not from him." She hitched her purse over her shoulder.

Rick's mouth tightened, but after a beat, he nodded and walked away. I didn't even watch him. Well, okay, I may have briefly let my eyes wander over his backside. Those soccer shorts made me remember why I'd caved when he'd asked me out. If only he'd been able to deliver on what those muscular glutes promised.

Tiannah muttered what I was thinking. "Damn waste of a fine ass."

I bit back my response, mindful of the many little ears around us.

"Let's go, Noah." I opened the car door for him, and he carefully slid into the back seat.

Tiannah put her hand on my car's front passenger door.

Guilt washed through me. "Really, Tee, I've got this. It's not our first trip to urgent care. You have enough going on with a toddler, a kindergartner, and a fifth grader to bathe, feed, and put to bed."

She opened the door. "But you don't have to do it alone. Besides, I want to hear all about your first day as a consultant."

I smiled despite the clench in my stomach. We'd worked together until she'd quit two years ago to be a full-time mom. I'd been planning it even then, and she was almost as emotionally invested in Weber Technology Consulting as I was. "Okay, then. Hop in."

Noah was still fumbling with the seatbelt, so I clipped it for him. He gave me a wobbly smile, and I closed the door. I got into the driver's seat of my Honda, waved at Coach, and slowly backed out of the parking space, watching for soccer balls and distracted parents.

I caught Noah's gaze in the rear-view mirror. "Tell me what happened, buddy."

He kicked his cleats against the bench seat. "Practice was over, and Coach made us run a lap. I was winning, and when I looked up, I tripped. I fell on my arm, and it hurt a lot. Miz Tiannah, do you think I still won, even though I fell?"

"Sure you did. Everyone saw you would've finished first."

In the mirror, I saw him lean back and smile. The competitive spirit ran deep in the Weber family.

The urgent-care office wasn't far, and the route was familiar. But this time, with Tiannah's soothing presence in the car, I wasn't panicked about Noah's injury or beating myself up over my parenting failures that might've caused it. So I walked into the lobby with a smile, holding Noah's uninjured hand. I froze when I saw the unfamiliar face behind the desk.

"Where's Ruby?" I stepped up to the desk.

"Not here tonight. What's the reason for your visit?" She stared at her screen, fingers poised over her keyboard.

"My nephew"—shit, I was going to have to go through all that with her—"injured his arm playing soccer. He's ten. Is Dr. Ruiz here tonight?"

"Yep." She typed the entry then handed me a clipboard. "I need you to fill that out, and we need a letter of consent from his parents."

"I'm his guardian. His parents are"—I stole a glance at Noah in the plastic chair next to Tiannah—"no longer with us. I'm sure we're in your system with the appropriate documentation."

Her smile was saccharine-sweet. "Fill out the paperwork. Don't forget the insurance information."

My heart dropped into my stomach. *Insurance.* How much was this visit going to cost? At least we hadn't gone to the hospital emergency room. Yet.

I took the clipboard from her and trudged to where Tiannah and Noah sat. I flopped down into the chair next to Noah and filled out

the form, taking out my new insurance card and carefully tran-
scribing the numbers.

Tiannah nudged me with her elbow. "What's wrong?"

"Nothing, just…right now, I'm missing my old insurance. You
know how good it was. I went for the cheaper plan while I'm still
getting my company off the ground. I should've known better than to
start up my company during soccer season. This copay is going to
hurt."

"Having your own business is worth it. You'll get through this."

After the meeting with Cooper and Jackson, I wasn't so sure.

I had to argue with the new receptionist about the parental note
until she found our paperwork in the system. Victorious at last, we
were taken back to see Dr. Ruiz, who palpated Noah's arm and told
us she needed to take him back for an X-ray.

When the door closed behind them, Tiannah hugged me. "It'll be
okay, sugar."

"I know." I squeezed her back. "He's a tough kid."

She leaned against the exam room wall. "You're tough, too, you
know. How was your first day?"

I snorted. "Terrible." I lifted my hair to show her the Lightning
McQueen bandage and told her briefly about the dysfunctional
founders of Synergy Analytics and the difficult task they'd set
for me.

She shook her head. "What'd Jamila say?"

"When? You mean two weeks ago, when she told me about this
gig?"

"You didn't call her after?"

"Today? No. I wore my big-girl panties today. I can handle this."

Tiannah rolled her eyes. "Always thinking you have to go it alone.
Jamila knows these guys. They all went to college together. She can
give you some tips. Pointers. Leverage. I bet she's got some serious
dirt on that Jackson Jones. Something you can use to get a leg up on
him."

Thinking about Jackson Jones and legs—the way those broken-in
jeans stretched over his thighs—made my cheeks hot. As usual,
Tiannah didn't miss a thing.

"Are they as fine as their pictures?"

"Head injury." I pointed at my cut. "I can't be trusted to make judgments like that."

Pursing her lips, she raised her eyebrows.

"Okay, yes, totally hot. Both of them. But Cooper's a glacier." I shivered, remembering the chill of his eyes. Jackson was the opposite: the warmth in those brown eyes as he'd blotted the blood from my face had felt like a crackling campfire on a crisp fall day, but they'd blazed into a wildfire when he'd learned I was there to take over his project. Dangerous. The flame had been doused after he'd spoken in the hall with Cooper. I still couldn't get a read on their dynamic.

"Oh, and I forgot to mention that I tried to ask Jackson Jones out, before I knew who he was, so there's that." I winced.

"Girl." She clucked her tongue. "I don't have to tell you to stay far away from all that."

"Nope. Nothing but downside for me in that situation. Good thing he turned me down." My stomach twisted with embarrassment. "And now that I've joined his project, Jackson's about as friendly as a bramble bush. Anyway, it's totally irrelevant. I'm there to do a job. Get in, get out."

"But?"

"I guess I thought it'd be different as a consultant. They hire me to be smart. I come in, I save the project, I leave. No fragile male egos. No company picnics. No happy hours. No performance reviews. Easy. Transactional."

"Honey." She gripped my hand. "Nothing's easy for women in a man's world. You'll be fighting the good fight against the patriarchy every damn day. I know you'll do your best. And you'll make Jamila proud."

I heard what she didn't say, too. That if I made a mess at Synergy, it'd reflect poorly on Jamila. I took a deep breath. "Do the job, get out. Don't rock the boat. I hear you." I'd tiptoed through the minefield of male egos my whole career. And this time, I was being paid double what I'd earned as a regular employee.

Fighting Jackson Jones, I'd earn every penny. And when Dr. Ruiz came in and told me Noah had fractured his ulna, and her assistant told us how much his treatment would cost with my rusted-tin insurance, I knew I'd need it, too.

3

JACKSON

"YOU WON'T FIND food like this in San Francisco." I leaned away to gauge Cooper's expression.

His lip curled so slightly that someone who hadn't known him for a dozen years might not have seen it. His gaze wandered from the "Keep Austin Weird" T-shirt of the person in front of us to the order taker, sweaty and with sauce on her apron, to the overcrowded kitchen, where an even sweatier man flipped a rack of ribs. "No, I don't think I would."

Ever since Alicia had swept into the meeting that morning—the meeting I'd thought was *mine*, proof Cooper finally trusted me again —all confidence and grace despite the ridiculous bandage I'd pressed to her forehead, I felt like I'd been covered in ants. Fire ants, which I'd discovered were a thing—a painful, ass-biting thing—when I'd tried to rest on the grass at the park after one of my runs. And that made me, as they said here in Texas, ornery.

So I'd brought Cooper to the smokehouse, with its surly service and sticky tables and self-service condiments, which I knew he'd hate. But I was no fool. The food, the best thing I'd eaten in the three months I'd been in Austin, was worth it.

My phone buzzed in my pocket, and I pulled it out. A reminder to call Sam. Marlee was a saint for setting the weekly reminders. I ignored the ones she'd set to call my mother and my other siblings, but I never blew off the one for Sam.

"Sorry, something I have to take care of. Order me the ribs, potato salad, and okra?" I chuckled at Cooper's horror-struck expression and ducked outside. I found some shade under a tree, tucked in my earbuds, and videocalled Sam.

She picked up after a few rings. The institutional gray walls surrounding her made her pale skin look greenish.

"Why can't you text like a normal person?"

"Favorite big brothers don't have to text first. Besides, I like catching people off guard. Where are you, anyway?"

"Stairwell at school. I was *working* when you called."

"On homework? Need any help?"

"No, Jackson." She rolled her eyes. "I'm working on my research project."

"That's programming, right? I can help. Like I used to do when I lived at home."

"When I lived at home, I wasn't doing convex optimization. And neither were you."

"Convex what?"

She smirked. "Yeah, they didn't teach that *ten years ago* to undergraduates, even at *Stanford*. Admit it, now that I'm in graduate school, I'm the programming guru."

"Of course. You've always been a natural. But are you sure you're okay?" She hadn't had those dark circles under her eyes the last time we'd talked.

"I'm fine. Though my dissertation project isn't going as well as I'd hoped. It's really hard, you know?"

"I barely got my bachelor's. What you're doing is hard, but you can do it. You're the smartest of us all."

She snorted, but I could tell she was hiding a smile. "Tell that to Mother."

"I will, next time I talk to her." Which wouldn't be until Thanksgiving if I could help it.

Her half-smile fell. "I wish I could come to Texas."

I jumped up and paced around the tree. "Why? What's wrong?

That asshole Stephen isn't bothering you again, is he? Because I'll fly back there and—"

"No, no. I just mean that Mother can be a lot. I could use some distance. Someday…"

My little sister was a lot like me, but she hadn't developed my fuck-it attitude toward our mother. "Don't let her bully you. And maybe distance is all you need from your project. You know our brains don't work the same as other people's. Take a drive. Or a run. Spend some time outside."

One corner of her mouth lifted. "You always excelled at escaping tough situations."

"Hey, I'm not saying it's the healthiest coping strategy, but maybe you need a break. Hell, I'll fly you here, Samwise. We can go to a honky-tonk bar. Drink tequila until we puke." Having a friendly face in Austin would be a relief after months of having people walk on eggshells around the company founder. At least at headquarters, they considered me a fuckup, nothing to be afraid of. Weston—and even Cooper—had made sure of that.

"That's nice of you to offer, but I'll pass. Too much to do here. Maybe I'll take Bilbo Baggins on a long walk, though."

"Okay." I didn't let my disappointment show on my face. "But if you need anything, you call me."

"Got it. When are you coming home?"

"Maybe Thanksgiving. Definitely Christmas." Cooper said we had to finish development by mid-November. I hoped that would end my exile. Then I could check on my sister in person.

"Good. I miss you. Love you, Jackson."

"Love you, too, Samwise."

I sighed out a deep breath. I'd call her and check up again next week. Make sure she was sleeping. I wished I could help with her programming. We used to program silly games together, full of magic and swordplay. I'd had a blast teaching my little sister to code. But she was right; she'd lapped me in her expertise. Programming was one of the things I was best at, but now even Cooper had lost faith in my skill.

I trudged to the wooden picnic table where Cooper had settled. Most of the day's heat had gone down with the sun, but it was still broiling for a couple of guys who'd grown up in the cool summers of Northern California. My AC/DC T-shirt stuck to my back. Cooper had rolled up his sleeves.

"I've been meaning to ask you all day." Cooper looked down at my feet. "What the fuck are those?"

"My boots?" I dropped onto the bench and propped up one foot to admire the ostrich vamp. That was what the cute girl at the boot store had told me to call the part that ran from the toe to the ankle, where the shaft started. We'd joked a lot about the shaft. But I'd bought my boots and left, declining to take her number. For all I knew, she'd show up the next day as our new receptionist. Which reminded me of how I'd almost fucked up with Alicia.

"I don't want to talk about the fucking boots. I want to talk about how you hired a consultant without telling me." One I'd almost asked out before I'd learned she worked in our building. I replayed our first few minutes together. The silkiness of her straight blond hair when I brushed it off her forehead. Her smooth skin, marred by that freakishly sharp piece of ice. Her prim black suit, nipped in at all the right places, paired with those sky-high dominatrix heels. A naughty schoolteacher-fantasy-in-distress that lit up all my buttons. But I wasn't about to repeat the mistake I'd made with Callie.

"You want to do this now?" His blue eyes glittered with ice chips. "Fine. The way you acted this afternoon was inexcusable. Yes, we're partners. And friends. But I won't allow you to undermine me or my decisions. Which includes Alicia."

"Only a fucking asshole springs *that* on his best friend in front of his team." Was it even my team anymore?

He had the grace to look embarrassed. "Sorry, Jay, I know it was less than ideal. I should've handled it better. I didn't know how to tell you without—"

"How about, 'Now you've managed to fuck up the one thing you used to be good at, so we'll bring in some rando off the street to fix it for you. Anyone could do it better than you, Jay.'"

"She's not a rando," Cooper growled. "She's fully qualified and certified, and she has a glowing recommendation from Jamila. You trust Mila, don't you?"

I didn't trust her if she was going to recommend someone who was clearly my kryptonite to work with me. Had Cooper told Jamila what'd happened in May, and now she was trying to punish me for it? But why would she do that? We were friends. Not like she and Cooper were, with their on-again, off-again dating. Last week, she'd come to see me here, in exile. She'd taken me out for tacos and hadn't said a word about Callie. Or Alicia Weber.

Was it a coincidence that she'd recommended Alicia, smart, competent, and maybe a good coder, too, who'd make going into the office a daily torture? Someone—the universe, maybe?—had set me up to fail.

No. I'd done it. I'd done it to myself by fucking up. If I hadn't gotten drunk that night, I wouldn't be in Austin. I'd never have met Alicia Weber or been replaced by her.

Our number squawked out over the speaker, interrupting the Randy Travis song.

I stood. "I'll be right back."

A minute later, I plunked an aluminum tray of charred chicken breast, pinto beans, and collard greens in front of Cooper. The look on his face was priceless, and the horror intensified when I set down my own tray of sauce-slathered ribs, fried okra, and creamy potato salad.

But he didn't say a word. He plucked a fork and knife from the can on the table, wiped them about a hundred times with a paper towel from the roll next to it, and then started cutting into his chicken with a delicate sawing motion worthy of my mother at a three-Michelin-star restaurant.

I tore a rib from the rack and bit into the tender meat. Delicious. Did I enjoy Cooper's revulsion as I licked sauce off my lips and my fingertips? Um, yeah.

We ate for a few minutes in silence. Aside from the five minutes I hadn't known Alicia worked in my building, they were the best part of my day.

Until he set down his knife and fork. "Since you came here—"

"Don't sugarcoat it, Coop. Since you exiled me here." I tossed a stripped bone into the pile in the corner of my tray.

He gave me a you-know-what-you-did scowl. "I thought by removing you from the...situation, it would help you focus on work. And yet I haven't seen any progress."

Heat built inside my chest, and it wasn't from the spicy barbecue sauce. "I'm leading by example. I'm keeping my head down and coding like you told me to do. The other guys are, too. We're making progress."

He lifted a bite of limp collard greens on his fork and squinted at it. I'd neglected to point out that here, "greens" didn't mean raw kale. "I had no evidence of that. Or confidence you'd finish on time."

"Don't you trust me, Coop?" Our friendship of over a dozen years should've been worth something.

"I—" He returned the greens to his plate and shifted them around. "I want to. But…"

He didn't have to finish. My most recent fuckup had been pretty epic.

He set down his fork. "Gurusoft has already announced their product. Our biggest customer told me last week that if we don't have ours ready to go by the end of the year, they're switching. We can't let that happen. Not in this business climate."

"When were you going to tell me that?" I grabbed a paper towel and scrubbed at my fingers.

"Last week. I wish you'd read your email."

Cooper sent me a lot of email. Usually, it was full of numbers and shit I didn't care about. "Fuck."

"This is our problem, right here, Jackson." His hand curled into a fist on the sticky wood of the table. "You don't take anything seriously. And our business is fucking serious."

I rolled my eyes up to the red-and-white table umbrella. He'd used my name, not *Jay* like he'd called me since we became best friends our freshman year at Stanford, like I was some coworker. Our business hadn't always been serious. It used to be fun. Back when we were just a pair of nerds in our dorm room, dreaming of changing the world.

"Look," he said more gently. "I know what happened to your dad gave you a certain outlook on life—"

"A fucking heart attack at age forty-one. That's only nine years older than us!"

Cooper glanced at the people at the next table who'd turned to stare. He held out his palms to me in a "whoa" gesture. "No one's saying you need to be a workaholic like he was. I need more communication. That's why I brought in Alicia."

I waved my hands over my head. "I text you almost every day!"

"Not about our business." His eyes narrowed at my elbow. "Why are you wearing a Lightning McQueen bandage?"

I'd forgotten it was there. "Funny story. Marlee—"

"Alicia had one, too." His eyes were slits. "Did you two—"

"No!" Did he think I fucked everyone I saw? And when would I have had the time? "She got caught in the hailstorm, cut her head. I gave her one of these. I was being nice. That was before I knew you two were fucking me over. Should've let her bleed everywhere." She'd have been the one judged unprofessional instead of me. Though not even an asshole like me could've left her there, bleeding. Not even if I'd known why she was there.

With one last pinch of his icy eyes, Cooper leaned back. "If I hear even the smallest hint—"

I snorted. "Not happening. I learned my lesson. I promise. Now, since you're replacing me here, can I go back home?" I'd be able to see Sam, make sure she wasn't working herself into the ground.

"I'm not replacing you. You're the best damn programmer I've ever known. Now that Alicia's here, you can focus on the code, and leave her to deal with everything else."

"Everything else?"

His gaze shifted to the side. "Managing the backlog, reporting, mentoring the team, you know, all that."

"But I do that. I'm the team lead." Well, okay, I was responsible for it. Maybe I hadn't done it as well as I should've. I'd been so shell-shocked about the thing with Callie that I'd been afraid to make any personal connections at all in the Austin office. I'd figured if we all just did the work, it'd sort itself out in the end.

He wiped his hands. "Now she's the team lead."

I slumped on the bench. It was happening again. I'd fucked up, and another piece of the company was being taken from me. But I'd never let Cooper see how much it hurt, and I wasn't about to start now.

"Here, try this." I held out a piece of okra.

"You know I don't eat fried food."

"It's a vegetable. Try it." I extended the crisp round to him. "Trust me." I'd never eaten it before I came to Texas, and the difference in texture between the crunchy outside and the gooey inside fascinated me.

He squinted at me but took the piece of okra from my hand. He stared at it for a second and then popped it in his mouth. After the first crunch, his mouth went limp, but he chewed it and swallowed like a champ. He gulped some water before spluttering, "That's revolting."

I picked up another piece and crunched it. "Maybe it's an acquired taste?"

"Focus, Jay. We need to talk this through." He wiped his mouth on a fresh paper towel. "I have full confidence in your coding ability, but sales of this product are going to make or break our first quarter. Remember how many people rely on us. The sales team. Marketing. Customer support. If we have products for them to sell, to market, to support, they have jobs. If we don't..." He spread his hands, palms up.

"You can't be talking about layoffs." My friend could be a cold bastard, but I didn't think he'd gone to the dark side. With fucking Weston, our CEO.

Cooper clenched his jaw. "Maybe you haven't noticed, but you haven't gotten a salary this year. Neither have I. The recession has been hard on our customers. Fewer people buying cars means less money for telematics systems, for manufacturing optimization software. Fewer people working means companies can't afford expensive business analytics systems. They're struggling, and now, so are we. I don't want to lay people off, but if this product is delayed, we might need to furlough some of them until it's ready."

The faces of my team members flashed into my brain. The senior developer, Amit. The new guy, Tyler. Even Ivan, the security guard. Marlee, my assistant back in San Francisco. She didn't really have anything to do now that I was here, but I'd refused to furlough her. She lived with her dad, who couldn't work, and they both depended on her income.

"No furloughs." I relaxed my grip on my knife and fork and laid them down on the aluminum tray. They'd left red lines on my palms. "I've got this, Coop. I won't let them down."

"I know, Jay. But Alicia's in charge now."

"Coop, give me another chance. I—" I wasn't ready to beg, but I'd do anything to get him to believe in me again. Not to be letting him down. "Tell me what I need to do to prove myself to you."

He stared at me, those freaky ice-blue eyes boring into my soul. He'd always seen me for who I was, no matter what smokescreen I hid behind. "Fine. Three things." He held up three fingers and ticked them off. "Produce good code on time. Earn the respect of the team. Work together to achieve your goals."

Good code, I could do. On time wasn't always guaranteed, but I'd try. The respect of the team? Easy. My reputation was legendary. The new guy, Tyler, practically worshiped me.

But work together? Not my strong suit. I'd learned a long time ago not to trust anyone except Cooper. He was the only one who'd never mocked me for my lack of focus, for my impulsiveness, for my disregard of authority that got me into trouble. Better to keep my head down, write my code, and rely on the other guys to do the same. But maybe if I spent a little more time interacting with the team, that'd be good enough for him. Besides, their jobs—everyone's jobs—were on the line. That was worth exposing myself to ridicule.

"Fine, I'll do it. You'll see. I've got this."

"I have full confidence in you and the team. With Alicia's help." Pushing his tray of half-eaten chicken away, he said, "Now, did I see a soft-serve machine?"

Cooper monitored his sugar intake with the same intensity that he followed his investment portfolio. He wouldn't touch self-serve, artificially vanilla flavored frozen dairy dessert with a ten-foot pole. So that was his signal we were done with this conversation, and his word was final. That was the way it'd been since Stanford. He made the decisions so I wouldn't fuck them up.

I reached across the table and gripped his wrist. "I'm trying to change, Coop. I won't let you down. I won't let anyone down."

When he nodded, I released him. We both knew that after coding, letting people down was what I did best.

Not this time. I'd prove to Cooper I could do this one thing without fucking it up.

4

ALICIA

I'D JUST LIFTED the steaming mug of Earl Grey to my lips—after a sleepless night with copays on the brain, I needed the hit of caffeine—when Jackson Jones sauntered into the communal kitchen, all long legs and athletic grace. I was glad I hadn't drunk it yet; I wasn't yet used to the wallop of seeing those soft, pink lips nestled into that dark beard, and the tea would've ended up on my blouse.

His lips weren't crooked up in a smile, not like when I'd met him yesterday before he knew I was replacing him as the team lead. They were set in a flat line. Gripping a green smoothie in a clear plastic cup with the straw still capped by the top of its wrapper, he approached to stand so close to me I had to crane my neck up to look him in the eye. Had he done it to intimidate me? If so, it wouldn't work.

"Morning, Jackson." I set down my mug and crossed my arms.

"Morning," he muttered.

My stomach curled into itself. I hadn't felt this way since middle school, when I'd gathered up every scrap of courage I could find to ask my crush, Ian Cameron, to the Sadie Hawkins dance, and he'd turned me down flat in front of the entire math class, saying he didn't date nerds.

Apparently, Jackson Jones ascribed to the same philosophy.

Checking that we were still alone in the kitchen, I jutted out my chin. "Don't worry. I'm not going to ask you out again. If I'd known who you were when we met, I wouldn't have done it in the first place."

I stood there, arms crossed, waiting for him to apologize for not telling me then that he was Synergy's cofounder. Or to say anything.

He tipped his chin at the counter behind me. "Mind if I—?"

I closed my eyes, wishing I could make myself invisible. I scooted away from the coffee machine. "Go ahead."

My cheeks tingled with heat. Fine. I was glad he'd turned me down. And I was glad he was acting like a jerk now. I'd remember this moment instead of staring at those kissable lips. No! They weren't kissable. They were just lips, slightly pouty at the corners. Used for talking. And frowning. I wouldn't be going anywhere near them.

I smoothed the wrinkles out of my skirt. "See you at the stand-up. Eight-thirty sharp."

"We always did them at nine. A little more humane, don't you think?"

I gave him a simpering smile. "But far less productive." I turned toward the door.

"Alicia."

I froze. People called me that all day. Why did I turn to jelly only when he said it?

"You forgot your...your tea?" He held it out to me, wrinkling his nose.

"Thank you." I snatched the cup and strode out.

The entire floor was open, and a line of potted trees separated our collaboration space from the rest of the office. Wide windows provided natural light. Three long, two-person desks arrayed with large monitors were arranged in a square with one side open.

Four of the seats were occupied. I tested myself on their names: Amit and Gary, the two senior developers; Kevin, the funny one; and Tyler, the junior developer. They faced the center of the open rectangle, which held a grouping of colorful, squashy pouf chairs. But we wouldn't have time to laze around in them. Much more useful was the whiteboard wall striped with swimlanes. My fingers itched for a pad of sticky notes.

"Morning, everyone." I set my bags on the empty center table. After turning my phone to vibrate, I tossed it into my purse and set it in the drawer. I pulled out my Synergy-issued laptop and connected it to the docking station. Tyler, to my left, peered around the side of my large monitor.

"That's it?" he said. "No knick-knacks? No pictures?" He gestured at his own workspace, where a collection of Star Wars figurines surrounded the base of his monitor.

"No." I'd learned long ago not to put pictures of Noah on my desk. Women with families got passed over. Only women who hid their life outside work ever got ahead in tech.

"So no kids?" Tyler swigged from a can of Mountain Dew.

I grimaced. "I do enough babysitting at work."

Tyler laughed. So did Kevin, who sat on the other side of him.

Jackson, who'd come around the corner, didn't. He stilled, his face a mask. Then he stalked around us to the seat on my other side. He didn't sit, and his knuckles whitened around his mug.

Shit, did he think I'd meant he needed a babysitter? It was only a joke, but now I wished I hadn't said it.

Jackson cleared his throat. "Shouldn't we start the stand-up, boss? Eight-thirty. Sharp."

The back of my neck burned like I was standing on asphalt at noon. But I'd never let him see he'd pricked me. "Absolutely."

I stood and circled the desks to the whiteboard, where the guys joined me. Good; I was glad that was one practice I didn't have to introduce.

Cooper emerged from the nearby stairwell, clutching a green smoothie. I didn't miss the way he scanned our group clustered around the whiteboard. Glad we'd started on time, I nodded at him. He returned my nod and lifted his smoothie to Jackson at the other end of the line. It seemed they'd made up. Good for them.

I dragged my attention from the guy who'd hired me to my team. "Before we start, I'd like to say a couple of words. First, I'm so excited to be working with you all. I know we'll do great things together."

Stepping up to the task board and its collection of colored sticky notes, I led them through a review of the backlog of work. Before we launched into a discussion of who would do what, I said, "I understand you're familiar with pair programming. I'd like to try that, at least on this first sprint. I know it's not the most efficient way to code, but it'll save us time in the end because the code will be higher quality. Okay? Now—"

"No."

All eyes swiveled to Jackson, who'd said it.

"No?" I raised my eyebrows.

"I code best on my own. I don't care if everyone else partners up" —he shrugged, hands in his pockets—"but it's not for me."

I took a deep breath through my nose. Was he resisting me because of the babysitting comment? "Jackson, I'd like everyone to try this. If it doesn't work, we can try something else for next sprint. Besides, we have an even number of people on the team. It'll work out well."

He hesitated, not even for a full second, but it was long enough for me to take back the reins. "Now, who's going to run with this first task?"

In the end, the other programmers paired up obediently. Only Jackson stubbornly refused to join up with anyone else. The words didn't want to come out, but I forced them to sound cheerful. "I guess that means you're with me, Jackson. All right, everyone, let's start."

The other guys rearranged themselves into pairs, but Jackson and I, already at the same desk, returned to our seats.

I unzipped my laptop bag and pulled out his folded, gray shirt.

"I got the blood out," I muttered, sliding it to him across the table.

"Thanks." His fingers brushed against mine for less than a second, but goosebumps still rose on my arm. I rubbed them away. *None of that.*

"Hey, Alicia?" Tyler's face hovered over the tops of our screens.

Had he seen me hand Jackson his shirt? I tried to smile at him, but the corners of my mouth wouldn't rise. "What's up?"

Jackson turned to his monitor and banged on his keyboard. The clacks of the keys rang out like crackling thunder.

Tyler asked a question about one of his tasks. I answered it, scanning his brown-green eyes for any hint of suspicion. His gaze flicked over to Jackson. Was it fanboy adulation, or did he think something inappropriate was going on between us? As a woman on a team of men, I'd been suspected before of secret relationships, of favoritism. I sent him off with a touch more vinegar than the question had merited.

After he went back to his desk, I logged into the Synergy network. Beside me, Jackson clacked away at his keyboard, but his stiff posture radiated tension. I wished I'd never said what I had to Tyler. We had to work together, damn it. And I needed to act like a leader, not one of the crew.

Softly, I said, "I'm sorry. About that comment I made. It was an attempt at a joke."

"A joke." The chill in Jackson's voice made me shiver. "Maybe you'd better leave those to me. I was always the class clown."

His tone was light, but the pain in those bottomless eyes twisted my stomach. "I meant it about me and my job, not about you."

Silence stretched between us. At last, he said, "Let's try to focus on the work." He turned to his keyboard.

Work. He was right. We were here to do work. Not to make friends. I'd apologized, and that was all I could do.

"Would you like to drive, or should I?"

"Hmm?" The bangs coming from his keyboard were so loud he might not have heard me. Listening to that all day would make me want to stab out my own eye with one of Tyler's action figures.

"We're a pair. How about I do the code entry—drive—and you navigate, by which I mean watch and comment?"

His fingers stilled, and he turned those dark brown eyes on me. They weren't melted-chocolate soft like they'd been yesterday but hard like polished mahogany. Quietly, he said, "I know what pair programming is. But I work best on my own. I'm not much of a team player, so I think we'll go faster if you do your work and I do mine."

My throat tightened. "Everyone can benefit from partnering up. We can learn from each other. Help each other."

He gave me a tight smile that only made his eyes seem harder. "I doubt you need help from someone like me."

Encouraging. "I guess that means I'll drive." I logged onto the coding interface and started typing. After a minute, he rolled his chair an inch or two closer, looming in my peripheral vision. The hairs on my arms rose again. He smelled. Like. Heaven.

Expensive leather. Something woodsy, like pine. Rick had smelled like the fragrance counter at Walgreens. But this didn't smell like it came from a bottle. He smelled like he could've ridden a horse through a forest earlier that day. He hadn't, had he? I sneaked a glance at his hands. Pale across the back except for a semicircle right below the wrist, and tanned fingers. All wrong for riding gloves, and callus-free, so probably not.

I shook my head. It didn't matter how great he smelled. We were colleagues. And not even friendly ones. Not even after my apology.

A few minutes later, he interrupted me. "I think we have some code for that method. You should call it."

"Oh." I searched the utility repository and found it. "Thanks."

"And maybe if you—"

"If I?"

He suggested a different way to organize the code. Unorthodox, but efficient. Grudgingly, I keyed it in.

"It'll compile a ton faster that way."

I shrugged. "Maybe you're right." He was definitely right. Damn him and his coding smarts. Would I ever reach his level?

He crossed his arms. He wore a Black Sabbath T-shirt that showed off his defined biceps and forearms and made me forget all about his brain. What would it feel like if I trailed a finger across his skin? Down over those strong wrists and—I swallowed—powerful fingers? I balled my hands into fists. I wouldn't be finding out.

Coding. I was here to code. I turned my face to the screen and started typing.

For most of the morning, we worked in silence, broken only by his suggestions for improvement. And although he'd said he worked best on his own, he acted more like a coach than a critic, making brilliant suggestions for how to make the code more efficient, more elegant. I felt like a clueless freshman around him, and I wondered again why I was there. Jackson could've coded the module we were working on with one hand tied behind his back while asleep.

Lunch by myself at a nearby deli was a welcome respite from Jackson's physical energy and intoxicating smell. I'd hoped for a few more minutes of peace when I returned, but no such luck. He was already there, his fingers clacking across the keyboard. *My* keyboard. Pair programming? Worst idea ever.

But I was the one who'd committed to it for at least the next two weeks, so I tucked my purse into the desk drawer and rolled my chair far enough away from him that I could sit down.

"I think we can finish this module today," he said. "You don't mind working after five, do you?"

"Actually, I have to leave by four. Every Tuesday and Thursday."

His fingers stilled, and he looked at me for the first time since the stand-up this morning. "You have another gig? Aren't we paying you enough?"

They were paying me plenty, more than double my hourly rate at my previous job, and I barely kept myself from snorting. "This is my only job. I quit my previous employer last month, when I'd saved up enough, when I'd done enough planning to go out on my own."

"So this is your first solo gig?"

Shit. I kept my wince on the inside. I'd revealed a weakness. "It is. But I've been planning this move for three years. It's always been my dream to be my own boss. You must know what that's like."

A flicker of something—pain?—narrowed his eyes. "I guess Synergy's recommendation will mean a lot to your business."

Was that sabotage lurking behind those flinty eyes? Regardless, I couldn't lie. Not even to someone who disregarded me as much as Jackson Jones did. "It will."

"And still, you're leaving work early two days a week?"

"When and why I leave work is no business of yours as long as I get the work done. You'll get your money's worth while I'm here."

He grunted. At least he didn't make another disparaging comment.

"Mind if I drive?" I indicated the keyboard.

He held up both hands. "Go for it."

We worked for half an hour or so as we had before lunch, me typing and him advising me in a way that made me wince at my own clumsiness. After a while, he asked, "Where'd you learn to code, anyway?"

"High school, and after that, UT."

"You're originally from Texas?"

"From Austin. I grew up just a few miles from here." I wasn't about to share that I lived in the same house where I'd grown up. With my mother.

"You've never left the state?"

"I didn't say that." My fingers stilled on the keyboard. "But no."

"No Disney World? No middle-school trip to D.C.? Graduation weekend in Paris?"

"Nope. We were more of a camping family."

"Camping's okay." He shrugged. "One summer, Cooper and I cycled through Europe."

Europe. It'd been my dream all through high school and college. But with money scarce, I'd put it off. And by the time I'd paid off my college loans, I had Noah and his college savings to build. No Europe for me. Though if Weber Technology Consulting took off, maybe we could finally take that trip I'd always dreamed of.

"And you've been working in Austin since you graduated?" He stretched his long legs under the desk, and his boots creaked.

"A lot of software companies are based here. I worked for several before I left and started my own business." It still gave me goose-bumps to be able to say that. *My own business.*

"How about I drive for a while?"

"What?" Was all the small talk a distraction to lull me into a false sense of security?

"It'll be faster if I type."

"No, I've got this." If I let him drive, he'd leave me in the dust. And for the next two months, I'd be running behind him, trying to wrest back control. I wasn't about to let Jackson Jones and his noisy, flying fingers snatch this project away from me.

5

JACKSON

I WAS glad to see the back of Alicia Weber. Not only because those red slingback heels and black pencil skirt did fantastic things to her ass. It meant I could get a minute of peace without the polished pink tips of those long fingers flying over the keyboard, without the wispy threads of her hair that escaped her bun at her nape teasing me, tempting me to touch them. Without the whisper of her ruby silk blouse setting my teeth on edge.

Without that judgmental set to her pink lips, showing she found me lacking, just like everyone else.

A babysitter.

Had Cooper told her I needed one? That she needed to watch me to ensure I didn't fuck up the project? That, if left to my own devices, I'd destroy the company I'd built, like some two-year-old with a tower of blocks?

Had my best friend told her he didn't trust me?

He didn't need to tell her that. Her presence at Synergy communicated that, loud and clear.

My hands poised over the keyboard, I gazed at the code we'd written that day. She was pretty good. Not as practiced as me, but who was? I'd been coding since I could read. Since Dad had given me that old desktop computer and a book on the Linux programming language. Still, together we'd produced more code in one day—a short one—than I'd done all last week. Something about working elbow-to-elbow with someone else, that subtle sense of competition, kept my brain from wandering. Why hadn't I thought to do it before?

Oh, right. *Does not play well with others.* I'd been getting that message since before I could read.

"Ah, Jackson?" It was the new guy looming over my desk. The one with glasses. Tyler. He still had to unlearn some of the crap they'd taught him in college, but he had potential. I hadn't hated some of his code.

"Yeah?"

"Is Alicia still here? I had a question."

"No, she left. She has to leave early on Tuesdays and Thursdays." And what was up with that? As a consultant, she could set her own hours, but I was sure Cooper had given her the same message as me —*this project can't fail*—so why not rearrange her schedule of manicures or girls' nights out or volunteer work with underprivileged puppies or meetings of the future dictators' club? Where the fuck did she go?

"Oh, okay," Tyler said. "Could you—"

I stood. "She'll be back tomorrow. You can ask her then. I'm getting a coffee." I tucked my laptop under my arm and strode toward the stairs. I'd figure it out. And if I couldn't, I knew someone who could shed light on the Alicia enigma.

In the small local coffee shop a few blocks away—not at the Starbucks across the street where anyone would think to look for me—I settled at a corner table painted in bold flowers.

I opened my laptop and flopped into the chair. *Alicia Weber University of Texas Austin*, I typed into the search box.

I found her middle name, Diane. The dean's list for every semester she'd spent at school. The scholarships she'd won. The programming prizes. Her page on a professional social network that listed her previous employers and projects. No wonder Cooper thought she was better than I was. She was a shining star.

I picked up my phone.

"Jackson! What's going on?"

God, I missed Marlee. She was the one friendly face I could count on at work. Who accepted me for who I was, fuckups and all. "Remind me again why you aren't out here with me."

"You know I can't leave Dad."

I knew. Still, I was a fucking selfish bastard. "How's he doing?"

"He's good. He gave a talk at the Young Astronomers' Club the other day. He did pretty well."

Even over the phone, I caught the slight hesitation in her voice. "What happened?"

"Nothing. He just mixed up Betelgeuse with Antares. And one of the kids had to correct him."

"Oh. But that's an easy mistake, right? Aren't they both...red?"

"Good Galileo. You've been listening to me."

"I always listen to you, Marlee."

"That's a damn lie, but I'll allow it today since you actually called me. Why *did* you call me, Jackson?"

"Just to hear your voice?"

She made a sound like the buzzer at a basketball game. "Try again, boss."

"Fine. What do you know about this new consultant we've hired? Alicia Weber."

"The one Cooper hired to save your ass, you mean?"

I winced. "He said that?"

"He didn't have to say it. Cooper's been pulling his hair out about that project. I tried to give him status updates, but when you don't call me for weeks, it's kind of hard."

"Fuck, I'm sorry. I should've—"

"It's okay. It's done. Alicia's there now. What's she like?"

"Annoying. Bossy. Brilliant."

"What was that last word? You mumbled, but it sounded like you said 'brilliant.'"

"I did, okay? She's smart. I feel a little...irrelevant."

"No, Jackson. You're important. Cooper needs you there. The company needs you. Don't disappear, okay?"

"Disappear? Wouldn't dream of it."

"You know what I mean. Don't give up and hide, okay? Don't run off to Amsterdam or Monaco or Rio or freaking Antarctica. You're important. You're worthy. People rely on you. Say it."

Too bad I hadn't had a Marlee back in school when I'd been the slowest kid in the class, unable to focus on what the teacher was saying or what I was supposed to read. The other kids had called me stupid. The best way I'd found to cope had been to laugh it off. Pretend I didn't care. Then run away and hide my tears. Once I left school, the world was full of ways to show I didn't give a fuck—booze, raves, yacht parties, bungee jumps—to hide how much I did.

I mumbled, "I'm important. I'm worthy. People rely on me."

"Good job. I miss you, you know. Work isn't nearly as fun when you're not here."

"My work isn't nearly as fun without you, either."

"Aw. But remember what I said: no hiding. Make friends. Go out and have fun. I bet Austin has amazing food."

"Yeah, it's not bad."

"You're remembering to eat, aren't you?"

Shit, she sounded like my mother. Not *my* mother, but someone's mother who worried about more than her family's perfect appearance. Without a mother of her own, Marlee had taken on the caretaking role at home for her dad. And since she'd joined Synergy a few years ago, she'd done the same for me, even though she was younger than me.

She must've interpreted my silence as a lack of recent nourishment. "I'm going to set a reminder on your calendar for mealtimes. Anything else you need, boss?"

"Yeah. If you get a minute, could you check up on Sam? I don't think she's sleeping."

"You got it. I'll drop by the university tomorrow."

"Thanks. I'll call you again soon, okay?"

"Yeah, right. Take care of yourself, Jackson."

"You, too. Tell your dad I said hi."

I stood, stretched, and went to the counter, where I ordered a sandwich. While I waited for it, I made another call.

"Hey, Jay." Jamila's familiar husky voice came through my wireless earbuds.

"Why the fuck do you sound so smug?"

"I may have made a bet with a certain friend of ours about how long it'd take you to call me."

"Cooper had more faith in me than you did?"

"My money was on our girl Alicia."

"So you did send her to be my kryptonite." What kind of game was Jamila playing? Cooper had said jobs were on the line.

"No, honey. Don't get your cables in a twist. I sent her because I think you two will work well together. She's smart, right? A stellar coder?"

"She's not as good as me. Or you. Better than Cooper, though."

Jamila's voice gentled. "She doesn't have to be as good as you. All she has to do is bring out your best. And the best of the rest of the team."

Before Alicia, that had been my job. And as Marlee had pointed out, and Cooper before her, I'd fucked it up.

"Look, I'm trying, okay? I just needed more time. Not some Stepford programmer to take over my team and make me look bad."

"From what I understand, Jay, you're out of time. Alicia is there to save your project and make you look good. When are you going to realize that you have so much more to offer than your programming skills? That it's time for you to step up and lead?"

The heat that had bubbled inside me ever since Alicia forced us to do goddamned pair programming boiled over. "When Cooper fucking gives me a chance to lead and stops putting babysitters in charge of me!"

My own labored breathing hissed through my earbuds. Jamila said nothing but left my angry words—unfair words, really, since he'd given me three months to prove myself and I'd blown it— echoing in our ears.

"Jay," she said at last in a voice so soft I put my hands over my earbuds to block out the other sounds in the coffee shop. "Alicia is a professional, a damn good one, and her job is to get the team working together to produce results. Including you. She won't be your babysitter unless you act like a child."

Serious Jay hadn't worked, so it was time to pull out fuckboy Jay. I tried to make my voice light, careless. "Me, act like a child?"

"I'm going to tell you this once. Don't fuck this up for her. She needs this job, this testimonial, to build her business. I'm going to be back out there in two weeks, and I'm going to check in with Alicia. If I find out you're sabotaging her—"

"No one said anything about sabotage."

"If I find out you're fucking with her, I will kick your ass. You know I'll do it."

"God, Jamila." She wouldn't actually kick my ass. But that tongue of hers would make my ears bleed for a week.

She gave me a sample of her ass-kicking tone. "Am I understood?"

"Loud and clear."

"I really do think you'll be great together."

A few more productive days like today, and they'd all realize they didn't need me at all. Cooper would figure out I was more trouble than I was worth, and we'd have a replay of what'd happened during the IPO. But this time I'd be out on my ass. Completely, not only demoted.

Not. Going. To. Happen.

"Still there, Jay?"

"Yeah, I'm here."

"I'll see you in a couple weeks."

"'Kay. Bye."

I let my head fall forward into my hands so I didn't have to look at my screen that showed a photo of Alicia in her cap and gown with her honors medallion and cord.

Cooper had told me to do three things: produce good code on time, earn the respect of the team, and some bullshit about working together. I'd show him. All he really needed was for me to produce good code on time. I'd do that. And I didn't need help from fucking Alicia Diane Weber.

6

ALICIA

THAT MORNING, I'd bravely tried the Cranberry Passion Blitz. The tea package in the break room claimed it was full of antioxidants. Maybe antioxidants would help me get through a day working side-by-side with Jackson Jones.

I lifted the steaming cup to my lips while the team gathered around me for our morning stand-up meeting. "Who'd like to go first?"

"I will." Jackson strode past me to the board, the scent of leather blowing away the nauseatingly fruity smell of my tea. But he wasn't wearing the boots today. Instead, he had on a well-worn pair of char-coal-gray-or-maybe-used-to-be-black Converse. He moved the sticky note with the name of the module we'd worked on yesterday from the "In progress" column to "Ready for Test." "This module was completed yesterday."

I choked down the scalding-hot tea. "No, we didn't finish. We still have to—"

"Correction: *I* finished it yesterday after you left. Progress shouldn't stop when you're not here." He crossed his arms over his chest.

My tongue wasn't the only thing burning. Heat radiated down from my scalp to my chest. Conscious of the rest of the team's rapt attention, I kept my voice steady. "That's not how pair programming is supposed to work. You could've checked through the code—"

"I did."

"—or helped one of the other pairs. Remember"—I faced the rest of the guys—"we're all on the same team."

"Completing code ahead of schedule means we can fit extra work into this sprint and finish faster." He plucked another sticky note from the "Backlog" column and moved it to "In progress." Without consulting me, his partner and team lead.

A new burn started in my belly and rose up my chest. My hairline prickled with sweat, and my half-healed cut stung. Angry words caught in my throat, but I swallowed them down. *Do the job, get out. Don't rock the boat.* It was what I'd promised Tiannah. I couldn't let Jamila down. I couldn't let myself down, either. And a shouting match with the company's cofounder in front of our team was a no-win situation for me.

I set my cup on the nearest desk and strode to the board, pulling the guys' attention from Jackson's smirking face. "Okay, then, let's hear from the other pairs."

The rest of the guys reported on their progress from yesterday and their focus for today. Tyler and his partner had encountered a problem, and after the meeting, I pulled up a chair to their desk to help them work through it.

It wasn't a difficult problem; more than anything, they needed a fresh set of eyes. But after I'd pointed out where they were going wrong and while they fixed it, my mind wandered to Jackson Jones.

He'd finished the code—*our* code—without me. Had I really been that much of a hindrance to him while we'd worked together? True, his brain went blazingly fast, and my fingers could hardly keep up. But I'd contributed some ideas, too. And he hadn't snarled at all of them.

He'd been so different under the awning that first day. When he'd sneaked that hailstone into his bag for safekeeping like an excited little boy. When he'd gently blotted at the cut on my forehead and pressed that ridiculous bandage against my skin. When he'd looked into my eyes like he cared whether or not I was okay.

Not anymore. If I'd given up and walked out, he'd have thrown a party to celebrate.

"Hey, Alicia, want to go to lunch?" Tyler was already standing, patting his pockets.

"Oh, I don't know. I haven't checked in with the other teams." I shot a glance at Jackson, who had his headphones on and was clack-clack-clacking away.

"Our treat," Amit said. "It's the least we can do since you helped us. We're going for tacos."

"Same team, remember. You don't owe me anything." Still, I stood. My stomach rumbled. *Tacos.*

Amit had to take his tacos to go so he could make it back to the office for a senior developers' meeting. Tyler and I sat on a bench in the shade to eat our lunch.

After scarfing his tacos, Tyler wiped his mouth and balled up his napkin and wrapper. "Alicia, can I ask you a question?"

I set down my taco. "Of course."

"What's the deal with—how do I—" He compacted the ball of paper further. "I'm just going to say it, okay?"

I nodded. "This is a safe space. I'll keep your confidence."

"Thanks." He pushed his glasses up his nose. "I've been working for Synergy for about six months. They recruited me from another company." He puffed out his chest. "I'm working at a company founded by *Jackson Jones.* How cool is that?"

Less cool than he'd thought it would be, if his experience was anything like mine.

"And then, three months ago, *Jackson himself* comes here, and I'm assigned to work on his project. I just about shit myself when I found out."

I'd have probably felt the same when I was a baby programmer. "But it hasn't turned out the way you'd hoped?"

He slumped. "No. He got here, and he seemed all pissed off, and he told us what to do and then sat at his desk with his headphones on. So we all did, too, but the code didn't come together. But now you're here, it already feels better. We've got direction. And help when we need it."

"Thanks for telling me." A frisson shot down my spine. I was making a difference. I wanted to dance right there on the bench, but I refrained. Tyler looked like he had more to say.

"I'd really like to learn from Jackson, but I don't know how to get close."

My internal boogie turned into the freeze. He wanted to learn from Jackson, not from me. It made sense: Jackson was an internationally famous programmer, and I was unknown outside Austin. His words pricked my pride. But last I'd checked, I was still wearing my big-girl panties.

"Keep trying to talk to him. You might wear down his walls eventually. I haven't known him long enough to really figure him out, but I'll work on it. If I come up with anything, I'll let you know."

"Thanks, Alicia."

I finished my lunch, and we ambled back to the office. I'd taken off my jacket in the September heat, and after eating chipotle-chicken tacos, I was still too warm to put it back on, even in the air-conditioned building. I draped it over the back of my chair and sat next to Jackson, who, true to form, had his headphones on.

At least he noticed when I sat down, staring for a second at my bare arms before meeting my gaze. His brown eyes were soft, unguarded for a second, the way they'd been before he'd known the cats I'd come in to wrangle were his. Like we really could be a team and not constantly snipe at each other. The tinny squeal of a guitar escaped when he lifted off his headphones.

I wanted to say something friendly. Something that'd keep that softness in his eyes, keep his jaw from hardening. But when I opened my mouth, the words that came out were, "Ready to get started on that new module?" The module he'd selected without discussing it with anyone, including me, the team lead. The cordial smile I'd intended became a grimace.

"I already started it. While you were off doing whatever." His eyes went flinty, and he waved his hand vaguely at Tyler, at the stairs.

"Okay, then," I forced out through my clenched jaw. "We can pick up where you left off. Want me to drive again?"

"No, I've got this. How about you check the code from yesterday? Or do the cleanup."

The cleanup? He might as well have asked me to sit quietly in a meeting and take notes while the men talked. I wanted to snap off my earrings and fight him right there in the open workspace. But I couldn't. My own irritating words echoed in my brain. *Don't rock the boat. Same team.*

"Sure." I didn't bother to smile this time. If that was how Jackson Jones wanted to play this, we'd do it. As long as we produced good code on time, it didn't matter how we got there.

Still, as I began to check through yesterday's code, that burn remained in my belly. Had I just given Jackson Jones room to run me over?

7

JACKSON

"GREAT JOB, TYLER." The wide, proud smile on Alicia's face was better suited to discovering the cure for cancer than to moving a sticky note from "In progress" to "Ready for Test" on the next-to-last day of the sprint. Her eyes were soft like the blue Texas sky that morning, not steely like they were when I'd picked up another new module from the backlog.

Was something going on between them? I rubbed my beard. Tyler was young—twenty-four—and Alicia was thirty. Though some people didn't care about an age difference. God, I'd hooked up with— No, I wasn't going to think about that now. No one here knew my shameful secret, and I didn't want the remorse to show on my face.

"Jackson." Alicia propped her hands on her hips.

I ripped my eyes up to her face. "Huh?"

"Is everything okay? You were making a face."

"Oh. Just thinking about all the work we have to do before the sprint review on Monday." A lie, but I couldn't tell her I'd been dreaming up ways to focus her proud, blue-sky gaze on myself instead of Tyler.

True to form, she nodded, her blond eyebrows squishing together. "There is a lot. But I know we can get it done." She brushed past Tyler and bent at the waist to move up a sticky note from the bottom of the backlog. I didn't miss how Tyler's gaze arrowed to the stretch of her narrow skirt over the curve of her ass.

"Tyler," I said, too loud, "how about you pick something out of the backlog to work on today and tomorrow? I bet if you and I partner up, we can knock it out by Monday."

Tyler's eyes widened behind his glasses. "Really? I mean, yeah, of course." He took Alicia's place at the board, scanning the sticky notes in the "Not started" column.

Alicia came to stand next to me, her nearness sending a shiver up my arm. In a low voice, she said, "It's great you're committing to teamwork, but do you think this is a good idea? He can't finish by Monday, not even if you help."

"Maybe I have more faith in him than you do." It didn't matter if he finished by Monday. We'd make as much progress as we could and then pick it back up in the next sprint. But Cooper had said I needed to earn the respect of the team, and coaching Tyler was one way to do that. No, it wasn't because I didn't like the way he looked at Alicia, all googly-eyed admiration.

Inspiration hit me in a flash. Cooper had also said some bullshit about teamwork. Back in San Francisco, he was always going on about teambuilding, and we had quarterly parties in the courtyard outside the building. I could do something similar here to show him I was trying. I'd tell him all about how I'd bonded with the team when he came out Monday for the sprint review. Soon, he'd be begging me to come back to San Francisco.

I waited for Alicia to end the meeting. Then, before everyone headed back to their desks, I said, "Hey, guys. How about we do a little teambuilding happy hour after work tonight? My treat."

"Really?" Tyler's face glowed. Like, it was literally pink. "That'd be lit."

"No one is getting lit," Alicia said, snapping a picture of the task board with her phone. "Tomorrow's the last workday of the sprint. I need everyone's best effort today and tomorrow."

"I'll have everyone home by ten, promise," I said. "You going to join us, Alicia?"

I half-hoped, half-feared she would. What would Alicia be like after hours? Would she finally let her hair down from that tight bun?

Could I get those blue eyes to soften again like they had before we'd known we were coworkers?

"No, it's Thursday. Next time." She flashed me an I-wouldn't-go-out-with-you-guys-if-the-world-was-ending, totally fake smile.

Fuck. I'd forgotten about her Thursdays. "We could do it tomorrow. An end-of-sprint celebration?"

"No, I have plans Friday night, too. You guys have fun." She turned away. Even her after-hours life was better than mine. I hadn't had Friday-night plans with anyone except my right hand since I'd left San Francisco.

But now I had Thursday-night plans with my team, and it was going to be amazing. I'd make sure of it.

Half an hour after Alicia left that afternoon, I gathered up the guys and led them to a nearby bar. I'd found it earlier in the summer and fallen for its collection of vintage arcade games. I stroked one as I passed. *Next time, Ms. Pac Man.* Tonight was for bonding with my team, not beating my high score.

We settled at a booth in the back. After I ordered one of every appetizer, I leaned forward. "Bucket of quarters to whoever tells the most outrageous story."

Four wide pairs of eyes stared back at me. Shit. I'd just asked a group of programmers to tell me a fun story. Might as well ask Ms. Pac Man over there to do it. She probably saw more action than they did.

"Okay, I'll start," I began, and proceeded to tell them about the time I'd unfurled the Stanford flag over the side of the Berkeley library.

Ninety minutes later, I leaned back against the vinyl seat back and propped my Converse up on the empty seat across from me. "That was a colossal disaster."

"Nah." Tyler went for his beer, missed, and tried again. "It was totally lit."

"That's bullshit." I pushed my own mostly full beer away. Someone had to see that Tyler made it home safely. I ticked off my failures on my fingers. "Amit doesn't drink. Who knew?"

"I knew." Tyler raised his hand like we were in class.

"And my idea to give quarters to the guy with the best story totally backfired." Kevin, who'd told us about the time he'd brought a pet goat to his mother's mah jongg party, had taken his quarters to the Galaga console. I'd given an out to the most interesting person at the table, leaving the rest of us to our lame-ass, awkward conversation. Amit and Gary had left after one drink, and now we had a table full of cold, soggy appetizers.

"What do you think Alicia does on Tuesdays and Thursdays?"

"Huh?" Tyler signaled for another beer.

"When she leaves early. Where does she go?"

"Dunno. I asked her, and she said she'd rather not talk about it. Maybe she's a spy."

"You think she's working for Gurusoft?" Fuck, that'd be the worst, if we were paying a consultant to sell our secrets to the competition.

"Nah. I mean, like, for the government. Cloak and dagger shit." Tyler took the beer from the server and winked at her.

"Alicia? I don't think so."

"Then what d'you think she does?" He took a long draw from his beer.

"I don't know." I'd thought about it. A lot. Too much. "Maybe she's getting her master's. Or doing volunteer work."

"Or modeling. God, she's pretty."

I picked up a sad, mushy jalapeno popper and examined it. "Who, Alicia?" I'd meant for my voice to be light and unconcerned, but it came out as a growl.

Tyler blinked at me. "Sure. But I meant her." He pointed toward the bar at one of the waitresses. Her hair was darker blond than Alicia's, and her eyes were the color of honey. She looked a little like Marlee, though I'd never seen Marlee in short-shorts.

"She has a friend." He pointed with his beer at another waitress standing at the well, this one dark-haired and curvy. "And she's looking at you."

I checked; she was. "I don't pick up women in bars anymore."

"Bad experience?"

"You could say that."

"Well, I'm going in." He pushed himself up and wobbled for a second.

"You sure about that? Maybe have some water first."

"Nah, I got this." He lurched off toward the bar. After signaling our waitress for the check, I surveyed our collection of congealed fried items and empty glasses. What an utter failure. I should've known better than to try to bond with the team. I'd always worked best solo.

"She's mine, asshole!" The loud voice at the bar caught my ear.

I glanced up in time to see a guy with a linebacker's build—he had to be six-six—punch Tyler in the face.

8

ALICIA

FRIDAY NIGHT, and I had a date for movie night.

I caught the first kernel of popcorn as it shot out of the air popper's chute. When I tossed it into my mouth, it singed my tongue, dry and flavorless. I had to find something to spice it up.

"Alicia, what are you doing?"

I looked guiltily back over my shoulder, like I'd done when I was eight and Mom caught me hunting for Oreos. This time, I wasn't standing on the counter, but I was leaning against it, the tiles digging into my stomach, hunting through the spice rack.

"Don't we have any flavored salt? Or anything with salt in it?"

Mom pursed her lips. "Esmy's blood pressure was high at her last checkup, so I got rid of all that stuff. People consume entirely too much salt. In fact—"

I interrupted her before she could go off on one of her nutritional diatribes. "How about butter?"

"We have olive oil. That's heart-healthy."

"On popcorn? Ew."

"Popcorn is perfectly delicious plain."

I wrinkled my nose. She hadn't cared nearly as much about all this nutrition stuff when she'd been married to Dad. Or maybe she'd never loved Dad enough to care what was happening to his arteries. She for sure hadn't loved him as much as she loved Esmy.

"Date night?" I asked as Esmy entered the kitchen wearing way more mascara than usual, skin-tight Wranglers, and her dancing boots.

"Dinner and then the honky-tonk." Her gaze lingered on Mom, whose plaid shirt was open one pearl snap lower than usual, revealing lace at her cleavage. "Don't wait up."

I unplugged the popper and grabbed the bowl of cardboard-flavored popcorn. I'd make a junk-food run to the store tomorrow. Too bad it'd be too late for movie night. "Have fun, kids."

Esmy leaned in and smacked an air kiss in my ear. "Cariño, there's a saltshaker in the cabinet behind the cookie sheets," she whispered.

"Thanks." I kissed her smooth, golden cheek.

"When's the last time you had a date, Alicia?" Mom speared me with a glare like she'd heard about the secret salt.

I popped a dry kernel into my mouth. It reminded me of Rick's passionless kisses. "Last summer, I guess. After soccer season ended."

"Rick is such a nice man. And Noah and Palmer get along so well together. I thought he might be the one."

"Mom, I'm not going to marry someone just because our kids are friends."

"There are worse reasons to get married."

Like getting knocked up. But we didn't talk about that. Before Esmy came into Mom's life, she never talked about feelings at all. Which was why she'd stayed married to Dad for so long.

She must've seen the thought pass across my face. "Don't start."

"Who started anything? I'm just standing here, eating delicious air-popped popcorn." God, what I wouldn't give for a beer. But I'd emptied our stash after last night's soccer game, feeling sorry for myself while Jackson and the team bonded without me. I'd sworn off the awkward company picnics and happy hours. I shouldn't have cared. And I didn't. Much. "Now go on, lovebirds. Have fun."

Mom narrowed her eyes at me. Esmy threw me another air kiss and hustled her out the door.

Grabbing two flavored waters from the fridge, I went to the living room, where Noah was already set up on the squashy old sectional.

Tigger nestled into his side, purring as Noah scratched between his ears.

"Did you remember the salt?" Noah asked. "Esmy hides it behind the cookie sheets."

"I'll go get it. And some napkins." He had a smear of Esmy's pink lipstick across his forehead. "Cue up the movie?"

"Space or superheroes?" He flicked through the options.

"Superheroes." After two weeks of working with Jackson Jones, I could use a hero. He was more the hot-villain type like Loki in *The Avengers*, secretly working against me. Like when he'd invited the guys out for drinks last night, on a night he knew I couldn't join them. I knew what he was doing; I'd seen it before. He was building up some bro-loyalty, and he'd cash it in when he needed to torpedo me.

Though, a too-rational voice in my brain said, *shouldn't he be building up loyalty with the team? It's his team, not yours. You're leaving when the project is over.*

Get in, get a paycheck, get out. Do not hang out after work with the dangerously attractive company founder. I should've put that on my business plan.

When I returned with the salt and napkins, Noah had the movie cued up, but even after I salted the popcorn and wiped the lipstick off his face, he didn't start it. He had his talking face on.

"What's the matter?" I asked. *Don't let it be about girls. Don't let it be about girls.*

"Do I have to go to school?"

"Tomorrow? No, it's Saturday." But he wasn't joking. He gave me a look that reminded me of Mom's pissed-off-about-the-salt one.

"I'm serious. Can't you homeschool me or something?"

"Oh." A dozen scenarios shifted through my brain, all terrible. "No, buddy. I have to work full-time to support us and to save money for your college. Grandma Diane and Grandma Esmy work, too. School is the best place for you. Why don't you want to go?"

He shrugged. "The kids aren't nice to me."

Not nice? What the hell? "What about your friends? Aren't Tamika and Palmer nice to you?"

"Yeah, but the other kids make fun of me."

Anger rose hot and swift inside me. "Why would they make fun of you?"

He shrugged again and started dissecting a piece of popcorn.

Who was I going to have to beat up? "I'll schedule a conference with your principal. We'll get them to stop."

"No! Forget I said anything. I'll handle it."

For the thousandth time, I wished Melissa were here. Or that she'd appointed someone better, someone wiser, as Noah's guardian. Or that she'd ever told us who his father was so I could drag him in here and make him talk to his son. Because I had no clue what to tell my nephew.

Tiannah was always telling me to let him fight his own battles so he'd learn to protect himself when he was older. Maybe that was the right path here. I'd certainly needed those skills.

"We'll check in next week, see how things are going. If it's not better, I'll schedule that conference. Okay?"

He shrugged again. Kid was going to give himself a repetitive-strain injury with the shrugging.

Maybe a story would help. Esmy told a lot of those. "You know how I've told you there aren't a lot of women in my field?"

"Yeah." He started shredding another kernel.

"Sometimes people—guys—try to bully me because I'm different. Or exclude me." Like Jackson had done yesterday when he'd taken the guys out for drinks. And, exactly like he'd planned, they came back this morning full of inside jokes and camaraderie. Jackson had a split lip, and Tyler, when he'd finally dragged in at ten, had a black eye. They'd assured me they hadn't fought each other, but no one would tell me what had happened.

And now Tyler looked at Jackson like he'd hung the moon. I should've been proud of Jackson for finding a way to bond with his team. I guessed I was, underneath my disapproval of his methods. And my jealousy. Jackson was doing what he should've done three months ago when he'd come to Austin. I should've encouraged it. But all I'd been able to do was glare at him.

"So what do you do?" Noah tossed the popcorn confetti into his mouth and finally met my gaze.

"I show them I deserve to be there, same as them. I work harder than they do. I never miss a deadline, and my work is always top-notch." I sat up a little straighter.

He wrinkled his nose. "That sounds like it sucks, never being able to make a mistake."

All the starch left my spine. "It kind of does."

"And what if they're still mean to you?"

"Then you have to tell someone."

"Like your friends? Or your family?"

If only it were that simple. "At work, same as at school, you tell someone in charge." I wasn't about to tell him that hadn't worked for me, either. In my first job after graduation, an older programmer had harassed me almost from my first day. I'd finally told Melissa, and she'd hounded me until I'd gone to my manager. He'd stopped the inappropriate jokes and the touches that made my skin crawl, but he hadn't stopped the dirty looks my male coworkers had given me, the grunt work I'd been assigned with no chance for recognition or advancement. I'd put up with it until Melissa died and I'd realized life was too precarious to stay in a job I hated. I'd quit, taken three months to get my head back together, and gone to work at a different company.

"Like a teacher?"

"Or the principal. One week, and if it's not better, I'm scheduling a conference." I'd stay on their asses until Noah felt safe again. No one was doing to Noah what had been done to me.

"What makes that guy so great?" I gestured at the superhero on the preview screen.

"He's, like, really strong."

"And what else?"

"When he gets knocked down, he gets right back up."

"That's right. And that's what we Webers do, too."

"Yeah." One corner of his mouth turned up.

"Let's watch him kick some bad-guy butt."

I might not pee standing up, but I was still a good programmer and an even better leader. At our review on Monday, I was going to show Cooper Fallon exactly that. And until this project was done, no matter how many times Jackson Jones and his bro-culture tried to knock me down, I was going to get back up.

9

JACKSON

"I'M SORRY. I'M SORRY." Tyler buried his face in his hands.

Alicia and I sat side-by-side at our desk, frantically searching through Tyler's fucked-up code for the bug. Her lips were compressed and pale, and a droplet of sweat trickled from her temple down the flawless skin of her cheek. I'd never seen her this rattled, not even when she'd been struck by a hailstone minutes before her first meeting with Cooper and me.

When we hit the bottom of the program, Alicia barked, "Again. From the top."

I rubbed my eyes. They ached almost as much as my toes in my fuck-you-Cooper boots. "No."

"What do you mean, 'no'? We have to find the bug and fix it."

"We're out of time. Cooper texted me he's coming up."

Alicia's eyes widened. "He's here? Already?"

"Promptness is kind of his thing."

"Shit," she muttered. "Shit. Shit. *Shit.*"

She wasn't so perfect now with the sweat trickling down her neck and her lipstick chewed off. I wished there was anything I could do to help—Cooper was going to rip all of us a new one, including Alicia, who was blameless in the mess—but the only thing that'd piss him off more than this code fiasco was if we made him wait.

"I'm sorry," Tyler said again. "I was trying to help. I felt bad about coming in late on Friday, and I decided to work over the weekend, add some new functionality. I didn't think I'd fuck it up so bad."

He'd already been in the office when I arrived that morning. His bloodshot eyes, stubbled chin, and grayish skin indicated he'd been there at least overnight. "You should've called someone, man. Me or Alicia. Or Amit. We'd have come in and helped you."

"I thought I could fix it." He laid his face on the desk. He lifted his head and dropped it with a thunk. "I should've been able to fix it."

"We're a team, Tyler." Alicia's words came out strangled through her clenched jaw. "We work together, not alone."

My chest tight, I stood. "Let's go in."

Slowly, the team gathered up their laptops and notepads. Tyler took his satchel like he expected to be fired on the spot and walked out of the building.

When I entered the conference room, Cooper looked up from his phone. "Jay!" He smiled, the real one he saved for friends. Then he caught my expression, and his smile dimmed. He raised his eyebrows, and I shook my head a fraction.

He squared his jaw and stood, offering handshakes all around. Tyler, who went last, wiped his hand on his jeans before offering it to Cooper. He looked everywhere but in Cooper's eyes.

"Okay." Cooper took a seat at the end with a direct view of the screen. "Show me what you've got."

No one moved to connect a laptop to the display cable. In fact, no one moved at all. Silence hung in the room for three…four…five seconds.

I stood. Might as well take the blame. It wasn't Alicia's fault. She'd tried to keep Tyler from taking that sticky note out of the backlog. I was the one who'd encouraged him. Besides, Tyler had only followed the example I'd set when I'd tried to show Alicia up by finishing our module solo. At the root of it, I was the one who'd fucked up. As usual. "Cooper, I—"

"We don't have anything to show you, Mr. Fallon." All eyes swiveled to Alicia, who'd also risen from her chair. "I'm still trying to set norms with the team, and there was a miscommunication. *I* miscommunicated. The code isn't ready today. We should have something prepared in a couple of days, and I can schedule a remote demonstration then."

That vein throbbed at Cooper's temple. The one that told me he was about to lose it. "I'm here now. Today. You couldn't have told me this on Friday?"

I paced along the wall. *Fuck.* He was building to one of his blow-ups.

Her lip trembled. "I'm sorry. We thought we'd be prepared, but at the last minute, unexpectedly, we—we weren't."

He splayed his hands on the table the way he did to keep from balling them into fists. "I'm sure you understand how disappointed I am. And you'll all ensure nothing like this happens again." He raked that icy blue stare over the team that encircled him. Tyler flinched. "But for today, this time will be best spent working on the code. Back to work, everyone. Alicia, a word."

I stabbed my hands into my pockets and paced back toward the table. She shouldn't have to take the brunt of Cooper's wrath alone. She'd stood up for us although it hadn't been her fault. She was being fucking *noble.* I'd never done a noble thing in my life.

"Cooper, I—" I started again.

But, not bothering to look at me, he said, "Jackson, you, too. We'll talk later."

I glanced at Alicia's pale face. Would she be able to handle it? Of course she would. She could match Cooper, word for cold, calculating word. Still, guilt gnawed my insides. "Alicia—"

She held up a hand. "Go on, Jackson."

I slunk out of the room, following the team.

When Alicia rejoined us half an hour later, she looked like her normal, not-a-hair-out-of-place self. Maybe he'd gone easy on her since she'd been on the job only two weeks. She set down her laptop and joined us where we'd all huddled around Tyler's workstation. Leaning over as if to get a better view of the screen, she whispered in my ear, "He wants to see you in his office."

My dread at her words battled the thrill of her breath on my skin. Goosebumps rose on the back of my neck and traveled down my arms. I brushed down the hairs that stuck up. What the fuck? My body had reacted like she'd told me she wanted to suck my dick, not that I was due for a very different kind of tongue-lashing.

No doubt Cooper had seen through Alicia's admission of guilt and knew I'd been the one who'd acted like Batman, some kind of lone avenger. I was glad. Alicia shouldn't take the blame for what was my fault.

I nodded at Alicia, holding her gaze for a second longer than I should've, trying to convey my gratitude for what she'd done. She'd been right, and I'd been wrong. It was time to let go of our petty rivalry. It was time for *me* to let it go and let her do what she'd come here to do: lead. Otherwise, we weren't going to make it.

She straightened, and I rolled my chair a few feet away from her before I stood up, discreetly adjusted my jeans, and headed to the executive offices.

Holding his phone in one hand, Cooper beckoned me in with the other. He held up a finger to show me he was almost done. He barked out a few more commands, thanked his assistant, and hung up.

"Jackson."

Uh-oh. He'd used my full name twice in a row. Not a good sign.

"Ms. Weber seemed to be under the impression that I didn't have anything better to do than drag my old bones all the way from California to Texas to hear her mea culpa. I'd have expected you to disabuse her of that notion."

"You're not old." I crossed my arms. "You're the same age as me. Thirty-two."

"That's what you want to say? Not, 'I'm sorry we wasted your time, Cooper'? Not, 'We fucked up, and I will personally ensure we turn this project around'?"

Anger boiled inside me, but on the outside, I shrugged. "If you're going to tell me what to say, why do I even need to be part of this conversation? You could've pulled up a picture of me on your phone, yelled at it, and left me alone to fix the fucking code."

"But that's the problem, isn't it? You're still acting like a lone programmer, and you haven't integrated into the team."

"Is that what Alicia said?" She didn't seem the type to rat me out, especially after she'd publicly taken the fall for all of us.

"No, but I've known you for almost fifteen years. I can guess what happened."

"We just fucking started. You can't expect us to get it done in two weeks."

"You've been here, working on this code, for three months. How much more time do you need to sort out the team and figure out what the *fuck* you're doing?" His voice had risen to a volume that must have carried outside the office.

The hot wave of anger broke through the dam I'd built. I slammed a hand on his desk. "More fucking time. You threw this curveball, a new project lead, at us, and we're adjusting. I'm trying. We're all trying. I'm going to try harder, okay?"

"Okay." He lifted his hands, palms out. "That's all I wanted to hear. But next time, I need to see results. Good ones. We can't afford to fuck around any longer. Understand me?"

"Yeah, I get it." My breathing slowed, and the heat in my chest slowly dissipated.

"You have plans for lunch?" That was Cooper. His anger went from zero to sixty faster than my Lamborghini Aventador, but it evaporated just as quickly.

"Yeah. Some fucker's making me work through lunch to fix the goddamn code."

"Not today. Today your best friend wants to take you out. Then you can fix the goddamn code."

"Fine." For the first time that day, I smiled. "I'll meet you in the lobby in ten."

On the way back to our work area to tell the team I was leaving for lunch, I heard familiar voices coming from the conference room where we'd had our asses handed to us earlier.

"I'm sorry. So fucking sorry. Sorry, so *freaking* sorry. And now Jay's getting his a— his behind chewed out, and it's my fault. I guess he was mad at you, too." Tyler's voice broke.

"It's not your fault," Alicia said so gently even I felt better. "Like I said in the review, it's mine. I let you guys think you could break our process. I took the easy way out. I won't do it again. And you won't go all Lone Ranger on me again, will you?"

"No. Promise."

Fuck. These were things I should've said to him. But here was Alicia, being a leader. Not like Cooper with his flashfire anger or like me with my jokes, but with gentle words that actually made Tyler feel better. She was a pro. I patted my pockets for a notepad.

"You're a good programmer." Behind the frosted glass, Alicia's form moved closer to Tyler. Was she touching his back? I wished I could see what she was doing. So I could take notes on her coaching methods. Not because I wished she'd rub my back and make it all better. "You've got a lot of potential. You just need to work on your discipline. I'd like you to partner up with Amit again next sprint. He's steady and careful, and he can teach you a lot."

Unlike me. I was a fuckup who couldn't teach anyone anything. I'd tried to turn it all around—the project, myself—and still failed. Shoving my hands in my pockets, I shuffled to our workspace, told Kevin I was headed to lunch, and walked back toward the stairs, keeping my eyes on the hardwood planks to avoid checking out the conference room where Alicia was making Tyler a better programmer, no expensive certification or thick coding guides required.

"Jay!" Before I had a chance to look up, I was enveloped in Jamila's jasmine scent and crushed by her embrace. I hugged her back.

"What are you doing here?" I stepped back, taking in her perfectly pressed, plum-colored business suit and cherry-red silk blouse. The colors blazed against her dark skin.

She grinned. "I told you I was coming to check on you."

"You didn't come all the way from California to check on me." God, I hoped not. If so, I was in deeper shit than I'd thought.

"Looks like I needed to. Those boots? Just no, honey." She shook her head.

I glanced down at them. If only I could give them up. But Cooper hadn't gotten the message yet. "When in Austin, do as the Austonians do, right?"

"Austinites, Jay."

"Whatever. Why *are* you here?"

"I'm giving a talk tomorrow at the Texas Women Engineers' Association. I flew out with Cooper a day early so I could check in with Alicia. And you. You treating her right?"

"Um—"

"Jamila!" Alicia jogged up to us, arms wide. For Jamila. What would it be like to have her look at me like that, open her arms to me? Heaven. I scowled and shoved my hands into my pockets.

The women hugged, and then Jamila stepped back. "This one's behaving himself, then?"

Alicia's eyebrows shot up her forehead. "Oh, I'm sorry. I don't think you've met. This is Jackson Jones."

Jamila roared out a laugh. "She's got your number, Jay." Hooking her elbow through Alicia's, she pivoted in her red-soled heels and strode toward the stairs. "Now, tell me everything."

I watched the tops of their heads, one blond, one black, disappear down the stairs. Two smart, successful women. One liked me—or at least fondly indulged me—and the other despised me. Especially after my role in today's disaster. And after being reamed out by Cooper.

I scratched my beard. Alicia had known me for only two weeks, and she already knew what a fuckup I was. She'd categorized me as an obstacle to be dealt with and corrected. Not an equal or a partner. And she was right: she'd stepped up as the leader today, not me. I could learn a lot from her.

I needed to keep my head down, do what I was told, do the fucking work. Act like her teammate, not a rival. Maybe she'd still hate me, but at least I wouldn't fuck up anything else.

10

ALICIA

"YOU MIGHT AS WELL TELL me about it. I'll find out from Cooper. Or Jay." Jamila neatly speared a thin slice of chicken and a folded piece of lettuce, popped the bite into her mouth, and stared me down as she chewed.

I poked my fork into my salad and moved a cube of pickled beet into a corner. Gross. My stomach was too knotted to eat, so I'd ordered what Jamila had.

She was right. Not about the disgusting beet salad, but that I was wasting an opportunity with my mentor if I didn't talk this through with her.

"We screwed up. *I* screwed up. We had nothing to show Cooper this morning. One of the programmers introduced a bug over the weekend that stopped the compile. Not only his module. The whole thing. And it's my fault."

"How is that your fault?"

I stabbed a tomato like it was Jackson Jones's face. "I tried to create a collaborative culture. I paired everyone up. But when Jackson went all cowboy-coder on me and started working solo, I didn't say anything. I didn't discipline him. I ignored it. Trying to get along, you know? And so Ty—the other programmer thought he could do the same thing. Surprise us all with new functionality. Impress Jackson and Cooper."

"Honey, you can't take the blame for that." She tapped her plum-tipped fingers on the tablecloth in front of my plate to draw my gaze. "That's not your fault."

"My job is to lead. To establish norms. To ensure everyone follows the rules."

Jamila shook her head. "Girl, you should know better than that. In their heads, programmers are half Bruce Willis in *Die Hard* and half Gandalf. They're artists who know everything. Trying to get them going in the same direction is like herding cats or rattlesnakes. Or rattlesnake-headed cats."

"I know. And yet I told Cooper Fallon I could do it."

"You can. It'll just take time."

Remembering the expression on his face in this morning's failed demo sent a shiver down my spine. And then his terse, angry words in his office sent a second shudder back up. "I don't know how much more time I have. Cooper was pretty disappointed." An understatement. He'd ripped me a new one, even questioned my qualifications.

And the worst part was that for a second, I'd considered letting Jackson take the blame. My heart had leapt when he'd stood and started to speak. I was almost certain he'd been about to tell Cooper he'd encouraged Tyler in his cowboy coding. But even if he was, I didn't want Jackson to ride to my rescue. Couldn't want that. I could only rely on myself. So I'd spoken right over him.

Jamila waved off my words. "Cooper's all wind and no rain."

I raised my eyebrows. "You're saying he's a big softy under all the ice?"

She snorted. "I did *not* say that. He'll do anything for his friends, but everyone else is either a tool or an obstacle to him. He knows you'll do your job and turn it around."

"You've told me no less than a dozen times that as women in a male-dominated field, we have to work harder, be faster, show better results. I'm"—not afraid, I wouldn't admit that—"concerned I'm not going to get a second chance. Not like Jackson will."

"In Cooper's mind, Jay can do no wrong. You're right that he'll get limitless chances and you won't. But you've got this. I have faith in you. Or I wouldn't have recommended you in the first place."

Jamila still believed in me. And that meant a lot. She was the smartest person I'd ever met. She'd gone from an underfunded public school in East Austin to Stanford University. She hadn't bothered with any of the job offers she'd been presented with months before graduation; instead, she'd taken her idea for an app and a small inheritance and built her own company. Jamila's face had filled the cover of one of the business magazines in the waiting room during Noah's check-up last week.

If she thought I could do it, it was worth another try.

"Thanks, Jamila. For both the recommendation and your support. I won't let you down."

"You'd never let me down, even if you quit today." She crunched into a carrot. "And I know you won't let yourself down. Or Noah. How's that adorable ankle-biter?"

Noah. Telling her about his broken arm reminded me of the doctor's bill that had arrived the day before. It was exactly the amount Dr. Ruiz's assistant had told me, but seeing that comma made it real. Even if I wanted to chicken out of the project, I couldn't. I had bills to pay.

Besides, what kind of example would I be setting if I gave up two weeks into my first consulting gig? If I gave up, I'd never get another opportunity like this. I needed Cooper's recommendation. I had to try harder. Like the superhero from the movie, I had to get back up even after today had knocked me down.

After lunch, when I walked Jamila to Cooper's office, I gave him my brightest smile. "I'll set up that remote demo, Mr. Fallon. You'll see our progress by the end of the week."

He didn't smile back or ask me to call him Cooper. "I'm counting on it," was all he said.

I trudged back to our team's workspace. We'd find that bug, we'd knock Cooper Fallon's socks off in our demo, and I'd earn that damned testimonial.

And it didn't matter that I thought for a second Jackson Jones might stand up for me. Or that I couldn't get his scent out of my nostrils even after I left the office. He was a distraction, an extra challenge, nothing more. I couldn't let him get in the way of my success on this project. And I had to succeed for Noah. For Jamila. And for myself.

11

JACKSON

ALICIA WEBER WASN'T PERFECT.

I mean, no one's perfect. Even Cooper had that temper thing. But Alicia swanned into the office every day, perfectly put together, not a hair out of place in that infernal bun, never late. She always knew what to say, what to do to motivate the team. Tyler found a reason to ask her advice almost daily.

Except.

She'd committed us to pair programming again the next sprint and said lots of words about collaboration, about teamwork, about asking for help and not going it alone.

That'd lasted a day and a half.

She and I'd partnered up again—just like in gym class, no one else had picked me—and she'd put up with my navigation for a full day and right up until lunch the next. Then, when everyone else had drifted off to the food truck that'd pulled up outside, she'd told me to go on, and she'd work a little longer on her own. Then, when I'd come back, she'd said why didn't I pull something else off the board to work on.

In front of the rest of the team, she pretended we were working together. But we weren't. Unless you considered working side-by-side, headphones on, on different parts of the program, working together.

It was fine. If what she wanted from me was to leave her alone, I could do it.

Except.

I'd found a bug in her code.

Tonight, I'd kept working after everyone else went home. I couldn't face going back to that lonely apartment, full of other temporary misfits and downtown divorcés. I was on good terms with my upstairs neighbors, and I'd met a workout buddy, Rick, in the gym, but I had no one I called a friend.

Even worse was going out on nearby Sixth Street. There, I found plenty of women. But Austin was a college town, and after last spring's intern scare, they all looked like college girls to me. And I was never, ever going to touch one of those again. Even the ones I was sure were older, who had a gray strand or two or traces of smile lines on their cheeks, didn't light my fire.

Maybe once you started, celibacy was addictive, like smoking. Or —I admitted late at night, my hand in my shorts—maybe I couldn't get Alicia out of my brain. No one else measured up. Not since my shriveled heart had fluttered to life when I'd laid a finger on her soft skin, when I'd brushed her hair over that ridiculous Lightning McQueen bandage.

So, with no after-work social outlets, I'd worked late again. And after I'd finished my code, I'd checked Alicia's, which she'd, of course, loaded into the repository like a good little coder. Since we were supposed to be working together, it only made sense for me to check it.

And I found a bug. It wasn't one that'd stop the compile like that gnarly one in Tyler's code on Monday, but it'd screw things up enough that we had to get rid of it.

But even I wasn't brave enough to muck around in Alicia's code.

So I texted her.

> Found a bug in your code.

Alicia: I'm sorry, who is this?

It's Jackson Jones.

Alicia: How did you get my number?

Your business card?

Fine. I'm the company founder. I have God-level access to our HR system.

The typing bubbles appeared and disappeared until I got tired of waiting.

Anyway, there's a bug in your code. Thought you should know.

Alicia: Are you going to tell me what it is?

Maybe. But there's a price.

Alicia: A price?

I hadn't meant to get flirty with her. I'd meant to call her out and then leave her to stew until she could fix it the next morning with no one but me the wiser. But something happened to my thumbs.

I think an exchange of information is in order. I'll tell you what the bug is, you tell me where you go on Tuesdays and Thursdays.

Alicia: I don't think so. I'll find it tomorrow.

No, wait! How about I get three guesses.

Alicia: What?

You give me three guesses, tell me if I'm right or wrong. Then I tell you about the bug.

Alicia: Two guesses.

Hot or cold?

Alicia: No.

Fine. You're an international spy, and on Tuesdays and Thursdays, you go to the Mexican Consulate to meet your lover/mark.

Alicia: I think you know that's a no.

Worth a shot

Alicia: Not really.

You're a part-time nun, and Tuesdays and Thursdays you use your cornette to fly around the city rescuing kittens and orphans.

Alicia: Cornette?

It's a part of a nun's habit.

Alicia: That doesn't even sound like a real thing.

It's totally real. How about a hint?

Alicia: You couldn't take a hint if it came free in a box of Cocoa Puffs.

Ouch! The woman had a pair of thumbs on her. But I had a pair, too, and I sucked it up and told her about the bug. She had the courtesy to thank me—I'd accused her of imperfection, not rudeness—texted that she had to go, and didn't respond to any of my texts after that.

I only sent two. Or maybe five.

I hoped she deleted them.

12

ALICIA

I PUT the key in the ignition, but I didn't turn it. Instead, I glanced into the rearview mirror at Noah's stormy face.

"Why didn't you tell me you were failing language arts?"

He shrugged. His neon-green cast flopped in his lap.

Noah wasn't going to make it to his teen years if he didn't stop shrugging at me.

"Did you know and fail to tell me, or did you not know?"

"I thought maybe I wasn't doing so good."

"And why didn't you tell me?"

He shrugged again.

"Is it because you were afraid I'd be angry? Because, after sitting in front of a panel of your teachers like some kind of inquisition, I'm pretty angry."

"Sorry," he mumbled.

"Sorry's a good start. How about, 'Alicia, I promise I'll never hide my grades from you again.'"

He stared down into his lap and mumbled.

"What's that?" I snapped.

"I promise."

"Okay. Good. And I promise, if you tell me you're in trouble, I won't yell at you. I'll get you help. Does that work?"

He didn't raise his eyes. "Yeah."

"Okay." I turned the key in the ignition and let Beyoncé fill the car.

Five minutes later, when we pulled into the driveway, he spoke again. "Are you going to tell Grandma Diane and Grandma Esmy?"

I turned off the car and rotated in my seat to face him. "I was planning to. I think this is an all-hands-on-deck, emergency-type situation. I think we can use all the help we can get, don't you?"

He shrugged for about the seventy-fifth time. "I guess."

"Don't be embarrassed about it. There's nothing wrong with asking for help. Understand?"

He made a face. He was a Weber, all right.

I pushed open the door and waited for him to clamber out of the back seat with his backpack that weighed more than he did. We went in through the back door, where I toed out of my heels and set my satchel and purse in the cubby I'd used for my own backpack when I was his age. While Noah took care of his shoes and bag, I walked through into the kitchen, where I took a deep sniff of Mom's cooking.

"Spaghetti and meatballs?" I leaned over the bubbling saucepot.

"They're vegan," she whispered. "Don't tell."

I eyed a kernel of corn that floated to the surface of the tomato sauce. "I think they'll figure it out. Maybe next time, try that fake meat stuff."

Spaghetti and vegan balls didn't fool anyone, but with enough cheese and garlic bread, they were a hit. Mom's favorite joke was that her homemade pasta sauce could save anything—except her marriage. That night, I thought she might be right.

Mom waited until Noah reached for a second slice of garlic bread to ask, "So, what was the conference about?"

I nodded at Noah, who gulped and took a deep breath. "'Mfailinglangauagearts," he said in a rush.

Like the meatless meatballs, it didn't fly. "You're failing language arts?" Esmy asked, setting down her napkin. Noah's dislike of reading offended her school-librarian sensibilities.

He nodded. At least he didn't shrug at her.

"What happened?" Esmy looked at me.

Now I shrugged. "The papers were all wadded up in the bottom of the bag. I was supposed to have signed them, but I never saw them. His teacher said I need to find him a special folder for work that needs to be reviewed and signed at home."

"That sounds like a good system."

"We've got extra folders in the desk drawer." Mom nodded toward the corner of the kitchen where she, Esmy, and I took turns doing the household finances.

"I think we need to consider"—I took a deep breath—"cutting down on extracurriculars."

"Extracurriculars?" Esmy said. "You already cut back on that. All he does now is…" Her eyes went wide.

"Soccer?" Noah set down his piece of garlic bread. "No. I love soccer."

"It's his only chance to get outside, run around," Esmy said. "Kids these days hardly get any time to play."

Mom remained silent.

"I don't even get to go out for recess most days," Noah grumbled. "My teacher makes me stay inside to finish my work."

"You're missing recess?" My voice was too high, too loud. I reached for my water and gulped it down.

"Yeah."

I shook my head. "Then I think—"

"I'll tutor him," Esmy interrupted me. "After school, I'll work with him on his homework."

"Esmy—" Mom began.

"No, Diane. I want to do this. So he can keep playing soccer."

Mom stood and picked up Esmy's plate, then hers.

"Noah," I said, "if Grandma Esmy does this for you, you need to take it seriously. We'll give it a few weeks, and if we're not seeing improvement, we'll talk again about soccer. Understand?"

"Yeah. Thanks, Grandma Esmy."

She patted his hand. "Put your plate in the dishwasher, and then we can start."

I got out a container for the leftover veggie balls and started scooping them in. Mom ran water in the sink. Even the rushing water sounded angry. "I'll take care of it, Mom. You cooked, I'll clean."

She glanced over her shoulder at the kitchen table, where Noah had opened a workbook. She said in a low voice, "I don't normally like to get involved in your parenting. You're his guardian, after all."

"You still can't let that go. After six years."

"Nope."

Mom and Esmy helped us a lot, even welcoming us both into their home. But Melissa had made Noah my responsibility, not Mom's. *Thanks, sis.* I set the container on the counter, more forcefully than I'd intended. "But what, Mom?"

"I agree with Esmy. Noah needs to run and play. He's only ten."

"Mom, I—" I stopped myself. What was I going to tell her? That maybe if she'd been sitting in the too-small chair at that inquisition, she'd have threatened to pull him out of soccer, too? That I agreed he should run and play like other kids, but that other kids weren't failing language arts and in danger of being held back? That the last thing poor Noah needed was another reason to be the object of ridicule at school?

In the end, I said something that was more honest than I'd intended. "I don't know what I'm doing."

She gave me a sad smile. "Sweetie, no matter what anyone says, none of us knows what we're doing. You have to take it a day at a time and do the best you can. I sure as hell didn't know what I was doing, pregnant at seventeen and married to someone I didn't love. But Melissa turned out okay. You did, too."

We'd never been hugging types, so I patted her arm as I walked to the refrigerator.

"Alicia, I think your phone's dinging," Esmy called out.

"Dinging or buzzing?" I asked.

"Definitely dinging. Oh. You know what? It sounds like that song, 'You're So Vain.' Who sang that, querida?"

"Carly Simon," Mom hollered back.

"Oh, boy," was the G-rated interjection I used as I passed by Noah.

"Shit," was what I muttered when I dug my phone out of my satchel and confirmed it was a text from Jackson. Had he found another bug? I knew we should have kept up the pair programming, but I couldn't take another one of his condescending corrections. He was usually kind about it, but did he always have to be right?

I leaned against the dryer and read his text.

> Jackson: Hey

> What

I was too irritated to bother with punctuation.

> Jackson: Just wanted to check on you. You don't normally leave early on Fridays.

I almost dropped the phone. Jackson Jones was worried about me?

> Jackson: I mean, did you have to rush off to your contact at Gurusoft to tell him how great our code is?

> Stop fishing. You have nothing to exchange for your terrible guesses.

At least, I hoped he didn't.

> You didn't find another bug, did you?

I held my breath while the dots popped up to indicate he was typing a response.

> Jackson: Not in today's code. Hoping to find something tomorrow.

> Sadist.

> Jackson: Only if that's what you're into.

My breath quickened. Was he flirting with me? I'd thought he might the last time we'd texted, but when he'd seemed perfectly professional at work, I'd dismissed the suspicion, thinking I'd read too much into his texts. But this last text had taken a giant step over the line.

And the worst thing was that I didn't hate it.

My phone sang again.

Jackson: Sorry. Don't know what got into my thumbs.

I blinked. *Okay, then.*

Don't worry about it. See you tomorrow.

As a woman in technology—a woman, period—I'd received plenty of drink invitations, sexual innuendo, and unsolicited dick pics, though, thankfully, never a coworker's cock. But Jackson's joke didn't make me feel like I'd been slimed, or ashamed like I'd let him think I was interested when I wasn't.

No, it felt like a couple of coworkers joking around, poking a little fun. Like my texts with Tiannah.

Or…that my coworker was checking on me. Like he cared.

And that was worse.

Because when the project ended, I'd go on to the next gig, and Jackson would go back to San Francisco. We weren't coworkers. He was a client, and I was a temporary consultant.

Jokes—friendship—caring—had no place in our relationship.

Get in. Get out. Get back to focusing on my responsibilities at home until Noah was straightened out. Go on to the next gig.

No time to lose focus now. I deleted the texts.

———

THE IMAGE on the video screen was so clear I could see the red creeping up Cooper Fallon's throat and hitting his sharp cheekbones. That chiseled jaw twitched.

Last week, Tiannah had sent me a link to a post on a thirst blog: "Thirty Sexy Nerds Who'll Give You a Brain Boner." She'd helpfully pointed out that Cooper and Jackson were numbers twelve and thirteen on the list, respectively.

Clearly, the blogger had never had their ass handed to them by Cooper Fallon. Twice. Because I could tell them from experience, there was nothing boner-inducing about it. My ovaries had to have shriveled up to the size of peas because he was making me feel too stupid to live, much less reproduce. And the curl of his lip said I was so far beneath him I wasn't worthy of having a lady boner in his video presence.

"This is the second code review. How do you have nothing to show? Again?" Cooper leaned his elbows on the dark wood desk in his office at headquarters. Behind him were shelves of books, interspersed with large conch shells and a few glass awards. It was much more opulent than the office he'd reamed me out in last time he was here. He rubbed his temples.

Tyler made a desperate sound, grabbed the wastebasket, and ran out, leaving Jackson and me alone in the conference room.

"Unfortunately—" I began.

Jackson interrupted me. "It was my fault. I was trying to do what you told me—"

"And what was that, exactly? Because I sure as hell didn't tell you to fuck up again. I'm pretty sure I'd remember that."

I winced, and so did Jackson. But he said, "You told me to earn the respect of the team. So I thought I'd do something nice for them. We were working late, and I brought in dinner."

"I said *earn* their respect, not *buy* it. But how did dinner result in utter failure?"

"I ordered sushi. We have a vegetarian in the group, but he eats fish."

"Sushi? In Austin, Texas?" Cooper's eyebrows lifted toward his hairline. "Alicia, how many miles from the ocean is Austin?"

"A little over two hundred miles from the Gulf. It's just over three hours, driving, to Galveston." We'd taken Noah to the beach this summer and had eaten our weight in shrimp. "We can usually get decent fish—"

"Three hours from the nearest body of water. Does ordering sushi in such a place seem like a smart idea?"

That hardly seemed like a respectful way to speak to a colleague, much less his business partner and friend. I stared hard into the camera beside the video screen. "Just a—"

"It's okay, Alicia." Jackson set a hand on mine, where I'd curled it over the chair arm. Warm and steady, his touch calmed me like a weighted blanket. Had I been about to stand up and get in Cooper's virtual face? No. At least I hoped not.

"Let's take it down a notch, Coop." Jackson's voice took on a low rumble that soothed my nerves.

"Take it down?" Cooper's voice rose. "I don't need to take it down. You need to take it up. Stop fucking around there in Austin and build fucking code. Have you forgotten the vital importance of this project, Jackson? Because I sure as hell haven't."

I gripped the arm of the chair. How could Jackson take this kind of abuse so calmly?

Jackson pressed my hand briefly and then lifted it when he shrugged. "Look, I didn't think about it, okay? I did what I would've done at home. I didn't know the sushi was going to make everyone sick."

He'd done it last Thursday, after I'd gone for the day. Everyone who'd eaten the sushi, including Jackson, had spent Friday and the weekend puking. After I'd read Jackson's pathetic text, I'd finished our module, but even though I'd put in hours on Saturday and Sunday, I hadn't been able to finish everyone's work. At least this time I'd emailed Cooper and told him not to come out to Austin. Half the team were still out today.

"Four weeks of our schedule have passed. We have only six weeks left. How are you going to finish on time if you keep falling behind?"

Jackson and I spoke at the same time. I said, "We'll take a look at the features, see what we can remove, and work hard to deliver the minimum viable product on time." Which was the correct response. The one Cooper wanted to hear. Jackson, on the other hand, said, "Software's an art. You can't put a schedule on it. It'll be done when it's done."

We looked at each other in shock. How the heck were we going to work together when we had diametrically opposing philosophies on software project management?

Cooper must have had the same thought. "How have you two not even talked about this? What the hell have you been doing all this time?"

Besides carefully avoiding coding with Jackson, mentoring Tyler, and managing the rest of the team? Worrying about Noah, obsessively checking his backpack every night, and keeping up a daily correspondence with his language arts teacher. But I wasn't about to say that. Cooper wanted to think of me as an automaton who shut down at the end of the workday, ready to power back up at eight a.m. the next day.

Cooper's eyes flared. "Jackson, you wouldn't. Not after what happened in May."

Wouldn't what? I looked between Jackson's pale face next to me and Cooper's red face on the video screen.

"Now just a minute, Cooper."

Finally, he was going to stand up for himself.

Color crept up Jackson's cheeks, and his eyes flashed. "You're out of line. What happened in May isn't relevant to our consultant."

He'd made *consultant* sound like a dirty word. Where the hell was all this coming from? Why was I suddenly the target of both men's derision?

"I can't believe you'd seduce our consultant. Fuck, now I have to find somewhere else to send you." He rubbed his temple. "Our office in Delhi, maybe."

I stopped breathing. Had Cooper Fallon accused me of sleeping with my client?

Jackson stood, fire in his eyes. "Now just a goddamned minute. I am not sleeping with Alicia. We are coworkers. That's all. You know I'd never lie to you, Coop."

The men stared at each other, Jackson's anger slowly melting Cooper's ice like a blowtorch. Silent words passed between them, the way Melissa and I used to speak without words, to know what the other was thinking. Though we'd never done it two thousand miles apart over videoconference gear.

I stood, too. "Absolutely not. We don't even like each other."

When Jackson looked at me, his eyes had lost their flash.

"I mean, we're strictly professional. I—I don't need to like you." I closed my eyes. Shit, I kept digging myself in deeper. One of them was going to fire me, for sure, and then I wouldn't be able to pay the life insurance premium that was due by the end of the month.

And the worst thing was that it was a lie. I liked Jackson. Or at least respected him. Although it drove me nuts to code with him, he was brilliant. And funny. He acted like he cared about the team. He'd thought to buy them dinner, even if he'd gotten unlucky with a batch of bad sushi. He'd checked on me the day I'd had to leave early for Noah's conference.

Did he act like a prima donna? Yes. Did he think he knew more about coding than I did? Absolutely yes, and, as much as I hated to admit it, he was right. Did he look down on me because I was a woman? Did he act like I threatened his ego because I had coding skills *and* wore skirts? No, and that set him apart from most of the men I'd worked with.

But what the hell had he done in May? That would've been right before he'd come out to Austin. It must've been pretty terrible to result in exile. I stole a glance at him, but he was staring at Cooper on the screen, the tops of his cheekbones stained red.

I shook my head. Regardless of our opinions about each other, we needed to work together to finish this project.

"Look, Mr. Fallon—"

"Cooper," they growled at the same time.

"—we've had a couple of setbacks. But I know with the talent on the team, we can turn it around and finish on time. Give us two more weeks. I promise, we won't let you down."

Cooper's gaze flicked over to Jackson, who dipped his chin a fraction of an inch.

"Fine. But I want a daily progress report, Alicia. Don't try to hide anything."

"I wouldn't dream of it. And I—we won't let you down."

He settled a long stare on me, and although my eyes burned, I didn't blink until he looked back at Jackson. "You stay," he said. "Alicia, I'll see you in two weeks."

On my way to our work area, I stopped at the refrigerator and grabbed as many cans of ginger ale as I could carry. We weren't stopping for anything until we had something great to show Cooper.

And as for Jackson Jones, there would be no more after-hours texts. I wasn't about to let even the whiff of fraternization near me. Nothing would prevent Weber Technology Consulting from earning Cooper Fallon's testimonial.

13

JACKSON

HOURS after the call with Cooper, I was in the zone, Led Zeppelin blasting in my headphones, when a tap landed on my shoulder.

Lifting off my headphones, I turned to see Tyler, his satchel strapped across his chest. "I'm taking off. Unless you need anything?"

We were the only ones left in the area, and the lights were turned off in the space next to us. "What time is it?"

"Eight-fifteen. Lose track of time?"

"I guess so." I'd almost finished the module I was supposed to have completed on Friday before the Bad Sushi Incident.

"Anything I can help with?" He tapped his fingers along the side of his jeans.

"No, I'm good."

"Oh." Nodding, he shoved his glasses up. "Okay." He nodded again but didn't move. "You doing all right?"

"You mean the—" I rubbed my belly. My abs were still sore from all the heaving I'd done over the weekend.

"Well, yeah, and, um...everything. Cooper."

No one on the team could've missed how I'd stayed behind in the conference room like a misbehaving sixth grader. Alicia had probably told them the meeting hadn't gone so well. My stomach twisted up, and not from bad sushi this time. From remembering what Cooper had almost told Alicia about me and the intern. Fuck, what would she think of me if she knew?

I wished I could take it all back. The extra shots of tequila that'd seemed like a good idea after my dressing-down by Weston, the CEO, over my behavior outside the office. Sure, I'd missed a day after the Grand Prix, and there may have been a tabloid photo or two of me, shirtless, with a pretty woman—or four. I'd gotten caught in a spray of champagne. Okay, it'd been my bottle of champagne.

After Weston had torn me a new one, I'd found the closest bar to the office and tried to take the edge off with tequila. All it'd done was blur my vision so I didn't see—or care—that the redhead winking at me from across the bar was ten years younger than me. A sense of recklessness had overpowered me when she'd caught me outside the men's room and whispered all those flattering things in my ear and palmed the front of my jeans. I figured I might as well act like the fuckup Weston thought I was. If I had to do the time, why not do the crime? He thought those pictures of innocent celebration were bad? Maybe some pap would catch me fucking this all-too-willing woman against the back wall of the bar. Try to cover up that one, Weston.

If only I could stand next to three-months-ago Jackson, take away that last shot of tequila, make him chug a glass of water instead, and tell him to walk out the door and go home. If I'd gone home, I could've laughed when I'd dragged my hungover ass into a meeting the next morning and found her, the redhead, taking notes on a tablet. I could've congratulated myself on my escape while we joked about hangovers.

But there'd been no escape for me. My skin had felt like it was covered in bees when I sprinted into Cooper's office and confessed about my back-alley hook-up with Callie. Although I'd never noticed her in the office before and had no idea she was our intern, I still should've avoided her. I'd deserved the reaming-out he'd given me.

Like always, Cooper cleaned up my mess. Exiled me to Austin. Let Callie finish out her summer internship at Synergy and sent her off with a nice bonus and recommendation letter.

But he wouldn't do it again. His threat about Delhi had been empty. This was my last chance. I knew it. Cooper knew it. That asshole Weston knew it. If I fucked up here, I'd be asked to take a leave of absence. Possibly a permanent one. Cooper wouldn't be able to protect me.

I focused my attention back on Tyler. "Yeah, I'll be fine." I'd keep my head down and work my ass off. Nothing would distract me. If it wasn't one of Cooper's three commandments—producing good code on time, earning the respect of the team, or working together—I wasn't doing it. No way I could get in trouble if I followed the path Cooper had set.

"And you and Alicia? You'll be fine, too?"

"Me and Alicia?" Maybe that's where the *working together* part came in. We'd sit there at that desk, staring straight ahead at our screens, the bitter citrus of her tea tickling up into my nose. Keeping up the front of pair programming so guys like Tyler wouldn't feel bad about needing help with their code.

But we absolutely would not cross any lines like Cooper somehow thought we had. I'd put a strip of masking tape—or a string of razor wire—down the middle of the desk if I had to.

"Alicia and I are fine. Separately, we are fine. As you can see, I'm fine here, and she's fine...somewhere else." At home? I'd never thought about Alicia's home before. Maybe she slept in a crypt like a vampire.

"Ohh-kay." He winked. I hadn't yet cracked the code of the Texas wink. At first, I'd thought it was flirtatious, but then the white-haired woman who scanned my can of deodorant in the checkout line at the CVS winked at me when she said, "Y'all have a nice day." And the bald, sweaty guy who manned the tamale cart always winked and said, "Buen provecho," when he handed me the bag. So I said nothing in response to Tyler's wink. Maybe it was like punctuation.

He hitched up his bag. "Don't stay too late. It'll still be here tomorrow."

I flashed him a tight smile. "Thanks. See you."

How many more tomorrows did we have if we didn't finish this project on time? Cooper had said not many. He'd said Weston was making noise again about trimming unnecessary staff to make the company leaner, nimbler. I'd thought we were pretty fucking nimble already, but Cooper and Weston were the numbers guys.

Would Tyler be one of those unnecessary staff on the list to be trimmed? He'd land on his feet, sure. But what about Alicia? Without Cooper's good word, she wouldn't get too many more high-profile gigs like this one. And I couldn't stand being the reason her business faltered.

I put my headphones back on and stared at my screen. I'd finish it for her. And for Tyler. And for Cooper. I wouldn't let them down.

14

ALICIA

THE SCRATCH of Noah's pencil against his paper made my eye twitch.

Jackson had his clacking keyboard and his leaky headphones. Tyler and the other programmers also coded to music. I, on the other hand, required silence. Especially when I was debugging.

But Noah was dutifully scratching out a book report for language arts across the kitchen table from me, and I wasn't about to tell him to switch out for a quieter pencil. Mom and Esmy had gone to bed, and we were united in working late.

When I'd tried to compile and run my code, it'd thrown up a runtime error. I'd reviewed my code but hadn't found anything. Then I'd checked the other modules one by one. And whose code was screwing with mine? Jackson's. I'd had to leave early for soccer, but I'd vowed to find and fix the bug before we returned to work the next day. If I was lucky, he'd never know, and we could keep working as a "pair" with the luxury of not speaking to each other. Exactly like he wanted.

Noah's head swayed, and he blinked his eyes hard. His pencil had zigged across the page, and he scrubbed the errant mark with his eraser.

"Hey, buddy, I think it's time for bed."

"But I'm not finished."

"You can work on it again tomorrow. I'll write you a note. You can show your teacher that you started it."

He grimaced and looked back down at the paper.

"It'll be okay. I promise. Go to bed. You'll feel better tomorrow if you sleep."

"Okay." He stood and stretched. "Night, Alicia."

"Night, Noah." He scuffed off to bed, Tigger trailing at his heels.

I focused my own bleary eyes back on my laptop screen. There was one piece of code that didn't look quite right...

My phone buzzed on my desk. I shot my hand out like a snake to grab it. It wasn't Carly Simon, and Jackson hadn't texted me since Cooper's chewing-out on Monday; still, I half-hoped it was somehow him. I'd tell him about the bug, and we could joke around like we'd done when he found that bug in my code. I half-smiled at the memory of his terrible guesses about what I did on Tuesdays and Thursdays. A cornette.

> Tiannah: We didn't get to talk at the game tonight. You OK?

I'd stayed in my car, one eye on the game and the other on my laptop screen. It wasn't an effective way to watch soccer or to debug code, but it was the working mother way of life.

> Sorry, had to work in the car. Miss you.

> Tiannah: You have a minute to talk?

I hadn't even finished typing out *Yes* when my phone rang. I swiped to answer. "Hey."

"Hey yourself. Mind if I vent for a minute?"

I leaned back in the stiff kitchen chair and smiled. "Shoot."

She launched into a story about the Evil P.T.A. Moms. A lesser woman—me—would've ceded the field years ago. But Tiannah wouldn't let them win. She fought them on everything from instituting a nut-free space in the lunchroom to diversifying the holiday concert program. She'd won some and lost some, but she always complained—or crowed—to me.

After she finished her story and I'd told her she was right, of course, she paused. "You okay? Diane said you were having a rough week at work."

I shifted in the chair. "It's fine. It's just…" I hadn't meant to tell her, but the words poured out of me. Tyler's screw-up two weeks ago. My failed pair-programming with Jackson. The sushi. Cooper's twin tongue-lashings. All the embarrassment, the frustration, the fear of the past four weeks that I'd held back from everyone, including my best friend, puked up like so much bad sushi.

"That Jackson Jones sounds like trouble," she said.

"He's not so bad." I bit my lip.

But Tiannah, my best friend, heard the words I didn't say. "Not so bad?"

"He's a great programmer, and he's taught me so much. He's trying to make nice with the team. Make them more cohesive. I guess I misjudged him at first. I don't hate him anymore." I winced, glad she couldn't see me.

"Whoa. You don't hate him? You mean you like him?"

"Not like that." But the words had spilled out too fast. "I respect him."

"Girl, watch yourself."

"I know. But he's different from the other guys I've worked with."

Tianna's silence stretched out, letting me know exactly what she thought.

"You know I'd never—"

"I know. But feelings are tricky things to wrangle."

"Just let me fangirl for a few more days. Then I'm sure he'll do something irritating and remind me why I hated him in the first place."

"They always do, honey. But I know you'll keep yourself under control. You'd never risk your business for dick."

"I didn't say anything about dick. I just said I liked the guy."

"Alicia." Her voice held a warning. "Remember what's important."

Noah. And Weber Technology Consulting. *Focus on that, not your smart coworker and his nimble fingers.*

"You've got this. You'll show everyone how smart and capable you are, and then you'll have to start turning down offers."

Turning down offers. I wished. For now, I had to finish the work I'd said I could do. And, as usual, I had to produce twice as much to get the same recognition.

"Anything I can do to help?"

Oh, you know, help me debug this code, figure out what's up with Noah and language arts, and talk some sense into me so I don't jump every time I get a text. "No, I'm good. Thanks for checking in. Love you."

"Love you, too. See you Thursday?"

"Yeah."

With a sigh, I turned back to Jackson's code, which, sadly, hadn't debugged itself.

15

JACKSON

I PAUSED the music and tugged off my headphones. I'd been searching all morning for the fucking bug in my code, but it was hidden better than that hairline crack in my Lamborghini's cylinder head. Alicia always coded in silence; maybe if I tried that, I could find the damned thing. I scanned through the program again.

A drop of sweat trickled down from my temple into my beard. It was hotter than hell in the office today. Had they turned off the air conditioning? It was fucking October, and it shouldn't still be in the nineties. The human body wasn't made to survive six months of heat like this. My body wasn't.

I glanced over at Alicia, typing primly in her slim black skirt and silk blouse. She sipped her tea. Hot tea in temperatures like this? The now-familiar smell of it wafted over me. Earl Grey. I'd sniffed all the bags in the kitchen one night to figure it out. It smelled bitter, like the time a kid at school had dared me to eat an orange like an apple, rind and all. I couldn't taste anything else for days.

She held the cup under her nose, letting the steam curl up around her face. It caressed her temples the way I had that first day. The way I'd daydreamed about doing again. She and her hot tea were making me sweat. I scooted my chair half a foot away from her, repositioned my keyboard, and stared again at my screen.

A few minutes later, my stomach growled. Ah. I needed some food in my system to make my brain work right. A few minutes away from the screen would do me good.

I stood, stretching, and pocketed my phone.

Alicia looked up from her perfect code. "You going to lunch?"

"Yeah." Then I had a brilliant idea. I could talk to Alicia about my code. Maybe it'd be that nudge that'd help me figure out what I'd done wrong. "Want to come with me?"

"Um." Her eyes drifted off my face. "I don't think—"

"Come on. You need a break and food, and so do I. Why not go together? Then you can be sure I come back on time." And I wouldn't mind some time out of the office with Alicia. Maybe she was less buttoned-up there. Would she grant me a few more guesses about her Tuesday-Thursday commitments?

She cut her gaze to the window behind me, like she could use the weather as an excuse. But it was hot and sunny, exactly like it'd been yesterday and the day before that and all fucking summer.

"I'll buy. And you choose the restaurant," I said.

She sighed like it was a huge imposition to be bought lunch. "Okay." She grabbed her purse from her desk drawer, quickly checked her phone, and then dropped it in. "Let's go."

When we emerged into the sunlight, I slid on my sunglasses. "Where do you want to go?"

She glanced to the left. "My favorite taco place is a few blocks that way. Are you up for a walk?"

"You're the one wearing heels." I made the mistake of looking down at them. Today, they were beige with an opening at the toe where one shiny, black-painted toenail peeked out. Alicia wore black nail polish? Did she have some sort of goth double-life? Maybe she did sleep in a crypt. Maybe Tuesdays and Thursdays were the nights she went to—

I almost smacked my forehead right there on the sidewalk. Of course! She had a boyfriend. It didn't surprise me that Alicia's dating life was regimented. Tuesdays and Thursdays—and probably Saturdays, but I didn't have any visibility to that—were date nights. How had I not figured that out over a month of working with her? Next

Wednesday or Friday morning, I could confirm it by checking her face for afterglow.

Afterglow? I clenched my teeth.

"Jackson?" She was already a few steps down the sidewalk. "You coming?"

"Yeah." I jogged a few steps to catch up and then walked beside her, my Converse silent next to the click-click-click of her heels. We passed clumps of students from the nearby university, a couple guys with skateboards, other tech types from the dozens of hardware and software companies that surrounded us, even a few suited politicians who'd wandered far from the capitol complex.

I rubbed the center of my chest, trying to ease the sudden burn. I didn't have any right to be jealous. Alicia, our consultant, was off limits. We couldn't date. It was probably a good thing she had a boyfriend. I'd done a lot of selfish things in my life, but I'd never tried to tempt a woman to cheat.

Besides, she'd told Cooper she didn't even like me. And that had hurt more than it should've. It definitely shouldn't have bothered me that she was seeing someone else. I tried to loosen my jaw.

Fuck, why was I even there, about to eat lunch with her, solo? I shouldn't see her anywhere but in the office. I stopped walking. I'd claim my gastric distress had come back.

She ran lightly up the steps to Linda's Taquería, a ramshackle single-story house with a giant wooden deck behind it. She turned at the door, her face flushed from our walk and the skin visible through the vee of her button-up shirt glistening. "Coming?"

Who was I kidding? I'd follow Alicia anywhere.

We walked up the steps and inside, which was blessedly dark and cool and smelled of cumin and chile. My stomach growled.

"Table for two?" the hostess asked.

"Yes, and can we sit on the patio?" Alicia asked.

The patio? My sweat-damp skin cried out for the air-conditioned dining room.

"Sure." She led us outside to the deck, which was shaded by a pergola. Flowering vines wove between the open wooden slats above, making it marginally cooler than the parking lot, where I could see waves of heat radiating off the gravel.

"Outside?" I flopped into the hot plastic chair.

She buried her nose in the laminated menu. "It's so nice today. And I figured we could use the fresh air."

Fresh air, my ass. Humidity clogged my lungs and made my T-shirt limp as a dishrag.

Alicia ordered unsweetened iced tea, and I asked for lemonade. I wished I could've ordered a margarita, but I didn't want to put up with Alicia's disapproving expression or the headache I'd surely get that afternoon.

After we'd ordered, Alicia folded her hands on her paper placemat and gave me a tight smile. "So, Jackson, are you enjoying Austin?"

"It's a little warm for my taste." I pulled the neck of my T-shirt away from my skin and flapped it to try to direct a breeze inside.

"Oh, sorry, I didn't even think— Would you rather eat inside?"

Yes. "No." I waved her off. "This is fine." If she was happy, she'd be more willing to help me with my code later.

"I guess I'm used to it, especially since it's cooled off now. It's not even supposed to hit ninety today. It'll be comfortable tonight once the sun gets low."

"Tonight. Thursday night." I dragged the words out slowly. "I can't believe it took me this long to figure it out."

She raised her eyebrows. "Figure what out, exactly?"

"What you do on Tuesdays and Thursdays."

"Oh?" She dragged a finger through the condensation on her tea glass.

"You have a date."

She blinked. "A date."

"You know, going out to dinner and a movie, or maybe staying in for a little Netflix and chill?"

"Netflix and chill?"

"You know what I mean. You have a boyfriend." Not a fiancé. She didn't wear a ring. When she didn't say anything, I widened my eyes. "Or a girlfriend."

She laughed, and it was the first time I'd heard it. She showed her teeth—another rare occurrence in my experience—and the sound started high and ended as a low chuckle. "You think my life is so orderly that I have dates every Tuesday and Thursday afternoon?"

I smiled, too, and shrugged. "You're just so...so organized." I pictured her, like the gathering-supplies montage in a heist movie, lining up a strip of condoms, a bottle of lube, a candle, perhaps, on her bedside table, and then, businesslike, starting to unbutton her silk blouse—*shit!* No imagining her doing a striptease. I rubbed a hand over my eyes to delete the image.

"Wow. Okay, sure. Tuesdays we play Bunco at his church, and Thursdays we catch the new release at the movie theater."

"See?" I pointed at her barely contained smile. "I knew it."

"Sorry, another bad guess. Though..." She bit her lip.

"What?" A hint had practically slipped out of Alicia's lockbox. Giddy anticipation made me hold my breath. She'd said her twice-weekly commitment wasn't a date. I was more relieved than I should've been.

"Nothing."

"A hint. A tiny one."

She considered for a moment, scanning my face. "Nope."

"Oh, come on." I flopped back in my chair.

"How's your code coming along?"

I hated that she'd changed the subject, but this was why I'd asked her to lunch. "I've run into a snag."

"Oh?" She squeezed another lemon into her tea and used a long teaspoon to stir it, the ice clinking.

"Yeah." I briefly described the issue to her, then all the things I'd checked and all the methods I'd tried to fix it. "Any idea what could be going on?"

She opened her mouth to speak but then looked over my shoulder and smiled. Our waitress set down a huge platter of enchiladas, beans, and rice in front of me and a paper-lined basket of tacos in front of Alicia.

I picked up my fork and cut off a corner of the leftmost enchilada. Chicken, spinach, and creamy white cheese sauce. Delicious.

Across the table, Alicia sprinkled hot sauce over her tacos before picking one up and biting into it with her straight, white teeth. She set it back in the basket and chewed slowly. I watched her swallow and pat her lips with her napkin. Lunch had been a bad idea. Too much focus on Alicia's tempting mouth. It was ridiculous to be jealous of a taco.

"Is your food okay?" She nodded at my plate with only one bite gone.

Shaking my head, I cut off a bite of the second enchilada, a cheese one. "Yeah, it's great."

"Knew you'd like it."

The red sauce was spicy. I chugged my lemonade. "Any ideas about my code?"

"Ah." She carefully wiped her fingers on her napkin. "I may have seen something earlier in the week."

"Something?"

"A bug." She explained it to me—God, I had to have scanned over the bad code a dozen times—and then she said, "I—ah—I fixed it in the development sandbox."

I let my fork clatter to my plate. "You what?"

"It was causing a problem in my code, so I fixed it so my module would run. I—I was going to tell you."

"When?" She could've saved my morning of frustration.

"When you asked, okay?"

That wasn't teamwork. That was betrayal. She'd never have done that to Tyler or Kevin or anyone else. "Why? Why the fuck would you wait?" My voice had risen too loud, and a few heads turned my way. "Why didn't you tell me?" I asked more softly, though anger still tightened my throat.

"This. Exactly this." She shoved her basket of tacos away. "Men don't want to hear criticism from their women colleagues. Working with a female programmer, I could tell her about the problem, and she'd thank me and move on. She'd respect me more for helping her. But men are infallible, and there's no way I, with my weak female brain, could figure out something you can't. And if I do, it must be because some man helped me." Her face was red, and a droplet of sweat dripped off her chin. "I thought—I hoped—you were different, but I can see now I was wrong. It's all about your ego, same as every other man I've worked with." She balled up her napkin and threw it on the table before scraping back her chair.

"Now wait a minute," I said, holding out a hand to her. "I didn't mean—"

"Oh, I think you did." Standing, she towered over me, the short hairs at her temple curling in the humidity and making her look like a flaming sun. "You invited me to lunch not as an equal but as someone who could help you. And then, when I helped you, you criticized me. I—I—" Without finishing her sentence, she turned and walked back through the restaurant, leaving me alone with my giant plate of enchiladas.

I hadn't fucking criticized her. I'd only asked her why she hadn't told me. Yeah, maybe I'd gotten a little loud. That was what people did when they—

Blotting the sweat from the back of my neck with a spare napkin, I slumped back in the chair. Fuck, I'd done exactly what she said. At least from her perspective, I'd been an asshole. Maybe I'd been an asshole from any perspective.

The waitress approached and scanned our table of uneaten food. "Is everything okay?"

"Yeah, just…would you mind boxing this up for us? Please?"

"Sure thing." She hefted my plate and Alicia's tacos. "Anything else?"

"An iced tea and a lemonade to go, please."

When I got back to the office, I set the sweating styrofoam cup of tea at Alicia's right hand. Leaning down, I said softly, "I put the rest of your lunch in the fridge. Your name is on it."

Without looking up from her screen, she said, "Thanks." Her tone was frostier than my cup of lemonade.

That night, after Alicia had left for her Thursday-evening commitment, when I went to grab my leftover enchiladas, I found the styrofoam box marked *Alicia* in the garbage.

16

ALICIA

DURING DINNER ON FRIDAY NIGHT, the doorbell rang.

Esmy wiped her mouth and scraped back from the table. "I'll get it."

"Maybe it's a guy with a giant check," Noah said, his eyes wide.

"Or one of those shirtless men in a kilt from the romance novel covers," Mom said.

"Cute." I smirked. They were all trying to cheer me up after my craptastic week at work. Monday: reaming-out by Cooper Fallon; Tuesday and Wednesday: working late to fix the code; Thursday: overreacting and bailing on the best tacos in the world because Jackson Jones had toppled off the pedestal I'd put him on with my fangirling.

Finally, Friday, the cherry on top of it all, Jackson had bugged me all day, trying to talk about God knew what, probably some other problem he was having with his code that he wanted me to fix and then yell at me after.

I knew I should've apologized for going off on him. Or at least heard him out. But with all the stress—not only work and Noah but also bookkeeping, taxes, and insurance for my new business—I was afraid I'd blow up at him again. I'd gotten a headache and left the office early, which meant I had more work to do this weekend. I balled my hands into fists under the table.

Esmy walked back into the kitchen carrying a white paper pharmacy bag. "Alicia, if I'd known you needed something at the drugstore, I'd have picked it up for you when I went after school today."

"But I didn't order anything from the drugstore."

"The kid said it was a delivery for you. Had your name and everything."

Weird. Had I ordered something a while ago and forgotten? I'd been so focused on work and Noah lately that I supposed I could have. "I'll check it out after we do the dishes. I'll wash, and, Noah, you dry."

"Aww," he groaned. "Weekends are the only time I get to play computer games."

"You can play after we put away the dishes. Now, show me your homework folder."

I waited until after we'd done the dishes, after Mom and Esmy had watched a show on TV while I finished up my daily report and emailed it to Cooper, and after I'd taken away Noah's gaming controller and sent him off to bed. Only then did I carry the package into my room.

It was the same room I'd slept in since we'd moved into the house when I was six until I'd left for college. And after Melissa died, leaving me, the occupant of a one-bedroom apartment in a downtown high-rise, as Noah's guardian, we'd both moved back in. I'd upgraded the canopied single bed to a double, but the white-painted dresser and nightstand were the same. The posters of boy bands were gone, replaced by botanical prints I'd picked up from a local art gallery. Noah slept next door in Melissa's old room, now decked out in superhero movie posters and a *Star Wars* bedspread, with a Jack-and-Jill bathroom separating his space from mine.

I flopped onto the bed and set down the drugstore bag. Popping the opening free from its staples, I peered inside. The bag held two items, plus a piece of paper.

I pulled out the bottle of ibuprofen first. I usually bought the store brand, and this was a name brand. It didn't seem like something past-Alicia would buy. The second item was a cardboard carton of hemorrhoid cream. *That* certainly didn't seem like me. Someone else's order had gotten mixed up with whatever I'd ordered. Someone with a burning butt and a headache was probably wondering what he could do with a box of tampons and a tube of Great Lash.

Maybe the receipt had the true recipient's contact information, and I could get the items to their suffering owner. I pulled the sheet of paper from the bag. It wasn't a receipt but a note.

Sorry I've been such a pain in the butt. You're a kick-ass programmer.
- Jackson

What? I let the note flutter down to my pale-blue comforter. Okay, it was a little sweet that he'd sent me medicine for my headache, but why the hell did he think I had hemorrhoids? He had to have crossed some sort of HIPAA line. Clenching my teeth, I snatched up my phone and jabbed in a text.

> What the hell, Jackson?

A few seconds later, my phone rang. He'd never called me, so it was the regular ringtone, but his name flashed across the screen.

I hesitated for a second. Texting was safe, almost anonymous. A phone call crossed a line. Hearing his voice, imagining him in his space, and him imagining me in mine, seemed intimate. Especially on a Friday night. Was I ready for that? No.

But he knew I was there. Ignoring the call would make me a coward. I tapped the answer button. "Hello?"

"Didn't you get my apology note?"

Oh, wow, he was jumping right in. "I got a note with two butt references worthy of a grade-schooler. And the, um, items. I don't need them." *Hemorrhoid cream. Overstepping asshole.*

My bra strap had been digging into my shoulder for hours, and my skirt waistband was tight after I'd gorged on Esmy's pupusas at dinner. I tugged my blouse over my head and tossed it toward the hamper, but it was too light and fell short.

Jackson's voice was gentle, soothing. "It was a joke. About how I'm a pain in the ass. I also considered diaper cream and lube, but I thought they might send the wrong message. For different reasons." He paused when I didn't say anything. "Did I choose wrong?"

I couldn't help smiling a little. I had a special appreciation for grade-school potty humor. I released the tight band of my bra, balled it up, and threw it at the hamper, thankful we weren't on video.

"As usual, you chose very wrong. A greeting card would've been much safer." I yanked open my dresser drawer, found a soft gray UT shirt, and pulled it on, feeling twenty percent better.

"I'm not really into safe." Jackson sounded a little breathless. "Except for sex. I'm very safe about that." He paused. "Though not too safe."

My skin tingled like he'd brushed his fingers over me. I shivered.

Jackson cleared his throat. "I probably shouldn't be talking to you about sex."

I'd unbuttoned my skirt, but now I felt weird about taking it off. No, he *shouldn't* be talking to me about sex. We worked together. We barely knew each other, spoke as little as possible in the office. Except for his questions about my Tuesday-Thursday commitments and clumsy fumbling about my dating life yesterday at lunch, he'd never asked me about my personal life. It was exactly what I'd wanted when I'd started my consulting business. Focus on the work. No need to get to know each other. No talk about families. The men I worked with would see me as someone exactly like them: no distractions or responsibilities that affected my work. And yet, his deep voice was turning on nerve endings inside me that I'd all but forgotten about.

He said, "Do I need to apologize again?"

I chuckled. "I was waiting to see how deep you'd dig that hole."

"I think I hit bedrock."

"Fine. You can stop now. I appreciate the apology."

We had to be almost done with the call, but I couldn't wait a second longer. I unzipped my skirt, let it fall to the floor, and stepped out of it. I rubbed at the red lines where the seams had pressed into my skin.

But he wasn't done. "I really am sorry about lunch yesterday. I'll admit, I did take you to lunch to get your thoughts on my code. Because I respect you. Because you're talented. But I should've made that clear when I asked you to go with me."

A warm glow started in my belly, and I smiled, even though he couldn't see me. I eased on a pair of sleep shorts. "Thanks. And I'm sorry, too. For blowing up at you. It's just—you hit a nerve. I"—I took a deep breath—"I've been on the receiving end of some pretty dismissive comments. At work. Because I'm a woman." I held my breath.

"You know I'd never—"

"I know. I think I do."

"I have a sister. She's a coder, too. She's told me some stuff. I'm sorry I triggered that for you."

The tension I'd been holding in my shoulders eased. "No more apologies, okay? We both did our penance when we missed out on Linda's tacos."

He laughed, low and sexy. *Not sexy!* "Next time, I promise lunch will be purely social."

I scooped up my skirt and blouse and tossed them into the hamper. Social lunches—especially with a man as attractive and brilliant as Jackson Jones—would complicate my orderly life. In fact, they were exactly the opposite of my goal: to keep my work and personal lives separate. No company picnics. No happy hours. Only work and a paycheck. "I don't think that's a good idea." Before he could press, I asked, "Did you find your bug?"

"Yeah. Thanks." Irritation roughened his voice. Good.

"Great. I'll see you Monday."

"Wait!"

"What?" What else could he have to talk about? Still holding my phone, I pulled back the covers and climbed into bed.

"'See you Monday' seems harsh after I sent you a gift." His voice was strangled.

I snorted. "You sent me expensive ibuprofen and hemorrhoid cream."

"It's the meaning behind the gift that counts."

"Meaning that you gave me a headache and you sent me something I won't use?"

His voice went playful. "Shit, should've sent the lube after all."

I couldn't think of a single appropriate reply to that.

"You could think of me while you used it," he continued. "Wait, I didn't mean it the way that came out."

I snorted. "Mayday, mayday, pull up."

"More like pull out. Shit! I meant my foot out of my mouth. Not…"

A few seconds of silence ticked by.

"I guess I'll climb back in my hole," he said. Then he groaned.

If I let him go on any longer, he might say something that actually offended me. "You should build yourself an app that censors your phone calls to coworkers."

"I'll get right on that."

I snickered. "You did it again."

"Oops."

"You're not sorry at all."

"You're right. I'm not. But I am about lunch. Thanks for saving my ass."

My chest expanded. "That's what I'm here for. To save your code, not your ass." I winced. "Don't respond to that one."

He was silent for a few seconds. "I'm glad you took this job, Alicia Weber."

Was I glad? Jackson Jones had been a giant pain in my ass. We both knew it. He'd admitted it and sent the hemorrhoid cream to prove it.

Good thing, too, or it'd have been too easy to fall for my brainy coworker who also happened to be hotter than Texas asphalt in July. But those two strikes against him—pain in my ass and coworker—meant I didn't need a third.

"I'm glad, too," I said. "Now, really, see you Monday." I tapped the end button and opened my book on small-business tax accounting.

17

ALICIA

I TOSSED my purse back in the drawer and heard my phone fall to the metal bottom. Screw it. I'd put it where it belonged next time I had to haul ass to the bathroom to change out my tampon. I tore open the paper packet of pain relievers I'd found in the first aid kit in the kitchen. This office full of guys might not stock feminine hygiene products in the ladies' room, but at least they had medicine that'd dull my cramps. I swigged it back with my tepid tea.

"Everything okay?" Jackson asked, low.

"Of course. Why wouldn't it be?" I slammed the drawer shut. He flinched.

"No reason." He stared at the drawer.

Screw him and his assumptions. I wanted to snarl at him and everyone on my team. And not only because they were all men. We had one week to finish the code for Cooper's next review, where we had to wow him. Or else. "Shouldn't you be coding?"

"Actually—"

Great, here we go. He's got some brilliant new idea that's going to disrupt the entire project.

"I was thinking maybe we could try pairing up again." He nodded at the other programmers working side-by-side at their desks. "It seems to be working well for the rest of the team. Maybe we'd be more efficient working together?" His voice rose, uncharac-teristically, into a question at the end.

Exactly. He wanted to change the process mid-stream. Even if it was what I'd wanted to do from the beginning, it was too late now. "I don't think so, Jackson. Our process seems to be working. I'll check your code when you're done." Maybe he could code the whole damn thing while I went and lay down somewhere. I rubbed a hand over my abdomen like I could iron out the stabbing pain.

His gaze followed my hand. "You sure you're okay?"

"Stop asking me that," I hissed. "I need to focus on work, and so do you." I thought we'd worked out all the post-phone-call weirdness that morning. And by *worked out*, I meant *completely ignored*. It was fine. He'd probably been drinking or playing a video game, half his attention on the screen while we talked. He hadn't really meant what he'd said about respecting me. Rather, respecting *my talent*. He'd only been saying what he thought I wanted to hear. I'd probably made up the softness in his voice, the kindness in his eyes this morning, the way he seemed to care about me. No, not *care*. I meant *concern*. He was only concerned that I was about to tear into him and the rest of the team with hormonal fury.

I dragged my attention to my screen and logged back into my computer. I scanned through the lines to see what I'd been working on before my trip to the restroom. Ah. I curved my fingers over the keyboard, thinking about what went next. The back of my neck prick-led, stealing my focus.

Rubbing it, I glanced over at Jackson. He snapped his gaze back to his own screen. Unfortunately for him, it'd timed out and gone black.

"What?" I snarled. If he said one word about PMS, I was going to whack him with my keyboard.

"Nothing. I... Can I get you anything? More tea?" His cheeks pinked.

I could only stare at him and his annoyingly pretty eyes, his dark eyebrows tilted into something that looked suspiciously like sympa-thy. Jackson Jones was being nice to me? At work? He had to have an ulterior motive.

And I was so tired of it all: the constant checks that I was doing the right thing, saying the right thing, acting like a man in a man's world. I'd been naïve to think being the boss of my own company would spare me all that.

"Can we just...not?" I curled my hands into fists and then flattened them over my keyboard. "Can we just act like coworkers and do the work? Without all the exhausting sparring? At least for today?"

His shoulders slumped. "I only meant—sorry."

Guilt speared through me, but before I could say anything, a rumble erupted from the desk drawer. I'd left my phone on vibrate as usual, and it made a sound like an oncoming train against the metal bottom of the drawer. I jerked it open and pulled out my phone.

Noah's school, the display read.

I grabbed it and answered, my voice low, as I speed-walked to the nearest empty conference room.

"Hi, Ms. Weber, it's Janet, the school secretary. I'm calling about Noah. He was in a fight this afternoon. We need you to come to the school."

"A fight?" My sweet Noah, in a fight? I imagined him lying on the blacktop, being kicked by bigger, meaner kids, and my heart shredded. Then it reformed into jagged shards of steel. He was in a cast, for God's sake! I was going to see that those kids got expelled. Or worse. Could you press charges against a ten-year-old? "Is he okay?"

"Just some scrapes and bruises. But we need you to come. Now."

"Right. Of course." Scrapes and bruises didn't sound so bad, but I might need to take him to urgent care again if she was downplaying his injuries. "Tell him I'll be there in twenty minutes."

Returning to our work area, I announced that I had a personal issue and needed to go home. Then I went to my desk and started packing up.

Jackson stood, nervous energy vibrating off him and colliding with my own anxiety. My teeth itched.

"Anything I can do to help?" he asked, low.

I set down my phone next to my keyboard. "Just—can you check in with the guys? Make sure they're on track? We can't fall behind."

"Sure, but I meant...for you."

For me? My heart, that traitor, thumped hard enough to twitch my blouse. "No. I'm fine." I slipped my laptop bag over my shoulder and grabbed my phone.

He nodded toward my side of the desk. "Don't forget your laptop."

"Oh. Crap. Right." I shook my head. *Focus.* Setting down my phone, I undocked my computer and slid it into my bag. Purse! I wouldn't make it far without my keys. I bent to pull it from the drawer and checked that my keys were clipped to the ring inside. "See you tomorrow."

I walked to the stairs as fast as I could without running and carefully descended the stairs. Scrapes and bruises. My stomach twisted. Had they reinjured his arm? We had only a week to go until the cast was supposed to come off.

Once I was outside, I ran across the street to the parking garage. Let them see me lose my cool. I had to get to Noah. Taking care of him was the most important thing.

――――――

JACKSON

NO, I didn't watch Alicia trot off toward the stairs, her swaying hips mesmerizing in that skinny black skirt.

Okay, fuck, yes, I did. Because Tyler had to punch my arm to get me to snap out of my trance.

"Hey, Jay, you okay?"

"Yeah, fine. Why?"

"I've been trying to get your attention. I didn't want to ask Alicia because she, um, didn't seem like herself, but I could use some help. Got a minute?"

"Sure." I hadn't been his first choice, but he was asking me for help. That had to be progress toward earning the respect of the team and working together, right? I followed him to his desk, pulled up an extra chair, and listened as he explained the problem.

As it turned out, it wasn't hard, and we resolved it in less than an hour, including some coding best practices I threw in gratis.

Going back to my desk, I felt almost as proud as when I'd fixed a gnarly bug in my own code. Tyler had come to me for help, and I'd helped him. Cooper would've been proud of me. He'd say I'd earned the respect of the team. My chest swelled with pride under my ZZ Top T-shirt.

Until I saw it.

Her phone. Alicia's phone, shoved half-under her keyboard.

A notification popped up on her lock screen. Was it something she needed to see?

I breathed in. Out.

Maybe it was a junk text, or a message from a political campaign.

Or maybe it was important, like the call she'd gotten right before she'd left, the one that'd turned her face pale and those blue eyes wide.

And she wouldn't get it until tomorrow.

Being separated from my phone made me itchy. She'd probably feel the same, that sick, sinking feeling when she realized she'd forgotten it. That missing-limb void when she reached for it but it wasn't there.

I picked it up, cool from its hour of abandonment.

It was only a phone. People had survived for thousands of years without phones.

But I'd make sure Alicia didn't have to.

18

JACKSON

THE BUNGALOW in the Cherrywood neighborhood not too far from downtown was painted a cheery sunshine yellow with a purple door. A rainbow flag jutted out from a pole anchored to one of the sturdy porch supports.

I squinted at the address on my phone and then checked the number next to the purple door.

Not the house I would've imagined for Alicia. She was straight lines and seriousness, a no-nonsense president of the homeowners' association out with a ruler to enforce grass-cutting height. Not whimsical pink flowers spilling out of cracked terracotta pots next to the porch steps.

But this was the address I had.

I jumped down from the truck's cab, my Converse slapping onto the street. I trudged up the short walk between a pair of twisted-looking trees covered in clumps of delicate lavender flowers. Two short steps, and I was on the shady porch, my finger poised over the bell. The scents of roasting chicken and garlic wafted from the open window next to the door, along with female voices. Screwing my eyes almost shut, I pressed the button.

Light, running footsteps approached the door, which swung open.

A skinny kid with a green cast on his arm smiled at me through the metal screen. The bruise under his eye matched the purple door. He couldn't have been more than eight, with straw-colored hair curling down over his ears. His eyes were brown, not the ocean blue of Alicia's; still, his mouth was the same shape as hers—I should know since I was low-key obsessed with it.

"Hey," he said.

I hadn't heard the woman approach. Her feet were bare, and she wore a flowered dress that hung almost to her ankles. Threads of white streaked her dark hair. The lines around her eyes deepened when she squinted at me. "Can I help you?" Her vowels were soft and colored with the bluesy music I sometimes heard in the bars on Sixth Street.

Maybe someone had fat-fingered Alicia's address into the Synergy payroll system? I looked at the house to the right. Nondescript red brick. Grass cut short like a putting green. Maybe that was hers. I checked the house to the left. A rusty washing machine sat on its peeling front porch. Probably not that one.

"Sir?" the woman asked.

"Um, hi. Does Alicia Weber live here?" I shifted my weight onto my back foot, ready to pivot down the steps and head to the house on the right.

"Yeah, she does," the kid said. "Who are you?"

Whoa. I balanced my weight. "I'm Jackson Jones. We work—"

"We know you." The kid squinted at me.

He knew me? It'd been a while since I'd been on the cover of any business magazines. And these people didn't seem the type to get *Car and Driver*.

"He means we know you work together." The woman's lips tightened, all the softness gone from her face.

Oh, shit. I could imagine the stories Alicia had told about me at home. Was this her...aunt? Much older girlfriend? The kid had to belong to Alicia because he and the older woman had no features in common.

"I, ah. She forgot her phone. At work. I brought it to her." I held out the device, my skin fizzling with the obliteration of my hopes of seeing Alicia.

"What are you two—" Alicia, also barefoot, had come up behind the woman. Her hair fell in loose, irregular waves around her shoulders, and she'd traded her silky blouse and tight skirt for a burnt-orange Texas Longhorns shirt and a pair of cutoff black sweatpants. I'd seen her knees before when she sat at our desk, her skirt inching up above them. But I'd never seen so much of her pale thighs.

"Jackson?" Her voice hit me like an electrical shock, and I ripped my gaze off her legs and onto her slack mouth. *Shit! Eyes! Look at her eyes!*

Her own gaze dropped to my still-outstretched hand. "You brought me my phone?"

"Yeah, I—you left it at the office."

She stepped around the woman and then gently moved the kid to the side so she could push open the screen door. Standing a step above me in her bare feet—my eyes burned to peek at those shiny black toenails—she stared me directly in the eye. Her fingers brushed my palm as she took it from me. "Thank you."

I shivered even in the sticky evening warmth.

"Aren't you gonna invite him in?" the woman said. "He came all the way out here."

"It—it wasn't far," I said.

"How did you even—" Alicia said at the same time.

"Your mama raised you better than that." Now the woman's voice held the bite of a hot pepper. "Jackson, would you like to stay for dinner?"

My mouth had been watering at the delicious smells that surrounded me. And was that cinnamon? I sniffed hopefully.

"He really can't—" Alicia began.

"Do I smell pie?" I said.

"Apple," the woman said.

I looked Alicia in the eye. "I'd love to stay for dinner."

Her pointy chin jutted out, but she said nothing, only held the screen door for me until I put my palm on it and stepped up into the house.

The setting sun streamed through the still-open door behind me, lighting up the bright colors inside. As they hustled me through the small foyer—really only a few squares of tile set into the carpet of the living room—and skirted the living room to enter the kitchen, I glimpsed walls painted yellow, orange, and turquoise; a red velvet sofa; and books double-stacked in bookcases with bowed shelves, piled onto tables, even towering in corners.

A tiny bell jingled as an orange cat jumped off the back of the red sofa and trailed us into the kitchen, where Alicia's older double carved through the crackling skin of a roast chicken.

I had to be stuck in the "Mirror, Mirror" episode of *Star Trek*. Because only mirror-Alicia would wear fucking *sweatpant shorts* that barely covered her ass. And have a kid. The Alicia I knew pretended like her life didn't exist outside Synergy Analytics' office.

Or was I the one who pretended her life didn't exist outside the office? I'd made a fuck-ton of assumptions. I was sure of that.

While I was trying to get my bearings, we'd all packed into the tiny kitchen. Seriously, my apartment's kitchen, the one I never used except to store a few six-packs of local beer, was bigger than this.

"Jackson." Alicia's eyes squinched up like she was in physical pain. "Meet my mother, Diane. Her wife, Esmy. And Noah. Everyone, this is Jackson Jones, whom I've mentioned before." She spoke very slowly and clearly when she added, "He *owns the company* where I work."

My presumed power didn't seem to have a lot of weight in the Weber household. Diane set her carving knife to the side but tented her fingers over it, ready to grab and stab. Esmy extended her hand to me, and when I automatically clasped it, crushed my hand. Noah stared at me, eyes narrowed just like Alicia's.

The cat sniffed the toe of my Converse, puffed up like a fluffy basketball, and hissed, baring its sharp teeth and flattening its ears. No one admonished it. Maybe it was the family's spokesman.

Someone had to break the tension. I said, "I can't remember the last time I had home-cooked food. I guess it was Easter, when my friend Cooper's mom cooked for us." I gulped down the saliva that filled my mouth at the savory scent filling the kitchen. "Thank you for inviting me."

Esmy, at least, cracked a sympathetic smile. "We're glad to have you."

Alicia didn't seem to feel the same. A steel band encircled my upper arm. "Dinner's ready. I'll show you where to clean up," she said.

She marched me back through the living room and into a dark hallway, past an open bedroom door, which she closed before I could peek inside, and into a narrow bathroom decorated in bright blue-greens with orange clownfish on the shower curtain.

Alicia followed me into the bathroom, shut the door, and turned on the water. She leaned in close and said in a low voice I had to bend to hear, "Listen to me. I keep my home life and professional life separate. Only a very few people I've worked with have been to my home. We will not be talking about any of this at the office tomorrow. Or ever. Do you understand me?"

"I guess? I mean, I don't talk about my family at work, but that's because everyone knows all about them. They're all over the business pages. And Coop—"

No, I couldn't tell her about Cooper's family. Not about his abusive father, at least. They hadn't spoken since we were in college, and Cooper mostly pretended he was dead.

"Your family seems...not terrible? You're not...embarrassed of them?" My gaze fell on the blue cup on the counter that held two toothbrushes, one red and the other shaped like Superman.

"No, of course not."

"Then why—"

"Look. I'm a woman in technology. Where we work, people have certain preconceived notions of women with families. If we say we can't work late, we're more committed to our families than we are to the company. Same if we have to take a long lunch to take a kid to the pediatrician or work from home when he's sick and can't go to school. Men—and childless women—get promoted because they're dedicated to their careers. Women with families don't."

"That's not—"

She shook her head. "Don't even say it. You might not think your company does it, but they do. It starts the moment a woman asks for maternity leave, and it follows her throughout her career. Did you know women with children earn fifteen percent less than women without? And don't even get me started on the pay gap between women and men. Or people of color and white men."

I shook my head. The second she'd said "maternity leave," my brain had stalled out, circling that concept. While I'd had her HR file open to get her address, of course I'd glanced through it. Anyone would've done that. No husband or domestic partner listed. Assuming Noah was eight, she'd been twenty-two when she'd had him. Practically a child herself. Starting a family didn't seem like the type of thing a twenty-two-year-old, fresh out of college, would do. Unless...

"Are you divorced? Widowed?"

Alicia blinked and took a step back. "What? *That's* what you took away from what I said?"

"No, no, I followed you. No talking about your family at work. I get it. But I don't understand where Noah came from."

She rolled her eyes. "You mean, where's the sperm donor?"

Wow, it was hot in the bathroom. I turned the tap to cold.

"We don't know. My sister never told us who Noah's dad was. And I think we've done just fine raising him in a household of working women. So don't start with your caveman ideas."

My jaw dropped. Noah was her nephew. Where was the sister now? But I couldn't ask that. Not yet. So I pulled out classic Jackson Jones. "Caveman? Me?"

"That's what I said. Wash up. We've been gone too long."

Silently, I pumped the soap. That was what she thought of me? After we'd worked together for a month, after I'd told her only three days ago how amazing she was? I scrubbed my hands under the water. "I don't think you know me as well as you think you do."

She pumped the soap, and when I moved to dry my hands on the blue towel, she washed her hands. "Maybe not. I've just had a lot of experience with guys like you."

"Guys like me."

"Hot-shot tech guys. Always the smartest guy in the room, thinking everyone's had the same opportunities as you, same priorities, and it's a weakness in someone else if they haven't made it as far."

"Wow." I handed her the towel, trying to keep my voice light despite the knot in my stomach. "You don't think much of me, do you?"

"I'm protecting myself and my family." Her smile was bitter. "I've been fooled a couple times. Never again."

I thought about leaving. About walking straight back down the hallway and out the front door. If she really thought I was like all those other assholes who'd passed her over, I should've. But the gleam in her blue eyes, the way her mouth turned up at the corner, hinted that she hoped I wasn't. And that was enough to keep me there, in that *Finding Nemo* bathroom, in the house she shared with her two moms and a nephew I hadn't known existed, determined to crack the code on Alicia Diane Weber.

She opened the door, and we returned to the kitchen, where her family sat around the round table at the edge of the kitchen.

"Thought you'd gotten lost," Diane said. She put one of the chicken legs on Noah's plate.

"My hands were extra dirty from all that code at work," I said. "All clean now." I held them up, palms out, for inspection.

Noah snort-laughed.

Alicia sat in the empty chair next to Noah, and I sat between her and Esmy. The table was sized for four, and it was a tight squeeze. My left knee rested against Alicia's right. Esmy passed me a bowl of mashed potatoes that smelled like garlicky heaven. I scooped out a moderate-sized amount and passed the bowl to Alicia.

"Tell us about yourself, Jackson," Esmy said.

"My friends call me Jay." I gave her my most winning smile.

Diane said, "Alicia calls you Jackson."

"That's right. Though I'm working on it." My smile faltered when Diane shot me with a Cooper-level withering look.

Esmy jumped in again. "Alicia tells us you founded the company she's working for now."

"My best friend, Cooper, and I started it when we were still in college. I was into cars, and I wanted to use computers to figure out how to make them go faster."

"Like our Honda?" Noah asked.

"Well, sure. Some of the major automotive manufacturers are our customers. We started out with Cooper's dad's old beater of a car, a 1995 deep jewel green metallic Ford Escort. We used her for a project in my mechanical engineering class. She was rusted-out and burning oil, but we turned her into a powerful, efficient, intelligently adaptive machine. Nothing we could do about the rust, though." I sat back in my chair, remembering the way Cooper and I had bonded over the project. "But what I was most interested in was race cars. You know Formula One?"

"Duh, yeah," Noah said.

Esmy asked, "Is that like NASCAR?"

Noah rolled his eyes. "No, Grandma Esmy. It's totally different." With very little help from me, he explained the differences to his grandmother, who at least pretended to be interested.

I was starting to like the kid. "Have you ever been to the race here in Austin?"

"Nah." He looked down at his plate. "I've watched it online, though."

"It's coming up next month. I have tickets, and I could—"

Alicia's knee collided with my thigh under the table. "Ah!" I rubbed my leg. Those knees of hers were sharp.

"Noah's too busy with school and soccer to spend all weekend at a racetrack," she said.

"Soccer! You play?"

"Yeah, we have games every Tuesday and Thursday."

Tuesday and Thursday. I shot Alicia a triumphant look. She pursed her lips to hide a smile and shook her head.

"That how you got that shiner?" I slid the last forkful of potatoes into my mouth. Absolutely delicious. I hoped there'd be seconds. Maybe thirds.

"No, just the broken arm." He held up his cast. "I got punched in the eye at school today."

"What's the other kid look like?"

"Jackson!" Alicia put down her fork.

"I got him in the mouth. Split his lip, but that's about it." He held up his left hand, which had a bandage across one knuckle.

"Punches to the face are hard to execute well. Next time—"

"Jackson!" She got me in the same spot with her knee. "Next time, use your words, was what Jackson was about to say."

I winced and rubbed my leg. "Exactly. What was the fight about? You steal his girl?"

This time, Alicia rested her hand on my thigh. Not in a sexual way —though my body reacted as if it were—but cautioning me to tread lightly.

Noah pushed a few black-eyed peas under his mashed potatoes. "He saw my paper with a D on it. He called me stupid."

"Which isn't very nice," Alicia said, "but not worth punching someone."

I leaned back in my chair and laid my fork across my clean plate. "You seem like a smart kid. Why'd you get a D?"

Alicia whipped her head around so fast her hair slapped my shoulder. Her hair. It smelled like oranges, like her tea. But there was nothing warm about the glare she pummeled me with.

Noah shrugged.

What had I asked him? Oh, right. Grades. "I didn't do so well in school, either, until my doctor figured out I had ADHD. I know what it's like to struggle. And to be frustrated. And to give up." I rubbed at a smudge on my watch's sapphire face. "But after I got the help I needed, I did okay."

A line creased Alicia's forehead between her eyebrows. She stared at me like she eyeballed misbehaving code. "You did better than okay. You went to Stanford."

"My family's rich. They paid for a lot of tutoring and test prep."

"Don't undersell yourself." Her tone was sharp at the top but soft underneath. "You're a smart guy. And you had to have worked hard."

I ducked my head. Not many people said that. When you grew up with every privilege, a lot of people assumed the path to success was easy. Sure, it'd been easier for me than it'd have been for Alicia or anyone whose parents weren't significant donors to the university, but having someone see my effort, see that not everything had been handed to me, meant something. Coming from Alicia, it meant everything.

"Mind if I finish the potatoes?" I asked, nodding at the last scoop in the bowl.

"Go right ahead." Esmy handed me the bowl.

When my stomach was taut with dinner plus an extra-large slice of apple pie topped with Blue Bell ice cream, Alicia walked me outside. Her chin was stiff again, probably to remind me not to mention this at work tomorrow.

But when she opened her mouth, she said, *"That's* your car?"

At the end of the front walk, the black Ford F-150 waited for me. "It's a rental. But, yeah, I figured, when in Texas…"

"Rent a truck?" She laughed. "To haul your fence-mending supplies? You leave your cattle trailer parked back at your apartment?"

I shoved my hands in my pockets, grateful for the dim porchlight that hid my blush. "It's fun to drive, way up above the other traffic. Surprisingly powerful. And if you ever need something hauled, I'm your guy."

She wrinkled her nose. "Is that why you have the boots?"

I wasn't about to tell her I only wore them to irritate Cooper. I hoped I'd earned some points with her tonight and didn't want to be docked for pettiness. "Yeah, I guess. I kinda thought more people would wear them at work. And that they'd be more comfortable."

She snorted. "They're comfortable once you break them in. Boots are a commitment, Jackson." Her smile dissolved as if she'd just heard what she said. She bit her lip.

"I can do commitment. All I need is a reason." What the fuck was I saying? I'd never committed to anything except pretending I didn't care what anyone thought about me.

She walked toward the truck. "I guess you've been committed to your company for a while."

True. "More than ten years."

"And Cooper?"

"Best friends since our first day at college." I considered. "Mostly."

"Mostly?" She'd reached the shiny black side of the truck, and now she turned, one corner of her mouth rising.

"It's complicated."

"Knowing what I do of Cooper, I can imagine."

I didn't contradict her. Neither one of us was easy to get along with. But no matter how much I fucked up, Cooper had never given up on me, and I wasn't about to let go of a friend like that.

The porchlight shone golden on her hair where it curled over her shoulders. Half her face was in shadow. Her lipstick was long gone, and her eyes drooped with tiredness. She looked soft and fragile though I knew she was tough as the truck behind her.

"Maybe I'll try the boots again," I said, like that was relevant to anything.

"You should. Though…"

"Though?"

"Not much time left before the project ends and you go back to San Francisco."

I scuffed my sneaker on the sidewalk. "Not sure I'm going back after the project ends. Cooper hasn't said I can."

"You're his partner. You let him tell you when to go and when you can come back?"

Pretty much. "He's the smart one. I'm just the programmer."

"You're not *just* anything." She stepped into my space and poked me in the chest. "You're the smart one, too. I've never met a more brilliant programmer. And you're good with the team. Tyler looks up to you. You could be so much more if you'd step out of Cooper's shadow and be the leader I know you can be."

I looked up from my sneakers to check if she was serious. Her jaw was set, and her eyes narrowed. She believed in me.

I closed the space between us, compressing our professional distance into nothingness. She tilted her face up, and I bent mine down. Cinnamon from the pie mingled in our shared breath.

Was I really going to kiss her? Was she going to let me? Her eyelashes fluttered down to her cheeks. I was close enough to touch her smooth skin, to bury my fingers in her unbound hair. I lowered my face to hover an inch above her plush pink lips. This wasn't like the text flirting, or even like our innuendo-laced phone call. There was no coming back from this. I inhaled the rich scent of sweet orange in her hair.

No. Squeezing my eyes shut, I stepped back. "Alicia, I—I fucked up."

She blinked her eyes open and took in the empty space between us. She crossed her arms. "What?"

"Right before I came out to Austin. It's why I said I couldn't go out with you that first day. Why I can't kiss you now."

A tiny furrow formed between her eyebrows.

I reached out to smooth it away and stopped, shoving my hand into my jeans pocket. "There were some photos of me from the Monaco Grand Prix in the tabloids. Weston called me into his office and yelled at me about how I was a representative of Synergy, even on the weekends, and I was pissed off. Cooper was busy, and he didn't want to hear me vent. So I went to the closest bar and got shit-faced." I ran my hand over my beard. "There—there was this woman across the bar. She, ah, she flirted with me, and then we, ah, went out to the back alley. You know?"

Of course she didn't know. She'd never done anything so irresponsible in her life. Still, she murmured, "Mm-hmm."

Now for the worst part. "The next day, I went into the office and saw her there. She was one of our college interns. Callie. I swear she was twenty-one. I freaked out. I ran straight to Coop's office and told him about it. And he—he fixed it. Made sure she was okay. She agreed it was consensual. Cooper set up a formal apology with HR there. And then he sent me here so I wouldn't have to see her. Or so I couldn't."

She swallowed. "Did you want to see her again?"

"No! I mean, I'm sure she's a great person. But it didn't mean anything. I had no idea she worked at my company or I'd ever see her again."

"Is that how you feel about me?" She looked down at her flip-flop.

"No. Never." I placed one finger under her chin and tipped it up until she met my gaze. "And that's why I can't kiss you."

Her smile was a little sad. "We both care too much about our businesses to let a kiss become anything more."

I jammed my other hand into my pocket to keep from smoothing it through her hair, from touching her soft skin. "I like you, Alicia. Do you think we could drop the office rivalry and be...friends?"

"Friends?" An inscrutable expression crossed her face. "I guess we could try."

It was tepid at best, but I'd take it. I couldn't pretend to hate the woman with the titanium core I'd taken a month to discover. I wanted to reach out and hug her—friends did that—but considering the rigid set of her shoulders, I stuck out my hand instead.

She shook it. "Thanks for bringing my phone." Then she turned and walked briskly up the walk, flip-flops slapping the concrete.

When she shut the purple door, I circled the front of the truck and clambered inside. I leaned my head back against the headrest. After four months in Austin, I'd made my first friend.

And yet, I wanted so much *more*.

19

ALICIA

> Jackson: Please tell me you're the coach so I can imagine you lording it over a bunch of 8-year-olds with a whistle.

I must've grinned because Tiannah elbowed me in the side. "What's that about?"

"Nothing." I dropped my phone into the cupholder in my nylon chair.

"Doesn't look like nothing. Looks like something's making you blush."

"Oh, you know. Just a text from someone at work." Shit, I shouldn't have mentioned work. Why couldn't I have pretended I'd met someone at the grocery store or in line at the DMV? I stared out at the kids running drills before the game, hoping she'd drop it.

"From Jackson Jones?"

Crap. Her eyebrows had all but disappeared into her hairline.

Esmy leaned around me. "He came over for dinner last night."

Tavon clambered up into Tiannah's lap and stuck his thumb in his mouth. She tucked one arm around him and plopped her chin onto her other hand. "Jackson Jones, multimillionaire, came over for meatloaf at Casa Weber?"

"He brought Alicia her phone," Esmy said. "Is he really a multi-millionaire?"

One-handed, Tiannah tapped out a search on her phone. She flipped the device around. In the picture, Jackson wore a red jumpsuit covered in patches for petroleum companies and an auto manufacturer, and his hair was disheveled and sweaty like he'd taken off a helmet. Below that was a figure so large I had to count commas.

At least she hadn't found the shirtless photo of him. I'd thought about searching for it last night, but friends didn't do skeezy things like that.

My mother whistled. "You'd think a guy with a bank balance like that would have someone to run phones out to people."

"Mom." I leaned back in my chair and fanned myself. All those commas had made my brain swim. "He's just a regular guy." At least, he'd seemed that way at work. His Converse had a hole in one side.

"Alicia. This is not a regular guy." Tiannah waved the phone under my nose again. "He paid more in taxes last year than you'll earn in, like, ten years. And that's *with* our unfair, regressive tax system that favors the rich. Jackson Jones is the freaking one percent. He's, like, the one-tenth of one percent. Think of how much he could afford to give to charity and not even feel it."

I slumped back in my chair, keeping my fingers well away from my phone. Until a minute ago, his ownership of the company had been abstract. A vague kind of power he could've wielded over me and the other guys on the team, over everyone in the building, but, so far, had not. He'd acted like your run-of-the-mill cowboy coder. And the money? What did a person do with all that money? Was it at the local credit union, like mine, earning minuscule interest every month? Or invested in the stock market and bonds like my IRA? Did he keep it in his mattress? That'd be some thick mattress.

"Have you asked him about it?"

"About the money? No, of course not. We're coworkers. And we're starting to be friends." The word still felt strange in my mouth.

She put her hands over Tavon's ears. "Oh, hell, no, you are not. What you are is delusional if you think you and that many-times-over-millionaire are equals. That is some dangerous game you're playing with your flirty texts and your home-cooked suppers."

She picked up the soccer ball under her chair and handed it to Tyesha. "Isha, take your brother to that empty field and practice dribbling the ball." Tyesha took Tavon's hand and led him away with the ball.

Tiannah leaned over the arm of her chair and said in a low voice, "Men like that don't think about how they hurt regular people like us. He wants to use those texts"—she nodded at my phone—"to get in your pants. And once he's ready to move on, he'll do it without a second thought for you or your career."

"But Jackson doesn't seem like that kind of guy. He's caring. Thoughtful. Even nice sometimes." I glanced at Esmy, but she'd discreetly started talking to Mom when Tiannah started whispering.

I'd thought about the story he'd told me about the intern for longer than I should have last night. In the end, I'd concluded that he'd made a mistake, and then he and Cooper had made it as right as they could.

It was a mistake to kiss Jackson like I'd wanted to do last night. It'd complicate things at work. If the team knew, it'd screw up the whole dynamic. Maybe the project, too. Not to mention my brand-new business. Cooper would flip a table if we actually did what he thought we had. There would go my testimonial. What if people in the tech community found out the CEO of Weber Technology Consulting threw in a little extra into her gigs? My cheeks heated, and it wasn't because of the warm, afternoon sunshine.

"Sure. He probably talked to Noah, too. Found some way to connect to him." Tiannah pursed her lips.

Cars. How had he known Noah was into cars? I nodded. "They hit it off. I wouldn't let him offer to take Noah to the Circuit of the Americas, though."

"Oh, girl." She shook her head. "He's got you figured out. The way to your coochie leads right through Noah."

"Ew, Tee. That's so gross."

"Doesn't make it less true."

Dammit, she was right. At least I hadn't caved and let him strike up a bromance with Noah. Jackson was leaving. His life in Austin was temporary. It'd be bad enough if I let him into my own heart. The worst thing would be if he and Noah got close and then Jackson left town. I checked the field and found Noah's knobby little sock-covered knees. He was dribbling the ball past Orlando, who was defending the goal.

My phone buzzed. As much as my eyeballs itched to see Jackson's latest message, I ignored it.

Tiannah shot it a stank-eye. "Not to mention the harm you'd do to other women in that office. Something happens between you and it gets out, and there's an excuse for management not to hire women as consultants or as employees. And then there's the women already working there who think you have to let a guy into your pants to get ahead."

"Oh my God." I buried my face in my hands. "I'm the worst." I knew, only too well, what even a hint of favoritism could do. All creepy Dr. Fletcher had to do was linger at my desk, touch my hand too familiarly, and praise my work too many times for the rest of the class to whisper about me, to exclude me from their study groups. To mark me as someone who'd given it up for a better grade.

"No, honey, you're not the worst." Tiannah laid her hand on my shoulder. "You're a strong woman, great at your work and a mama-bear guardian to Noah. Never forget that you're under the micro-scope—to Noah, to your clients, and to everyone else at that company. I wish it wasn't like that, but it is."

She knew what she was talking about. As one of the few Black women programmers in the area, Tiannah faced even more chal-lenges. She'd worked through two pregnancies and come back to the office after both, at least in part, she'd told me, because she'd wanted to prove to everyone—including herself—that Black women could be rock star programmers and mothers at the same time. By the third pregnancy, she was exhausted. Not even proving herself was worth it once she had three little ones at home.

"I know. I'll be strong like you."

"No, honey. You don't need to be anyone else. Be you. You are strong. I know you'll do what's right."

I smiled at my best friend and clasped her hand.

The whistle blew, and we turned our attention back to the field. Noah was playing forward on the far side of the field. He stared intently at the ball.

Focus. I needed to keep my focus on the ball, like Noah did. And the ball was not some undertaxed multimillionaire who played with expensive sports cars for fun. It was my job, my company, and my future. My family's future.

20

ALICIA

FRIDAY, with Cooper's in-person demo looming on the other side of the weekend, I went straight to my workstation after the stand-up meeting. Between leaving early on Monday and juggling Noah's mandatory three-day out-of-school suspension for fighting, I'd fallen behind. I'd allow myself no refills on tea, no trips to the restroom. I wasn't moving from my chair until after I'd checked in my code. During the meeting, I'd made the same rule for everyone else who wasn't done. Minus the no-restroom-break rule. I was a tough manager, but I wasn't a monster. Our demo was going to be flawless. Cooper would have no reason to take us out behind the woodshed this time.

Jackson planted his palm on the desk beside me and leaned over to peer at my screen. The short sleeve of his Queen T-shirt strained around his biceps, and I followed the vein that twisted around his forearm to his wrist. What would that strong arm feel like wrapped around me? I shivered.

"Still working on your code?" he asked. Jackson had already moved all of his assignments to the *Done* column.

"I am."

"Let me help. We can get it done faster if we work together. We'll try pair programming again."

Tyler and Amit had their heads together, scanning through their code. It had worked great for them. And Jackson was fast. With me checking his code as he flew through it, we'd be done by the end of the day.

"Okay. I'll try it. In five minutes." I brisk-walked downstairs and located the IT cave. When I returned to our desk, I handed Jackson a box containing a brand-new keyboard that proclaimed it was whisper-quiet. "I'll even let you drive."

Grinning, he plugged in the keyboard, and I rolled my chair closer to him. He opened up the program, and we started to work. He still managed to click the less-than-whisper-quiet keys, but it didn't pound into my brain the way it had that first day. Or maybe it was his leather-and-piney-woods smell that enveloped me and made me forget everything that used to irritate me.

"Alicia?"

"Hmm?" I yanked my attention to Jackson's face, turned toward me over his shoulder.

"I asked if you were okay with what I did there. It's a little unusual, but I think it'll get us the results we need more efficiently."

"Oh, ah"—I scanned the code and saw the part he'd asked about—"it looks good to me. Maybe add a comment in case someone questions it later."

He turned back toward the screen, and I inched my chair away. Friends. That was all either of us could commit to. My traitorous lady bits needed to get on board with that.

A few hours later, Jackson's stomach growled.

I checked the clock on the wall. It was almost one. "Why don't you take a lunch break? I'll keep working." I'd brought my lunch from home, knowing I couldn't waste a minute today.

"No lunch." He flexed his fingers over the keyboard. "Your rule." His stomach gurgled again.

"Fine. Want half my sandwich?" I pulled the insulated bag out of the drawer. "It's Esmy's homemade pimento cheese."

"Pimento cheese?"

"If I tell you what's in it, you'll think it's disgusting. But it's spicy and delicious. Want to try?" I set half the sandwich on a napkin and handed the rest to him, still encased in plastic wrap.

"Okay."

When he took the sandwich from me, it was just low blood sugar that made my skin tingle. I bit into my sandwich, and he did the same. We'd both feel better in a minute.

He swallowed. "That's really good. Sure you won't tell me what's in it?"

"Not a chance. Hey, watch that extra white space."

At four o'clock, music started downstairs. One Friday a month, Synergy had its own happy hour for employees with beer, snacks, and music. As our team wrapped up their coding and got the green light from the automated testing system, they meandered down, leaving only Jackson and me finishing up our code. After another half hour of work, he tapped the button to send the code to the testing process.

Jackson leaned back in his chair and rubbed his shoulder where it met his neck. He glanced at the board and the dwindling backlog of work. "Another two sprints after this. I think we might even have time for some refactoring."

I chuckled. "Let's not get crazy. Four weeks isn't a lot of time. Anything could happen."

"Come on. You know you want to make this code sing."

I rolled my wrists. "Okay, yes, I do. I want it to run so fast it makes Cooper's head spin."

"If we finish up the new features in the next sprint, we can spend the last one supercharging it."

What would it be like to impress Cooper Fallon, tech superstar, with our demo? Pretty damned good. "Okay. If we finish all the features early, we'll do it."

He grinned at the progress bar on the screen.

The testing routine finished with a clear report. Jackson checked the code into the repository, and I used my own computer to check that everyone else's code was where it belonged.

He stood. "Come on."

"What?" But I stood, too, stretching out my back.

"We need to move." He walked along the open hallway and turned left toward the sliding glass door that led out to Synergy's small second-story deck that overlooked the river. With everyone else at the happy hour downstairs, the deck was empty, as were the desks inside that faced it. He strode to the railing and leaned his elbows against it, staring out at the trees and the sparkling water beyond.

I took off my jacket, laid it over the railing, and mirrored his stance.

"So what are you doing after?"

I tilted my head toward him. "You mean tonight? Going home. Movie night with Noah."

The corner of his mouth quirked up, and I wanted to trace it with my finger. "No, I meant after this project. Have you lined up your next gig?"

"Oh. Yeah, a local hospital needs some help with their records system. A former coworker recommended me. Should take me to the end of the year." It wouldn't have the cachet of the Synergy project, but it'd be a paycheck. I could leverage Cooper's recommendation for the gig after that and start moving up the ladder of big-name companies. Maybe I could even swing an assignment out of town next summer. I could finally travel the way I'd always wanted.

"Nice." He leaned over the railing and scanned the green space below.

"What are you doing after the project?" I asked.

"We'll have some loose ends to tie up. Let the test team have a whack at it. Then, I don't know. It all depends on Cooper."

"You really think he wouldn't let you go back to headquarters if you wanted?"

"Depends." He shrugged. "If he's still mad at me, no."

"Why do you let him treat you like that?" I thought back on my first day at Synergy, when Cooper hadn't told Jackson I was coming to work on his project. "You're partners. Equals."

He stilled. "He's better at the business stuff than me. Besides, he always has to fix it when I fuck up."

"You don't—" But then I remembered the intern. He'd said Cooper had fixed the situation for him. Still, it didn't seem all that bad. She'd finished out her internship and gotten a recommendation. "I'm sure Cooper's made some mistakes, too."

"Not like mine." He looked at me, his brown eyes full of something that made my heart go heavy. "The IPO. The night before we met with the bankers, Cooper and I went out. We got sloshed. Usually, he's the grumpy drunk, and I'm the happy one. But for some reason—the stress of it all, I don't know—I argued with a cop outside. Ended up in jail. Cooper'd already gone back to the hotel and passed out, and he didn't get my message until the next day. He sprung me, but I showed up to our meeting in last night's clothes, smelling like jail." He wrinkled his nose at the memory. "The bankers said we had to bring on someone else as CEO. Someone they picked." His face pinched when he said, "Weston."

I searched his face. Would he have made a good CEO? We'd had a rough start on the project, but in the last few weeks, he'd shown true leadership. He had potential. Too bad he'd put so much effort into trying to prove he didn't care about a company he clearly loved. I put a hand on his arm. "You haven't fucked up anything here. You've been great with the guys. A leader. You could be so much more." I wanted to say *if you'd stop letting Cooper keep you down*, but he might not be happy if I told him what I truly thought of his best friend. I'd have clawed the eyes out of anyone who tried to say a word against Tiannah.

"You've made me a better programmer. A better leader." He faced me, his brown eyes earnest, demanding. "We work well together. Admit it."

"We do."

He tilted his head. "I thought you'd disagree with me."

"No. I don't lie. I tried it when Melissa—my sister—was sick. I tried to tell her she'd be fine, she'd recover, and we'd go back to doing everything we used to do. It was what I hoped, anyway." I stared out at the river, flowing sluggishly toward the Gulf. "She told me I was full of shit, and she didn't have enough time left to waste it listening to me."

"Ouch."

"Yeah. Melissa didn't have a lot of patience for lies—either those we tell others or those we tell ourselves. It's why I got Noah. She never forgave our mother for staying with our dad so long. Waiting for him to leave us." I swallowed with difficulty. Where had all that come from? I never talked about Melissa. Certainly not to work colleagues.

"I think she'd be proud of you now. For breaking out. For starting your own business. Don't you?" He put a hand over mine, still resting on his arm.

"It's part of the reason I did it. For her. And for Noah. To show him we Webers can do anything we set our minds to."

He squeezed my hand. "Alicia, I—"

"Hey!" The shout came from below us, and I snatched back my hand. Tyler stood on the grass, a red cup in his hand. "Party's down here, you two!"

I set a hand over my racing heart. Had he seen me touching Jackson in a not-so-coworkerlike way?

"We're on our way," Jackson shouted down. "Just needed the fresh air."

Tyler held up his cup in a toast and then trudged around the corner of the building toward the music.

"I should head home." I picked up my jacket and shook it out, willing my cheeks to cool.

"One beer. You can have one beer with me. With the team."

A beer sounded good on a Friday after writing all that code. After the soul-baring we'd done. "One beer with the team." I shot him a teasing smile. "You can be there, too."

"You've made me the happiest nerd in Austin." He crooked his elbow at me. "Shall we?"

No matter how much I wanted to take his arm, I couldn't. Neither one of us could afford the mistake of being perceived as anything more than friendly colleagues.

"Come on." I sidestepped him and slid open the glass door. "Let's go join the rest of the nerds."

21

JACKSON

I LIFTED my legs onto the seat next to me at the high-top table and crossed my ankles, putting my boots practically in Cooper's lap.

He looked at them like they were a pair of shit-encrusted work boots but then lifted his glass of expensive bourbon. "To turning around the project. I'm impressed, Jay."

I turned my glass in a circle, watching the golden extra añejo tequila slosh against the sides. "It's all Alicia. She's amazing."

He raised his thick eyebrows. "When I met with her this afternoon, she said it was all you."

"I guess we work well together. And we're both modest."

He snorted. "You've never been the modest type. The first time you got an A on a paper in our freshman lit class, you 'accidentally' showed it to the whole class." Bastard had the balls to do air quotes. I'd tripped over the untied lace of my Converse, and the paper had fallen out of my hand. I just took the opportunity to let it fall grade-up.

"That was a team effort, too. I'd never have passed that class without you. Fuck, I'd never have graduated."

"There's nothing wrong with needing a little help. I wish you..." He shook his head and sipped his whiskey.

I narrowed my eyes at him. "You wish I what?"

"I wish you didn't always try to go it alone, be a cowboy." He nodded at my boots.

I lifted my legs off the chair and hooked my boot heels around the crossbar of my stool. When I worked alone, I didn't expose my shit to anyone else. Or take them down with me. But Alicia hadn't laughed at me, not once. Not even when I skipped around in the code or the day last week I couldn't seem to focus on anything and she'd caught me staring into space five separate times. She'd gently reminded me what we were working on and picked it back up. In fact, the whole team seemed to be coding faster and better. We'd done more together in the last two weeks than separately in the previous four.

There were only two other people I trusted not to mock me. One was my sister, Sam. "You and I always worked well together."

"True." His blue eyes burned into me, a little pink at the edges from the bourbon. "We make a great team. That's why we called the company Synergy. Remember?"

Yeah, I remembered. Vaguely. We'd been drinking cheaper booze then, the night before we pitched the venture capitalists. A flash of memory: Cooper slurring out "Ssssynergy. Thassit." I might've kissed him after that. Or maybe it was only that one time in college. We'd been younger then, and the hangovers hadn't been as painful.

"To you and Alicia Weber," he said. "A partnership that's going to save the company."

This time, I raised my glass, too, and drained it. I'd floundered for so long before Alicia joined us. No matter what she or Cooper said, she was the difference. She'd turned the project around, not me. But for once, I didn't resent needing help. I signaled the server for another round.

"I think, after you finish this project, you ought to come back to headquarters. We've got a couple of initiatives that could use your expertise. Maybe you could work on both in an advisory capacity. Start acting like a vice president of development instead of a senior programmer."

I blinked at him. "Seriously?"

"You can finish up this project remotely. You'll be home in time for Thanksgiving dinner with your family."

The waitress set our drinks on the table, and I drank half of mine down in one gulp. The glass still in my hand, I pointed at Cooper. "You're coming to Thanksgiving, too."

The tops of his cheeks turned pink. "Sure. I'd love it."

Of course he would. My mother adored him. Unlike her own son, he was perfect.

I shoved the thought aside. I was being sprung from exile. I was going home. Back to Synergy headquarters and my office on the top floor where no one bossed me around. Okay, except for my assistant, Marlee.

But there'd be no Alicia to subtly shake her head when I pulled too many sticky notes from the backlog. To comb through my code with those sharp blue eyes. To encourage me to be my best. To believe in me.

No wonder I wasn't excited.

———

THE HOUSE WAS dark when I pulled up outside. Shit. I checked my watch. After eleven. I turned off the truck and sat in the silent blackness for a minute.

Maybe she wasn't asleep yet. I typed out, *You up?*

After a minute, she texted back, *No.*

Fine. I hovered a finger over the ignition button. But my phone buzzed with another text.

Alicia: Need to talk?

Can you meet me on your porch?

The curtain twitched at an upstairs window, and a few seconds later, the porchlight flicked on. I scrambled out of the truck and sprinted up the walk and the front steps.

Alicia stood behind the screen door, her arms crossed over a tank top. She wore a pair of sleep shorts even shorter than the cutoff sweatpants she'd worn the last time. "What are you doing here?"

"I needed to talk. And we're friends, right? Friends talk."

She hesitated for a moment before she pushed open the screen door and stepped outside. She headed toward the swing on one side of the porch, and I followed. It creaked when I sat on the other side of the bench.

Alicia tucked her knees up under her chin and circled them with her arms.

"You cold?"

"No, I—"

Her arms were covered in goosebumps. I lifted my sweater over my head and handed it to her. She stared at it for a second and then, reluctantly, took it and slipped it over her head. She tucked her nose inside the neck.

"Sorry, it probably smells like the bar."

"No. It's perfect. Thank you. What did you need to talk about?"

I tugged down my T-shirt that had ridden up when I took off my sweater. "Cooper says I can go home at the end of the project."

I couldn't see her mouth, hidden by the sweater. Her voice was muffled when she said, "That's good news."

"Is it? It's what I've wanted for a long time. But when he said it, I felt… I don't know what I felt."

"Vindicated? Relieved?"

"Disappointed."

She tugged down the neck of the sweater so I could see her face again. "Why disappointed?"

"I think I'll miss it here. I'll miss the team. I'll miss you."

Her lips lifted in a smile, but her eyes seemed sad. "The team will still be here. Maybe you could collaborate with them remotely. Or ask some of them to transfer to headquarters."

"But—but not you." She'd be off to her next consulting job at the hospital.

"I was always going to leave you. This is just a gig for me."

A sharp sting, like a papercut, zigged across my chest. "Would you ever consider making this gig…permanent?" What would it be like to work alongside her every day? To have her encouragement even when no one else believed I could do it? Heaven.

"Been there, done that, have the emotional scars to prove it." Her eyes glittered in the porchlight.

"But Synergy's not like that. We value our female employees. Hell, our trans and nonbinary ones, too. We have employee resource groups—"

She reached across and laid a hand on my arm. A thrill rose all the way into my chest, making my heart beat faster.

"I'm sure working at Synergy is great. But having my own company gives me independence. Flexibility. The power to say no."

My chest tightened. "The power to walk away."

"No, that's not—" She bit her lip. "I guess that's part of it."

"Why is that important, Alicia?" It was unfair of me, especially after she'd told me she didn't lie. But I couldn't keep the question inside. Someone had hurt her, and I wanted to know who.

She paused a long time before speaking, so long I wasn't sure she'd tell me.

"My dad left when we got Melissa's diagnosis. I don't know if it was because he couldn't deal with the stress or if he already had one foot out the door, and that was the last straw. Except for the divorce papers, we haven't heard from him since. Then I saw what happened with Noah's dad. Melissa said he was already gone when she found out she was pregnant. And then, the cancer came back, more serious than ever, and she—she left, too." She tucked her hands into the too-long sleeves of my sweater. "I guess after that, I wanted to be the one who did the leaving. The ending. Tiannah—she's my best friend—says I come up with ridiculous reasons to end relationships."

"Really?" I couldn't imagine it. Solid, steady Alicia telling someone to hit the road because he chewed with his mouth open? "Give me an example."

She smiled, and I was glad I'd lightened the mood. "Okay, here's the worst one: the last guy I dated was perfect. Gets along great with Noah, even has a kid his age. Nice ass."

"But?" I drew it out.

She smirked at my weak pun. "But, when we finally slept together, it was...not good."

Heat rose up from my core, and I balled my hands into fists. "He didn't hurt you, did he?"

"No, no. It was just...meh." She shrugged. "I couldn't imagine wanting to do it with him for the rest of my life."

My hands relaxed. "I'm no sex therapist, but maybe you should've talked to him about it?"

"Maybe I should have. But it was easier to end it. Less painful than if I'd let myself get too involved, and then he left me. I know that sounds terrible. But"—she shrugged again—"prove me wrong."

"Is that an invitation?" What was I saying? I was Mr. One-Night-Stand. Alicia ended things before they went too far; I never let them get started.

"You know we can't. It'd be a professional disaster. For both of us."

"It's only a gig for you, remember. We'd be free to date once the project is over."

"You just told me you were going back to San Francisco."

"I said Cooper said I could. I could stay. If I had a reason." My chest felt lighter as soon as the words left my mouth. I could stay. Here. With Alicia. I could sit on this swing with her. Hold her hand. Kiss her the way I'd wanted to the other night.

"I'd be a reason to stay." Her tone was flat, unbelieving. Hell, I hardly believed what I was saying.

I reached over and took her hand, nudging back the sleeve of my sweater until our palms touched. "You're the only reason I'd need."

Her blue eyes, so much warmer than Cooper's, softened. "Let's talk about it when the project ends. If we still want to try it then. See how it goes for a couple of weeks."

A test run, like we did at the racetrack. To ensure the car was fit to race. Only in this case, I was the car. "Okay."

I lifted her hand and kissed her knuckle. Then I stood. "G'night, Alicia."

"Night, Jackson. Wait, your sweater."

I was already down the porch steps and walking back to my truck. "Keep it." As proof I wasn't going anywhere.

22

JACKSON

I PROPPED my phone on the kitchen counter, leaning against the giant plastic jack-o'-lantern, and let the bags of decorating shit fall to the floor.

"You really can't make it out a day early?" I added a hopeful twinge to my voice, like I wanted him to come.

I didn't.

"No, I've got a benefit tonight." On the screen, Cooper weaved back and forth, sweat dripping off the darkened ends of his hair as he pedaled his exercise bike. "You always have your party *on* Halloween, not the day before."

I almost felt bad. *Almost.* Cooper and I hadn't missed a Halloween together since freshman year of college. From the keggers we'd hosted in our dorm room to more over-the-top warehouse blowouts to that one memorable weekend in Amsterdam—well, at least the part I hadn't blacked out—Halloween was my thing. No Jones family obligations, only the anonymity and lack of accountability that came with costumes and a lot of booze. Yeah, I'll admit it: those ragers fed right into the playboy image I'd tried hard to cultivate. The parties, the racing, the women, all of it layered into a hard shell I'd built around the insecure kid who couldn't focus, the company founder who regularly disappointed people.

Not even Cooper saw through it.

"The last time Halloween fell on a weeknight, I had to send Marlee after you the next morning. Remember?" he asked fondly. "Where'd she track you down?"

"On a chaise next to Weston's pool." For some reason, I'd thought it was a good idea to show up at the CEO's place early on November first, but I'd passed out on his deck before I'd accomplished whatever prank I'd gone over there to play.

"Marlee's a lifesaver."

Didn't I know it. One of the many reasons I'd refused to furlough her. I lifted a package of spider garland out of one of the bags. I'd hang it over the door to the patio so people could brush through it on their way to get a beer.

"Some of the people I'm inviting have kids. They wouldn't come to an adults-only party on Halloween. So I did it a day early." I'd almost danced, right there in the office, when Alicia said she'd come.

Cooper's pedaling slowed. "That's actually kind of considerate of you."

I shrugged. "I guess I'm growing or something." I pulled out a package of eyeball ice molds. "I love these!"

"Growing," Cooper grumbled. He sped up. "Maybe I can come out early tomorrow. We could go for a ride. Or a hike."

If all went well tonight, I'd hoped Alicia might invite me over to her place for Halloween. Together, she and I could walk Noah around the neighborhood trick-or-treating. I hadn't done that since my sisters were little. I'd imagined acting like friends. Not colleagues.

Now that I'd decided to stay in Austin, I had weeks, if not longer, to spend with Alicia. Maybe she'd let me come to one of Noah's soccer games.

"Sure. Let's do it." I'd spend the next day with my best friend, who'd be in town for only a night or two.

Cooper slowed again and beamed at me. "I'll be there by noon. And, Jay, I'm proud of you."

I smiled back, not quite as broadly. "Can't wait."

———

ALICIA

I'D GOTTEN a twinge in my belly when I saw Jackson's address in the emailed invitation. There were a lot of apartment complexes on that street. It couldn't be the same one. I couldn't be that unlucky.

But I was. The twinge turned into a full-on sinking feeling as I parked in front of Jackson's building. I glanced toward the other side of the complex, past the swimming pool, sport court, and clubhouse. I couldn't even see the building that housed the apartment where I'd slept with Rick that one time. I deliberately slowed my breathing. This was a risk I could avoid. If I stayed inside Jackson's apartment, especially if I left early, the chances I'd see Rick were minuscule.

I got out of my Honda, smoothed down my costume, and fluffed my hair. Taking a deep breath, I scanned the building until I located his apartment number—though the AC/DC blaring from his door gave it away—and walked in.

The apartment was dark except for colored lights pointed at the ceiling, the uplights giving everyone a spooky glow. Garland was strung everywhere: splayed across the walls, dangling from the peninsula that separated the kitchen from the living room, fluttering across the open slider to the patio. There didn't seem to be a theme to it, other than things you could find at a pop-up Halloween shop: there were skeletons, spiders, bats, even a few *very* creepy clowns. Plastic jack-o'-lanterns sat on every flat surface, battery-powered candles flickering inside.

Jackson bounded up to me, wearing jeans and an untucked pink polo with the collar popped to show off a gold chain around his neck. A backwards baseball cap covered his dark hair, and sunglasses glinted across the top. And, of course, he wore his now ever-present boots. His expression was the same as Noah's had been last year as we'd stepped off the porch on Halloween night, about to go trick-or-treating: boyish delight. Jackson reached out as if to give me a hug, but at my warning expression, his hands dropped to his sides. Sure, friends hugged. But coworkers didn't, and I'd already spotted Kevin in the corner, an orange plastic cup in his hand.

"I'm glad you're here." He looked me up and down. "Eleven from *Stranger Things*, right?"

"Yeah." I'd found the geometric-print shirt at a vintage shop and paired it with high-waisted jeans and suspenders. "Are you...also eighties-themed?"

His face fell a little. "I'm a *bro*grammer. Get it?" He made jazz hands.

"Oh. Totally." I scrunched my nose to keep from giggling. It *was* a little clever.

"Can I get you a drink?"

"Um, okay. A beer?"

He led me outside, through the dangling spiders, to a cooler. He named off the beers, I chose a local IPA, and he dug it out of the ice for me and popped the top.

He pulled a bottle of water from the other cooler and leaned against the post that supported the balcony above. He tilted his head, watching me.

"What?" I checked my costume. All the buttons were still fastened, everything in order.

"I've seen you in the office. And at your house. But this is the first time I'm seeing you here, at my place." One corner of his mouth kicked up.

He hadn't mentioned Linda's Taquería. "And?"

The other corner rose. "I like it. We could try going other places together."

"Jackson, I—"

"Hear me out. We're friends. I could go to one of Noah's soccer games. See some of that Tuesday-Thursday magic."

"No, Jackson, I—I want to keep Noah out of it. I understand you're going back to San Francisco"—I held up a hand—"eventually. But he won't."

His smile drooped. "Okay, then, you'll have to show me some of Austin's landmarks. Like the Capitol. And the Alamo."

I almost spat out my beer. "The Alamo is in San Antonio."

He scrunched his nose. "It is?"

"A ninety-minute drive in light traffic. And you'll be disappointed. People who aren't Texans or history buffs always are."

"I like driving. And if I were with you, I couldn't be disappointed."

He was a good six feet away, much farther than when we worked elbow-to-elbow in the office. Still, a warmth started in my belly and dipped lower, tingling at the juncture of my thighs in my high-waisted jeans. I clenched my center. *None of that.*

"I shouldn't keep you from your guests."

He shot me a glance like he could see right through me. "Let's go inside. I'll introduce you to some people."

"Who's here, anyway?" Besides Kevin, I recognized a few other faces from Synergy. No Cooper Fallon yet, thank the Halloween spirits. But there were many people I didn't recognize. How did Jackson have so many friends in Austin?

"People from work. People I've met around here. Come on."

He introduced me to his upstairs neighbors, the guy who managed the condo complex, and a couple of folks who worked at the Formula One track south of town. We were still talking to his neighbors, who hadn't realized they lived above a world-famous programmer until I told them, when a heavy arm landed on my shoulders.

"Hey, guys." Tyler's breath in my ear was liquor-scented. "Wha's up?"

"Hey, man." Jackson, who was now also holding Tyler upright, patted his shoulder. "Having fun?"

"Oh, yeah. I was playing Fuzzy Duck with your neighbors over there." He waved at a group of young men, all dressed as Tom Cruise in *Risky Business*, with white button-downs, boxers, and shades. One lay half-on the sofa, another swayed where he stood, and two more sat on the floor, talking earnestly.

"You invited the college boys?" Jackson's neighbor June asked.

"No. I think they're naturally attuned to the frequency of party music. Couldn't keep them out if I wanted to."

"They're grrreat," Tyler said.

"Unlike you, they're able to walk home. Let's get you some water," Jackson said.

"I've got it." I ducked out from under Tyler's arm. He swayed but remained upright, leaning on Jackson. Out on the patio, I plunged my hand into the half-melted ice and drew out two bottles of water. I wished I could plunge my head into it to dispel the haze I felt around

Jackson Jones. Since I couldn't do that, I'd drink the water and then go home, where I'd be safe from the tingling I'd started to feel whenever he was near.

But when I stepped back through the spider garland into the apartment, I saw something that made me wish I'd chosen a beer or something stronger.

"Alicia!" Jackson had been standing between the couch and the sliding glass door. He took one of the waters and handed it to Tyler, who now slumped on the couch next to Tom Cruise number one. He grasped my icy hand and pulled me to his side. "Let me introduce you to my workout buddy.

"Rick, this is Alicia. We work together."

I stared into the last pair of eyes I'd wanted to see tonight. "We know each other," I said, my voice tight.

"We've been seeing each other on and off," Rick said at the same time.

I stared at him. "On and off? We ended it four months ago."

He shrugged. "I figured you didn't want to date during the season, and we'd pick up where we left off after."

Jackson's hand convulsed in mine. "Alicia's the woman you told me about in the gym?" His cheeks were pink, and he didn't look at me.

Shit, what had Rick told him?

"You didn't say you were seeing anyone." Rick's gaze arrowed to where our hands were still joined.

"We're not—" I began.

Jackson dropped my hand. "Alicia and I work together."

A chill settled in my chest.

"Rick. You and I are not getting back together." My voice crackled with frost. "Not when the season's over. Not ever."

His green eyes flared. "You were a bad lay, anyway, Ice Queen."

A fraction of a second later, Jackson was in his face. "Out."

"But I—"

"Out." Jackson used his larger body to herd Rick toward the door, ignoring the people they jostled along the way.

I stood where they'd left me, my feet stuck to the floor like I was exactly what he'd called me, an ice queen, a statue. I'd tried to be open with him. I'd let him into our lives. He'd met Mom and Esmy. We'd even taken the boys on a couple of our dates.

But had I really let him in? Had I held something back, not giving him a chance? Would I always be holding part of myself back, like Mom had with Dad?

Had it been me who sucked in bed, not him?

I wrenched the cap off the bottle of water and chugged it, the cold liquid burning my throat. By the time Jackson rejoined me, I'd emptied the bottle. I shoved it into his hand. "I'm going now. Thanks for inviting me." My voice was two-dimensional, like my heart.

"Don't go." He rested a hand on my arm below my shoulder, not pinning me there, but comforting me with a squeeze. "I'm sorry about Rick. I didn't know he was the one you told me about."

"Yeah. Well." I stared at his boots. "I shouldn't have come."

"Alicia." His big body shielded me from Tyler and the college guy lolling on the couch, as well as the rest of the party. His voice was low, urgent. "I'm glad you came. I want you here. Please don't let that asshole Rick ruin this for you. You're a strong woman, one of the strongest I've ever met. I'm honored you've allowed me to be your friend. Letting people get close to you is your choice. Not mine, and not his." He nodded at the door he'd muscled Rick through.

My throat closed up, and the words piled up behind it like water behind a dam. Even though we were surrounded by people, by loud hair-band music, by the ghoulish uplights, we two were all alone under Synergy's awning, his gentle fingers blotting away blood at my hairline. I reached down and tangled my fingers with his for a moment. I hoped he could see the gratitude shining out of my eyes.

"Ouch." He winced.

Gentling my grip, I lifted our joined hands. His knuckles were red, and one had an abrasion that was starting to well with blood.

I stared at him, my eyes bugging.

He shrugged. "Punches to the face are hard to execute well."

A groan from Tyler ripped through the moment. I let go of Jackson's hand and peered around him. "Tyler, are you okay?"

"Spinning," he mumbled.

Laying a hand on Jackson's chest, I said, "Maybe we should get him to your bathroom."

One corner of Jackson's mouth lifted in not quite a smile, and he shrugged one shoulder. "Guess I'd rather not have to clean up puke tonight."

He said something to the college guys, and they shambled to their feet, propping up the collapsed one, and shuffled toward the door. The apartment had started to empty, and the music seemed louder now that there weren't as many bodies to absorb it.

He crouched next to Tyler, draped one of his arms over his shoulder, and levered him up. I hurried to support Tyler's other arm, and we lurched down the hall. Jackson passed the open bathroom door and opened the door at the end of the hall.

I could tell it was his bedroom from the gray Converse and satchel piled on the floor. Jackson steered us toward an open door on the left, which led to a spacious bathroom that was almost as big as my bedroom at home. When we reached the toilet, I lifted Tyler's arm from my shoulders. "You've got him from here?"

Jackson nodded. "Wait for me in the bedroom?"

"Okay."

I had only a few seconds to check out his bed with its generic white duvet tossed across it and the pile of laundry that overflowed from the closet before Jackson joined me, closing the bathroom door. "He says he's good."

No sounds came from the bathroom.

"You won't let him drive home, will you?"

"No, he can sleep it off in the guest room."

"Good. Then I think it's best if I—"

"Stay. We'll...talk." Taking two steps, he closed the space between us. His lips twisted into a sinful smirk. I imagined the many, many things he could do to me with those lips. Not one of them involved talking.

"Maybe just for a few minutes."

He took my hand like we did this every day and led me out to the living room.

June, his upstairs neighbor, waved from the front door. "Everyone's going to the bar across the street for karaoke. You coming?"

"Maybe later," he said.

When she closed the door, leaving us alone in the apartment, he turned down the music. "Huh. My parties usually last longer than this."

Orange cups and bottles littered every flat surface. An item of clothing lay discarded on the kitchen floor next to a sticky-looking spill of red punch. A bag of chips in the corner of the carpet had exploded, and crumbs coated a four-square-foot area.

"Let me help you clean up."

"I'll take care of it in the morning. Tonight, I'd rather relax. With you."

"Relax?" I brushed crumbs from the sofa cushion before I sank down onto it. "I'm not sure I know that word."

He chuckled. "Here. Give me your hand."

"My…hand?" Was he going to kiss it again, like the hero in some old black-and-white film?

"I give a great hand massage. It eases stress and helps counteract all that time we spend typing." He held out his hand, palm up. "May I?"

"But—your hand." He'd put another one of those Lightning McQueen bandages across the split knuckle.

"Doesn't hurt anymore. Not when I'm with you."

I snorted at the line, then I touched my palm to his. What harm was there in a little hand massage? "Okay."

He turned over my hand and pressed his other thumb firmly into the center of my palm, making tiny circles. Slowly, he increased the pressure until my hand felt warm and loose.

I leaned against the sofa cushions. "You do this with all your coworkers?"

He looked up from my hand. "Nah. Just my sister, Sam. She's a coder, too. She gets sore wrists." He turned over my hand and made the circles on the back of it.

So that's where the patience had come from. Why he'd coached me instead of berating me for my subpar skills. I started to ask about his sister, but he spoke first.

"And my dad. When he was with us."

"He left?" We had more in common than I'd thought.

"No." He increased the pressure slightly as he moved down to my wrist. "He died."

Way to put your foot in it, Alicia. "I'm so sorry." I wished I'd searched him online the way I'd been tempted so often to do.

He shrugged. "It was a while ago. Summer after my freshman year in college. Heart attack. Anyway—"

"No, Jackson. I really am sorry. No matter how long ago, or how old you were, it hurt. I understand."

He looked up, and our gazes held. Melissa's death had been slow and painful, but at least we'd been able to say good-bye. Jackson might not have had that chance. "I know you do. Thank you."

He made long, slow strokes between the tendons and pressed the skin between each finger. "Before he started his company, before he became a CEO, Dad was a programmer, too."

"Like you."

"Like me. And his hands would hurt. He used to rub them. So I watched a couple videos and learned how to do it for him. And we'd...talk."

He was right about its being good for stress. I felt like he'd removed my spine, and I was a throw blanket spread over his sofa. "Talk. Like you and I are doing now."

"Yeah, between his startup and my three siblings, it was usually the only one-on-one time we had." He sandwiched my hand between both of his, letting his body warmth suffuse into it. "It's nice to give a massage again. And remember."

Shared experience. That's what that phantom string that connected him to me was. It had to be the reason I felt alive near him and empty when we were apart. I levered up from the couch cushions and surged past our joined hands to kiss his cheek. His beard wasn't prickly as I'd anticipated but soft and warm. He held very still with my lips against his cheek. "Thank you," I whispered.

I should've sunk back down into the cushions, but I didn't. I'd found the nexus of his intoxicating scent, and it held me there, curling around me like a third arm. I was so close to him, the stiff fabric of my shirt brushing up against his polo, that I could almost feel his racing pulse in my chest. It thrummed at his neck.

"Alicia, I can't—"

"I know." He'd said the same words that day we'd met. When he knew I worked at Synergy, and a relationship was off-limits. I knew all the reasons my lips shouldn't have been within inches of his, my hand pinned between his, my own pulse throbbing between my legs.

"No. I mean I can't stop." His lips touched mine.

It was soft, tentative, at first, giving me time and space to pull away. But that was the last thing I wanted. Lifting a hand to the back of his neck, I tugged him closer and felt a corresponding hand on my back, pulling me tighter against his heaving chest. My heart sped up, pounding between us.

Finally. I was kissing Jackson Jones. And it was heaven.

I licked the corner of his mouth, and he opened, letting me delve inside. He tasted like candy corn and sin. The shorter hairs around his mouth prickled my lips while my tongue slid lightly across his, like a dance. Meanwhile, my pulse had become a battering rhythm through my body, urging me to go faster, go deeper, to straddle him and soothe the ache inside my Mom-jeans.

When I pulled back to catch my breath, he dragged his lips across my cheek and down my neck, leaving a blazing trail of heat. I threw my head back, clearing the way for him to kiss down to the hollow between my collarbones. Tingles shot from everywhere he touched right down to my core. My cheap polyester-blend shirt was going to melt right off me.

"Alicia," he murmured between kisses, "I want more." He traced his hand up my ribs to my breast and covered it, rubbing soft circles over my nipple through my shirt.

God, I wanted to give him more. I wanted to tell him exactly what to do to make my body sing. With both hands, I guided his face back to mine and kissed him, setting a rhythm with my tongue against his. A promise of how we'd be together, the joining of our bodies, the perfect push-pull that'd build to an explosive climax. I tangled my fingers in the hair at his nape and trailed my other hand down the nubby fabric of his polo.

"Jay?"

We turned our heads at the same time, our chests heaving against each other, and our cheeks stuck together with a sheen of sweat.

Tyler leaned against the wall in the hallway, his eyelids drooping. "Mind if I crash on your couch?"

With a last, regretful glance at me, Jackson said, "Sure, buddy." He stood and crossed to Tyler, gripped him by the upper arm, and led him back down the hallway and into the second bedroom. I followed and paused in the doorway. Tyler flopped back on the bed and flung his arm across his eyes. "Night, Mom. Night, Dad."

Jackson ruffled his hair, and I entered the room to slip off his sneakers and set them on the floor next to the bed. I led the way back out into the hall, and Jackson closed the door behind us.

Jackson glanced at his bedroom door. He must've had the same thought I did, to continue where we'd left off. But we both knew it was a terrible idea. Tyler had caught us. Good thing he was too drunk to remember in the morning.

"Jackson, I—" God, I wanted to. My body hummed for him. Two weeks. We had only two weeks until the project was done. "I'm going to go now."

"Okay." With a whisper of whiskers, he kissed my cheek. "See you Monday."

"See you Monday," I said. "Thanks for—for everything. I had a good time."

He gave me that smirk again, the one that set me on fire. "Me too."

Before I melted right there into his carpet, I forced my feet down the hallway, out the front door into the night. The cool air prickled against my cheeks, an echo of the abrasion of his beard.

We'd agreed to be friends. I touched my skin, still warm from our kisses. But after we finished the project, was there a chance we could be more?

23

JACKSON

I GAZED up at the stairs to the second floor, my lower half already twinging from the short walk to the office. Why hadn't I said anything during our ride yesterday, asked Cooper to stop for five minutes to adjust my bike?

Because he was Cooper, and I was me, and that was how we worked. And now I was paying for it with shooting pain in my legs and...other areas.

But I didn't have to be brave today. I took a shuffling step toward the elevator.

"Jay! How was the ride?" Tyler bounded up beside me.

"Excellent. Thanks for the tip."

I'd had to boot him out of my apartment late Sunday morning because of my scheduled ride with Cooper. When I'd told him our plans, Tyler had recommended the bike rental place near the Barton Creek Greenbelt.

He tilted his head toward the stairs. "Going up?"

I glanced at the elevator and sighed. "Yeah."

My achingly slow pace didn't escape Tyler's notice, and by the time we made it to the kitchen, he had the whole story out of me.

While I went for coffee and ibuprofen, he went to the fridge. "Want an ice pack while I'm in here, old man?"

I shot him the finger.

He had the balls to laugh. "Just thought you'd want a faster recovery so you can perform at your best with—morning, Alicia." He stuck his head back in the refrigerator like he didn't already have a can of Mountain Dew in his hand.

"Morning, Tyler." She lowered her eyebrows at him. "Sorry, I didn't mean to interrupt y'all."

My pulse pounded in my ears, and not in a good way. Not like when I'd kissed her the other night. "You didn't interrupt anything," I said. I glared at Tyler, daring him to call me "old man" again.

Tyler closed the refrigerator and came to stand next to me at the coffee counter. I repressed a growl. He didn't drink the stuff. Why was he getting between Alicia and me?

"You've got something on your face," I grumbled.

Blushing, he rubbed his hand over his chin. "Did I get it?"

I squinted. "No."

Alicia sighed. "Tyler, he's ribbing you about your beard."

"*That's* a beard?" Kid looked like he had dryer lint stuck to his face.

He went even redder. "It's a work in progress."

Alicia mouthed, *Role model*, behind his back.

Fuck. "Um, looking good." I scratched my own beard.

"Thanks, man." Tyler crossed to the center island and lingered in the kitchen like an old-fashioned chaperone, getting himself a napkin and taking his time making his selection from the fruit bowl.

Alicia strode to the coffee station and stood next to me to prepare her morning tea. I inhaled the herbal scent of her hair swinging next to her ear.

"You're wearing your hair down today," I murmured. Had I told her I loved it down? Had she done it for me?

She grimaced and drew the curtain of it away from her neck, where a red rash bloomed. *Beard burn*, she mouthed silently.

"Oh, fuck," I said loud enough for Tyler to look up from the fruit bowl. "Sorry," I mumbled.

She flashed me a quick smile. "Worth it," she whispered.

My chest swelled. Our code review could've crashed and burned later that morning, and I'd still have been the happiest guy in Austin.

But we had an audience, so, to hide my grin, I looked down at the ibuprofen still in my hand, the orange coating starting to melt onto my skin. I popped the pills into my mouth and washed them down with coffee.

"You're not hungover, are you?" Alicia asked quietly, still dunking her tea bag.

"No, just a little twinge from a bike ride yesterday." I wiped my hand on my jeans.

"Are you all right? Do you need ice, or a heating pad?"

Yes, please. Make me lie down on a couch in a dark room, and kiss it better.

Tyler snorted and muttered something about "old bones."

"No, I'm good." To prove it, I hobbled across the kitchen and flicked the back of Tyler's head.

"Ow!" he yelped, feigning injury.

"Jay, what's going on?" Cooper stood tall and straight in the kitchen doorway.

Fucking perfect, leave it to Cooper to catch me acting like a twelve-year-old. "Nothing. Just bonding with my teammate." I gripped Tyler around the shoulders and rubbed my knuckles into his hair.

"Let's try to bond without physical contact." Cooper's smile was tight.

Tyler and I both froze. Slowly, I released him. He took a step away and combed his fingers through his hair.

"You okay, Tyler?" Cooper asked.

"'M fine," he mumbled.

"Good."

Tyler scurried out of the kitchen. Alicia started to follow him, but Cooper stopped her by saying, "Good morning, Alicia."

"Morning, Cooper. Did you have a nice flight?"

"I did, thanks."

Their small talk was making me sweat. Would Cooper see the beard burn on Alicia's neck and somehow know the beard in question had been mine? Would he pick up on the sexual tension zapping between the two of us? I needed air. And for the three of us never to be in the same room again.

When I calmed my breathing and tuned back into their conversation, Cooper was saying, "Jay and I went for a ride yesterday at Barton-something."

"Barton Creek. You biked at the greenbelt?"

"We did, though this guy overdid it a little." Cooper chuckled and gave me a fond smile. "Feeling better today?"

"Much." My face felt too tight.

Alicia looked between us. "Well, I'm going to check on the rest of the team, make sure we're ready for the demo."

"Before you go, Alicia—"

Fuck. Fuck fuck fuck. Somehow, he'd found out. Who could've seen us kissing and reported it to Cooper? Frantically, I cast my mind back on the party.

"—I thought we'd bring in lunch after the review. And I have a surprise for you."

"For me?" She put a hand on her chest. Maybe her heart was trying to beat its way out, too.

"For you. Better go on, or I'll be tempted to spoil it."

With a last, worried glance at me, she hurried out, clutching her tea.

"A surprise? I hope it's a good one." Like, not being outed for kissing me.

"She'll like it. You will, too."

"Give me a hint."

"Sorry, Jay. My lips are sealed."

Why'd he have to mention lips? Now I'd be staring at Alicia's mouth while she presented the demo.

He closed the distance between us and nudged me with his elbow while he poured a cup of black coffee. "Really, you're okay?"

No. "Absolutely."

———

ALICIA

I EXPECTED to see the standard selection of sandwiches and a giant bowl of salad arrayed on the credenza near the conference room's door. What I didn't expect to see was—

"Jamila!" I squealed and rushed to hug her.

"Hey, girl, how've you been?"

I ached to pour out all my troubles and confusion, but a couple of the guys were already in the room, and, besides, what would my mentor think of the mess I'd gotten myself into on my very first gig, one for which she'd recommended me?

"Good," I said, my voice too high.

She raised a delicately sculpted eyebrow. "Come sit with me." Grabbing my hand, she led me toward the back of the room, away from the food.

"Cooper tells me you've been a rock star." She crossed one long leg over the other, her champagne-colored skirt rising to her knee.

"The team's been great. We've really come together." My cheeks went hot when I recalled how Jackson and I had come together at his party.

Jamila's voice went low and urgent. "Alicia, you have to own your success. No one else will. Say, 'I'm a rock star.'"

"I'm a rock star," I parroted.

"She is a rock star." Jackson's hand landed half on the back of the chair and half between my shoulder blades. He smiled down at me.

Jamila stood and hugged Jackson. "It's been a while, Jay. Join us, and we'll catch up."

"I'll get some food first," he said. "Alicia, would you like this? I grabbed you one of those chicken Caesar wraps you like."

He'd made me a plate. My favorite sandwich alongside a pile of green salad with balsamic dressing, and he'd even left off the disgusting pasta salad. Parked on the side was a double-chocolate-chip cookie. My eyes prickled, and I blinked, fast.

"Thank you. This is perfect."

He shot me a grin and sauntered back to the food line.

Jamila raised her eyebrow again. "He fixed you a plate."

Like me, Jamila had grown up in Austin. She knew our ways. Jackson didn't, and it didn't mean anything. Though...maybe it did. Jackson tried so hard to hide it, but I'd seen him reveal how much he cared. Like that green smoothie he'd gotten Cooper the day after the kickoff. Food poisoning aside, he'd bought the guys dinner when they'd worked late. He'd talked to Noah about cars. And now he'd brought me lunch even though I was perfectly capable of getting it myself.

"He—"

She nodded. "You've trained your team well. I think you're doing just fine."

"Just fine?" Cooper had swept up silently on Jamila's other side. "She's doing great. Our code review this morning was impeccable." He set down his plate.

"Oh, you brought me a plate. How sweet," Jamila said. "Come back and join us when you've got your lunch."

A micro-frown crossed his face, but he turned and joined Jackson at the food table. Jamila stared at the plate he'd brought, piled high with salad and lacking a cookie. "Northern boys." She shook her head but picked up the fork and stabbed a bite of salad.

"You've known them a long time, haven't you?" I said.

"Forever. Since our freshman year at Stanford. We were in some of the same classes together. I met Jay first, and he introduced me to Cooper, who was his roommate. I guess I've stayed closer to Cooper over the years. He and I come from a similar background. We understand each other. Jay's a little…different. He doesn't let many people close. Only Cooper, really."

A warm glow settled inside me, right next to the chicken Caesar wrap. He'd told me about his ADHD. About his father. I'd become one of his select few friends.

The chair next to me pulled away from the table, and then Jackson sat in it. I didn't even have to look to know it was him. I could tell from his scent and from the way he took up space behind me. Shit, I was developing Jackson Jones radar.

Cooper sat on Jamila's other side. "Jamila, you haven't been trying to pull Synergy trade secrets out of Alicia, have you?" He chuckled at his own joke.

"No, Coop, just checking that you're taking proper care of my girl."

"What's the verdict?"

She smiled at Jackson. "I think you are."

My heart went straight from a nervous trot to a full-out canter. Did she know him so well she could tell something was going on between Jackson and me? That I'd kissed him the other night?

Jackson's knee pressed against mine under the table. "Breathe," he whispered.

I nodded. Drawing in a shaky breath, I held it for a second and let it out.

"So, Jay, did you throw one of your legendary Halloween ragers this year?" Jamila asked.

"Sure did. Though it was pretty low-key. Music, decorations, and beer."

Cooper said, "Jay told me he invited people from the office. Did you go, Alicia?"

"I—I did." Shit, had he heard something?

"So you can tell us whether it was legendary or low-key."

Some of my tension blew out with my breath. "I'm not much of a party person, so I'm not a good judge."

"I think Jay would consider a party low-key if everyone kept their clothes on," Jamila said with a smirk.

"Definitely low-key, then." My voice shook. I'd kept my clothes on —barely.

"That's too bad," Jamila said. "Though I'm sorry I missed it. I hope you'll be back in San Francisco next year so I can go."

"You won't have to wait too long for Jay to be back in the Bay Area," Cooper said. "He's coming back to headquarters when the project's buttoned up in a few weeks."

I shot a glance at Jackson. He'd told me he'd stay in town longer. So was he lying to me or to his best friend?

Jackson slashed a hand through the air. "Coop, let's—"

"In that case," Jamila said, "we need to make sure you get the full Austin experience. Ever played Chicken Shit Bingo?"

Jackson wrinkled his nose. "Can't say I've done that yet."

"What about you, Coop?"

He shook his head. "We're not talking actual—"

"Tonight. Alicia, you come, too."

"Tonight?" The evening routine of dinner and homework spun through my head.

Jamila read my mind. "Diane and Esmy can handle it," she murmured.

But it was Jackson's hopeful smile that convinced me. "Okay."

"Chicken shit." Cooper shook his head. "The things you two get me into."

24

JACKSON

"NINETEEN!" Cooper roared, throwing his arms into the air.

On the overhead TV screen, the chicken pecked at the number and then wandered to the corner of the cage.

"Fuck." His hands thumped to the top of his head.

I nudged Alicia. "I can't believe he's being competitive over where a chicken shits. Can you—"

She shushed me and muttered, "Come on, honey."

A thrill ran through me. She'd never used an endearment for me before. It was probably best if we didn't until the project was over. I turned and found her eyes fixed on the screen. "Do it on number five," she whispered.

I tried to catch Jamila's gaze across the high-top table, but her attention was on the screen, too. She gripped her wooden chit painted with the number twenty-two.

I scraped my chair back across the patio pavers. "Anyone want a refill?"

All three of them shushed me, so I took my empty and wandered toward the bar. But something caught my eye before I reached it. I went over to investigate.

Away from the bingo cage and the crowd were a few poultry cages, and the strangest creature I'd ever seen pecked at a bowl of seed inside one of the cages. Tawny like a lion, it looked like it had fur instead of feathers, but it had a sharp, blue-black beak. Its feet were hidden by puffs of fluff, and another pouf on the top of its head obscured its eyes.

I bent to examine it. "Is that a chicken or a tiny llama?"

A teenage girl with a voice as thick as molasses drawled, "That's Leo. He's a Silkie."

"So what is he?"

She laughed. "He's a rooster. A chicken."

I straightened. "Is he yours?"

She flipped a red pigtail behind the shoulder of her plaid western shirt. "Since he was an egg. I raise them."

"You raise them?" When I was her age, I wasn't responsible for as much as a fish. I still wasn't.

"Yeah, these guys aren't too hard. Friendly. Calm. Goes right in his cage when it's time to come out here."

"Does he—?" I tilted my head toward the bingo cage.

"Nah. The bar owner asks me to bring my birds to show the kids. You know, in case they get bored. Some of the parents can get kinda into it, y'know?"

"Oh, I know." The bar patrons roared. The chicken must've done her business. "Nice meeting you—?"

"Bonnie." She flashed me a shy grin.

"Jay. Good luck with the chickens." I headed toward the bar.

Four longnecks in hand, I returned to the table. Jamila took one and started whispering in Alicia's ear. I handed one to Cooper, who muttered, "A little young, even for you."

"What are you talking about?" I set a beer in front of Alicia and took a swig of mine.

"That girl over there can't be older than seventeen."

I glanced back at Bonnie, who'd hefted up a toddler to look into Leo's cage. "We were talking about chickens. That's Leo, and he's a Silkie. What the fuck, Coop?"

The women paused their conversation to look over at us, and Cooper held back whatever he was going to say.

Jamila laid a hand on his arm. "Hey, Alicia, maybe you and Jay should go check out the music inside."

"Good idea." Alicia brushed past me, and with one final scowl at Cooper, I followed her through the doors into the darkness of the bar. She led me to the edge of the small dance floor, where a few couples spun to the lively song playing over the speakers.

"Hey, you okay?" She gripped my forearm and spoke right into my ear, her breath tickling my cheek.

"Not really. He actually fucking accused me of flirting with that… that child."

She bit her lip. "You guys aren't what I expected. Is he always so…feisty?"

"Me and Coop?" Jamila said we were best friends with a bite. "I love him like a brother. And we fight like brothers. I trust him with my business; I'd trust him with my life, too."

"Still, you deserve to be treated with respect. You know that, right?"

I shrugged. I understood why he'd made the comment. I'd fucked up pretty big with Callie. He wasn't going to let me forget it anytime soon.

Her voice went fierce. "Jackson Jones, you are worthy. And don't let Cooper make you think anything else."

I glanced away from the dancers into her eyes, blue as the hot springs down by Santa Barbara. She believed in me the way no one else ever had, not even me. I wanted to kiss her, right there in that bar full of people, where Jamila or Cooper could walk in any minute.

But I didn't. Instead, I grabbed her hand. "Teach me to dance?"

"You want to learn to two-step?" She tilted her head.

"I want to touch you, and this is the only way I can do it with him here." I tipped my head toward the bingo patio.

Her cheeks pinked, but she held up our joined hands and put the other on my shoulder. She didn't have to instruct me to put my hand on her waist. I'd been watching the other couples.

"I go backward, you go forward. Slide your feet. Start with your left. One-and-two step. One-and-two step."

In a minute, we were shuffling across the floor, part of the circle of other dancers. The soles of my boots slid across the wood dance floor, and Alicia lifted on her toes so her heels didn't trip us up.

"Stop watching your feet. They're doing it right."

"But I don't want to step on—" I realized it was a mistake as soon as I looked up. Her eyes, blazing in the darkness of the bar, sucked me in until I couldn't see anything else. Even the twangy music faded. Alicia believed in me. She believed I could dance. That I could stand up to Cooper. That I could lead the team and even the company. That I was worthy of holding a treasure like her in my arms.

"Alicia, I—" I lowered my head until our lips were inches apart, until I could feel the heave of her chest against mine, could imagine what could happen if we were alone like we'd almost been at my apartment on Saturday night.

"Hey, y'all." Jamila's voice cut through the haze of my thoughts. "I think we should go. Cooper lost again, and he's cranky."

I ripped my head up and stepped away from Alicia. Her cheeks had gone red. She untangled her fingers from mine. "Yeah, time to go."

Jamila missed nothing. She took in Alicia's blush, my fingers that still reached for her. But she didn't say a word as we traipsed back through the bar, not even when we joined Cooper, silent and broody, in his rental.

On the drive back, close enough in the narrow back seat to smell Alicia's sweet orange and line-dried cotton, I wondered what would've happened if Jamila hadn't interrupted us. We were dancing a fine line between friendship and something I wanted more than anything, something I couldn't have.

Or could I? She'd been breathing as hard as I had, her burning gaze a reflection of my own. We were better together at coding. Could we pair up outside work, too? And not for one night but for an endless string of them? More than a couple weeks' trial. Forever?

Was that what I wanted?

My galloping heart answered for me: *it is it is it is.*

25

JACKSON

SO FAR THAT AFTERNOON, the Wednesday after our stellar code review and those magical moments on the honky tonk's dance floor, Alicia had accidentally kicked me under our desk—twice—knocked over her tea, and snapped at Tyler for asking an admittedly dumb question. I was almost relieved when she stood at ten minutes after three.

"I'm headed out." Her voice was steely, and her hands balled into fists.

"What's going on?" I asked her, too low for the other guys to hear.

"I told everyone this morning I had to leave early today." She slid her laptop into its bag.

"I remember. I mean, what's going on with you?"

She yanked out her drawer so hard her purse slammed into the back of it. "It's not your concern, Jackson."

"You're...nervous or something. I want to help."

"It's not something you can help with. It's not a piece of code or a party."

I smiled through the stabbing pain in my chest. "I can help with other things."

Her nostrils flared. "Not with this." She whirled, almost taking me out with her laptop bag, and stomped toward the stairs.

I grabbed my keys and wallet and jogged to catch up. "You're upset."

Not breaking stride, she said, "Not upset. Apprehensive, maybe."

"Why? Where are you going, Mordor?"

Her jaw was set, stony. Glancing behind us to ensure we were out of the team's earshot, she said, "Another conference for Noah. His teacher has a long list of…of concerns."

"Concerns?" From what I'd seen the one time I'd met him, Noah was a great kid. Except for the fighting, maybe. "Did he get into another scuffle?"

We'd reached the top of the stairs, and she slowed her pace to pick her way down in her heels. "No. It's things like failing tests and disrupting the class. Staring into space when he should be working. She asked me if he was on drugs. He's ten!" She had to slap her badge twice on the reader to get it to turn green.

I'd known a kid or two who'd smoked some weed behind our elite private school in fifth grade. Fine, I'd been one of those kids. And Mother had plenty of conferences with my teachers to talk about similar concerns. But I didn't think those facts would be helpful to Alicia right then.

I held the front door for her, and she strode out into the sunlight. After checking for traffic, she jogged out into the street. I followed. On the other side, she turned.

"What are you doing?"

"I'm going with you. I think you're too upset to drive."

"I am not!" She jabbed the elevator's down arrow by mistake before hitting the up arrow.

"I think you are." I stepped into the elevator with her, and we rode up to the third level. She strode to the world's most generic gray Honda Civic and fumbled with the key fob.

"Let me. Please?" I held out my hand for the keys.

"How are you going to get back?"

"I'll take a rideshare. I promise I won't inconvenience you."

She rolled her eyes. "You're not inconveniencing me. Other than making me late because of this argument."

I winked at her, something I was trying on in Texas along with the truck and the boots. "I promise you won't be late."

She shook her head but dropped the key in my palm. I slid the driver's seat all the way back and adjusted the mirrors while she settled into the passenger seat. Once she'd buckled her seat belt, I pulled out of the parking space and carefully exited the garage. I didn't turn on the making-up-for-wasted-time speed until we were on the main streets.

"So I take it this isn't the first time his teacher's called you in?"

"We had a regularly scheduled conference with his teaching team last month. She had some concerns then. And then, of course, the fight, but that was with the principal. I—I don't know what to do. I wish kids came with instruction manuals. Or a customer service line. You know? It's a lot."

"Your mom and Esmy don't support you?" They'd seemed great the other night.

"No, they do." She bit her lip and turned to look out the window. "But Melissa appointed me as guardian, and Mom's always been a little prickly about it. So I do most of the guardian stuff alone. And raising Melissa and me, Mom didn't really have to deal with issues like Noah's."

I chuckled. "I imagine not." Alicia would've been the perfect student, perfect daughter. Like my brother, Andrew, and my youngest sister, Natalie. Nothing at all like Sam or me. "From what I saw that night at your house, you're doing great with him. He seems happy and well-adjusted."

"He does, doesn't he? I can't figure out what's going on at school."

"Have you talked to his pediatrician about it?"

"His pediatrician? No. He's fine during his checkups. And, frankly, the folks at the urgent care place know him best. We've spent a lot of time there with all the soccer injuries and the playground bumps and bruises he used to get."

"He's accident-prone?"

"Aren't all boys?"

I glanced at her. "Not all boys."

"Oh." She bit her lip, and all I wanted to do was hug her, make her feel better.

"So you've never had him tested for a learning disability or a neurological issue?"

"No." She looked at me, a frown creasing her forehead. "Should I?"

"I told you I had a lot of trouble in school. In the bottom of the class, I figured out there were two types of kids down there with me: kids who didn't care about school because they had bigger problems, which doesn't seem to be the case with Noah, and kids who had undiagnosed learning disabilities or neurological differences. That was me before I was diagnosed with ADHD. Maybe you should talk to his doctor."

"But if I—if they discover he's different, they'll pull him out of class for special education."

"Yeah, I didn't love being singled out for help. But that help made the difference between failure and success for me. I never would've made it to Stanford without the study skills, without the organizational help I got from my resource teacher. Besides, once they've identified Noah as someone with a 'disability'"—I made air quotes since I preferred to think of it as a difference rather than a disorder—"he gets special accommodations at school. Extra time for standardized tests. Things that'll help him succeed."

"What if…what if they prescribe medicine for him? I've heard it changes kids' personalities. I don't want it to stunt his growth, either. He's already on the small side."

"Medication isn't right for everyone. You and Noah's doctor have to decide what's best for him. But I don't think I could've started Synergy without the focus it gave me."

"You still take it?" Her eyes widened. "Sorry, that's private medical information. Forget I asked."

"I don't mind. I don't take it every day. Only when I notice I'm more distracted or impulsive than usual." I grinned. "Okay, I probably should take it all the time. I'm pretty impulsive." I waved my hand at the interior of her car. I definitely hadn't checked in my code before I'd run out of the office.

She went silent, speaking only to direct me to Noah's school. The school grounds had that no-kids empty feeling, but the teachers' lot was still full.

She took a deep breath and put her hand on the door handle. "Thanks, Jackson. I appreciate the advice. And the ride."

"Can I—do you want me to go in with you?"

"In with me? No." She wrinkled her nose in that expression I found adorable.

"For moral support."

"No, I— Fine. If you want."

We got out, and I locked the car and handed her the key. She led me inside, where we signed in. The scents of disinfectant and books and kids' smelly sneakers took me right back to my own school days. I half-expected to see Baron Sinclair and his gang of bullies come around the corner, threatening to smash my nose in. But the silence, broken only by a pair of quiet adult voices down the hall, told me no kids were in the building.

We walked down the hall decorated with leftover construction-paper jack-o'-lanterns to a door marked *Mrs. O'Reilly, 5th Grade Language Arts.* Alicia knocked and opened the door.

"Ms. Weber. Come in." Mrs. O'Reilly could've been one of my old teachers. Her hair was a pinkish red, but the wrinkles around her downturned mouth gave away her age. She sat behind her desk and gestured at a pair of kid-size chairs in front of it. Alicia perched delicately on one. Mine squealed when I sat, and my knees rose almost to my chest.

Mrs. O'Reilly looked over her half-rims at me. "And you are?"

"A family friend," I lied.

"This is highly—"

"Mrs. O'Reilly, I know we have only twenty minutes," Alicia interrupted her, making the teacher frown. "I'd like to hear your concerns about Noah."

"Noah isn't doing well in my class. While his grades have improved"—she gave Alicia a pointed look over her glasses—"slightly, he's been disruptive. Speaking out of turn, tapping his pencil, talking to the other children. Not to mention the fight on the playground last month."

"I—I'm sorry," Alicia said, her face pale. "What do you think we can do to help him?"

"I've done everything I can think of," Mrs. O'Reilly said. She gestured at a desk at the back of the classroom with a cardboard divider surrounding it. "I've separated him from the other children.

I've disciplined him." She pointed at the edge of the whiteboard behind her with a list of children's names and either smiley faces or frowny faces. Noah's name had a lot of frowny faces next to it. "He's been sitting inside during recess all week to finish his classwork."

"Sitting inside at recess?" My blood pressure had risen as she'd listed each intervention. When she'd mentioned recess, I thought my head might explode. "That's the worst thing for him."

"Your name?" This time, she took off the glasses and speared me with a beady-eyed stare.

"Jackson Jones, ma'am."

"Mr. Jones, I don't know why you're here, but I'm speaking to Noah's guardian."

"It's okay," Alicia said. "Why is recess such a big deal, Jackson?"

"If he's got ADHD, he's got to expend his excess energy somehow. Sitting inside all day is only going to make it worse. Even if he doesn't have it, kids need exercise. They need to run around. Socialize. Take a break. No wonder he's acting out." I stood and paced behind the chair. This classroom and its reminders of my own elementary-school misery made me twitch.

Mrs. O'Reilly shifted so she faced Alicia. "I understand Noah's father doesn't live with you."

"No. We, ah. No."

"Children who grow up in single-parent homes are more likely to use drugs."

I spun on my boot sole. "Where did you get that statistic?"

She glared at me. "Everyone knows that."

Alicia cleared her throat. "He also lives with his grandmothers."

Mrs. O'Reilly's thin eyebrows disappeared into her forehead wrinkles. "Is he receiving discipline of any kind at home? Or is he playing video games all night?"

Alicia's face went from pale to red faster than was probably healthy. "Of course we discipline him. And he isn't allowed to watch videos or play games until he finishes his homework."

"Maybe stronger discipline and a more structured home life would help." Mrs. O'Reilly shot me a calculating glare. "I'm not sure Mr. Jones is the best person to provide it."

Alicia sucked in a breath. I laid a hand on her shoulder to stop her from saying something she'd regret.

"Does the school have a guidance counselor?" I asked.

"Yes, of course," the teacher said.

"Alicia, I think you should set an appointment with the counselor. Maybe the principal, too. Talk about ways the school can help him." As much as I wanted to, I didn't say that Mrs. O'Reilly was entirely the wrong teacher for a kid like Noah.

Alicia narrowed her eyes at Mrs. O'Reilly. "I think that's an excellent idea." She stood. "Thank you, Mrs. O'Reilly. I'll talk to Noah about some of these behaviors. I'll talk to his pediatrician and the counselor, too. We'll get him some help."

The teacher's smile was tight. "Excellent. We all want what's best for Noah."

"We do." Alicia rose. "Have a good night." She strode out, and I scurried to keep up.

When we escaped the stuffy confines of the school for the fresher scents outside, I jogged around in front of her, forcing her to stop. "Are you okay?"

Her eyes glittered with tears. "No."

Cautiously, like I'd do with a wild deer or a feral cat, I reached out and stroked her arm. "You did great in there."

"Until I stepped into that classroom today, I had no idea how awful it was. It wasn't like that at Open House. No wonder Noah hates school."

"Was his teacher last year like—like her?" I only barely kept myself from calling Mrs. O'Reilly a name I'd regret.

"No. I mean, yeah, we had some issues, but nothing like that. That was a great idea you had. To talk to his counselor. And the pediatrician. I'll call both of them tomorrow. Thank you for coming with me."

My chest filled up with warmth. This was one thing I hadn't fucked up.

"I wish I could promise that a diagnosis or medication will solve all his problems, but they didn't for me. I struggled. I still do. But you're doing the right thing. Taking steps. Helping him."

She stepped closer and put her arms around me, resting her cheek against my shoulder. "Thank you. I wish—"

"What do you wish?"

She hugged me tighter and then stepped away. "Nothing."

What did she wish for? I'd give her anything she wanted. Would she let me hire a tutor for Noah?

When Alicia started walking to her car, I remembered I needed a ride downtown. I pulled up the app and requested a car as I followed her.

"You're really good at that. Advocating for kids," she said. Her eyes were dry now.

"I am?" I couldn't contain my grin.

"Have you ever considered funding organizations that help kids with learning issues? Or founding one yourself?"

Me, found a charitable organization? I almost laughed, but then I saw the stubborn set of her jaw. "Uh, no."

"You've got considerable resources. Both mental and financial. You should use them for good."

I stumbled back. "What?"

"You're a very wealthy man, Jackson. You could never hope to spend everything you have. You could use it to help others."

"But I—" *I'm a fuckup*, I wanted to say. Unsociable. Unreliable. Barely housetrained. But if Alicia said I wasn't...

"Think about it." She leaned on her car. "You could do a lot of good."

No one had ever said anything like that to me before. No one, not even Cooper, had believed in me like that.

A black Nissan pulled into the lot. My ride.

"I'll think about it." I stared into her blue eyes, so kind. I didn't even want to kiss her. Okay, I did. But the gratitude I felt outweighed the low level of lust simmering in my veins. She believed in me.

Maybe I could believe in myself, too.

26

ALICIA

AT ALMOST FIVE ON FRIDAY, the Synergy ladies' room had that empty, end-of-the-day feeling. The primpers were gone, already settling in at happy hour. Those who had families had slipped out with the rest, eager to get back to their loved ones. I should've been among them.

I propped my foot on the arm of the sofa to tie my sneaker. How had I let him talk me into this?

I knew exactly how. I was falling for Jackson Jones. Between his coding-smarts, the kindness he tried to hide with his outrageous bluster, and the moral support he'd provided in the conference with Mrs. O'Reilly, he'd broken through every defense I'd put up, and now I couldn't help but hope he'd really stay in Austin like he said he would, and we'd take our friendship to the next level. The one that involved not only more helpful advice about Noah and more envisioned possibilities for Jackson beyond coding, but also more kissing. Because although Jackson Jones might be the greatest programmer I'd ever met, he was an even better kisser.

My cheeks flamed. I pulled a baseball cap out of my bag and tugged it over my hair, which I'd taken out of its bun and braided. The bill hid some of the blush. But it was getting late, and I couldn't wait for it to fully fade.

I pushed out the bathroom door and came up against a hard chest wearing a Pantera T-shirt. Jackson hadn't had to change clothes for this.

"Ready?" he asked, bouncing on his toes.

"Yeah. Let me stow this at my desk." I held up the tote.

He took it from me. "I don't want you to get distracted by your laptop. They might go early tonight." He pounded across the wood floor to our workspace and jogged back. "Let's go."

I couldn't repress my smile. "You're just as bad as Noah."

He started toward the stairs, and I fell into step beside him. "Have you taken him to see them?"

"Not specifically. We've been on the trail once or twice when it happened. Going to see them on purpose is kind of a tourist thing." I bit my lip. I hadn't meant it to come out so condescending.

"No one will believe I was in Austin if I say I never saw the bats. Are we going to make it in time? What about traffic?"

"We're walking. We're ten minutes from a prime viewing spot."

"Ten?" He glanced at his phone. "The sun sets in twenty-five minutes."

"Now you're starting to sound like me." In sneakers, our footsteps were silent in the empty lobby. "If only you'd be this concerned about project deadlines."

"I am concerned about project deadlines." He held the door for me, and I stepped out into the late-afternoon sunshine. "I'm concerned that they take our focus off what's really important, which is the quality of the code. My name is on the company website. Every line is my reputation."

I nudged him toward the crosswalk. "I guess I never thought of it that way. Still, without deadlines, we'd never release anything. We'd spend the rest of our careers perfecting it."

He grinned. "You get it!"

Shaking my head, I zipped up my jacket.

"You cold?" He wasn't wearing a jacket.

"It's a little nippy, don't you think?"

He gripped my hand and veered out into the street, weaving among the traffic-stopped cars. "This is the most comfortable I've felt since I stepped off the plane from San Francisco. It's perfect."

The lakeside trail was easy to find, and we followed it until it broke out from behind the trees to give us an unobstructed view of the water and the Congress Avenue bridge. It wasn't tourist season, and it was getting too cold for locals, but clumps of people were silhouetted on the bridge against the setting sun. We stepped off the trail toward the water until the ground started to soften under my sneakers.

"That's where they come out?" Jackson pointed at the bridge.

"Yeah, but they're less reliable this time of year. They've already started to migrate. Don't be too disappointed if they don't emerge at all, okay?" Though I'd hate it if my hometown disappointed him. *Don't let us down, bats.*

"Is that one?" He pointed overhead at a dark shape against the thin, pink clouds.

"That's a hawk. The bats are tiny. They brought some into my school once. They fit in a kid's palm."

"Ah." He stared out over the water toward the bridge.

I knew we had a few minutes, so I let my gaze wander across the trail. A pair of bikers whizzed by, then a woman pushing a jogging stroller. It was a popular spot for bikers and runners. In fact, I'd have been surprised if Jackson hadn't jogged down here himself. His apartment complex was close to an access point to the trail. Rick had told me he often ran here, and sometimes he biked to work along the trail.

As if the thought had conjured him, a familiar rangy form emerged from the trees. I gasped. "Rick!"

He did a double-take and stopped, panting. "Alicia." Then he tensed. "Jay." He had a greenish spot on his jaw, which he rubbed against his shoulder.

Jackson spun away from the water and stepped in front of me. "Rick." He seemed to expand until I couldn't even see my ex. I peered around Jackson's arm.

"Nice night for a jog." Rick used his forearm to wipe sweat from his brow.

"I guess so." Jackson's voice was hard like I'd never heard it. His ever-present sense of humor had fled.

"Hey, Alicia, how's—"

"Shouldn't you move along? Don't want those muscles to lock up. You might trip and fall." Jackson crossed his arms.

Rick ripped his gaze from me to Jackson. "Right. See you." He sprinted away.

I laid a palm on Jackson's rock-hard biceps. "What was that all about?"

He relaxed, but his eyebrows almost met in the middle. "Are you okay?"

"I'm fine." Rick hadn't stuck around long enough to say anything obnoxious. Now that I thought about it, I hadn't seen him in a while, not even at the end-of-season pizza party for Noah's team. I'd dreaded his making a surprise appearance. Had Jackson had something to do with it?

When I looked up to ask him about it, I saw a speck swoop across the sky. "They've started."

He whirled away from the trail and gazed across the water, sparkling in silver and rose-gold from the setting sun. The sun kissed the horizon, sending up its final citrus-colored salvo. Above us, the sky had gone a pale blue.

From beneath the bridge, millions of tiny creatures streamed into the sunset sky. They swooped into an S shape, then spread out, then looped back toward the bridge, spreading into a stippled cloud. One moment, they were a flock of birds, wheeling together, and the next, they diffused into the sky, searching out their insect meals.

As one group of them fluttered overhead, their clicks and cheeps drowned out the traffic on the streets nearby. Jackson held up his phone to capture it. I stood still, trying to discern patterns in their flight.

At last, they dispersed, though the occasional bat flapped overhead in search of its dinner.

"That was amazing." Jackson still stared into the sky. A star or planet winked bright in the darkening blue.

"It was, even for a jaded local like me."

He tore his gaze from the sky. "Thanks for bringing me on my tacky-tourist quest."

I smiled, though he probably couldn't see it in the dark. "That's what friends do."

He stepped closer. "Aren't we more than friends?"

"Not until the project's over." I crossed my arms.

Jackson rested his hands on my shoulders and slowly rubbed them up and down my biceps, warming my chilled arms. "Not long now."

"One more week."

"And then?" His thumb brushed over the top of my breast, and even through my jacket and my shirt, his touch sent an electric current straight down between my legs. My sex clenched. Without thinking about it, I shuffled closer so that our sneakers bracketed each other. Our knees and hips bumped together, and I leaned my chest against his, chasing the sensation.

"I guess it depends," I murmured.

"On what?" He dipped his head closer until I felt his warm breath on my cheek.

"On whether you're staying in town or going home."

"Home? Home is here. With you." He touched his lips to mine, and in the dark, with the pink fading into purple in the star-dotted sky, a flame ignited inside me. If I could've opened my eyes, I'd have expected my fingers to glow against his chest. The bats and the roosting birds made soft music around us.

Jackson had taken my hometown and made it more. He'd brightened the sunset, added an extra twang to the honky-tonk music, and made me feel alive at work the way I'd never felt before.

And he was staying. When the project ended, a week from Monday, I'd keep the new-and-Jackson-improved Austin.

"Alicia," he muttered, kissing across my cheek to my ear, "I can hear you overthinking. Let go. Enjoy the moment." And then he found a place on my neck that lit me up like the neon signs on Sixth Street. I curled my hands behind his neck and hung on for my life as he nosed lower to my jacket collar and then back up and found my lips again.

We sipped, we tasted, we devoured each other. When I swiveled my hips against his, the steely ridge of his erection rubbed promises against my belly.

He tipped his forehead against mine, breathing hard. "One week."

Damn. If he hadn't pulled away, I'd have dragged him off into the bushes. I sighed. "One week."

He dipped down and picked up my ball cap, which had fallen off at some point, probably when I'd tried to dry-hump him in a public park. He placed it on my head backward and then kissed me gently on the temple. "Maybe after the project's over, you'll show me the Alamo?"

"Remember, it's in San Antonio. Ninety minutes each way."

"We'd have to stay overnight, I think." One corner of his mouth kicked up.

A hotel room. And Jackson Jones. I shivered, though I wasn't cold anymore. "Okay."

"Promise?" Just like tonight, he'd be excited as a little boy.

"Promise."

"It's still early. Want to go to dinner?"

"Might as well. I know a great place for tacos."

He grinned. "Of course you do. Let's go."

Placing my hand in his, I led him back onto the trail and toward the bright lights of downtown.

———

"HEY."

The following Friday, Jackson's voice startled me. I glanced up from the code I was checking. He held a red plastic cup, and the sharp scent of hops curled into my nose.

"Party was a dud?" I asked.

He smiled. "Yeah. You weren't there. So I brought the party to you." He plunked the cup onto the desk beside me.

"That's sweet, but I—" I waved at the screen. I was not going to screw up what I hoped was our final demo to Cooper Fallon. I was scanning every line of code, even after it'd passed the automated testing process. Leave it to Cooper to perform a key sequence the quality assurance process didn't test.

"You know what they say about all work and no play."

"You mean that it makes for a flawless demo?"

He scrunched his eyebrows together. "Not what I had in mind."

He reached out and hovered his hand an inch from my shoulder. "May I?"

I looked around. The floor was deserted. Not even a key clicked on the other side of the row of potted trees. "I guess?"

He squeezed the muscles that connected my neck to my shoulder and then dug in with his fingers. "This okay?"

I groaned. It. Was. Heaven.

"You've got to relax your shoulders while you're typing. You carry all this stress in your neck."

I hung my head to give him better access. "I carry a lot of stress, period. Less talking. More neck massage."

"Yes, ma'am." There was a smile in his voice. He stepped behind my chair and put both hands on me, rubbing my shoulders. The muscles loosened under the pressure and the warmth of his hands.

I lifted my head to resume my review of the code, but it was no use. The letters and numbers swam together on the screen. His thumbs wandered to either side of my spine, between my shoulder blades. Magical.

"I'm going to put one hand in front of your shoulder and use the heel of my hand to—"

But the second he put his big hand below my collarbone, his sneaky little finger caressing the upper slope of my breast, I rolled back my chair, bumping into his boot, and stood.

"Ow! Why'd you—"

"Not here," I whispered. I was standing too close to him. So close, I felt the heat of his body. My nerves still tingled from his touch and cried out for more. In my heels, I was eye-level to his lips. Those soft, pink lips I'd kissed last week on the shore of Lady Bird Lake. All I wanted to do was reacquaint myself with them.

His lips parted. "Where, then?"

I turned and strode to the main hallway. Not sensing him behind me, I turned. I beckoned toward myself. *Come here,* I mouthed.

He blinked and jogged to catch up.

I turned left into the smaller hall with the restrooms. When I pushed open the door to the ladies' room, the motion-sensing lights flicked on. I reached out and tugged Jackson in behind me, then I flipped the bolt on the door.

He looked around. "Hey, we don't have a couch in—"

Pushing him against the door, I rose up on my toes. "Less talking, more kissing." I pressed my lips to his.

After a second of shocked stillness, Jackson's arms came around me, and his lips softened under mine. Like we'd kissed at his place on Halloween, but *more*. The tang of beer on his tongue. The leather and pine on his skin. The roughness of his beard chafing my cheeks and my nose. Plus the heightened sense of urgency because we were kissing at work where someone might bang on the door any minute. I gripped a double handful of his T-shirt. What was the band today? Didn't matter. All that mattered was the slide of his tongue against mine, the press of his solid chest into my hard nipples, the tingles that told me my panties wouldn't be dry for long.

He broke from the kiss to run his lips down my neck and bury his nose in my collar. "Fuck, Alicia, I—I want to pick you up and carry you over to that couch." His thumb flicked open the top button of my blouse, and he nosed deeper into my cleavage, his beard scratching the swell of my breast over my bra. "I want to tug up your skirt, rip off whatever you're wearing underneath, and taste you." He flicked his tongue over my skin, and my knees went weak.

Yes yes yes. My brain had become a cheering section for Jackson Jones's dirty talk. He wouldn't have to pick me up. I'd sprint over there willingly, sprawl over the couch, and let him rip away.

"But." He dropped a closed-mouth kiss in the shallow valley between my breasts and then fastened the button he'd loosened. "I'm not tasting you for the first time in the ladies' room."

"You're—you're not?" The cheers inside me turned to boos.

"No, baby."

The last thing I needed was for him to call me *baby* in Monday's code review. "Don't—"

He put a finger over my lips, and then he kissed the corner of my mouth. "You're not some bathroom hook-up. I want more." He rubbed his thumb under my lower lip. His own lips were stained the same pink as my lipstick. "You deserve more. All night."

The throb between my legs repeated it. *All night all night all night.*

"Promise?"

He kissed me one last time, a closed-mouth brush of his lips. "Promise."

I tried to straighten up my kiss-slacked mouth. "I'll hold you to it, Jones. After we finish the project."

"After we finish the project." His hands caressed my hips and then dropped to his sides. "That code is fucking perfect. Check it back in and go home."

He was right. It was done, and the last thing we needed was for someone—me—to inadvertently introduce a new bug. "No touching it over the weekend, right, cowboy?"

"Not the code. I can guarantee I'll be touching something else." He shifted his hips, and a ridge pressed into my belly.

An inch or two lower, and I could've rubbed against him. It'd probably take less than a minute to get myself off. Maybe to get us both off. But he was right. We were at work. Assuming the demo went well, the project would end on Monday. And we'd no longer be coworkers. We'd be free to touch wherever we wanted.

"Save some for me." I winked.

His eyes went wide, and then they flicked to the couch. "On second thought—"

Quick as a rattlesnake, I unbolted the door and pulled it open. "See you Monday," I called over my shoulder, laughing as I trotted back to our desk. Even Jackson Jones wasn't bold enough to walk through the office with a hard-on in his tight jeans. And I was out the door before he returned to our workspace.

27

JACKSON

IT WAS what I'd been waiting for since I'd been exiled to Texas five months ago: Cooper's rarest, wide smile, the one I only ever got when I'd somehow *not* fucked something up.

"This is amazing, everyone." Cooper stood at the end of the conference table. We were in the same room where it'd all started, where Alicia had walked in with a still-bleeding nick on her forehead and I'd thought we didn't need her. I'd thought *I* didn't need her. I'd never been more wrong.

Someone flicked on the lights and turned off the projector. "I'm really proud of all of you," my best friend said. "You pulled together and built something truly special."

My chest was going to explode, or I was going to do something ridiculous like cry with joy if I couldn't move. When I stood, everyone looked at me expectantly. Were they looking for me to say something...leaderly? Cooper usually did the things and said the words, not me. I stole a look at him, and he dipped his chin in an almost imperceptible nod.

I cleared my throat. "Um...I want to recognize each of the team members for your contributions. You guys are superheroes." Slowly, I circled the table and said something important that each person had done for the project. It got easier as I went, so by the time I got to

Alicia, I felt comfortable and loose. "Finally, Alicia. She managed to pull us all together, supported each of us when we didn't think we'd make it. She showed us what true leadership looks like."

She blinked quickly and sniffed. Her lips trembled when she smiled at me, but those blue eyes shone proud and fierce. I yearned to sweep her up in my arms and kiss her right at the conference table. But Cooper would've had something to say about that.

He rose from his seat. "You'll all see a little extra in your paychecks next pay period, a token of our appreciation. And I know it's only Monday, but I'd like to take you all out for drinks and dinner to celebrate."

The guys cheered. Cooper repeated my circle of the table, starting with Alicia, shaking everyone's hand and saying a few words to each of them. Slowly, the room emptied, leaving only Cooper and me. He extended his hand, and when I clasped it, he pulled me in for a shoulder-clapping hug. "You did it, Jay."

I shook my head. "We couldn't have pulled it off without Alicia. And the rest of the team."

Cooper raised his brows. "The team?"

I drew myself up straight. "Tyler has grown a lot. I think he'd be an asset to our automotive analytics group in San Francisco. Would you ask him if he'd be interested in a transfer?" He would; I'd already felt him out. But Cooper made the hiring and firing decisions.

"Sure." He twisted his lips to the side. "I'm surprised you care. You don't normally take an interest in human resources."

I shrugged and pushed in my chair. "I guess I'm growing again."

"That's great." He laid a hand on my shoulder. "When you get back to San Francisco, we'll talk about building you a role that'll help you continue that growth."

My chest didn't tighten. I didn't get a sick feeling in my stomach. Leadership didn't sound like a sure way to follow my dad to an early grave the way it used to. Or something I'd be sure to fuck up and have my name splashed across the business magazines as the Jones who'd tried but couldn't cut it.

Alicia had shown me leadership was something I was capable of. I might make mistakes along the way—that bar fight with Tyler was one—but I could recover. *We* could recover if we all worked together toward a common goal.

Fuck, exactly like Cooper had told me the day of the project kick-off. He'd been right all this time.

I didn't need to be CEO. Or Chief anything. I wouldn't mind over-seeing development, taking a strategic look at our products and how we might take the best parts of each to make them all better. Nurturing young programmers like Tyler to help them grow, too.

But I was staying here. Maybe he'd let me build my new role from Austin. When I opened my mouth to ask, he was giving me the look he only gave me when we were hanging out together, the one that'd become so rare at work. Caring. Friendship. I missed that look. And I couldn't wipe it away by saying I wanted to stay here, where my best friend wasn't. Not today, anyway. I'd tell him tomorrow. "I'd like that."

His phone buzzed, and when he looked down at it, he frowned. "Weston. What the hell does he want?"

I might be a leader, but I wasn't about to let our CEO spoil my team's celebration. "I'll meet you at the restaurant. Don't let that asshole make you late."

He nodded absently and raised the phone to his ear. I scooted out of his office.

Back at our desk, Alicia had stacked her badge on top of her Synergy-issued laptop. Seeing it made my insides crumple in like one of Tyler's aluminum cans of Mountain Dew.

"I guess this is it." I shoved my hands in my pockets.

One corner of her mouth turned up. "I guess it is. I didn't really think about how sad it'd be to leave a company after only a couple months. Occupational hazard."

"You don't have to leave. You could stay."

She glanced around at the other programmers, packing up for the day. "The team is breaking up. Amit says he's going to work in the data modeling group. It wouldn't be the same."

"I'm staying. You could work with me."

"Cooper seems to think you're going back to San Francisco." She tucked her phone into her purse.

I kept my voice low. "I'll talk to him tomorrow. I promise."

The light came back into her blue eyes like sunshine on Lady Bird Lake. I wanted to see that light every day. I wanted it to be the first thing I saw in the morning and the last thing I saw at night. I wanted it on workdays and weekends.

Fuck. What was this? It wasn't friendship, not even the kind I had with Cooper. And it wasn't lust. I'd never wanted to stay and see my partner in the morning, her makeup on the pillowcase and her hair mussed. And I certainly hadn't wanted them to see me, naked, all pretense of power gone, just Jackson Jones and his fucked-uppery.

Alicia wasn't like that. She saw past the figurehead position and the cash in the bank. She'd seen me humiliated, and she'd seen me soar. She believed I wasn't a complete waste of space. That I had value. That I could be more than I was. And maybe I could, with her by my side.

"So...celebration?" Both corners of Alicia's mouth kicked up. And it hit me. The project was over. Alicia no longer depended on Synergy for a paycheck. We could be together now. As in, be. Together.

"Yeah." After the team dinner, I'd take her to my place. We could finish what we'd started on my couch after the Halloween party, in the park with the bats. In the Synergy ladies' room.

Her eyes widened at what must have been a starved-wolf expression on my face. And then her smile broadened. "Walk me out?"

Right then, if she'd asked me to walk her into the depths of hell, I'd have said the same thing. "Yeah." Then, louder, "Hey, guys, I'm going to walk Alicia to her car. We'll meet you at the restaurant."

I grabbed the keys to my truck, my wallet, and Alicia's laptop. She hefted her purse over her shoulder and checked the desk and drawers one last time. When she was ready, we walked downstairs to the IT cave, where she turned in her equipment and her badge. She had a kind word and a thank-you for everyone we met, from the IT intern to Ivan at the front desk.

I walked her to her Honda, parked a few spots down from my rental. I flipped my key fob around my finger, suddenly reluctant to let her out of my sight. What if she changed her mind and decided to go home to her family? "Want to ride over with me?"

She opened her car door. "No, I'd rather have my car in case the party goes late. But you can ride with me if you'd like."

I bounded to the passenger door and slid inside. Even in the shadowed garage, her eyes glittered so brightly I almost slipped on my sunglasses.

"You were amazing on the project," she said.

"We're a good team. I wish you'd think about—"

She stopped my words with a kiss, devouring them in a blaze of heat. And I was no fool. I went with it, sliding my hand up her shoulder, around the back of her neck, holding her to me so I could delve inside her softness, tasting her passion and sweetness again. I'd stay here, inside her cramped Honda, my knees smashed against the plastic console, the nubby cloth headrest catching on my beard, until my limbs cramped and I couldn't meet her lips anymore.

The whoop-whoop of a car alarm startled us apart.

"Want to get out of here?" I caressed her hand where it lay on my inner thigh.

She cleared her throat. "I could use a drink."

"I've got beer at my place. Unless you'd rather go out with the team?" *Please don't say you'd rather go out with the team.*

"Perfect. I'll text Tyler and say I'm going home. You'll text Cooper and tell him you're not coming?"

I nuzzled behind her ear. "You could tell Tyler we're both ditching."

She rolled her shoulder, and I stopped kissing her soft skin. Not looking up from her text, she said, "I still need that testimonial from Cooper. I'd rather he didn't find out about us until I have that up on my website."

My not-so-shriveled heart swelled. She'd said *us.* Maybe she felt the same strange feeling I did.

While she drove the few blocks to my apartment, I couldn't keep my hands off her. I rested my hand on her knee, playing with the hem of her skirt and watching her breath quicken the higher I inched it. I caressed the soft skin of her inner thigh the way I'd wanted to do since dinner with her family. Goosebumps rose on her skin, and I smoothed over them. When we stopped at the light right before the turn-in to my complex, she gripped my hand, leaned over, and kissed me fiercely. "Stop that. I want us to get to your apartment safely. Then I'll let you fulfill that promise you made on Friday."

"Promise?" I whispered. I remembered it. I'd promised her all night. I wriggled in my seat, my jeans suddenly too tight.

She didn't reply, but one corner of her mouth tugged up.

I sat on my hands, but she hadn't said anything about my eyes. I catalogued each part of her I wanted to touch, to taste: the curve of her neck, the soft swell of her breasts hidden behind her button-up—I gulped—shirt, those thighs that'd teased me when she wore her cut-off sweatpants. The insides of her ankles.

When she pulled up in front of my building, I was ready to leap across the console and maul her. Instead, I bounded out of the car and circled to open her door.

She swiveled her long legs out of the car and planted her shoes— the red power slingbacks she wore when Cooper was in town—on the pavement. I held out a hand, and she placed her palm on it and levered up.

Her face was inches from mine. Cooper couldn't see us here. So I kissed her, pulling her against me and letting her feel my desperate arousal, pouring my new feelings—whatever they were—into the kiss.

Finally, she pushed against my chest and laughed breathlessly. "Let's take this inside."

I had to have set a land speed record between her car and my front door. I dropped the key on the first attempt but managed to unlock the door on the second. I pushed it open, flicked on the light, and let her precede me through.

The second the door closed, I pressed her up against it, pinning her hands on either side of her head. I kissed her neck, her jaw, the vee of her collarbone revealed by her button-down shirt. Her skin tasted like heaven, and I wanted to devour every inch. I nosed inside her shirt to flick my tongue along the upper swell of her breast. I needed more—more skin, more taste, more of the soft sounds she made when I sucked the tendon between her neck and her shoulder.

"Jackson," she gasped. "Stop."

I froze and released her hands. I backed away half a step so I could see her face. "Stop?" Had I hurt her? Or was she having second thoughts?

"I need to call home first. Check on Noah."

"Right." She had responsibilities. I hoped it didn't mean she'd lost interest.

"Meet you in your bedroom in ten minutes?"

"Fuck, yes." I bounded off to my bathroom, where I brushed my teeth and took the world's fastest shower. Then I padded into the bedroom, pulled the unopened box of condoms out of the bedside drawer, and set them on top of the table. Casting my gaze over the rest of the room, I cringed. The bed was unmade, and there were clothes everywhere. How much more time did I have?

I scooped up the clothes and jogged toward the closet. Sliding open the door, I chucked them all onto the floor. On the top shelf was an unopened package of sheets, the spare set I'd never used. Yes, I had washed my sheets in the five months I'd lived in the apartment— I wasn't a monster—but I'd always put the freshly laundered ones back on the bed. I ripped open the package, found the fitted sheet and two pillowcases, and replaced what was on the bed. I balled up the dirty sheets and tossed them on top of the pile of clothes and slid the closet door shut. I kicked the comforter into the corner of the room.

Had I used up Alicia's ten minutes? She hadn't changed her mind, had she? I tugged on a clean pair of sweatpants and walked back down the hall to the living room.

She was sitting on my sofa, staring at her phone. "Hey."

"Everything okay?" I sat next to her and put a gentling hand on her back.

"Yeah, it's good. I—I don't do this a lot. I mean, with a partner." Her cheeks went red.

All the blood rushed out of my brain and straight into my groin at the thought of her touching herself, using a toy on herself. Damn, I wish I'd thought to buy a vibrator. It would've been a good way to ease into it. And then, of course, I thought of easing my way into Alicia, and my sweatpants hid nothing about how I felt about that.

I kissed her gently on the lips. "We can go as slow as you want, baby. We don't even have to fuck. I can just hold you. Would you let me do that?"

She tugged away. "Do you think that's what I want? That I don't want sex because I'm—I'm frigid?"

"No, baby." Fuck, I'd fucked up the one other thing I was good at

—fucking. "I think you're gorgeous and sexy. And all I want is to make you feel good." I touched her jaw lightly, and when she didn't pull back, I cupped her face in my hand. I kissed her again, less gently this time, trying to communicate, in a way I couldn't with my clumsy words, what I felt for her.

When she gasped for breath, I kissed her cheekbone, her throat, the place I'd found at the side of her neck last time. When she moaned, I grinned. Maybe I wouldn't fuck this up.

I lifted her onto my lap and leaned back to let her take the lead, spreading my arms along the back of the sofa. She stared at my bare chest for a moment and then reached out a finger to catch one of the drops that had run from my damp hair onto my neck. She smeared the wetness over my left nipple, raising it to a peak. Electricity ran straight to my groin. I hadn't thought I could get any harder. I'd been wrong. I gripped the cushions to keep myself from ripping off her blouse.

"I think I'd rather we both make each other feel good." And she shifted so she rubbed her ass against my dick.

I threw my head back to keep from tossing her onto the couch and shoving a hand up her skirt. I'd decided to follow her lead, and if she wanted to tease me, I'd let her.

She stood, and I missed the weight of her, the brush of her hip against me. Then her fingers tangled with mine. "Let's take this to the bedroom."

I was up in a flash, leading her down the hall to my hastily cleaned bedroom. I sprawled on the center of the bed and waited for her to make the next move.

She knelt on the side of the bed. Then she prowled on her hands and knees to me, letting her skirt lift higher and higher as she approached. Finally, she lifted her skirt enough to straddle my hips.

"If I do something you don't like, tell me to stop, okay?"

My eyes widened. What the hell was she going to do to me? What was past full-mast? Because my dick hardened to stone and tried to jab a hole in my sweatpants. "O-okay."

Then she touched me. Her fingertips trailed lightly from my collarbone over my pecs and twirled into my chest hair. And it set me on fire. My skin hungering for more, I twitched.

With the pad of her thumb, she flicked over my left nipple. Dutifully, it rose to a peak. She pinched it, not hard, but enough to make me suck in a breath.

"You like that?"

"Oh, yes." It came out as a sigh.

She trailed her fingers over to my right nipple, swirled a finger around it, and pinched.

"Harder," I grunted.

She raised her eyebrows, but she did it, making white-hot pain sear down from my nipple straight to my groin. I groaned. God, now I wished I'd rubbed one out in the shower. I was going to shoot off the second she touched my dick.

Then she caressed my nipple, soothing the tingling pain. My chest heaved with the effort of gripping the pillows to keep from touching her—or myself. I wasn't used to delayed gratification. The pulse throbbing in my cock ached.

She glanced back at the tent in my sweatpants. Her smile turned devilish. "Anxious to get started?"

"Please, will you—can I see you?"

She bit her lip but nodded. She unbuttoned her cuffs and then started with the button at the top.

"Slowly?" I gasped. I'd been dreaming of those fucking buttons, jerking off to my own fantasy of her slowly releasing them and revealing what was underneath. This businesslike undressing was too much.

Her fingers froze, and then they moved to the hem. She toyed with the lowest button. "Like this?"

I couldn't speak past the tightening in my throat, but I nodded, my eyes bugging.

Ever so slowly, she released the buttons on her blouse, giving me peeks at the skin of her stomach and a flash of white lace. I clenched every muscle in my body when she reached the last one. Then she lifted off me and swiveled on her knees to turn her back.

"One more button," she said with a saucy glance over her shoulder. She splayed her hands on the back of her skirt and slid them to the button at the back. Her long fingers released it, and then they moved to the short zipper below. I saw only a vee of white before she sucked in her breath, whipped off her shirt, and threw it over my face.

"Oops," she muttered. "I wasn't planning—just a sec."

I shook my head to try to dislodge her blouse, but all I could see was white fabric. I heard rustling, and then she snatched her shirt off my face. I blinked. She was completely naked.

I took in the sight of her—smallish breasts, nipped-in-waist, wider hips. The paler skin in the shape of a not-at-all-revealing one-piece swimsuit that made me imagine warm breezes and lying beside her on blinding-white sand. A trim triangle of dark-blond hair concealing her sex. I trailed my gaze up to her face. She was biting her lip again.

"Can I—can I touch?" I uncurled my fingers from the sheets.

She released her lip and smiled. "Only with your mouth."

"Fuck, yes."

"I left my shoes on," she said. "Is that okay?"

"Oh, my God." The red slingbacks. "Yes, please."

She knelt on the bed. Then she straddled my chest. Too far away. She curled over me so her breasts hung like ripe fruit over my face. I licked one pink nipple, then the other. She bowed her back, pushing them down toward my face. Slowly, carefully, I raised my hands and pressed her breasts together, swirling my tongue in a figure-eight over the tips. She moaned and ground down over my chest.

I caught one of her breasts in my mouth and sucked hard on the nipple. She gasped but pressed toward me. I crowed inside. She was losing her grip on her control. Because of me. I snaked my hands down her ribs to where her hips flared, then I ran my thumbnails lightly over her ass cheeks. She shivered.

Boldly, I trailed a hand around the curve of her ass to the valley between her legs. Even before I reached her center, my fingers slipped through her slickness. I mapped her with my fingers: lips, her beck- oning slit, and her swollen clit. She stilled when I touched it.

"Can I"—I had to swallow to croak the words past my suddenly dry throat—"can I taste you?" I knew it was unfair, but I thrummed her clit as I asked the question.

She straightened. "Um, I guess?"

"You guess?" I knew they were out there, but I hadn't met too many women who didn't like oral. Could Alicia be one of them? I hoped not, but even if she was, I'd find something she'd like. "Scoot up closer. We'll try it, and you can tell me to stop whenever you like."

She grabbed the headboard and scooted up. Not close enough. I lifted her ass and inched myself down until my target was directly overhead. I turned my head to the left and licked the slickness on her inner thigh, long and slow. Salty, musky, sweet. I turned right and repeated the motion. Then, gripping her hips, I swirled my tongue directly over her center and straight up to her clit, which I flicked with the tip of my tongue. She gasped.

Encouraging. "That okay?"

"Yes." The word was crisp enough, but her voice was high and breathy.

I went to work like I'd tackle a tricky bit of code, testing as I tasted, checking what worked—what made her twist and moan—and what didn't. Developer's note: there was very little that didn't work. Soon, she gasped as I sucked her clit, my middle finger sliding in and out of her.

I let go of her nub for a moment and ghosted it with a puff of cool air. "You can be as loud as you like. There's no neighbor on this side of the apartment."

She groaned as I raked my teeth across her sensitive skin. Then, as I gently squeezed my index finger inside her, she made an incoherent sound. She moaned my name, and I sucked harder on her clit and closed my teeth on the base.

She made a keening sound—not loud, but it was enough. My dick, trapped by my sweatpants, pulsed, and my vision went black for a second while I came. I grunted and released her clit, giving her long, flat licks to ease her down. My breath rasped across her, and she shivered.

"So I guess that was okay?" I couldn't hide my cocky grin when she looked down at me.

She flopped onto her back beside me and flung an arm over her eyes. "Is there anything you're not good at? Besides humility?"

I shrugged and then lifted my sticky pants away from my skin. "Impulse control?"

28

ALICIA

"WATER?"

I'd been drifting somewhere between completely blissed-out and trying to replay the best orgasm of my life when Jackson's voice pulled me from the haze. I moved my heavy arm off my face and blinked my eyes open. He leaned over the side of the bed, holding out a bottle of water.

Propping myself on my elbow, I accepted it from him. I took a swig and then handed it back. He chugged down the rest of it.

He'd shucked off his pants, and he was naked for the first time. Rather, the first time I'd seen him naked. He'd been wearing those gray sweatpants to tease me, surely. They were positively indecent, hiding nothing while he'd sat beside me on the couch. And his obvious arousal had given me the courage to forget what Rick had said about me, to have confidence that with Jackson, sex might be something special.

Wow, had it ever.

Sex with Rick was like the ancient Buick Melissa had passed down to me when she went off to college. It started out okay, but eventually, I was stranded by the side of the road, having to make it to my destination under my own power. Jackson had convinced me he'd be more like my Honda, a dependable ride that went the distance. But, oh my

God, he was the Corvette one of Melissa's boyfriends had driven us to school in that one time. All power, leashed on the curves and ready to roar at the next straightaway.

And I hadn't even had his dick yet. I stared at it as he capped the empty bottle and set it on the nightstand. It looked a little softer than it had been. Had I turned him off?

Chills broke out over my skin. I'd let myself be so vulnerable, showing him my body, even my secret places, as I rode his face. I covered my breasts with one arm and crossed my legs. Why didn't he have a top sheet so I could cover myself?

"Cold?" he asked.

"Mm-hmm."

He turned away, giving me a flash of the sexy dimples at the top of his ass. Then his full ass—oh, my God, it definitely rivaled Rick's—as he bent to pick up the white duvet from the floor. He held it out toward me, and I snatched it and burrowed inside.

The mattress dipped next to me. "Are you okay? Did I do something wrong?"

"No." I poked my head out of the comforter. "Was it okay for you? Want me to…" I let my gaze fall to where his cock lay on his thigh.

"Fuck, no. I mean, I'd love it if you wanted to. But this isn't a transaction. We're making—we're enjoying each other. You have no idea how long I've wanted to touch you like that. To taste you. To hear the sounds you make when you come. I came without either one of us touching me. You were amazing."

"Yeah?" I didn't know guys could do that.

"You had a great time, too, right?"

I'd seen stars. "Of course. I haven't come like that in…ever."

He rolled closer and laid a hand on top of the comforter that covered me. "I love"—he swallowed—"how honest you are."

My heart raced. Was he about to tell me he loved me? That wasn't what this was about. Was it? Like he'd said, we were two consenting adults, enjoying each other's bodies.

"You think there's room in there for me?" He nodded at the duvet. "It's a little chilly out here, and I'm a cuddler."

"I don't believe that for a second." Still, the hopeful expression on his face melted me. I opened one side of the comforter, covering my torso with the rest. "Come on, then."

He nudged inside and then spooned around me. One arm tucked under my head and the other draped around my waist. The comforter twined around us, making an uncomfortable lump under my hip. I wiggled and tugged to straighten it out, and by the time my hip was flat against the mattress, my butt was snugged up against Jackson's stiffening erection, and his breath was hot in my ear.

His hand crept up to cradle my breast. "Could I interest you in a second round?" He flicked my nipple.

That flick sent a shock straight to my center. I gasped at the intensity. Every part of me was on board with his proposal. "You said you wanted to cuddle," I teased, squirming against him again.

"That was before you ground your beautiful soft bits against my not-so-soft ones." Proving his point, the head of his cock slid between my legs.

I held back a moan. "I was just trying to get comfortable."

"This is pretty comfortable, don't you think?" He drew his hips back and then pushed them forward, sliding his cock over my pussy.

My sex clenched, hungry for him. Teasing time was over. "Feels good."

He trailed his fingers down my stomach and cupped between my legs. "How does this feel?" He thrummed his fingers across my clit.

I flung my top leg over his and let out a groan.

"Okay," he whispered against my neck. "I'm going to interpret that as 'fucking fantastic.'"

He strummed me higher and higher until I held my breath, waiting for the orgasm that dangled tantalizingly out of reach. "Jackson," I murmured, "make me come."

"What do you need, sweetheart?"

"I—I don't know."

"What about—" He kissed me, right at the juncture between my shoulder and my neck, and then I felt the bite of his teeth on my skin. The small pain, paired with a pinch to my clit, rocketed through me and sent me over the edge with a shriek.

When I came back from my star-spangled orgasm, he was kissing the spot he'd bitten and gently pressing on my clit.

I tried to say his name, but it came out as an unintelligible mumble. My mouth wasn't working. None of my muscles were.

"You good, baby?"

My skin fizzed at the endearment. He could call me that all he wanted now that we weren't working together. No more chances for him to slip up in front of the team. I nodded.

He rolled away for a second, and I heard paper rip. He shifted back under the comforter and knelt between my knees. But instead of plunging right in, he scooted down toward the foot of the bed and bent so his chin hovered between my legs.

"Can I taste you again? I'll be gentle if you're sensitive."

Still in the trough of post-orgasmic bliss, I nodded.

Before he touched me, he felt under the comforter until he found my ankles. I was still wearing one shoe. The other had fallen off somewhere between orgasms. He snugged them around his torso and ensured the point of my red heel rested in the crease of his hip. "Go ahead and spur me," he said with a grin. "But watch out for the dangly bits, or you might miss out on another orgasm."

He bent and scraped his bristly jaw along my inner thigh until he reached my center. Spreading me with his thumbs, he lapped my pussy inside and out. My legs started to tremble, and I dug my heels into his hips.

"That's it, baby," he said against my sex. "Give it to me again."

My hips rose, and I ground myself against his face. What was it about this man that dissolved my resistance, that arrowed through the chinks in my armor? I focused solely on my pleasure and how he heightened it.

He slid a finger or two inside me, pulsing, and moved his lips to my clit. He started slow, with kisses and gentle licks. My legs shook harder.

"Hold on to me, sweetheart," he said. "Can you take more?"

"Yes, yes." The words burst out of me.

He flicked his tongue over my clit, revving it back up, before he closed his mouth over it and gave a long, hard suck that bowed me off the mattress.

Then his fingers were gone, replaced by a blunt pressure at my entrance. Cradling my hips with his hands, he slid inside me on one long, slow thrust. My aftershocks squeezed around him.

"Oh, God, baby, yes. Feels so good." He remained motionless, gripping my hips.

At last, I opened my eyes. I wished I hadn't because everything showed in his eyes, soft with longing. His expression mirrored the ache in my chest, the one that'd only get worse when he finally went back to California.

We stared at each other in silence for a long moment. He broke away first, looking down to where my legs splayed across the bed. One of us had flung off the comforter. He lifted my foot and worked off my shoe. Then he set my ankle against his shoulder. He lifted my other leg and placed it on his other shoulder. Then he pulled his hips back and thrust inside me again, lighting me up deep inside. A sharp squeak escaped me.

"Okay, let's go with that," he said with a smirk.

He set a moderate rhythm that allowed us to savor the friction as he slid in and out. My legs shook against his shoulders until he gently laid his hands across my ankles. He turned his face to kiss one, and then the other, so tenderly that tears prickled the backs of my eyes.

"What was that for?" I lifted my palms to blot away the moisture at the corners of my eyes.

"I've been wanting to do that all afternoon. I've got more spots I want to kiss." He thrust twice more without speaking.

"You going to tell me?"

"I'll show you," he said. "Later."

His mouth tightened, and he sped up his rhythm. One hand drifted down between us, and he thumbed my clit. Paired with the deepening pressure inside me, his touch made me clench around him. He sucked his thumb and pressed it back on my clit, circling. My legs slipped off his shoulders, and I counterthrust against him, once, twice, before I shouted out my climax.

He stilled, and I couldn't tell if the pulses inside me were his or mine. Then, gripping my knees around his waist, he rolled so my body draped over his. My hair had come out of its bun and stuck to his skin. *I* stuck to his skin, and I wanted to stay there, adhered to him, forever. I stroked the side of his chest and then let my arm flop to the mattress. He whispered my name into the top of my hair.

I may have dozed because I was only dimly aware of his shifting out from under me, going to the bathroom, and returning.

When I blinked my eyes open sometime later, the golden afternoon light was gone, and the room was dark. "What time is it?" I mumbled.

"Not too late. Seven thirty. Are you hungry?"

Only for more of him. More of his warmth wrapped around me. More of his soothing words about how amazing I was. More of the softness in his eyes that reflected what I felt.

Love.

A tiny scream started in my brain. I'd fallen in love with Jackson Jones. With a man who'd said he'd stay although his job, his company, was almost two thousand miles away. Maybe we could play at being together for a little while, but he'd need to return eventually. He belonged there as a leader.

The curse of the Weber women had caught up with me.

Stay cool, I told that screaming voice. I'd put that pesky emotion away in a box. Sure, it'd rattle when Jackson left. But then I'd leave it alone, let it get dusty. Maybe the moths would get to it, like they'd done with Mom's wedding gown in the attic, leaving it ridden with holes like Swiss cheese so we didn't feel bad about tossing it in the trash.

The scream got louder. Who was I kidding? What I felt for Jackson was new, but it was too big to keep in a box. It was like the giant baby monster the superhero had fought in one of Noah's favorite movies. Too innocent, too oblivious, to understand the destruction it was causing. It'd smash everything in its path, leaving me a ruin.

If I stayed, I was sure to confess it. Jackson may have made me lose control of my body, but I wasn't prepared to let loose my emotions like that.

"I need to go." I glanced at the floor. Where had I tossed my underwear, the giant, unsexy white briefs with "Big Girl Panties" printed across the butt, the ones Tiannah had gotten me as a joke my last birthday, the ones I'd forgotten I was wearing until I'd attempted that striptease for him?

"You can't stay? Not even for dinner? There's a great Thai takeout place near here. They're really fast."

I scooted away and sat up. "I can't. It's a school night, and I'd like to see Noah before he goes to bed."

He caught my hand. "Want to take a shower?"

I envisioned his face between my legs as I pressed my cheek to smooth tile. "Tempting, but I really do need to get home."

"No funny business. I promise. Just getting clean. You can even shower alone if you want."

My lips tugged up into a smile. Who'd have thought Jackson Jones, rockstar programmer and international playboy, would be begging me to take a shower with him after giving me who-knew-how-many orgasms? Me, the sex goddess formerly known as the Ice Queen? "All right," I said. "Come on."

His shower was plenty big enough for two, and it would've been easy to go another round. But the only touching we did was soaping each other's backs. When Jackson asked if he could shampoo my hair, I let him. The warm water pelted my chest and my belly, and I closed my eyes while his big fingers massaged all the tension out of my scalp. I'd let him in, both emotionally and physically, and he hadn't turned it against me. Instead, he made me feel safe, cared-for. Cherished. After so many years of caring for myself—and Noah—I wanted it to go on forever.

How long could we do this? A couple weeks until Thanksgiving separated us? Or longer? Would we go out on Saturday nights, strolling along Sixth Street, holding hands and sampling the music outside each bar? Could I spend lazy Sundays at his place, wearing his T-shirts and lingering over coffee in his kitchen?

The water beat at the crown of my head and my lower back, Jackson's big body warming my front. Too soon, he'd rinsed the suds from my hair and reached around me to turn off the water.

After we dried off, I slicked my hair back into a bun. Jackson insisted on doing up the buttons of my blouse—which was totally unnecessary—but also helpfully did the back zipper and button on my skirt. He found a fresh shirt and shorts somewhere in his bedroom and then made me sit on the edge of the bed while he slid on my red slingbacks like I was Cinderella.

He tugged me to my feet. "When can I see you again?"

The best thing was that I didn't have to make up a fake reason to end things with Jackson. We had one already built-in. "You're leaving."

His eyes sharpened like a scalpel, cutting away my defenses. Damn. He knew about the excuses and why I made them. "I told you I'm staying."

"For how long?"

His mouth tightened for a second. "Long-term was never my thing. I'm more of a one-night guy. I've never been with anyone—never let myself be with someone—who's challenged me the way you do, who's beautiful and smart, too. Someone I respect."

"You don't mean I'm not like other girls, do you?" I crossed my arms.

"No." A blush spread over his forehead. "I mean, of course you're exceptional. But I—I didn't think I could be with anyone who'd—"

"Call you on your bullshit?"

He snorted. "Exactly. What I'm trying to say is that this is a first for me. I'm probably going to fuck it up. But I—I want to try. I was already planning to talk with Cooper tomorrow about continuing to work from Austin. I want to give this a chance. Give us a chance."

"You're not going to say anything to Cooper, are you? About... us?" Was there really an *us?*

He shuddered. "Not yet. We'll get him to write that testimonial for you first."

I uncrossed my arms and joined my hands with his. "Thanks." It wouldn't hurt to see him a few more times before he left. Either way, I'd be ruined. And I liked the way with orgasms better than the one without.

"My next gig doesn't start until next week, so I'm free the rest of this week."

"Cooper's staying through tomorrow. But I could play hooky the day after that."

"I'm off the project for one day and you're already playing hooky?"

"I'm a fuckup." He shrugged. "Everyone expects it."

My stomach clenched. I wanted to shake him. "Listen to me,

Jackson Jones. You are not a fuckup. You are a star. Cooper praised you, and I get the feeling he doesn't do that a lot. You built that software and made it sing."

His face softened. "I know. But it sounds better when you say it."

I kissed him hard on the lips. "And you deserve a day off once in a while."

His arms wrapped around me. "So do you. You need to spend time with your boyfriend, who also happens to be the best lover you've ever had."

A thrill shivered through me. "Let's not get ahead of ourselves here. You haven't even taken me out on a date."

"Day after tomorrow. I'll take you out Wednesday."

"Okay. Text me." I leaned in to give him a peck on the lips, but he captured my mouth in a devouring kiss that made my knees weak and stole my breath. It made me forget why we'd waited so long to sleep together.

Cooper. Thinking about his judgmental face made ice flow through my veins.

"What? Why'd you say 'Cooper'?" Jackson murmured into my neck.

"Oops." I stepped around him, out of the bedroom. He followed, his bare feet silenced by the carpet.

"Hey," he said when we reached the living room. "Maybe you, me, and Noah could do something together. We could go to a basketball game. Or hiking. Even one of those obnoxious places with animatronics and cardboard pizza."

It'd be bad enough for me when Jackson left. I couldn't face another one of Noah's yearning expressions like the one he had whenever we saw Rick. "I—I don't want to confuse Noah. So I'd rather not involve him."

Jackson's face fell. Then he gave me a half-smile that didn't brighten his eyes. "Whatever you want, sweetheart."

I wanted to take it back and see him smile again. But I couldn't. I couldn't let him hurt Noah. I took his hand and squeezed it. At last, the other corner of his mouth kicked up.

"Text me tomorrow?" I said.

"I'll text you tonight."

Tipping up on my toes, I kissed him, a long, languorous, we-have-all-the-time-in-the-world kiss. For now, we'd both pretend he'd stay long enough to give us a chance. Maybe if we pretended hard enough, it'd come true.

"I'll text you back. Night, Jackson."

I stepped out into the cool November night, my cheeks glowing with the thought of playing hooky with Jackson the day after tomorrow. It wouldn't last forever, but he'd called himself my boyfriend, and the thought of kissing him again made my knees weak.

How long could he stay here in Austin? I didn't know, and I didn't think he knew, either. But for once in my life, I wasn't going to worry about a year or even a month from now. I'd enjoy this new thing with Jackson Jones as long as I could.

Then I'd break.

29

JACKSON

AFTER ALICIA LEFT, my stomach felt hollow. Digging through my drawer of restaurant delivery menus, I pulled out the one for the Thai restaurant I'd tried to tempt her with, but I laid it back in the drawer next to the plastic-wrapped forks, chopsticks, and ketchup packets. Even Thai food wouldn't fill the emptiness inside me.

In the bedroom, I sniffed both pillows. One smelled faintly of sweet orange, so I brought it with me out into the living room. I stretched out on the sofa so my feet hung over the arm, tucked the pillow under my cheek, and picked up the remote. What was I in the mood for? Sports? Comedy? Something sexy and romantic?

I let the remote fall from my hand. Nothing could measure up to the replay of my afternoon with Alicia. I rubbed a hand over my Led Zeppelin T-shirt. One nipple still stung from her pinch. I wondered if I'd left a mark on her neck. If she'd be a little sore tonight. If she'd smell her skin for traces of me.

Wednesday. I'd see her Wednesday. Maybe we could go for a walk along the river. Or she could take me on a tour of the Capitol. I'd be the goofy tourist, buying the most ridiculous tchotchke I could find in the gift shop, and she'd be my sexy tour guide.

Or maybe we'd rent a hotel room overlooking the river for the afternoon and make love against the windows.

Make love? I meant fuck. Knock boots. Plow her field. Kneel at her altar. Go downtown.

Fuck. I squeezed the pillow. Who did I think I was bullshitting? Not myself.

This thing with Alicia was different. Sure, I'd been attracted to her since that first day, when I'd brushed her hair aside and blotted her wound with my T-shirt. And then I'd resented her. Well, not her, exactly, but everything her presence meant about me. Until the resentment had given way to respect. Admiration. And something softer that lit me up every time I looked at her.

Fuck. Was I in love?

I'd never been in love before. I'd never dated anyone I could connect with like that. It was safer to date women I didn't care about. If I didn't care, it wouldn't hurt when they laughed at me and left me.

But after all we'd been through together, I didn't think Alicia would do that to me. I'd seen that expression on her face in the shower, after I'd washed her hair. She'd looked at me like she cared, too. Like if I knocked at her gate long enough, she might eventually let me in. If I was persistent and trustworthy, she might even let me into her life. Except the part with Noah.

She didn't trust me enough for that. Maybe it was fair, considering I still fucked things up. And there was no room for error with a kid. Poor guy had enough fucked-up things in his life, considering he had no parents and probably ADHD.

I hadn't fucked up that conference, though. I'd helped Alicia through it. And maybe, once she pulled Noah out of that awful classroom and got him treatment, he'd do better in school.

Could she trust me then?

I let myself imagine it: riding bikes on the greenbelt. Or taking them with me to San Francisco and doing tourist shit like Alicia had done with me and the bats. Watching the sea lions with Noah. I wouldn't take them to Alcatraz; that was creepy. We'd sit in Golden Gate Park listening to music or walk along the beach or tour the California Academy of Sciences. We'd be a family.

Was I ready for a family? Was that prickling in my fingers excitement or terror?

At dinner with Alicia's family, she'd been so strong, so confident.

The way she always was at work. At work, we'd become partners. Could we do it with her family, too?

I flopped back on the sofa and let myself fantasize. I'd introduce them to my mother. She'd be enchanted by Alicia's maturity and drive. Would we spend the holidays with her family or mine? Maybe Christmas in the Alps would be best. Or the Caribbean. I pictured Alicia in a bikini. Walking hand-in-hand on the beach with the moon glistening on the water, listening to the roar of the surf, warm water lapping at our toes. I lost myself in the fantasy.

So that's why I was huddled under my comforter, cocooned in Alicia's scent, when three sharp bangs rattled my door.

Grumbling, I threw off the comforter. Only one person knocked like that. I padded to the door and looked through the peephole. Sure enough, Cooper stood there, still in his work clothes, staring daggers at the door. Fuck, what'd I done now?

I opened the door. "Hey, Coop."

He stepped inside and scanned me from my T-shirt to my boxer briefs and bare feet.

"Is she here?"

"Who?" I shut the door. He was wearing his about-to-yell-at-me face.

"Our former consultant, Alicia Weber."

Fuck. She needed his testimonial. I never lied to Cooper, but this one time, I could obscure the truth a little.

"Why would she be here?" I went back to the couch and tossed the comforter and pillow behind it. He wouldn't be able to smell her, would he?

He sat in the chair facing the kitchen. "Really? You're going to lie about this to your best friend? At least, when you slept with that intern, you came clean about it."

How the fuck had he found out? Alicia wouldn't have called him. And she and I were the only people who knew what we'd done a couple of hours before. I flopped onto the couch. "What are you talking about?"

"When you weren't at dinner—"

Fuck. Alicia had asked me to text Cooper to tell him I'd miss it.

"—Tyler told me that you two have been carrying on for weeks."

"*Tyler* said that?" I'd never have thought he'd snitch on us. Of course, I'd thought everyone was oblivious to how close Alicia and I had become.

"He said he thought it was common knowledge."

"What was common knowledge?"

But Cooper wasn't having any more of my innocent act. His face was red in the lamplight. "That you've been fucking the consultant I hired. Frankly, I thought she was too professional, too mature, to fall for your"—he waved a hand at my boxers—"charms. Jamila said she was unimpeachable. The pinnacle of integrity. I guess Alicia fooled her, and she thought she could fool me, too. But as they say here in Texas, I didn't just fall off the turnip truck."

"They say that here? I've never heard it." I had to stop him before he really got going.

"I'll see that she never works for a reputable company again. She won't be fucking her way through Austin's tech leaders if I have anything to say about it."

"Now wait a minute—" I stood. I really wished I was wearing pants. And my ass-kicking boots.

"You'd done so well. Three months here without an incident. And then she shows up, and you fall off the wagon." He narrowed his eyes at me. "She's not even your type."

"Listen to me, Cooper. I did not fuck Alicia while we were on the project together."

"Tyler seems to think you did."

Pain stabbed through me. "We've known each other for fourteen fucking years. And you believe a junior programmer over me, your best friend?"

"Yes, we've known each other for fourteen years, and I've never known you to show the slightest bit of restraint where your dick was involved. You fucked every heterosexual woman in our freshman dorm."

"I was eighteen fucking years old. Don't you think I've changed since then? This afternoon, you said I'd grown."

"That was before I knew you and Alicia were here fucking instead of joining us at the team celebration."

"She and I were nothing but colleagues in the office. Alicia is a consummate professional."

"Apparently, she didn't seem to think that professional integrity extended to events outside the office. Tyler said you two were together at your Halloween party."

My blood went cold. Had he seen me kiss her? We'd been careless in front of him, thinking he was too hammered to remember. No, *I'd* been careless. And now I had to pay for it.

"Tyler was drunk that night. He ended up sleeping in my guest bedroom. But he misunderstood what he saw. Yes, I pursued Alicia, but she didn't reciprocate. I kissed her at the party. She was too nice to slap me, but she told me she wasn't interested. She left."

"But you two left the office together tonight."

I gritted my teeth. I hated lying to my friend, but Alicia's business, her fucking career, was on the line. "I asked her for a ride. I tried to kiss her again in her car. She pulled over and kicked me out. I walked here. I guess neither of us felt like celebrating after that. She must've gone home."

Cooper rubbed his temples. "Fucking hell, Jackson. Now I've got to protect the company against a sexual harassment suit. On top of—"

"I—I don't think she'll press charges. She probably just wants her testimonial." I sank down onto the coffee table in front of my friend.

He scrubbed his face. "This isn't even my biggest problem today."

"What do you mean?" I held my breath. If he had a bigger problem than me, maybe he'd go back early to San Francisco and leave me alone.

"Weston. He's got an all-hands-on-deck situation back at headquarters. We've got an activist shareholder questioning our relationship with that offshore outfit."

I stiffened. "The one Weston brought on because they were cheaper than our team in Singapore?"

"That's the one. Looks like they weren't paying a living wage, and now we've got to do damage control."

"And fucking reparations."

He lowered his hands and stabbed me with his steely stare. "That's why you're going with me."

"I'm—what?" I couldn't go with him. Alicia and I had a date on Wednesday.

"All hands on deck includes our new VP of Development, under whose purview relationships with offshore developers fall."

"What?" The gears in my brain were slipping.

"This is your fucking problem, too. You're coming with me to fix it."

"I—I can't."

"And why is that? We're partners. Synergy is half your company."

Because I lied to you, and I'm fucking our former consultant. Nope. *Because I've fallen in love with our former consultant.* True, but it still wouldn't fly.

Fuck. Alicia wanted me to be a leader. Being a leader sucked.

"Fine. Are we leaving tonight?"

He stood. "Tomorrow morning. We'll stop in the office for a quick talk with Tyler to straighten him out, and then we'll head back on the jet. Pack your things tonight. The team will finish up here. No need for you to come back."

"But—"

"When we get home, if I hear even a rumor of sexual harassment, I'm sending you to that monastery in the mountains near Big Sur. You can send your code down by donkey."

Donkey? I was the one about to act like an ass.

30

> Jackson: I didn't want to leave, but I had to. I'm
> sorry.

I stared at Jackson's text for longer than I should've, all alone with my mug of tea in my mother's kitchen the next morning, parsing the words and trying to find the meaning behind them. The why.

But the why didn't matter. Not really.

All that mattered was that he was gone.

He'd said all those perfect things yesterday. About how he was imperfect. How he'd never had a relationship before but was willing to try.

And then he'd left even before the beard burn on my thighs had faded.

I shuddered and stood, tugging my robe more closely around myself. I set my cold tea in the microwave and waited for it to heat.

Mom would tell me I'd given him what he'd wanted, so there was no reason to stay.

Tiannah would put it more bluntly. She'd tell me my coochie and I had fallen right into his trap.

Melissa would tell me she was proud of me for putting myself out there, even though it hadn't worked out.

I scrubbed a tear off my cheek. Jackson Jones wasn't worthy of my tears.

"Cariño." I hadn't heard Esmy come into the kitchen. "Is something wrong?"

"No." I sniffed. "Must be allergies."

"In November?" She clucked her tongue a few times and put the back of her palm against my forehead. "This doesn't have anything to do with your date last night, does it?"

"Date?" I opened the cabinet and pulled down the bottle of honey.

"I've been out of the dating scene for a while, but back in my day, when I came home with wet hair and wrinkled clothes, it meant I'd got some action." She pressed the button on the microwave. "And that tea's not going to heat up unless you turn it on."

I grimaced. "You and Mom are always telling me I should date more."

"And you should. But you aren't glowing today the way you were last night."

Last night, I'd practically floated back inside the house. This morning, since I'd read Jackson's text, I had lead in my veins.

"I'm fine." And I would be. People had one-night stands all the time. And that's all the night before had been. I just had to convince my cracked-open heart.

And, apparently, Esmy. She squinted at me. "You're sure?"

"Positive." The microwave beeped, and I pulled out my tea. "I'm going to clean out some closets. I'll see you later."

The work did me good. I blasted Rihanna through my earbuds while I went through Noah's closet and drawers and bagged up anything that looked too small. I hosed off his soccer cleats in the back yard and set them on the back patio to dry. I tackled my own room next. Jackson's sweater, the one he'd told me I could keep the night we sat together on the porch swing, went into the donation bag with Noah's outgrown SpongeBob pajamas.

That night, to show Esmy I was fine, I cooked King Ranch chicken, Noah's favorite, in the kitchen I'd scrubbed.

Still, she pursed her lips whenever she looked at me across the table.

Wednesday wasn't so good. After Noah got on the school bus, I looked at my phone once an hour, hoping to see a text or missed call from Jackson. Something in response to the text I'd sent him.

> Are you coming back?

Nothing.

Still, I managed to get dressed before Noah came home from school, and I even made spaghetti for dinner.

Thursday after I walked back from the bus stop, I scooped up Tigger and curled around him on my bed. What had I done wrong? Had I been bad at sex? I'd gotten weird for a while, hiding inside his duvet. And then I'd said all those things that made me sound not at all like the Wonder Woman persona I'd tried so hard to project. Maybe he'd decided I wasn't worth the effort.

I probably wasn't.

Tigger kneaded my scalp, running his claws through my hair and reminding me of Jackson's shampoo-massage in his shower. He'd been so tender, so caring. Had he been putting me on? Pretending?

That line he'd used about never letting himself be with someone he respected, until me, had destroyed my defenses. But that's all it had been: a line. Had he used the same one on that intern? Maybe he used it on everyone he wanted to sleep with.

I wasn't special. Not to Jackson Jones. If I were, he'd have kept his promise.

Gently, I lifted Tigger off my pillow and wrapped it around my head. I let loose a scream—muffled by the feathers—and another, and another until I was hoarse. Maybe a tear escaped. Or maybe two. My pillow soaked them up, and no one was the wiser.

I hid under my bedspread well into the afternoon. At last, I dragged myself into the shower and was reasonably normal-looking by the time Noah walked inside.

I found some fish sticks and tater tots in the freezer for dinner. Esmy bit her lip but didn't say anything.

Finally, on Friday, I looked at the bags under my eyes from my second sleepless night and decided I needed help.

Tiannah answered her door with Tavon on her hip. "You look like you need a margarita."

"It's ten-thirty in the morning."

"A mimosa, then. Come on, we're going out."

While Tiannah buckled Tavon into his car seat, I picked Cheerios out of her minivan's footwell.

She peeked over my shoulder. "Don't worry about it. Orlando and the kids wash my car every Saturday. He'll get those."

Tiannah had Orlando, who loved her enough to vacuum Cheerios out of her car. With his scalp massage on Monday, Jackson had fooled me into thinking he cared about me. Yet he couldn't even be bothered to answer my text.

A tear plunked onto the leather seat. Another followed it. Then a sob so violent I had to lean my hands on the car door to keep from collapsing right there onto the sticky seat.

"Oh, no, honey, what's the matter?" Tiannah rubbed my back.

"It's just—just—Jackson."

The side door rolled back, and a few seconds later, Tiannah gently turned me away from the van. "Come on. Let's go back inside."

We sat on her couch while Tavon banged away at a toy musical keyboard.

"Tell me about it," she said.

I wiped the tears off my face with the crumpled tissue she pulled from her jeans pocket. "So, Monday, after the end-of-project review with Cooper Fallon, we were supposed to meet the team at a restaurant for dinner. But instead, Jackson and I went back to his place."

Her eyebrows rose. "And?"

"We, ah"—I glanced at Tavon—"we went to bed."

"Girl..." She shook her head. "All right, how was it?"

"Good. I thought. And then I felt...weird."

"Weird? You mean physically?"

"No. Too exposed, you know?"

"Vulnerable. Okay."

"And then he made me feel better. Safe. Cared-for. I thought it m-meant something."

She walked to the bathroom and handed me a box of tissues. "And then?"

"We said we'd do something Wednesday. But he texted Tuesday to say he'd left. And when I asked if he was coming back, he didn't respond. He g-ghosted me." I hiccupped.

She rubbed a circle on my back. "Maybe something happened to him." From the way the words came out through her clenched teeth, it sounded like if something hadn't happened to him, she'd see to it that something did.

"The good thing about dating someone famous is that you pretty much know if something happened to them. I, ah"—I closed my eyes and sighed—"I set a Google alert for him. Nothing. Go ahead, you can tell me you told me so."

"Why would I do that to you?" The circles didn't stop.

"Because you told me not to get involved. That nothing good could come of this for me. That I'd get hurt. You were right."

"I'm not going to kick you while you're down. Love hurts enough."

"Love?" I blotted my eyes. "I'm not in love." Sure, I'd thought I was for a second. But I could erase it, pretend it never happened.

"Honey, you're too smart, too driven, to have risked your career for anything less than love. I know you didn't roll into bed with your coworker—"

"Former coworker."

"And the best friend of the person who's supposed to write you a testimonial. You wouldn't have done that for lust. Love makes you do stupid things. If it hadn't gone so wrong, I'd say I was proud of you for letting someone in."

It'd only been a crack, but he'd shoved through it with his broad shoulders and left me gaping wide and bleeding out. The tears started to fall again.

Tavon pushed himself up, toddled over, and hugged me around my knees. I ran my hand over his soft curls.

"I won't be making that mistake again."

"Oh, honey. I know it hurts now. But didn't it feel good for a minute? To care about someone and feel cared for?"

I tugged Tavon up into my lap and hugged him. "I guess."

"Someday, you'll find the right man who's emotionally mature enough to talk about his feelings. Who won't leave when things get hard."

"There are guys like that? Couldn't prove it by me."

She pursed her lips. "You had a couple of bad examples."

"This, right here?" I waved at my puffy eyes and tissue-roughened nose. "This is what happens when I let myself fall for a guy. You always make fun of me for dumping guys for trivial reasons. But that's better than this."

"Let it all out, honey."

"Maybe I should start dating women, like Mom."

"Maybe you should. But don't get any ideas. I'm not about to start cheating on Orlando with your skinny, white booty."

I chuckled, and then Tavon giggled, and I started laughing so hard I couldn't stop.

"I've got orange juice and V-O-D-K-A. How about a screwdriver?"

I couldn't stop laughing, but I gave her a thumbs-up.

After Tiannah went into the kitchen, Tavon gave me a sticky hug. Eventually, my hysterical laughter subsided. I inhaled his baby-shampoo scent. What had I done? Why had Jackson seemed so caught up in his feelings, too, and then...nothing?

I picked up Tavon and brought him to the kitchen, where I buckled him into his highchair. Tiannah set a sippy cup in front of him and scattered Cheerios across the tray. She handed me a drink.

"To my best friend, wise in the ways of the heart." I clinked my glass against hers.

"You'll get over the sleazeball. Once you start your next project, you'll be so busy you won't get all stuck in your feelings."

My phone jangled in my purse. I didn't jump for it like I'd done for the past three days whenever it rang.

"You're not gonna get that?" Tiannah asked. "What if it's—"

"It's not." It wasn't his ringtone. "It's probably Jamila."

"Did you tell her? She's probably calling to let you know she's almost done whooping his A-S-S."

"No! And don't you tell her, either. I don't want her to know what a—what a fool I was. She's calling about a job. She's left some messages."

"A job here in Austin?"

"No. It's at her San Francisco office. A long gig starting in the new year."

"You should do it. Take your mind off things."

Being in San Francisco, where Jackson lived, wouldn't take my mind off anything. "I can't leave Noah. Or you."

"It's temporary. We can manage Noah for you."

"Tee." I reached over the table and laid my hand over hers. "I'm not going." I drained my glass.

"You need a refill." She picked up my glass.

"More V-O-D-K-A this time, please?"

"You got it." She fixed the drink, this time with only a splash of orange juice. "How about you and Noah come over tomorrow? Orlando'll grill some steaks, and we'll let the kids run around the yard."

When she handed me the glass, I sipped, the strong drink burning my throat. "That sounds good." It'd keep me from driving past his apartment—again—looking for his truck.

She gripped my hand. "You'll get through this."

I shook my head. "I don't think so." I wasn't sure the wound would ever close. That I'd ever stop hurting. "I guess the good thing is that I learned something: I suck at relationships. I was right all along to stay away from them."

"Honey, that's not—"

"I'll be what Rick called me, an ice queen." I imagined it. Though it really wasn't too different from the persona I'd used in my early days at Synergy.

"He called you that?" Tiannah bristled.

"At Ja—at the party." But I didn't want to think about the way Jackson had stood up for me and punched his former workout buddy. "Who needs a partner when there's such a variety of battery-operated toys? Maybe I'll order a new one." Someone had to make one that sucked my clit the way Jackson had.

"Fu—screw Rick. I never liked him, anyway."

"You said I should give him another chance."

"I didn't know he'd called you that. I'll give him a piece of my mind the next time I see him."

"I'll bring the popcorn."

"The right guy's gonna come along. It's not Rick, and it's not Jackson Jones. But he's out there."

"Doesn't matter. I'm done with men." I wouldn't be giving anyone else the chance to hurt me.

She picked up my glass. "I'll make you another. We'll get good and sloshed before lunch." She twisted her lips. "I'm proud of you, you know. For being vulnerable. For letting someone in far enough to hurt you."

"You're proud that I was foolish enough to get hurt? How many of those have you had?" I nodded at the empties in her hand.

"Sugar, being vulnerable doesn't make you weak. Acting like a woman who has feelings doesn't make you weak. Weakness is hiding yourself away from hurt. Never taking risks to get something you want. You took a risk. It didn't work out this time. But next time, it might. And I don't want you to miss that."

Goddamn motherly wisdom.

31

ALICIA

I SNATCHED a fortifying glass of champagne off a waiter's tray as I strode into the lobby of the Synergy Austin office on the first of December. The winter darkness outside the large windows reflected the blackness inside my heart.

I scanned the room. Normally, I wouldn't have attended a client's launch party. As a contractor, I was supposed to do my job unobtrusively, expecting nothing other than a paycheck. But after I'd refused every one of his lunch invitations over the past two weeks, Tyler had begged me to come, saying he needed to tell me something in person. So here I was.

I'll be honest: I was looking for closure, too. I'd finally be able to confront Jackson Jones and tell him what I thought of his lack of emotional intelligence.

He wasn't there in the lobby, and neither was Tyler. Still sipping my champagne, I walked upstairs.

I found Amit and Kevin near the balcony doors. After a few minutes of small talk about their new projects and the hospital gig I'd been working on, I excused myself to continue my prowl.

Cooper Fallon was standing near our old work area. They'd reconfigured it from its former U-shape, and now the desks were all bunched together. Someone else sat there now.

I owed Cooper thanks for the very nice testimonial he'd sent me about a week after my last day at Synergy. It'd been like him: cold, detached, and professional. But the same day I'd added it to my website, I'd gotten three calls from potential clients.

I caught his eye, and a change came over his expression: a flash of surprise, followed by narrow-eyed suspicion. What the hell?

I needed another glass of champagne before I could brave a conversation with him. I headed toward the kitchen, where I found a fresh glass, but no Jackson. Where was he? What right did he have to stay away, to hide from me? He should've at least had the balls to show up and give me my closure.

I stalked along the fronts of the offices, glancing inside each one. I wouldn't have put it past Jackson to have found some new coworker to seduce and to be making out in one of them, the dog.

Not that I cared. What Jackson Jones did wasn't my business anymore.

Since my breakdown at Tiannah's, I'd been my pre-Jackson, buttoned-up, professional self. But I'd learned a thing or two from working at Synergy, and I'd implemented a few stylistic changes. I accepted the happy hour invitations. I'd even gone to a fundraiser for the hospital I was working for. One of the administrators I'd met had a kid with ADHD, and we'd shared stories. We were going to lunch the following week.

I was warm. Friendly. And still professional.

Too bad I hadn't found that balance at Synergy. If I had, maybe I wouldn't have gotten my heart broken. I wouldn't be wandering the halls like some suit-wearing Miss Havisham, looking for lost love. *He'd* done that to me. *He'd* reduced me to this seething, champagne-clutching, tunnel-vision version of myself. I should've been enjoying myself at this swanky party, secretly patting myself on the back for my contributions to the project, chatting up other potential clients. Jackson had to be here somewhere, hands in his jeans pockets, rocking on the toes of those ridiculous boots, soaking up praise and adulation.

I glanced back toward the stairs and caught a glimpse of tousled, sandy-brown hair. Tyler. I strode that direction. He was going to tell me where Jackson was, and then I was going to get my damned closure.

———

JACKSON

"FUCK," I muttered when the error flashed again on my screen. Somehow, I'd managed to forget everything I knew about coding. That or, like Pavlov's dogs, I'd been conditioned to code when I smelled Earl Grey tea, and without it, I was lost.

Maybe I could ask Marlee to make me a cup to set on my desk, and it'd reset my brain so I could code again.

Like she'd read my mind, she tapped gently on the door. She never used to walk on eggshells around me. When I was bad-boy Jackson, she'd pushed and pulled me until I did the right thing. Most of the time. But even Marlee couldn't handle model-programmer Jackson, who showed up at my sixth-floor office at 8 A.M. to code, kept my head down, and went straight back to my lonely apartment when the cleaning staff arrived late at night.

And managed to produce nothing but crappy code.

It didn't matter so much. Cooper had assigned me a couple programmers to "clean me up." Their code, while clunky and unin-spired, at least functioned, error-free. It wasn't anything like the elegant program I'd produced with Alicia.

I'd never write code like that again.

Alicia. What was she doing right now? Probably kicking ass on her hospital project. And hating me.

"Jackson?" Marlee poked her head in.

"Yeah?" I peered at my screen. The error message hadn't gone anywhere.

"I brought you a sandwich. And a cookie." She held up a white bakery bag.

"Not hungry."

She set it on my desk. "You need to eat."

"I said I'm not hungry," I growled. I hadn't felt like eating since that last night with Alicia. The Adderall I was taking to help me focus on work probably wasn't helping.

"How about a walk? We can go to the park, and you can meditate."

I'd tried that, too, but I couldn't clear thoughts of Alicia out of my brain. "No."

"The fitness center, then. Exercise always makes you feel better."

"What the fuck, Marlee? Why are you trying to distract me?"

She made the mistake of glancing at my screen, the empty one with the time and date app in the corner. Four in the afternoon on December first.

December first. Two thousand miles away, the Austin office was hosting the launch party. For the product our team had produced. And they were doing it without me.

I should've been there. Except I didn't deserve it.

Was she there? Was she looking for me?

The night before that Wednesday morning I'd been supposed to meet her, after four hours of furious silence on the company jet, after another eight hours of all-hands-on-deck solving Weston's problem, Cooper had dropped me at my place. He'd knitted his eyebrows at me like he was worried. I guessed he'd expected me to rage at him, to argue. To sulk. To run.

I'd wanted to tear off my own skin while I was stuck in that conference room with Weston and our public relations team when I should've been back in Austin making plans for my date with Alicia. But I'd stayed. It was the right thing to do for my company. For Cooper, for Marlee, for everyone at headquarters and the entire team back in Austin. It was even the best thing for Alicia. If I could've told her what I was doing, she might've been proud. But I couldn't. Not a word of the offshoring fiasco could get out into the media. Weston had shut us up tighter than his own asshole.

While Alicia's testimonial hung in the balance, I didn't dare contact her. Her text sat on my phone, torturing me. It was what I deserved after nearly ruining her business.

So she thought I was a douchebag. I'd have let her down sooner or later anyway. And in the back of her mind, she knew it, too. She'd known not to trust me with Noah. Too bad she hadn't been so careful with herself.

Who was I to think I could be a man and step up as a parent to Noah? I couldn't even keep my own shit together.

The next day, I'd blocked her number and then deleted it from my phone to avoid the temptation to call her back. And then I'd stomped down to the dumpster and tossed in the useless hunk of technology. It'd landed with a gratifying smash against the metal bottom. What the fuck did I need a phone for? I'd be a drone, shuttling back and forth between the office and my apartment. No temptations. No social life, no friends. No illusions I could be more.

Still, I couldn't keep from torturing myself.

On my computer, I opened a browser window and pulled up a social media site.

"Jackson, don't," Marlee said, flexing her fingers like she'd stop me. "Please."

"Did he ask you to keep me away from it?" I searched for the #SynergyLaunch hashtag. Photos of the familiar Austin office flooded the screen. People drinking champagne. Kevin and Amit at the buffet table. I almost smiled. I missed those guys. Upstairs, a group of posed employees, beaming.

"He said it'd only upset you."

I barked out a bitter laugh. "Upset me?" How the fuck could I be more upset than I already was?

I scrolled through a photo of Cooper standing near our old work area with some suit. Cooper with some grinning employees. Same employees, no Cooper, though I spotted him in the background, scowling at—

I zoomed in. A hand, clutching a glass of champagne. Most of her was out of frame, and her face was obscured by an outflung elbow.

But I'd know that hand anywhere. Long and pale. I'd watched those slender fingers fly silently over her keyboard for weeks.

I scrolled through more photos. There she was again, in the background of a photo of the IT team. She had her hand on someone's arm. Tyler's. His face was blurry, but his tousled hair was the same as it'd been at the party at my place. A few photos later, I spotted them behind the glass of a conference room wall. They were out of focus in the background of another picture, but I knew the curve of her hip. The hip she'd revealed to me when she'd dropped her skirt. The hip I'd caressed, reverently, while I'd coated myself in her essence. The hip I'd cradled after she'd shown me what lay behind her shield, after she'd fallen apart.

In the foreground, Cooper smiled. Like he'd toiled for months in Austin's summer heat to build the fucking software. Like he hadn't swooped in at the end and shredded the first happiness I'd found in a long time. Like he hadn't forced me to act like all the other men in her life and disappoint the best woman I'd ever known. Like he didn't fucking care. Some partner he'd been.

"Jackson?" I'd almost forgotten Marlee was still there. "What happened in Austin? And why is there a chunk of ice wrapped in a sock in the employee freezer?"

"He didn't tell you how I fucked everything up? Again?"

A line formed between her delicate eyebrows. "It's not fucked up. Look how happy everyone is. Customers are lining up to buy the new version."

I clicked on the photo of Alicia with Tyler. Zoomed in until it was so pixelated I couldn't resolve her features. But I remembered. I remembered the slope of her nose. The perfect curve of her barely-there blond eyebrows. Her eyes so blue and deep I could have drowned in them. The trusting, hopeful smile she gave me when I'd promised to text her.

"Her." I jabbed my finger at the screen. "She's the reason the project was successful. That everyone is so happy. That I was happy for a while." I tried to swallow, but my throat closed.

Marlee dragged one of my guest chairs around to my side of the desk and plopped down into it. "Tell me."

And I did. I let it all go. The good parts and the bad. And then the worst part where I let her down exactly like she'd expected.

When I finished, Marlee squinted at me. "And why are you like this?"

"Like what?"

Her lip curled. "Here, acting like a robot, and not at a race in Brazil or on a sailboat in the Mediterranean or surrounded by women in a hot tub at a ski chalet. You know, doing what you always do when you fuck something up."

I blinked. "I—I thought about it. But I guess I'm not that guy anymore."

Her eyes widened. "She did this. She changed you. Like in the novel I'm reading!"

She ran out of my office and returned with a battered paperback. On the cover was a bare-chested guy in a kilt. She waved it at me. "She completes you. And that makes you a better man." She sighed and closed her eyes for a minute.

"So fucking what," I snarled. "Did the dude in that book also happen to punch his love interest right where she was already hurting? I can't hit control-Z on this and undo it."

Marlee sat up. "No, you can't. But you can make it right. You have to grovel. And then, *then* you'll live happily ever after." Her lips curled up in a smile, and her eyes went soft.

"No!" The word shot out of me like a Formula One car at the starting grid. "How long could we make it work? Two weeks? A month? And then I'd fuck it up like I do everything else. I can't do that to her."

"Why not, Jackson?" she asked. "She wanted to try."

"Because I care about her too much. Because I love her." I turned away from the screen and stared out my window at the ugly building across the street.

"She loves you, too."

"You don't know that."

"I do know that. She's a smart woman. She wouldn't have jeopardized her testimonial for you if she didn't love you."

"She'll get over it." I never would, though. My own heart was shattered in pieces like my goddamn phone.

"Jackson Jones." When she stood, the chair legs screeched across the wood floor. "I put up with a lot of your shit, but I will not put up with this. It's time for you to stop hiding behind that I-don't-give-a-fuck veneer. I know showing you care about something is hard. It opens you up to ridicule. And heartbreak. But if you care about Alicia, you need to man up. Believe in yourself. Believe that together, you can be stronger."

In Austin, Alicia and I had been a team. We'd accomplished more together than we ever could have separately. But that'd been for only two months. Could we sustain it for longer, for—I gulped—forever? Because that's what Alicia deserved. What she needed.

"She has a kid, you know. He's ten. I don't know anything about kids."

"You practically raised Sam from the time she was only a little older than that. She turned out great. I think you're smart enough to figure it out."

Sam had never fit into Mother's expectations, either, not like Andrew and Natalie had. So I'd spent a lot of time with her. Taught her to code. Maybe I could do the same for Noah. It'd be a start.

"You really think I could be a—a dad?"

Marlee smiled. "I bet Alicia's got the parenting part covered. Aim for big-brotherly role model. At least to start."

A tiny seed sprouted in my brain. *Big brotherly role model.* "Marlee, I need your help."

She pulled out her phone. "Do you want the jet, or do you want to fly commercial to Austin?"

"No." I laid my hand over hers, stilling her fingers on her phone. "I need an appointment with my financial adviser. Like, now. And I need a list of charitable foundations that help kids. Preferably neuro-divergent kids. And if they use computers or coding to do it, even better."

Marlee's mouth went flat and exasperated again. "Jackson, she doesn't need you to prove you're worthy by giving away a ton of cash. She only needs you."

"I need to prove I'm worthy. To myself. Before I can ask her to take me back."

She shook her head. "Always the hard way with you."

I lifted one corner of my mouth. "You wouldn't want it any other way."

Finally, I earned her smile. "No, boss, I wouldn't." She sank back into the chair. Her fingers flew over her phone screen.

"Thanks, Marlee. For everything." I'd have hugged her, but I didn't want to interrupt her research.

"You can thank me by groveling to Alicia until she takes you back and then bringing her here to San Francisco. I want to meet this woman who's changed you."

"You'll love her. I do." I had a fuck-ton of work to do before I could achieve the goal Marlee had summed up for me. But like Alicia had taught me to do, I'd break it up into tasks and knock them down one by one. Though I didn't think she'd be impressed by a win-Alicia-back task board. I'd keep that quiet and focus on the grand gesture Marlee was always talking about in her romance novels.

Marlee looked up, her eyes sparkling. "We need a code name for this project."

"Don't you think that's a little—"

She tapped a finger against her lips. "In most of the movies, the hero has to serenade the heroine to win her back. You don't sing, so you could always do a *Say Anything* with a boombox. We could call it—"

"No singing. No boombox. And we'll call it Project Cowboy Up."

She grinned. "Sounds good, boss. Your financial planner will meet you here in an hour."

"I've got to run to my place first. For my boots."

"Your—"

"Boots." I'd committed to the fucking boots. It wasn't the same as what I was going to do with Alicia, but they'd remind me of what she'd taught me and of how I was going to live the rest of my life.

"Got it, boss. Project Cowboy Up is going to be one for the books."

I didn't care about books. Or movies. Only Alicia and whether I could get her back.

———

ALICIA

"YOU *WHAT?*"

Tyler hunched and shoved his hands into his pockets. He glanced at the closed door of the small conference room I'd dragged him into like he was considering a jailbreak. "Cooper was asking where you two were, and I said you'd probably rather celebrate alone. It was an offhand comment. I didn't know it was a secret. I thought he knew. I thought everyone knew."

"It wasn't a secret," I said through gritted teeth, "because there was nothing to tell. Jackson and I weren't a couple."

"But I—but you kissed. At the party at Jay's place."

Heat rushed to my cheeks. "Okay, we did that. I didn't realize you saw us. Or that you'd remember. But it didn't mean we were together." I thought back to that Monday night in Jackson's apartment, when I'd hoped we could start something real, if only for a while. But he hadn't wanted even that.

"God, I'm sorry. Really. Do you know where he is? I've been dying to apologize."

"He's not here?"

Tyler's forehead wrinkled. "Not since the day after the project ended. He came in to apologize to the team for creating a hostile work environment. And now he doesn't pick up when I call, and he doesn't text back. Do you think he hates me? Because—" He ducked his head. "I got a promotion. And a transfer to San Francisco. I'm going to work in his department. And it'll suck if he hates me."

"No, Tyler. He thinks you're a great guy. And congratulations on the new job." I reached out a hand to lay it on his shoulder but froze. The blinds to the room were open, and I didn't want anyone to see me —the office's scarlet woman, apparently—touching him. A hostile work environment? Maybe a couple of our glances had lingered too long. Maybe our kisses—outside work and in places we thought no one could see us—threatened Tyler and the rest of the team. We hadn't been as circumspect as I'd thought. If only they knew the rest of it. Jackson and I had barely waited for my company access credentials to be deleted from the system before we'd fallen into bed together. My face burned.

And yet, Cooper had given me the testimonial I needed, despite behavior he clearly saw as unprofessional. Why? I needed to find him. I'd thank him for the valuable words. And I'd apologize if I needed to.

"Have you seen him tonight?" I peered out the room's tiny window.

"Who?"

"Cooper."

"Yeah. He's around somewhere. I was going to ask him about Jay."

"Do you mind if I talk to him first?"

"Go ahead. I'm really sorry I said anything."

"Don't worry. It'll be fine." I opened the door and strode toward the stairs. Would it be fine? Or would Cooper tell anyone who called for a reference that I'd engaged in an improper relationship with a coworker? I supposed I'd know if I showed up to my next gig and they were all wearing chastity belts.

I spotted his dark blond hair, rising above the rest, downstairs. Keeping my gaze locked on him, I descended and made my way to where he was standing, talking to a group of people. Executives, from the quality of their clothes. I fidgeted with my own skirt, making sure it covered my knees. I wished I'd worn pants.

Cooper's gaze connected with mine. He winced. Not good.

I hovered outside the circle until, eventually, he excused himself and stood in front of me.

"Ms. Weber. How's business?" He shook my hand, his fingers icy.

"Doing well, thanks. I'm on a project with a local hospital right now. Thank you again for the kind testimonial. I posted it to my website, and it's been a help in bringing in business."

"I'm glad. Could we speak for a minute?" He tilted his head toward the small conference room next to the security desk.

I nodded and followed him.

When the door closed, he said, "I should have reached out to you earlier, but we had something of an emergency at headquarters. I'd like to apologize for Jackson's behavior. We don't condone sexual harassment, and he's being disciplined."

I blinked. "Sexual harassment?"

"He said you resisted his advances on multiple occasions, including the day the project ended. I appreciate your discretion and hope the testimonial I gave will smooth over any unpleasant feelings he engendered."

What. The. Hell? What had Jackson done?

"He told you I refused him. That what Tyler said he saw was nonconsensual."

He held out his hands, palms up. "Jackson's always honest with me."

I barely contained a snort. Jackson's entire persona was a lie. I supposed Cooper knew Jackson used many layers of nonchalant, reckless swagger to hide his soft, squishy, caring self. But now I knew something Cooper didn't.

If I were a different person, I'd take advantage of the fear in Cooper's eyes that told me he'd settle out of court for a sum that'd make my family and me comfortable for many years. Private-school tuition for Noah. A nice nest egg for college and retirement.

But that wasn't who I was.

"Mr. Fallon, Jackson hasn't been completely honest with you about the nature of our relationship. It was consensual. Jackson didn't do anything wrong."

"Are you telling me you, a consultant, had an affair with your client?" His jaw had turned to stone.

Oh, shit.

I wished I could cool my burning cheeks with my cold hands. "Not exactly. Our relationship was almost completely platonic during the project." Except for the kissing. I bit my lip.

"Unfortunately, it didn't have the appearance of a platonic relationship. Others on the team noticed."

"I know, but—"

"You may not realize this"—his eyes were like ice chips—"but this isn't Jackson's first...office indiscretion. And it likely won't be his last."

Wow. My eyes bulged, and I wouldn't have been surprised if they'd rolled out of their sockets and onto the industrial carpet. I guess you had to have balls of steel and icewater in your veins to grow a company from your dorm room to a multinational juggernaut.

"Jackson has returned to headquarters. I'd advise you to forget about whatever happened here in Austin. Since you confessed to reciprocating his...advances, I don't think Synergy owes you anything further. In the future, Ms. Weber, think carefully before you get involved with your clients' personnel. Not everyone will be as understanding as I am."

He turned on the heel of his Italian loafer. He had one hand on the door handle when I said, in a voice as sweet as Esmy's tea, "I don't think I have much use for your understanding, Mr. Fallon."

He froze and turned. His wide eyes told me not a lot of people spoke to him the way I had.

"Jackson Jones is an excellent programmer and an underutilized asset to this company. Someday he's going to figure out exactly how much he's worth and how little you deserve not only his partnership but also his friendship." I propped my hands on my hips and stared up at him, pretending I was six-foot-something and could actually look down my nose at him.

He glared at me for ten of my racing heartbeats. Then he yanked open the door and stormed out, leaving me gasping in his wake.

"Fuck you, Cooper Fallon," I muttered. It made me feel a little better. I'd done all I could: I'd stood up for the man who'd stood up for me. Who'd lied to protect me.

But I hadn't asked him to do that. I'd asked him to stay. And he hadn't.

Grinding my teeth, I glared at the phone on the conference table. I wanted to call him. Yell at him. But he wouldn't answer. He hadn't answered any of my calls. Maybe he was depressed. Or angry.

My hands shook. Well, fuck him. I was angry, too. Mostly at Cooper and his high-handed assholery. But also with Jackson. Who was he to decide what was best for me, to take the fall himself for something I'd wholeheartedly agreed to? And then to run away without a word, like a ghosting douchebag?

Just like my dad. Like Noah's dad. Taking the easy way out when life got hard.

Guess what? There was nothing easy about my life. And there was no room in it for someone who couldn't be bothered to stay.

32

JACKSON

"IT LOOKS GOOD." Cooper set the tablet on my desk and leaned back in my guest chair.

"You think it'll work?" I leaned my elbows on the desk.

"Are you asking if I think it's a viable plan for a foundation, or..."

"Yes." I didn't want to hear his *or*. "Will it achieve my goals of helping neurodivergent kids?"

"I think so. It's a lot of cash. You'll need someone to step up and manage it."

"I've got more cash than I could ever spend. But who can I get to manage it?"

He shrugged. "You could hire a search firm. They'd find you someone qualified."

"I need someone I can trust. Do you think..." My mouth dried up before I could say her name.

"She's a programmer, not a nonprofit executive director."

"She's a great manager. She can do anything she wants to."

His eyebrows bunched together. "Are you doing this to help kids or to get Alicia back?" His lips twisted when he said her name. He was on board with the foundation, less so with Alicia, even though he'd told me she'd told him the truth at the launch party. Which was weird because my two favorite Type-As should've gotten along great.

"I'm doing it to help kids." Though if I impressed Alicia, that'd be good, too.

"Then get yourself a qualified director."

I sighed and glanced toward the window at the rain pouring down and obscuring the building across the street. It hardly ever rained when I was in Austin. I wished I were there right then, breathing the same clean, dry air as she was.

Soon.

"I'm proud of you, Jay."

I swiveled my head so quickly my neck cracked. "What?"

"You heard me. Not only the project in Austin, but this foundation of yours. You really have grown."

"Thanks." I wished I had some papers to shuffle or a hard drive to take apart, but Marlee had cleaned my desk while I was in Austin. There was nothing to hide me from the intensity of his laser gaze.

"And you deserve...love. Hers, if that's what you want." He flicked invisible lint off his dress pants.

"Really?" We never talked about this shit.

He looked tired. He had wrinkles under his eyes and shadows I'd never noticed before. I'd just opened my mouth to ask about it when the voice of the person I hated most carried into the office.

"Oh, I'm sorry, I thought this was a meeting of company executives, not an episode of *Gossip Girl.*" Our CEO, Harris Weston, sauntered into my office. Hadn't the door been closed before?

Fuck, how much had he heard? Enough, if I correctly interpreted the knowing glint in those beady eyes. My feelings for Alicia were private. My best friends, Cooper and Marlee, knew about them, but they weren't for Weston to collect in his hoard of secrets, for his manicured hands to paw through and use to his own advantage.

I stood so fast the chair spun out behind me and collided with the credenza. "What do you want, Weston?"

He glanced down at his Patek Philippe wristwatch. "I thought we had an appointment, Jones."

Fuck, we did. Why hadn't Marlee warned me it was time? Weston had probably called her off to distract her, and without a phone, I couldn't get her SOS texts.

Cooper stood. "I'll leave you to it, then. Unless you need me, too?"

I had to give him credit. Cooper didn't share my loathing of Weston, and he usually tried to act as a buffer between us.

"No, thank you, Fallon. I'm checking in with Jones here, now that he's returned from—" He coughed, and I couldn't tell whether he'd said *Austin* or *exile*.

With one last, steadying nod, Cooper walked out and shut the door.

Weston ignored my guest chair and, with his typical reptilian smoothness, eased into one of the wing chairs in my seating area. He held out a hand to the neighboring chaise. Fucker was telling me where to sit in my own office.

I stomped over and sat in the wing chair across the coffee table from his. I crossed my arms. "What do you need, Weston? Marlee already submitted my project report."

"Thank you for that." He smoothed down his beard, which had gone mostly gray with a few brown threads in an inverse ratio to his hair. "But I came to speak with you about something more...personal."

Heat rose from my chest up my neck. Had Cooper told him about Alicia? If he was going to try to use her against me—Alicia, the best person I'd ever met—

"I understand you're about to sink a significant amount of your fortune into a foundation. What a worthy effort."

I blinked, knocked on my ass. Was that a compliment? "Thank you?"

He nodded, a king granting a boon. "As you know, I support many worthy causes. Once your foundation is ready to receive donations, I'll happily write you a check. Would ten million be acceptable?"

I couldn't help it; my eyes bugged. Not even Cooper, not even my mother, had offered that much. I felt like George Bailey in *It's a Wonderful Life*, sitting in the low chair while Mr. Potter offered me twenty thousand a year. I wished I could've done what George did and toss it away. I didn't want Weston's oily hands in my foundation, but that money would help a lot of kids.

I swallowed. "Yes, thank you."

"I'm happy to help." He spread his hands in a wide, generous gesture. Then he leaned forward. "I also understand you've met someone. Someone who requires a little more"—he chuckled—"wooing."

I stiffened. How the fuck did he know that?

"As someone with a little experience in that area"—he chuckled again, an attempt at self-deprecation, since everyone knew he had a couple of ex-wives dripping in diamonds—"I can tell you, wives and girlfriends aren't inexpensive. Like one of your fine automobiles, they require maintenance to keep them purring."

Was Alicia like that? Did she want diamonds and mansions? Racing thoroughbreds, like one of Weston's ex-wives owned? She was from Texas, too, I remembered.

"Between setting up your foundation and bestowing gifts on this deserving young woman, you might feel a bit strapped for cash."

I pursed my lips. He was right; I'd planned to donate most of my liquid assets to give the foundation a healthy start. I hadn't even thought about buying Alicia jewelry or a big house or even a fancy car. I'd assumed, once I'd proved myself worthy, she'd just want… me. Was that naïve?

"I can help you." Weston leaned back in his chair. "You own a significant number of Synergy stock shares. I'd be happy to take them off your hands at market price. For safekeeping."

Fuck. Like Potter, he'd wrapped me up like a cobra and tried to hypnotize me. This wasn't about helping me or the foundation. It was a stock grab.

Between Cooper and me, we held fifty-one percent of the shares, enough to keep control of our company. We'd promised each other to hold onto it no matter what. No one could take away what we'd built together.

I jumped to my feet. "I'm not interested in giving up my stake in Synergy."

Weston stood and shrugged. "I'm trying to help. Regardless, my donation offer still stands."

He sauntered to the door and paused, his hand on the knob. "Let me know if you change your mind. After…everything, you might need a gift to smooth things over with your paramour."

The asshole closed the door, leaving me hollowed-out. How did he know how badly I'd fucked things up with Alicia?

But he didn't know Alicia. If she wouldn't take me back for me, no amount of diamonds or horses or private-school education for Noah would convince her. I had to strip all that away and prove to her something immensely more difficult: that I was the kind of man she could depend on. One she could trust to be in it for the long term. For her and for Noah.

And after I'd fucked everything up so badly, I had no idea how to do it.

But I was going to try.

33

JACKSON

I HAD zero experience with groveling.

Every other relationship I'd had—and I'm using the term *relationship* loosely here—I'd fucked up somehow, either intentionally, like by taking off in the middle of the night without leaving a note, or unintentionally, like the time I'd called a woman Caroline instead of Catherine. While she had my dick in her mouth. Ouch.

But each time, I'd shrugged and moved on. I'd never cared enough to want to fix things.

Okay, I'm not proud, but that was Old Jackson.

New Jackson didn't want to fuck this up.

And that meant I needed to learn how to grovel, fast.

Marlee, clutching her stack of romance novels, had tried to coach me every day for the past week. She'd said things about admitting fault and being vulnerable and expressing my feelings. She'd mentioned a spectacular entrance, gifts, sweeping her off her feet— and I got the weird feeling she meant literally.

Cooper had no advice for me. He'd stared out the window in the car on the way to the airport and in the jet all the way to Texas. It didn't bother me. We never talked about feelings.

His silence had given me time to work through a few dozen emails. Setting up a foundation was fucking hard. Who knew you couldn't do it in three weeks? Once I got someone on board to lead the foundation, we could set up some camps. Until then, we'd funnel the cash to organizations that helped kids with ADHD, dyslexia, autism, Tourette's, and OCD. I was sure I'd discover other causes related to neurodivergence, too.

We split up at the airport. Cooper headed for the office's holiday party, and I went straight to Cherrywood.

The clouds hung low over the Webers' yellow house that afternoon. They weren't green like they'd been the day I'd met Alicia outside the Synergy office, but the bottoms were dark and heavy. It'd be fitting if Austin decided to unleash some fresh meteorological hell on me.

My mission was too important to be deterred by hail or tornadoes or raining bats. I squared my shoulders and strode up the Webers' front walk clutching a bouquet of grocery-store flowers. Give me a little credit; they were from the fancy organic grocery store I'd passed on the way from the airport.

I knocked on the purple door.

The porchlight turned on, then the door opened. Alicia's mother, Diane, leaned in the doorway in a pair of jeans and a striped sweater. She squinted at me through the screen. "What are *you* doing here?"

So much for Southern hospitality. Not that I deserved it. "Good afternoon, Ms. Weber. Is Alicia here?"

She crossed her arms. "No, she's at work."

Silence stretched between us. "Do you know when she'll be home?"

"I don't know that that's any of your business, Mr. Jones. She said things didn't end so well between you two."

End? I gulped. But of course no one thought I'd come back. "No, and that's my fault. I'm here to apologize. Mind if I come in?"

"I don't think so, Mr. Jones. I think you've hurt my daughter enough. You can wait in your car. Or, even better, I'll tell her you stopped by, and she can call you if she wants to speak to you."

She closed the door, leaving me staring at purple paint. Shit, I should've brought wine or chocolates to ease my way into the Weber household.

"I guess I'll wait," I muttered. I plunked myself down on the top porch step and stared out into the street like she'd be arriving at any moment. I laid the flowers next to me and shoved my hands in my pockets. A raindrop splatted on the toe of my boot.

The trees were bare now, their twisted limbs curling up into the darkening sky. Coolness seeped through my jeans from the wood floorboards of the porch, making me shiver. A few more raindrops pattered down, and I tucked my boots closer under the porch. Suffering had to be part of groveling, right? It had been my frenemy since I'd left Austin over a month ago.

The front door groaned open again, and this time the screen door swung out. Slow footsteps approached.

"Want some coffee?"

I smelled it at the same time he said it, and the scent of the brew made my spine straighten. "Yes, please."

Noah handed me a mug. He held another mug in his other hand, hot chocolate from the smell of it. He sat beside me.

I smiled. One member of the Weber household didn't hate me. "It's pretty cold out here, buddy. And wet. You going to be okay?"

He snorted. "You going to be okay? Seems like I can go back in the house whenever I want while you're stuck out here in the rain like a loser, waiting for Alicia to come kick your ass."

Oh. So it was going to be like that.

I looked down into my mug of coffee and sniffed it. Could you smell rat poison? I set it aside. "How's school going?"

He shrugged. "It's okay. I'm in Ms. Fraser's class now. And I'm taking some medicine to help me pay attention in class."

"Is it working?"

"Maybe. I got an A on my math test last week."

"That's great. And the other kids are leaving you alone? No more shiners?"

"Nah. The school counselor did a lesson on treating others with respect. And Alicia made me practice using my words." He sipped his cocoa. "Seems like you should've used some words, too."

"I guess she told you what I did."

"She didn't have to. First you came around here, saying you'd take me to the racetrack. Help me with homework. Teach me how to throw a punch. Then you were gone. Alicia said you went back to

California. And she got this look on her face when I asked about you." He wrinkled his nose and pursed his lips like he'd sucked on a lemon. "Like that."

"I guess when you look at it like that... No. Any way you look at it, I'm an asshole."

"Yep. So. What are you doing here?"

"I came to grovel."

"What's that?"

"I'm going to apologize for what I did. Tell her I love her. And ask her to take me back. Think it'll work?"

He ran his gaze over me. The collared shirt. The flowers. The flashy but worn-in boots. "I don't know. You don't seem like the other guys she's dated."

I ducked my head. "She's dated a lot of guys, huh?" A fantastic woman like Alicia had to have a line of guys waiting to date her.

"Not a lot. Some. My friend Palmer's dad, Rick. He wears a tie to work. Took her out to dinner and stuff. Took all four of us out for hamburgers and ice cream once. You ever take her out?"

"Not—not exactly." She'd taken me to see the bats that night. Then I'd blown the opportunity to take her out and show her I cared.

He squinted one eye at me. "I don't think your chances are too good, then."

"I brought flowers." I held them up. One of the big chrysanthemums drooped.

He curled his lip. "Did she say she likes flowers?"

"I—I didn't ask." Marlee liked flowers. She squeed whenever I sent them for Administrative Professionals' Day. And she wore floral prints all the time. But I'd never seen Alicia in a print at all. Only solid colors. None of them particularly flower-like. Crap.

"Know what she likes?"

"What?" I'd run out and get it. I had time.

"Dudes who aren't assholes."

"Oh." I slouched. He was right. What the fuck was I doing there, freezing my ass off on her porch?

He slurped the last of his hot chocolate. "I'm going in to get warm. If I don't see you again, bye."

I gave him a half-smile. "Bye, Noah. But I'm staying until she gets here."

He shrugged. "Suit yourself."

The screen door slammed behind him. A light flared above me—Christmas lights. The old-fashioned multicolored strand ran across the eaves of the porch in a straight line. Alicia's work, I guessed. Lights flicked to life in the pair of trees growing closest to the house. Those were pink, blue, and purple, and their haphazard pattern hinted at another family member's effort.

A car pulled up under the carport across the street. A man got out and squinted at me before he turned and walked into the house. A minute later, a phone rang inside Alicia's house, but I couldn't hear the person who answered. The rain had picked up into a roaring downpour that splashed my boots and the bottoms of my jeans. I tucked myself further under the porch's overhang.

A meow came from behind me, and a fat orange tabby cat wearing a blue collar squeezed through the flap in the door. Was this the same cat who'd hissed at me the night I'd had dinner here? What was his name?

He tiptoed around me, sniffed the wilted bouquet, and plunked himself down on the porch, an arm's length away. He meowed again. I stretched out my arm and let him sniff my hand before I stroked him between the ears. He closed his eyes, and I glanced at the tag on his collar. Tigger. Yes, he was Alicia's cat.

"You don't hate me, do you, big guy? You know I'm here to try to make it up to her, right?"

He meowed and rubbed the side of his face against my hand.

"Yeah, we're pals. You'll vouch for me. Tell them I'm not a complete asshole. And then we'll be best friends. I'll bring you tuna treats."

He stopped rubbing my hand. His eyelids burst open, my only warning before he nipped my forefinger.

"Ow!" I snatched my hand back. "Not a fan of tuna, huh?"

He turned around, swished his tail at me, and bounded through the cat door with a snap.

Two drops of blood welled up on my knuckle. "Tough crowd." I stuck my knuckle in my mouth.

A few pickup trucks and a delivery van rumbled past. I checked my watch. It was after five. Maybe Alicia would come home soon. I should plan what I wanted to say.

I leaned back on my elbows and stared up at the ceiling. It was painted a comforting robin's-egg blue. Maybe someday I could have a front porch with a blue ceiling. Alicia and I could sit in the porch swing—

The screen door slammed shut again. Noah stomped out, but instead of sitting beside me, he leaned against the post. "Still here, huh?"

"Yeah."

"I brought you a sweatshirt. It's Alicia's, but it's pretty big." He held out a gray hoodie with an orange longhorn symbol above the kangaroo pocket.

"Thanks." I took it from him and wrestled it on. Maybe it was big for Alicia, but it fit snugly on me. Instantly warmer, I breathed in Alicia's familiar, clean smell.

He bounded back through the door, and I settled in to wait.

Close to an hour later, Alicia's Honda rolled down the street. I didn't know right away it was Alicia's—she drove the world's most nondescript car—but I hoped. And when it turned up the driveway, I knew my gut hadn't misled me.

I stood, wincing at the aches that rocketed through my muscles. My ass tingled as the blood flow resumed. The car door opened, and a black umbrella poked out. The car door closed, and the umbrella made brisk progress along the walk and up the porch stairs. Then it tilted back, and when she saw me, her face blanched.

Alicia wore black slacks and boots—city ones, not western ones like mine. Her raincoat hung open, showing a light-blue blouse with a few rain splotches on it. Her hair was swept back from her face in the bun she always wore at work. Her makeup did a poor job of covering the purple smudges under her eyes, and her lipstick had worn off, leaving her lips pale. I wanted to kiss the tremble out of them, to fold her in my arms, wet coat and all, and warm her up. Undress her slowly and put her in the shower. Tuck her into bed where she could sleep off the week. Hold her close until the shadows faded from her eyes.

But I'd hurt her. If I was the reason she was exhausted and miserable, I didn't have the right to do any of that. Not yet. Maybe never.

I took a step toward her, my hands dangling, useless, at my sides. "Hi, Alicia."

Her lips tightened. "Why are you here, Jackson?"

I tried to flash her a winning smile. Not too much. Friendly, but not too snake-oil-salesman. But my face was chilled, and I managed only a grimace. "To apologize. I left Austin without saying good-bye. I didn't text you back or call to explain. For all that, I'm sorry."

"Why'd you do it? Why'd you leave?" She leaned the umbrella against one of the porch posts and crossed her arms.

"Partly because—well, I can't tell you about it or Cooper will have my nuts. But mostly because I wasn't ready. I wasn't good enough for you, and I didn't want to ruin your business or—or your life." I gestured behind me at the purple door. "But, you see, I've taken some steps to change. I've set up—"

She stopped me, mid-reach for the foundation charter in my pocket.

"I didn't want you to change. I wanted you just the way you were, here in Austin. The man I—I fell for."

My heart revved like a racecar at the starting line. "But I had to change. For me. I had to feel worthy myself before I could try to convince you I deserved another chance." I poured all the hope, all the love I had into the gaze I locked onto her. *Give me another chance.*

Her lips thinned. "It's too late."

"Too late?" Marlee hadn't told me a grovel could come too late. She said the heroine always forgave the hero.

"I can't do this." She looked away, an unshed tear sparkling green in the Christmas lights.

"You can't do forever with me? Because that's what I want." Fuck, I should've bought her a ring. Even Marlee said it was too much, too fast. But I wanted to give her the happily ever after part, and didn't that always come with a wedding?

"Forever?" She laughed, bitter, and when the tear rolled down her cheek, she swiped it away like she was angry at it, too. "We both know I was only one of your flings. You were in it for the chase, nothing more. Well, you caught me. And, like a fool, I fell for it. I fell for you. I thought I was in love. But now I know better. And I won't make that mistake again." She took a step toward the door.

My heart pounded. She loved me. Or she had, once. I touched her arm. "Alicia, I love you, too. Give me another chance. I'll prove I've changed."

She looked at me then, her blue eyes glistening. "I can't. You'd better do what you do best and leave." Then she yanked open the screen door, pushed through the purple door, and was gone.

The rain roared like the static in my brain.

She'd said no.

Actually…I replayed her words to me. She said she couldn't. Similar, but not exactly the same. She'd told me she loved me. Past tense. And then she'd told me to leave.

Oh. I sank down again on the top step where the downpour soaked my knees and the toes of my boots.

She didn't trust me not to leave again. Like her father. Like Noah's dad. I'd made three of a kind with those dickwads.

The foundation didn't mean anything to her. Neither did my coming to see her. The only thing that'd prove I was different was to stay.

So I'd fucking stay.

34

JACKSON

AS IT TURNS OUT, there's a fine line between showing persistence to the woman you love and being a stalker. And not only would being a pest not win me any points with Alicia, winding up with a restraining order or in jail wouldn't prove anything.

So I brought them breakfast. And then I left. Every day.

The first day, a Saturday a week before Christmas, Noah answered the door. The cat, Tigger, stood at his feet. They both squinted at me through the screen. "I thought she told you to go away."

I winced. "She told you?"

"Nah. We were all listening in the dining room. Alicia went straight to her room after and didn't come out." He squinted at me. "So why are you back?"

I smiled at the kid, even though I wanted to crumple. She'd spent the night away from her family? I hated myself for hurting her again.

"Breakfast." I handed him the drink carrier—two coffees, a hot chocolate, and Earl Grey for Alicia—and the sack of pastries. I glanced behind him, but I couldn't see anyone but the cat. "I'll be back tomorrow. Let me know if you have any special requests."

Then I did the hard thing: I turned around and walked back down their porch steps. I got into my rental—a boring blue sedan this time

—and drove to the empty office, where I worked half the day on code and the other half answering emails about the foundation.

On Monday, I arrived even earlier so I could drop off breakfast before Alicia went to work. This time, Diane opened the door, wrapping a robe over her pajamas.

No good-morning, no thanks-for-the-bagels. "She doesn't want to see you."

"I understand." I handed over the drink carrier. "How do you take your coffee?"

She narrowed her eyes the same way her grandson had done. "Doesn't matter. You won't be back." She shut the door in my face.

But the next day, as I handed her a fragrant tray of cinnamon-spiked Mexican coffees and hot chocolate, plus Alicia's tea, she said, "Black. But Esmy takes cr—milk and sugar. Skim." Then she shut the door.

I grinned.

Friday—Christmas Eve—Esmy answered the door. "You came!" She took the tray of drinks and the bag of kolaches, plus a canister of liver-flavored cat treats, and set them on a table inside. Then she actually stepped out onto the porch to hug me. "Thanks for the cream. I haven't felt indulged like that in months. But you aren't spending the holiday with your family?"

I let my arms go around her back. Her hug was strong and soft at the same time. And until she'd touched me, I hadn't realized how starved I was for physical contact. Tyler—a hugger but still on my shit list—had taken the transfer to San Francisco. Cooper had gone home to spend the holiday with his mom, and the office had been a ghost town all week.

"No. I'd rather be here. Where she is. How is she?"

Esmy leaned back. "She's okay. Eating better. Though that might be because of the holiday foods. Do you want to come over tomorrow? We always make tamales for Christmas."

My heart leapt, and my mouth watered. "Does she want me there? Did she ask you to invite me?"

"Well…" She studied her slipper.

"I won't come in unless she wants me," I told her gently. "And please don't ask her to invite me. I'll wait as long as she needs me to."

Esmy pursed her lips. "My money's on you, mi querido."

"Wait, what? Are you guys betting on me?"

Grinning, she shut the door.

I spent Christmas alone in the extended-stay hotel. They had a sad little tree in the lobby. A few noisy families were staying at the other end of the floor, and children's feet pounded past my door in a race to the ice machine.

On the video call I made that afternoon, I had to put up with Mother's wrath about not being home and Sam's accusing glare. I sucked for abandoning her there with our perfect siblings. But I'd stay in Austin as long as Alicia needed. I'd promised her forever, and maybe that was how long it'd take.

But it wasn't all bad. After the call, I bit into one of the tamales from the paper sack Esmy had handed me that morning. I imagined the four of them sitting around their tree—would they have put it in the living room in front of the windows or right in the middle of the room?—opening gifts with Christmas music playing.

I wished I could've taken Esmy up on her offer to be there. I hadn't seen Alicia in over a week, and I wondered if she was better rested, if her skin had regained its glow. I didn't want her family to tell me she was okay; I was desperate to see it for myself.

But this wasn't about me or my desperation. It was about what Alicia needed. If she decided she didn't want me, if she told me to go away again, I'd hate it, but I'd do it. At least she'd know that she was worth staying for. She might never forgive me, but maybe I'd restore her faith in men, and she might not push away the right guy—the one who wouldn't fuck things up the way I had—when he came along.

I was crumpling up the bag when my phone rang. I leapt for it. Then I sighed. It wasn't her.

"Hey, Coop, what's up?"

"Don't sound so thrilled to talk to me. Merry Christmas."

"Merry Christmas. How's your mom?"

"Good. She made enough food for you, too. I guess I forgot to tell her you weren't coming."

"Sorry, man. I'll call her tonight."

He gave a noncommittal hum. "So when are you coming back?"

My stomach tightened. "Don't know."

"I could really use some help here. I'm presenting to the board in early January, and I'd like you to join me."

"Really?" He hadn't asked me to do that in a few years. I hated getting up in front of the board, but having Cooper trust me enough to ask might make it worth it. Except— "I can't. I'm staying here for a while."

"How long? You could take a break from your sexfest to do some real work."

I let myself imagine it for a minute, what could've happened if Alicia had forgiven me. We could've slept together every night. If it weren't for the holiday, we could've spent a lazy weekend in bed. I'd be curled around her right now, breathing in her scent, letting her hair tickle my nose. I rubbed my hand across my chest. "I wish."

"You—what?"

"I'm still waiting for her to forgive me. To trust me. It's going to take some time."

"And you're sitting on your ass in Austin waiting for her to come around? That's the most ridiculous thing I've ever heard."

"You ever been in love, Coop?"

He was silent for a while. "Yeah."

Huh. I wondered who it'd been. Some girl in high school before I'd met him? Or a relationship I hadn't even noticed while I was self-ishly focused on my own problems? "So you understand why I'll wait as long as it takes."

"You can wait here in San Francisco."

"No. I need to stay here, prove to her she's worth staying for. Sorry, Coop. I'll do whatever I can to help you from out here. We can get on a video call tomorrow."

"You know you're being an idiot."

"Who said, 'We are all fools in love?'"

"Jane Austen. *Pride and Prejudice*. Freshman year literature. Though you only watched the movie."

"Right. Right." Maybe I'd watch it again, get some tips. Maybe Weston was right, and I needed a fancy mansion. It'd worked for Mr. Darcy. My apartment in San Francisco wasn't going to woo anyone, especially since I'd spent a month there losing my mind over Alicia and not caring about the mess. "Call me tomorrow. We'll work on your presentation then."

"Fine." That word carried the weight of others, but I didn't want to hear them.

"Remember, Coop, get your donation into my foundation by the end of the year. Marlee can tell you how."

"Fuck off." But there was no heat, only fondness in his tone.

"You know I'll bug you until you do."

"Looking forward to it. Night, Jay."

"Night."

In the middle of the next week, between Christmas and New Year's, I pulled up behind an idling, sporty black Lexus. A man sat inside, his head bent like he was looking at his phone. Was he an actual stalker?

Leaving the Webers' breakfast in the car, I walked slowly up to the driver's side window.

Rick, my former workout buddy, sat in the driver's seat, texting. He wasn't here to bother Alicia, was he? Or—my heart stuttered—at her invitation?

I tapped on the window.

Rick's head shot up, and when he saw it was me, his hand went to his clean-shaven jaw. He lowered his window halfway. "Jay."

"Rick. What are you doing here?"

"I'm picking up my kid. He slept over. I guess I know what you're doing." His lip curled.

"Oh, yeah? What's that?" I put my hands on my hips.

"It's no secret you fucked things up. You've been crawling here every day like a loser, trying to win her back. Pathetic," he sneered.

Blood pounded in my temple. "I don't have to explain myself to you."

"No, you don't. But when you drag your ass back to California, your tail between your legs, guess who's still going to be here?" He didn't wait for me to unclench my jaw. "That's right. Me."

A kid, bulkier than Noah and with Rick's green eyes, hopped down the porch stairs and ran to the passenger side of Rick's car. He tossed his backpack into the backseat and slid in behind it. "Alicia said thanks for the flowers."

She didn't like flowers. And yet she'd taken them from Rick. Fuck. Maybe he was right. Maybe he could outlast me. Maybe proving he was good with kids would win him points I could never hope to earn.

Rick smirked at me. "See you around, Jay. Maybe." He didn't wait for me to step back before he pulled forward.

I fetched the coffee and muffins from my car. Gritting my teeth, I carried them up the front sidewalk and braced myself for whichever hostile Weber would answer the door. Maybe I was making a fool of myself. Maybe I'd fail in the end. But for now, I'd keep trying and hope that Alicia would remember how good we'd been together, that she'd loved me once, and give me another chance.

Cooper's donation hit the foundation's account on New Year's Eve. Along with Weston's donation and several others, we had an excellent start, and I doubled the total with my own donation. I might've been the worst one-day boyfriend ever, but I was doing what I'd said I'd do for kids.

I toasted the new year with a local IPA and went to sleep.

On New Year's Day, I strode up Alicia's front walk with a sack of donuts and a new sense of purpose. I'd spend the day researching neurological studies and earmark a few scientists to ask to join my foundation's board. Then maybe I'd—

I froze on the bottom step. Alicia stood behind the screen door wearing another UT hoodie and a pair of soft-looking lounge pants. Her hair was down around her shoulders, and her face was makeup-free. Two spots of color bloomed high on her cheeks. She was beautiful.

"Come on inside." She rubbed her arms. "It's cold out there."

"Cold?"

She pushed open the screen door, and I bounded up the stairs and crowded into the foyer with her. She looked more delicate than I remembered, swallowed up by her oversized sweatshirt. Or maybe my brain had mixed up her physique with her strong spirit.

Standing there, the bitter-orange scent of her tea filling my nostrils, I was back in the Synergy communal kitchen the Monday after I'd kissed her the first time, desperate for more. I gripped the drink carrier and the paper bag to keep from touching her.

"Happy New Year." Her feet were bare, and she had to look up at me. Not like in the office, when her heels took her almost to my height. I wanted to drop everything and take her in my arms, kiss those pink lips, bury my fingers in her silky hair. The cardboard drink carrier trembled.

"You can set that in the kitchen." She nodded at the drinks and then turned to shut the purple door.

Something brushed against my ankles. I looked down, and the cat twined around my leg, looking up at me. He meowed. Good thing I was wearing jeans. When he attacked me, he'd only shred the denim. I braced. But then the little fucker purred.

"Good boy," I whispered.

He unwound from my leg and stalked toward the kitchen.

I followed him through the living room and past the tree. Ornament boxes lay on the carpet around it, and one side of the tree was bare.

I set the donuts and drinks on the round kitchen table and turned. Alicia stood on the threshold between the kitchen and the living room, the tree lights sparkling behind her in a halo. Was this real, or was I still sleeping? I dug my fingernails into my palms, but everything was numb.

If it was a dream, I didn't want to wake up.

————

ALICIA

HE WAS STARTING to scare me. I didn't think I'd ever seen him this quiet, not even when he was coding. "You haven't said a word. Are you all right?"

"I—" His voice came out hoarse, and he cleared his throat. "I didn't expect to see you. Maybe I got into an accident on the way here, and this is all a figment of my head trauma. I was afraid if I said anything, I'd wake up."

"The way you drive, it'd be no wonder." I smiled, but he didn't. He only stared like he was trying to consume me with his eyes. My cheeks burned. "I sent everyone out to breakfast and a movie. I figured it was time for us to talk." I crossed the threshold into the kitchen and pulled out my chair.

He set a cup in front of me and sat in Noah's chair, shoving his hands between his knees. His face had gone a little gray. "Talk?"

I lifted off the lid and sniffed. Earl Grey. He'd gotten it right every time. "I can't believe you noticed my favorite kind of tea. The first day, I thought it was a coincidence. But you brought it every day."

"You drank it every morning in the office. Except that one day I pissed you off by finishing our module on my own. You drank something sweet that day. But Earl Grey every day after. I'll never—" He gulped and shut his mouth.

"It was kind of you to bring us breakfast. The pastries earned you points with Noah. He doesn't usually get sweets in the morning." He'd gotten so jittery I'd made him drink a giant glass of water and then jog around the block.

"Oh." He winced. "Did I fuck up?"

"No, it's the holidays. A few extra treats are okay. But why did you do it? Guilty conscience?"

"I—I wanted to see you. Know that you were all right. I let you down. And I'm sorry. I wish I could go back and—but I can't. This was the only way I could think of to show you that you deserve someone who stays. I was a brainless ass to leave in the first place and let you think anything else. But I won't leave you again. I mean, unless you tell me to go. I'm not a stalker."

Each cup of tea, each kolache or bagel, was a stone rolled away from the fortress around my heart. After a week, I couldn't stir up enough anger at him to scowl at the arrangement of breakfast foods Esmy laid out on a platter. And after two weeks of showing up, of putting up with Mom's forbidding silence and Noah's taunts, he'd cleared a way to my heart. All that was left was for me to invite him in.

"If I told you to go and never cross my path again, would you?" I held my breath.

"Of course I would. I care about you, and I don't want to hurt you ever again. Is that what you want? For me to leave?" Those brown eyes of his rounded, pleading with me to say no.

"I asked you to leave. That first night I came home and found you waiting on my porch. In the rain." I'd thought for sure I'd hallucinated him. I'd thought about him so often that I could've conjured him there.

"I didn't think—I hoped you didn't mean it. But if you ask me to leave now, I will. I promise."

"You'll leave. You'll go back to California, and I'll never see you again." He'd done it once, and it'd broken me. Even speaking the words made my heart wring itself out in my chest.

"Is that what you want?"

I thought about lying. It'd be easier. It would confirm what I'd thought for years. And I loved being right.

But then Melissa's voice whispered in my brain. *Ask for what you want. And then take it.*

"No. I want you to stay. I want to trust you again. Can you earn my trust?"

His cheeks went red above his beard. "I made a mistake. I thought I was bad for you. That you shouldn't want me. And then I remembered how smart you are. That you know what you want, and I shouldn't decide for you. I was a dick. And I'm sorry. I'm not good enough for you. I know that. But I want to try." He reached across the table but stopped before he could touch me, his palm facing up. "You showed me how to be a better man. And I want to keep working at it. Because I love you."

A fizz started at my scalp and cascaded down through my body. I laid my hand over his, and he clasped it. "You were already a good man, Jackson Jones. You just needed to see it." I thought back to what he'd said before, on the porch in the rain. "What were you going to tell me the other day? Something you set up?"

A new spark lit his dark eyes. "Yeah, I started a foundation for neurodivergent kids. Like Noah. Like my sister and me. I want to try to set up some coding camps. But first I need someone to run it. Like, the day-to-day stuff. I don't suppose you're interested?"

"I don't know the first thing about nonprofits or leading a foundation. Besides, I'm doing what I've always dreamed of doing, running my own business."

"I know. And you're great at it. I wish…" He looked down at our joined hands.

"What do you wish?"

"I wish we could work together again. We were better together. You taught me how to lead."

I squeezed his hand. "You're a good leader all on your own. You only need to believe it. And I'm the one who got a masterclass in coding."

He locked his fingers into mine. "I don't want to talk about work. Or the foundation. I only want to talk about you and me. I love you. Will you let me love you?"

My heart beat like it wanted to leap right out of my chest and into his. It knew what it wanted. The rest of me hesitated. Accepting him mean opening up every part of my life, including Noah. Could I trust him? I sipped my tea, the familiar scent wafting over my face.

I scanned Jackson Jones from his anxious, hopeful expression to his polished boots. He'd probably screw up again. So would I. But we'd figure out a way through it. Together.

"Okay. Let's try it."

His face lit up with hope. "You mean it? I'm not dreaming all this, lying on your kitchen floor with Tigger eating my entrails?"

I snorted. "Don't be so dramatic. You two are going to get along great. Now come on." I stood and led him to the couch. We sat, side by side, and his arm went around my waist. Tigger jumped onto the sofa and curled against my other side, purring. I laid my head on Jackson's shoulder and let my gaze go soft until the Christmas tree lights blurred.

"I can do my job from Austin," he said at last. "Cooper and I'll work out some combination of leading projects here and the management stuff he wants me to do for headquarters."

"No!" I sat up. "They need you at headquarters."

He pulled me back against his chest and inhaled. "But I need to be with you. I need to prove that I can stay."

I rubbed his chest over his sweater. I'd thought about it over the past week, when it was clear he wasn't going anywhere. I was willing to try long-distance for a while. And when the time was right, I'd consider moving to San Francisco. That was where he belonged as Synergy's leader. And although I'd been more or less happily stuck in Austin all my life, I'd always wanted to see the world. San Francisco would be a first step. "We can be together and not be…together. At least for a while. As long as you're with me. Here." His heart beat strong and steady under my hand.

"Always." He kissed my temple. Turning my face up to him, I captured his lips. The spark was still there, igniting between us. But it wasn't as desperate as it'd been before, when we knew we had a time limit. It was the warmth of a roaring bonfire, able to burn for hours, not the flash of a scrap of paper blazing into nothing.

He cupped the back of my head, and I angled toward him. For the first time in weeks, I touched his skin, caressing his neck and the softness of his beard. He was mine to touch, mine to hold, mine to kiss, as he'd said, "Always." I took my time reacquainting myself with the softness of his lips, the scratch of his beard, the taste of him. The heave of his chest against mine.

He groaned and slid a hand under me, shifting me to straddle him. I ground my hips over his, and he trailed his lips down my neck, murmuring my name. Goosebumps broke out over my skin. My panties were soaked, and my lounge pants would soon follow, especially if he kept kneading my ass like that.

"Jackson." I pulled away. "We are not doing this here on the sofa where my family could walk in at any moment."

He shifted the hand that wasn't on my ass to my waist and slid it up under my sweatshirt. "I thought you said they were at a movie."

"Stop." I gave him my sternest glare. "What I want to do to you will take more time than we have. Hours."

His Adam's apple dipped. "Hours?"

"Hours. At your place. Tonight."

"All night?" His fingers teased the lower curve of my breast.

"Tomorrow, too. It's the weekend."

"All weekend in bed? I like the sound of that." The low tone of his voice hit something inside me, and my sex clenched.

I clambered off him and tugged down my sweatshirt. "But now, we have work to do. You do the top of the tree, and I'll do the bottom."

He frowned. "But I—"

"Jackson Jones. Do you or do you not want to spend all night and all day tomorrow in bed with me?"

His face went slack for a moment. Quickly, he said, "I want that."

"Then you'll do what I say. Start with the star."

"Yes, ma'am." He bounded off the couch, and I watched his tight ass all the way over to the tree.

"Mmm-hmm," I purred, picking up the empty box.

He reached easily for the perforated tin star and plucked it off the top. He set it into the box I held and then kissed me. "Better together, right?"

"Always."

EPILOGUE
THREE MONTHS LATER

ALICIA

WEARING the visitor's badge Jackson had left for me at the front desk, I stepped out into the courtyard behind the Synergy office in San Francisco. Music and voices bounced off the brick pavers and the sides of the surrounding buildings, making me wince. It had been a long day of work and travel, and a headache lurked behind my eyes, ready to flare. Maybe I could find Jackson and convince him to slip away to somewhere quiet so I could tell him my news. My stomach fluttered in anticipation.

I scanned the party. It was my first time at Synergy's headquarters. The few times I visited Jackson, he met me at the airport and whisked me straight back to his place. But he'd forgotten about Synergy's quarterly celebration when I arranged this trip. Tired as I was, I was curious to observe him at headquarters.

People sat at the tables scattered across the courtyard, shaded by pergolas. Others stood in clumps, swaying to the music that played over the speakers. Inside, I'd passed a long table full of snacks; out here, another smaller table served as the bar. A queue of employees stretched across the courtyard, empty cups at the ready. Behind the bar was the reason for the line. Instead of professional bartenders, Jackson and Marlee filled cups with beer. Their foreheads glistened with sweat despite San Francisco's April chill. What were the company founder and his executive assistant doing there when they should've been mingling with the employees?

I skirted the line and approached the table. Marlee saw me first. She dropped the spigot. "Alicia!" She held out her arms for a hug. We'd met the last time I'd visited Jackson, taking part of our precious weekend for a girls-only shopping trip. I liked her a lot. Plus, she was important to Jackson. I could see us becoming friends, especially considering my news.

I stepped into her arms and kissed her cheek. A trickle of sweat dripped from her temple to her chin. "What's going on?"

Her eyebrows slammed down. "Bartenders didn't show. The caterer is sending replacements, but we have thirsty people here." She waved at the line.

"Want me to help?" I'd never poured beer from a keg—the library had been more my scene in college—but it didn't look too difficult.

"Absolutely not." She pumped the handle, then picked up the spigot and reached for the next cup. She nudged Jackson with her elbow. "Take a break, Jackson. Alicia's here."

He looked up, and the cup he was filling overflowed, splashing his jeans. "Alicia!" He shoved the cup at the waiting person, sloshing her hand, and with a quick apology, dropped his spigot and folded me into his arms.

He smelled like beer and sweat, but under that was my Jackson's leather and soap scent. I breathed him in and then lifted my face for his kiss.

His beard was freshly trimmed, and it scratched at my cheeks, contrasting with the soft press of his lips and tongue. He tasted like hops and orange peel from the beer. I tunneled my fingers through his hair, tugging him closer. His hands pressed into my lower back, bringing me right up against the hard planes of his stomach. Something else hard nudged against my lower belly.

One of his hands slid down my silky skirt. During our shopping trip, Marlee had convinced me to buy the flouncy, short skirt, so different from my usual slim, professional ones. Its cheery floral pattern was much better suited to Austin, where it was already spring, than to wintry San Francisco.

He kissed over to my ear. "I like this skirt. I think it has room for both my hands."

"Told you it was a great skirt," Marlee said.

I gasped and pulled back. "You can't feel me up in front of your employees." I tilted my head toward Marlee, who grinned at us.

"Marlee doesn't mind," he said. "She tried to help me with my grovel."

"It worked, didn't it?" But she wasn't looking at us any longer. She gazed up into Cooper Fallon's face.

His jaw clenched when he saw Jackson's hand on my ass.

"Hey, Cooper," Marlee said. Her voice had gone high and breathy, and her pink lips parted. Was she *flirting* with the guy? Her fluttering lashes and sweet smile were no match for the six-foot block of ice that was Cooper Fallon, CEO and certified hard-ass.

"Jay, I—" he began.

At the same time, Marlee said, "Want a beer?"

Without looking, she gave an enthusiastic pump on the tap. But she must have hit it at the wrong angle. It popped off, and foam rocketed out of the keg into her face.

"Blasted beastly Robert Boyle!" she howled, leaping back and shielding her eyes from the spray.

Jackson gripped me tighter, turning his back to the geyser to protect me.

Tyler Young sprinted in out of nowhere, vaulted over the table, and jammed the tap over the volcano of suds. He wrestled against the pressure for a moment, his forearms straining, until he finally clamped it into place.

His chest heaving, he looked up at Marlee. Not Jackson, his boss, or Cooper, or even me. Beer glistened on his hands and bare arms and darkened his gray T-shirt. "Are you okay?"

Marlee's cheeks were pink under the white foam. She tugged the soaked fabric of her pink blouse away from her skin. "I'll live. Cooper, it didn't get you, did it?"

He wiped a spot of foam off his cheekbone. "I'm fine. Though I think"—he looked at the table, at Jackson, anywhere but at Marlee—"you might want to find some dry clothes."

Her pale-pink blouse had gone transparent, and her lacy, red bra showed through.

Her cheeks went full red. "I—I—"

"Come with me," Tyler said. "We'll dry you off. I mean, you can dry off. Inside." Now his cheeks went pink. Interesting.

She glanced at Cooper again. Even more interesting.

But a second later, drill-sergeant Marlee was back. She pointed at the next pair of guys in line. "You and you. Take over."

Obediently, they stepped around the table and took up their posts at the keg.

With one last glance at Cooper—holy shit, did she have a thing for the Snow Miser?—she trudged toward the door, beer dripping from the ends of her hair. Tyler trailed her like a hungry puppy.

"You okay?" Jackson murmured.

"I'm fine. You?" I buried my fingers in his hair, which turned out to be damp.

"It's just a little beer. I'm fantastic now that you're here." His hand crept back down toward the hem of my skirt.

Despite the penetrating cold, being near Jackson warmed me from the inside out.

However.

"Easy there, cowboy. Everyone's watching."

"They understand. I haven't seen my girlfriend in two weeks." His hand crept lower, teasing at the back of my thigh and making my skin zing.

"I might be wearing something special underneath, and I'd rather not flash your employees, if you don't mind." I smiled when he froze, his pulse beating wild against my cheek. "Maybe we can find some-where more private?"

He sucked in a breath, smoothed my skirt down, and whisked me away to the other side of the courtyard. He tugged me behind a tree in a planter bigger than Noah, then leaned against the side of the building and hiked me up against him. The tree shaded us, throwing the corner into semidarkness.

"Now, where were we? As I recall, I was about to discover some-thing special." His big hand trailed over my ass and teased the hem of my skirt.

I slapped my hand over his, stilling it. "First, I have some news. Want to hear it?"

"Good news?" He searched my face. "You booked your next gig?"

"Hey, no fair guessing." A little of my excitement leaked out. I'd wanted to surprise him.

"No more guessing." He tightened his grip on me. "Tell me."

With my fingertip, I traced the curve of the lips on his Rolling Stones T-shirt. "I booked my next gig. And it's here in San Francisco." I dared to look up. For the last month, he'd been begging me to come live here so we could stop the endless travel and separations that exhausted us both. But was it really what he wanted? His expression was blank and still.

"Jamila asked me last November to do a job for her, but I turned it down. She ended up delaying the project, and now it's available again. It's a—a year-long gig." My voice faltered. Why didn't he look happy?

"I was thinking I'd bring Noah when the school year ends. He'd stay here through the summer, and if things work out, he could start school here in the fall. If...if that's what we want." My voice had dropped to a whisper.

"You're telling me you're coming to San Francisco for the next year? Maybe longer?" His voice rumbled through my chest, pressed against his.

"Yes?" It was barely audible.

He crushed me to his chest, lifting me off the ground. "I don't believe it. That's the best news ever." He set me back down and stared into my face. "It's real? That beer tap didn't hit me in the head and knock me out? Better pinch me."

I pinched his nipple a little harder than I should. "You scared me! I thought you were upset. That you didn't want me here after all."

He gasped at the pain. And then he crashed his lips onto mine, bruising them against my teeth. His tongue invaded my mouth, and his fingers marched right past the hem of my skirt, teasing the bare skin of my ass revealed by my red thong. I'd worn a different style of big-girl panties for my big-news weekend.

He was steel against my stomach, and I rubbed against him, needing more. When he nudged one leg between mine, I ground against the roughness of his jeans. My thong dug into my swollen flesh, lighting me up in pleasure. If he kept kissing me like that and caressing the edge of my panties, I might come right there against his jeans. I ground harder into him, chasing the sensation.

"Jay. Are you back here?"

Cooper's voice was decidedly unamused. Still, he gave us a minute to compose ourselves. Jackson straightened my skirt and then adjusted his jeans. I rubbed my pink lipstick off the corner of his mouth and then smudged a thumb around the outline of my lips.

"Right here, Coop." He stepped around me, shielding me from his partner.

"Sorry to interrupt. I assume you'll be leaving soon, and I wanted to check the talking points with you for the speech."

I reached for Jackson's hand. "Stay. Do the speech. I'll wait." Jackson had worked too hard to assert himself, to become an equal partner over the past two months, to lose this opportunity to appear before his employees as a leader.

When he turned to look at me, his gaze was soft and grateful and full of love. "We'll do it now. I'll just be a minute."

"Alicia." Cooper's gaze flicked away from my face. I must've missed a smudge of lipstick.

"Cooper. Congratulations on the year-end results." They'd announced them a few days ago. I wished my ratios were that good. But I'd get there. Eventually.

"Thank you." He flashed me a glance that wasn't as subzero as usual. Not quite friendly, but closer than when he'd stormed out of that conference room at the launch party. Could he and I eventually get to be friends?

"I'll get a beer and find a spot to listen to your speech," I said.

I stepped up next to Jackson to pass him, but he stopped me, whispering in my ear. "You must be tired from the flight. Go up to the sixth floor. You can relax in my office."

Taking off my heels sounded pretty fantastic. I nodded and crossed the courtyard to reenter the lobby. After taking the elevator to the top floor, I stepped out into a bright, airy space. The converted mill's original wide-plank floors glowed with the reflection of the skylight above.

Which way to go? There were four corner offices; surely the company's cofounder had to have one of them. I strode across the floor toward the nearest one, weaving between the workspaces in the center.

The office was unlit, and the door was closed. The nameplate read *Cooper Fallon*. Cooper was downstairs, so I risked a peek through the glass wall. It looked the same as it had on that disastrous video call after the bad sushi incident. The day Cooper had accused us of an affair, and I'd told him I didn't even like Jackson. I never lied, but I'd lied that day.

A chime sounded from someone's workstation behind me, reminding me I was staring into the COO's office. I glanced around. One of the other executives or their admins might still be up here. Weston, the CEO, whom I'd never met but whom Jackson had told me all about, might be prowling the floor. I backed away and went to the next corner office.

I'd lucked out. This door had Jackson's name and his new title, VP of Development, on the plate. The door was closed, and the scanner light next to it glowed red.

Tentatively, I pushed the handle, but it didn't budge. Jackson had told me to wait in his office. Were there cameras capturing my every move? Would a security guard burst onto the floor and escort me out? I tried to keep the apprehensive wince off my face as I extended the visitor badge clipped to my neckline toward the scanner. The light flashed green, and the lock clicked. With a victorious smile, I pushed the door open.

Unlike Cooper's sunny office, Jackson's was overshadowed by two adjacent, taller buildings. Still, some natural light filtered in from the two enormous windows and the glass front of his office.

A rug anchored a small seating area with a couch, a chaise, and two armchairs. Through a half-open door behind it, a small bathroom was visible. On the opposite wall, a bookshelf was stuffed with pieces of computer equipment: a pile of hard drives and another of circuit boards, a couple of disassembled laptops, a clear acrylic tray filled with screws.

Predictably, Jackson's desk held a similar array of electronics, plus a few stacks of papers adorned with sticky notes and flags that said,

"Sign here." The enormous wood rectangle was big enough to support a docking station for Jackson's laptop plus three big screen monitors. The monitor edges butted up against each other so Jackson could code without distraction from the windows or the front glass wall. It was a good setup for him. Marlee had probably arranged it.

"Alicia." Jackson's voice, breaking the stillness of the sixth floor, made me jump. I whirled around.

He stepped closer and interlaced his fingers with mine.

Without a word, he tugged me into his office. He closed the door behind him and flipped the bolt to lock it. He flicked a switch on the wall, and blinds rustled down, blocking out the rest of the office. He prowled toward me.

"How'd it go?" My voice came out high and breathy.

"Huh?"

"The speech."

"Fine. But that's not what I want to talk about now."

"Oh?" He wanted to talk? He looked like he wanted to rip my clothes off and ravish me right there on the chaise. I couldn't stop the smile that spread over my face or the tingle that started between my legs when I caught his hungry stare.

"I want to talk about how many times I can make you come here in my office before I have to carry you out."

I shivered. "Oh."

"Want to start on the desk?"

I pictured bending over the desk while Jackson entered me from behind. My thighs slicked; the thong was doing nothing to contain my arousal. We'd done it half a dozen times that way on his kitchen counter, Jackson so deep inside me my vision had blacked from the intensity of my orgasm. Somehow, though, that enormous expanse of wood was different.

I lifted my chin. "That desk is steeped in patriarchy. I'm not about to bend over it like some virgin in one of Marlee's books."

"'Steeped in patriarchy?'" He chuckled. "Sounds serious."

"Don't laugh. Synergy has an appalling lack of female executives."

His smile dissolved. "Something Cooper and I are working to address now. And Weston." His lip curled as he said the CEO's name.

"Maybe when your gig with Jamila is done, I'll be able to lure you into one of those executive positions."

"Lure me into an executive position?" I quirked an eyebrow.

"Now who's not being serious?" He took two strides toward me, lifted me, and dropped me on the edge of his desk. I laughed until he spread my knees apart and kneeled in front of me. "How's this for an executive position?" He teased a finger along the scrap of fabric that covered me.

"I'll take it."

Without another word, he tugged my thong aside, spread me, and landed his mouth on my clit, circling it with his tongue in that figure-eight pattern I loved. His beard scratched against my thighs, warming them in a way I'd feel hours later. I leaned back on the desk, propped up by my arms. When his teeth scratched lightly across me, my back bowed.

He flattened his tongue over me and then sucked, stretching my clit. He popped off. "More?"

"More." I'd gotten so used to coming silently on my vibrator in my bedroom next to Noah's that I wasn't used to giving the feedback Jackson craved. I tightened my thighs on the sides of his head. "More sucking."

I felt his cheeks rise in a grin before he did exactly that. The pleasure radiated up from my clit, sparked my heart into a faster rhythm, and made my pulse pound in my ears. I curled my hands into fists. "Yes, Jackson, yes," I whispered as I spiraled up and up into blackness and white noise. My body stiffened, and my mouth gaped in a silent scream.

When I floated back inside my body, Jackson was beaming up at me, his eyes glowing and his beard wet with me. He kissed the inside of my thigh, pink from beard burn. "Think we've crushed the patriarchy out of this desk?"

My voice was scratchy when I said, "It might take another session or two to fully eradicate it."

"I'm up for that." He rose to stand in front of me.

"I can see you're up for it." I set my hand on his belt buckle. "Want me to—"

He laid a hand over mine. "Not here. Let's go back to my place. I think there might be some patriarchy hiding out in my bed."

"Maybe some reverse cowgirl would take care of it." I slid off the desk and twitched my hips, setting my skirt swinging.

"I can get behind that plan." He stepped up behind me and smoothed his palms from my ribs down my front and between my legs.

"I thought we were going home?" Still, I pressed back against his erection.

"Home. I like the sound of that."

"Me, too."

He took my hand, and we stepped out of the office, knowing home wasn't his apartment or even my mother's place back in Austin. Home was wherever the two of us could be together. And soon, we'd be home all the time.

THANK you so much for reading *Work with Me!* Please consider posting a review on your favorite retailer or Goodreads.

Not ready to let go of Alicia and Jackson? Join my newsletter at michellemccraw.com/Work or use your phone's camera to take a picture of the QR code below to download a bonus epilogue!

The next book in the series, *Friend Me,* is a friends-to-lovers, fake-dating romance featuring Jackson's assistant, Marlee. Read on for a sneak peek.

FRIEND ME, SYNERGY BOOK 2
CHAPTER 1

I'D WATCHED a lot of women come and go from Cooper Fallon's office, but this one was the worst. And she wasn't going quietly.

When her shriek—something that ended with "asshole"—escaped his closed office door to echo all the way down the hall to my desk, I pressed my lips together to hide my grin and pulled up the staffing agency's contact information.

Since his long-time assistant retired five months ago, the Chief Operating Officer of Synergy Analytics had gone through eighteen temporary assistants. Some stormed out, like this one was about to do, some slunk out, and some just didn't bother showing up the next day.

I swear, it was all his own doing. At first. After temp number five keyed the cherry surface of his desk on her way out, he asked me to select the next one. As a favor. And I just took advantage of his own high standards—and raging temper—to ensure that none stuck. I became the Statue of Liberty of San Francisco temps: *Give me your amateurs, your idlers, your novelists and poets yearning to slack off...*

So I might not have been the most impartial person to hire Cooper's assistant.

Because I had a plan. One that relied on, well, unreliable help.

As I composed the email to the agency—I had to be vague enough about why we were firing this one so they'd send us another just as terrible—a voice behind me asked, "Are they okay in there?"

I spun in my chair toward the familiar voice, banging my bare knee against the leg of my desk. I squinted at my work-buddy, Tyler Young, haloed in brightness from the hazy light coming through the converted mill's top-floor skylight.

I rubbed my knee. With Cooper bellowing from the corner office, I hadn't heard the soft approach of Tyler's sneakers. "I was just about to bust out the popcorn."

Flashing his adorable dimples, he came around to the front of my desk, as he always did so I didn't have to stare into the skylight. When Cooper's low growl cut across the temp's higher voice, Tyler shoved up his black-framed glasses and asked, "Are you sure? Do we need to—?"

I tilted my head to listen. The temp was giving as good as—or better than—she got. All the swearing was on her end. "No, they're pretty evenly matched. At least she's not a crier." I'd raided my desk drawer for chocolate and tissues to console the one he'd fired last week.

When the temp's shouting escalated into a high-pitched screech, Synergy's other founder, Jackson Jones, emerged from his office and ambled to my desk. "Hey, Marlee. Who picked"—he checked his Omega—"four o'clock?" My boss leaned his big hand on my desk and plucked a piece of candy from the ceramic bowl.

I snorted. "Someone down in payroll. I'm guessing she'll win it."

"Poor Cooper." He wadded up his candy wrapper and handed it to me to throw in the trash. "Not everyone can have San Francisco's best assistant. He's jealous I found you first."

My cheeks warming, I smoothed my rosebud-pink skirt.

Cooper, the COO of one of the world's hottest tech companies, demanded a lot of his employees. He was an alpha billionaire, just like in my favorite novels.

Total romance-hero material. I just wished he were mine.

That first day I'd met him, when I was still a part-timer figuring out what exactly analytics software did and how the building full of scruffy young programmers had made it onto the Fortune 1000, my jaw had dropped and my knees had gone weak. He was more than handsome; he looked like the model on the cover of the romance novel I'd been reading. Blond hair, blue eyes, the perfect amount of stubble, impeccable clothes—though lacking a broadsword—and tall as a redwood. I'd spent my first three days at Synergy staring at him. By the end of the second week, it was a full-blown crush.

Not only was he one of Northern California's most eligible bachelors, but he was a considerate, caring, honest man. He knew the names of all of his employees, from the executive floor down to the mailroom. He'd started a foundation to help kids from lower-income families go to coding camps. And most important—

"You going to get that?" Jackson asked, leaning a hip against the soapstone lab table I used as a desk.

Cooper's line was lit up on my desk phone, ringing, but since both people who should've answered it were screaming at each other, it was up to me.

"Cooper Fallon's office. Marlee Rice speaking."

"Hi," said a husky female voice. "This is Jamila Jallow. Is Cooper available? He's expecting my call."

He was? My heart thudded. Why was top-of-their-Stanford-class, could've-been-a-model, on-all-the-forty-under-forty-lists Jamila Jallow, Cooper's BFF, calling him today?

"No, I'm sorry. He's tied up at the moment. Can I help you?"

"Sure. Could you let him know my plans changed and I *can* go with him to Jackson's wedding?"

Holy Stephen Hawking.

"You can?" Although Jamila and Cooper had attended more than one industry function together, he never brought a date to Synergy events. And while my boss's wedding next weekend wasn't an official company function, I'd been sure he'd go stag.

"I can. But, you know, I'll just text him. Thanks, Marlee."

My ears buzzed. I'd figured Jamila would go to Jackson's wedding. They'd been friends since college. What did it mean that she'd go with Cooper? Was it a friends-date or a date-date?

It'd be just my luck if she snapped up Cooper right as I'd finally found the courage to do something about my three-year-old crush.

"Um, Marlee?" Tyler asked, straightening his glasses. "Are you okay?"

I blinked to focus. "Fine." I turned to Jackson. "That was Jamila Jallow. She says she's coming with Cooper. To your wedding."

His eyebrows shot up. "He never brings anyone to my parties."

"I know, right? What's going on?"

Cooper's door swung open, thumping into the wall, and the temp stormed out, her face as red as her silk blouse. I'd been a little afraid when the gorgeous woman had walked in on Monday with her designer clothes and shoes that cost more than my weekly salary, but she'd been too preoccupied with fluttering her fake eyelashes at Cooper to answer his calls. She snatched her buttery leather handbag off the desk outside and flounced past us toward the elevators.

"Bye, Lynley," I said.

"Fuck off." She veered right, yanked open the door, and disappeared into the stairwell.

I exchanged a glance with Jackson.

"Yeah," he said, "Cooper has that effect on me, sometimes."

Tyler said nothing. He hadn't spent enough time up here on the sixth floor to know that Cooper's moods were a summer thunderstorm: loud but quickly spent.

The man himself stepped out of his glass-walled office, his nostrils flaring, his jaw like marble. He shoved his hands into the pockets of his tailored black slacks and, gaze on the reclaimed-wood floor, approached us. I ran a hand over my pendant and sat up straighter in my chair.

Rubbing the back of his neck, he turned his crystal-blue eyes on me.

"Marlee?" He shifted on his feet. "It seems Lindsey—"

"Lynley," I corrected him.

He grimaced, showing straight white teeth. "She and I have agreed she's not a good fit for Synergy."

"That's one way of putting it," Jackson said.

Cooper's stare stabbed his friend. "If you'd just reconsider sharing Marlee with me…"

"I'd be happy to—" I began.

"Not happening," Jackson interrupted me. He stared at me, hard. "Marlee has plenty of work already. And you might as well ask to borrow my right arm. Find your own Marlee." He shrugged. "Or keep one of the temps she finds for you."

Before he spoke, Cooper took a beat to relax his hands, which had balled into fists. Then he looked at me. "Do you think you could—"

"Done." I clicked to send my email to the staffing agency.

"Thanks. You know I adore you, Marlee." And there it was, the heart-stopping smile that turned me to goo on the floor every time. I wanted to dance my fingertips over his strong, stubbly jaw and into his short, sandy hair. Run my hands over his gray striped dress shirt to touch the toned shoulders underneath. Drag my nails down his back and squeeze his—

"Anyway, Jay—" He turned to Jackson, and that was when I realized I'd been eye-fucking Cooper again. "Can we start our ride early? I have a foundation event tonight."

"I'll go change." Jackson shot me a look—he hadn't missed my wandering eyes—and then gripped Tyler's shoulder. "Let's talk tomorrow about your ideas for the fuel burn module." Because I was watching Cooper, I saw his gaze follow his friend's hand and then narrow at Tyler. Cooper tended to be the jealous partner in his bromance with Jackson.

"Sure thing." Tyler grinned at our boss, looking exactly like a Labrador Retriever who'd been told he was a good boy.

Jackson had created the company's flagship product—an automotive analytics package that made cars perform better and more safely —ten years ago in the dorm room he shared with Cooper at Stanford. A programming legend, he inspired admiration among the developers, and Tyler was president of the fan club. Though Tyler was a legit programmer himself. Jackson didn't have the patience to mentor many programmers, but he made time for Tyler.

When the two executives returned to their respective offices, I beckoned Tyler closer and checked that no one else was nearby. "I heard Sanjay's leaving."

"Yeah?" His lower lip pushed out into an almost-pout. "He's a good boss. I'll miss him."

"Sure, but..." I paused for effect. "That opens up a manager position. And I know a talented programmer who's ready for a promotion."

"Who, Grant?"

I snorted. "No, you dork. You."

He rocked back on his heels. "I'm not ready. I've been here less than a year."

"It doesn't matter how long you've been here. What matters is how much you know about programming and how good you are with people." And Tyler was good with people. Unlike most of his colleagues, he didn't look down his nose at me because I was an admin.

His eyes narrowed, uncertain.

"Think about it. HR will post the job next week."

He gave a noncommittal grunt. Plucking a peppermint from my candy dish, he twisted the ends tighter. He opened his mouth, took a breath, and then let it out slowly.

"Oh, right. The fuel-burn module. Want me to schedule a meeting with him tomorrow?" I clicked to Jackson's calendar and searched for a free slot. "How's two-thirty?"

A soft drumming was my only answer. His long fingers tapped out a rhythm against the side of his jeans.

"Tyler?" I prompted him again.

"Right. Sure." He dragged his gaze off my desk and met mine. "A few of us are—I thought you'd like, maybe, to, uh—"

"Yes?" I typed up the meeting invitation and sent it while he hesitated. I glanced at the clock in the corner of my screen. If Jackson was leaving now, I could just make the early train. Definitely a good idea, considering the problems we'd had lately. A few weeks ago, Dad had tried to help out by making dinner but had ended up burning through a pot on the stove and setting off the smoke alarm.

"It's three-dollar pint night, and..."

We both startled when Jackson slammed his office door and shouted down the hall, "Coop, get your ass in gear!"

Cooper emerged from his office, duffel bag thrown over his shoulder. Like Jackson, he wore a T-shirt that skimmed over his chest and ended just below the hip of a pair of tight-fitting bike shorts. My eyes trailed up his toned leg to the hint of a bulge just under the hem of that shirt. I swallowed.

"See you tomorrow." Jackson waved lazily in our direction before he jogged to the stairs and held the door for Cooper. "After the ride, let's—" The door shut behind them, cutting off Jackson's words.

I blinked hard and then turned back to Tyler. "Sorry, what did you say?"

He took off his glasses and rubbed them on his T-shirt. Without his glasses, his eyes were dappled with specks of brown, blue, green, and gold, like Earth seen from space.

"I was thinking about going to the pub on the next block after work. Want to come with?"

"I'm sorry, I can't tonight. Who're you going with?" When we hung out together at the quarterly Synergy parties, the other programmers orbited Tyler like satellites. Most of them were okay, but a few wouldn't even speak to someone without "developer" in her title. They scanned past me like I was some sort of exotic pink insect, completely beneath their notice.

"Oh, um. I hadn't invited anyone else yet."

I paused my packing. It was just like Tyler to build the gathering around me and my preferences. Such a sweet guy. If I were anyone else, I'd have jumped at the opportunity to spend time with him after work.

But I had responsibilities. And plans. "Maybe some other night?"

As soon as he nodded, I strode to the elevator and jabbed the button.

The doors slid open right away, and when I turned to press the button, I glimpsed Tyler's downturned mouth as he watched me go. I gave him an apologetic smile and finger-waggle.

He'd be fine. He'd go out tonight with his other friends. He was like most people our age who worked at Synergy—dedicated and hardworking with few responsibilities outside the office, and with plenty of cash to party when the work was done.

Even though we'd been friends for the better part of a year and best buddies for more than six months, Tyler didn't know I wasn't like him. I hoped he didn't think I was making up a fake excuse, like all my friends from college had. They'd slowly dropped out of my life after too many refused invitations, too many last-minute cancellations.

But from the moment he'd rescued me from that evil beer tap,

Tyler had been different. He'd kept asking me places even though most times, I refused. He was a good friend. One worth keeping.

I'd take him to lunch the next day. But right then, I needed to woman up for my second job.

———

Friend Me is available in paperback from your favorite retailer.

ACKNOWLEDGMENTS

Y'all, this has been a journey. Since I started this book almost five years ago—it was called *Distracted* then—so many people have read it that I can't possibly thank them all without doubling the length of this book. But I know who you are, and I'm grateful for your feedback. You helped make this a better book.

But I do have to call out Lauren Accardo and Dr. Bella Ellwood-Clayton, two of my very first critique partners. They've read this book almost as many times as I have. Thank you both for your patience, for your support, for the many emails and DMs that kept me pushing ahead on this long journey to publication.

And I want to thank my Twitter squad of RChat cheerleaders, especially Meka James and Coralie Moss, who have shared so much knowledge, answered so many of my newbie questions, and rah-rah-rahed me over the finish line at last.

Finally, thanks to my family, who put up with me for the past six years as I've written at the kitchen table, on vacations, and even in my head as they were talking to me. I know you'll never read this kissing book because I didn't put nearly enough dragons in it, but I appreciate your support all the same.

CREDITS

Editing

Angela James

Proofreading

April Bennett, The Editing Soprano

Cover Design

Qamber Designs

ABOUT MICHELLE

Michelle McCraw loves reading kissing books and working in tech. One day, she decided to combine her two interests, and now she writes steamy, nerdy contemporary romance that just might make you laugh. Her books feature characters who unashamedly love science, engineering, and technology.

A native Texan, Michelle has shoveled snow during nor'easters and knows the proper response when someone yells, "O-H." She now calls Georgia home, where she doesn't miss snow AT ALL. She enjoys reading, travel, drinking bourbon, and spoiling her extraordinarily ill-behaved but adorable dogs. She has been a finalist in the RWA Vivian Contest, the Contemporary Romance Writers' Stiletto Contest, and the Windy City Romance Writers' Four Seasons Contest.

For updates about upcoming books and more free reads—plus guaranteed puppy pics—subscribe to Michelle's newsletter at michellemccraw.com. You can also follow the author on Facebook and Instagram.

facebook.com/MichelleMcCrawAuthor
instagram.com/MMOWriter
amazon.com/author/michellemccraw
goodreads.com/MichelleMcCraw
bookbub.com/authors/michelle-mccraw

BOOKS IN THE SYNERGY SERIES
CAN BE READ IN ANY ORDER

Work with Me

She's got a checklist for every occasion. He's never met a bad decision he didn't make. Can straitlaced single mom Alicia find a way to work with billionaire tech genius Jackson and save her business—without falling for him first?

"Slow burn magic!" (5-star review)

Friend Me

Romance-obsessed executive assistant Marlee has a plan to woo her crush, icy and aloof San Francisco tech executive Cooper Fallon. But it all goes wrong when her fake date, instead of making her crush jealous, sparks more-than-friends feelings. Kissing the wrong guy? Not in her plan. Neither is falling for her best friend.

"Un-put-down-able" (5-star review)

Trip Me Up

Nerdy computer scientist Samantha Jones didn't mean to end up on a book tour trying to pass off her artificial intelligence-written novel as one written the old-fashioned way. And she certainly didn't mean to fall for her flannel-wearing, poetic tour partner. Opposites attract in this road-trip romance.

"This book had me hooked right from the start and up until the wee hours devouring their story!" (5-star review)

Boss Me

Frosty billionaire philanthropist Cooper Fallon would never start a fling with his off-limits assistant, Ben...or would he?

"OMG...If you like forbidden romance this is the book for you!!!" (5-star review)

Forget Me

She doesn't remember their night together. He can't forget it. When Mimi's prospective boss mistakes Mateo for her boyfriend, she's shocked when he rolls with it. But when their fake romance becomes real, will buttoned-up Mimi let down her guard for love?

"I absolutely love this twist on the grumpy sunshine trope." (5-star review)

Tempt Me

When a gaffe caught on camera threatens her company, a no-nonsense tech CEO calls on her bestie's little sister for help. But falling for her sunshiny public relations assistant could get her into even more hot water.

"THIS WAS FUN!!" (5-star review)

BOOKS IN THE 40 AND FABULOUS SERIES

Fashion and Passion

After a disastrous self-help seminar, Carly finds friendship, empowerment, and maybe love with a younger admirer. Get swept away by sparkling banter, new besties, and spicy seduction, perfect for a bubbly escape.

Frenemies and Lovers

When Carly needs a date to her ex's wedding, she agrees to a deal with Andrew, a devilishly handsome younger man. Her frenemy's son. Who happens to be her one-night stand. What could go wrong? Who says you can't be fabulous over forty?

"Total catnip" (5-star review)

Books and Hookups

Writer Lucie's life is looking up: she has a new book deal, fabulous friends, and a bar where everyone knows her name. The last thing she needs is a surprise (geriatric?) pregnancy with her much-younger neighbor.

Conspiracies and Chemistry

Secretive billionaire Tessa seeks redemption from the biggest mistake of her life by betting it all on a groundbreaking biotechnology company, which happens to be run by her younger nemesis. And who knew lab coats were so sexy?